AMBASSADOR 8: THE ALABASTER ARMY

PATTY JANSEN

GET FREE EBOOKS

Visit pattyjansen.com
or scan the QR code below with your phone to get four series starter
ebooks for free!

DID YOU KNOW?

Ambassador 8: The Alabaster Army is also available in audio. Click the image or visit https://pattyjansen.com to find out more.

1

———

A COUPLE OF WEEKS in the hospital, even if some of those were spent barely conscious, was far too long for me.

But that was all behind me now, and I was on my way home.

Thayu came to pick me up, uncharacteristically alone, and shortly we sat on the train, which barrelled its way from the main island of the city of Barresh to the *gamra* island, zooming low over the water.

It was midafternoon, and the position of Ceren's two suns made the water look like a bath of silver. People were out on boats, carrying big bags of lily bulbs and other produce on their way to the market. Some people were fishing with spears, Pengali style.

The train carriage was full of chatter.

There were groups of domestic servants going back home with items they had bought, as well as some of the delegates in *gamra* blue who had been to the city for lunch or for business meetings.

Some of them gave me strange looks as if they wondered if they should say anything.

I was not wearing blues. I hadn't worked for almost a month.

Thayu opened the window to let the fresh air come in. It wasn't warm, although I had the feeling that it should be, because it was the middle of summer and the air was humid with the promise of a late thunderstorm. Sunlight on my skin, breeze in my hair. They were things I'd had to do without for far too long.

"You're not paying attention," she said.

"Aren't I?"

I was just so happy to be out of that horrible hospital where the air was always dry, heavy with obnoxious antiseptic smells and where everybody seemed continuously obsessed with my well-being. There had been very good reasons for this, but to be honest I was over it and wanted to go back to work.

Thayu held up her reader and informed me—again, apparently— that she had finally set up the formalities for me to be initiated into Asto's Domiri clan as her father, Commander of Asto's air force and head of that clan, had urged me to do.

I wanted it. Thayu wanted it, being Domiri herself.

It was quite rare that a non-Coldi person was inducted into a Coldi clan, but not the first time by any means, and I'd had no idea that this would entail so much filling out of forms. It was almost worse than *gamra* bureaucracy.

Neither had I imagined that I would need to choose a name.

"What do you mean—a name?" I'd asked Thayu when she first told me.

"A name. A proper Domiri name, to be entered into the register."

The naming of Coldi children was a subject that I was not terribly familiar with. By the time his son Ayshada was born, Thayu's brother Nicha had already decided on his name. He had not spoken much about choosing the name, since there had been so many other things to talk about at the time.

But because there were only thirty-six Coldi clans, people wanted to make sure that their first names were unique.

So enter the hallowed register.

Thayu proudly presented me her reader, which had a list of currently unused and available names that she'd pulled out of that register.

All of which meant that I was left with the unenviable task of having to choose my own name. It was weird.

I felt a bit uneasy about some of the names, because they sounded too much like the names of some of the people I knew and respected. I would never get away with Raya because that altogether sounded far too much like Daya, who had been one of the most hallowed citizens of Barresh, and naming myself after him would sound arrogant.

I didn't like Neida, because we already had a Reida in the household. In fact, none of the names on the list jumped out at me, and looking at the screen of Thayu's reader made my eyes flash with annoying spots of light.

"Let me think about it when we come home," I said, handing the reader back to her. The flashings lights usually came with a sharp headache and blurred vision. I didn't want to admit weakness to her. Damn it, I was supposed to be getting *better*.

The sweat broke out over my back.

Thayu went, on, oblivious to my discomfort. "We do have to decide about it fairly soon. I need to give notice and they will need to move all sorts of bureaucracy in order to let you come. The date hasn't yet been set, but there are only certain dates that will work."

Despite the fact that Coldi were not religious, they attached a curious amount of superstition to the positions of the stars in relation to naming ceremonies. "Yes, I know, and I'll decide within the next few days."

I leaned back in my seat, eyes closed.

"Are you all right?" Thayu's voice was concerned.

"Fine. Just . . . the light bothers me a bit."

The breeze brought a whiff of her scent to me. It was distracting, because my nose had become so much more sensitive to smells. I could smell the fruit in the bag that the woman across the carriage had bought at the markets. I could smell the wet scent of the mud in the marshlands. I could smell the scent of the impending thunderstorm in the air. I could smell the overwhelming *female* scent that hung around Thayu, the scent that made my heart speed up and my breath catch in my throat, that made me want to draw her into my embrace and do all kinds of things that were inappropriate behaviour in a train carriage.

It was disturbing.

"We're almost there," she said.

She sounded anxious.

Unfortunately I didn't remember much of my first week in hospital, but everyone had told me that they had feared for my survival.

It was the end of a long story that began with our desire to have a child.

Aghyrian scientist Lilona Shrakar, who had abandoned the

Aghyrian ship to stay with us, had outlined several methods she could try to make it work. They all involved invasive genetic treatments for me, each more invasive than the last. First it was just the sperm. Thayu fell pregnant, but miscarried later.

Buoyed by that initial success, we tried a different method to treat sperm, but that also didn't work. Tantalisingly, those attempts had resulted in three short pregnancies and miscarriages, and this had given us the hope that it would be possible.

The third possible treatment had not been tried before. The doctors were interested. They wanted to do it.

About fifty thousand years ago, Aghyrians on Asto had artificially created the Coldi race by grafting modified genes onto the large sections of junk DNA in the basic human genetic code. They had done this because they wanted to produce a race that was hardy and suited to the worlds that they planned to colonise. That Coldi toughness had been a boon to their ability to survive when the Aghyrian—and Coldi—homeworld Asto had been hit by a meteorite that had wiped out all the Aghyrians but spared a group of Coldi people who were being prepared for colonisation projects.

Because Coldi DNA had been grafted directly onto Aghyrian genes, the theory was that this graft should work for all humans who were descended from Aghyrians—and people on Earth branched off the Aghyrian main branch well over a hundred thousand years ago, but were still clearly related.

Supposedly, this gene treatment could be localised to fast-growing areas in an adult body, like reproductive functions, but this was where the experiment had become interesting.

I'd gone into the hospital and received the treatment—painful, but so far, so good. Initial tests on my sperm looked promising. I'd gone home a day after the treatment, and then things went downhill fast. Light started flashing in my eyes. My temperature spiked. Two days after the treatment I collapsed in the hall. I didn't remember anything of the frantic rush back to the hospital and the week I'd spent in a coma, apparently bleeding out of my eyes amongst other fun things.

The verdict: the graft was spreading throughout my body. The Coldi genes were taking over.

We were in uncharted territory. No one knew what it would mean for me, but I had recovered for now, albeit without hair and with some added new sensations.

The train slowed and slid into the tunnel underneath the artificial *gamra* island. To my eyes, the darkness was almost complete.

I knew there were lights in the carriage, because I had seen them many times before. But the only reason I knew that they had come on was that no one else complained about darkness. Right now I could not see them and I could not see the people who were getting up from their seats in order to get out. I could feel the train slowing down and coming to a stop. I could feel Thayu next to me, getting up. She took me by the elbow.

"Come on, we're there."

I protested. "I can't see anything." I held out my hands, hitting the back of the seat in front of me. I could see the faint glow of the ceiling lights in the carriage, but that was it.

"Welcome to the club."

She must see more than I did, because she guided me out of the carriage. I bumped my leg a few times and hoped that I was not going to get some more of those horrible bruises I had acquired last week from bumping into a table at the hospital. I was turning into an old man.

She helped me down the step onto the platform. I could hear the voices echo in the hall. I could hear the hissing of air out of the train's pressure pads. And I could still see little more beyond shapes moving about.

I stumbled with Thayu up the stairs, because I sort of knew where the stairs were. Only when we came out into the daylight, in the middle of the square that was the centre of the island, could I see again.

Thayu laughed when I breathed out a sigh of relief. "Now you understand what it's like to try to do things at night."

I asked her, "Do you really see that little?"

"We know where everything is. And we usually wear the eyepieces that allow us to see a little bit more."

Yes, they usually wore infrared eyepieces.

Damn.

I thought of all the times we'd gone out at night, and they'd actu-

ally shot at people—while seeing as little as this? That was somewhat
. . . disturbing.

We walked through the leafy avenues of the island.

Several people gave me strange looks. Yes, my long hair was all
gone.

There was only one reason men from most *gamra* worlds cut their
hair: when they spent time in jail.

Mine was now barely a fingernail width in length, and in combination with the fact that I had lost a lot of weight, I probably made
quite a sight, or, should I say, a convincing ex-prisoner.

I was keen to get home, but I wasn't quite up to normal strength
yet. I was fading, feeling alternately hot or cold, which, I had learned,
was a sign of fatigue. I struggled with the sharp differences between
sunlight and shadows. Judging distances was hard.

But finally, we made it into the large atrium of the building.

The first thing I noticed was the sheer humidity of the air in here.

Then the scent of the flowers that bloomed on the wall next to the
artificial waterfall that kept this room . . . almost cold.

I'd never experienced any part of this building as cold.

The scent of flowers, of the water constantly rushing over the
mossy rocks, the scent of *water* almost overwhelmed me. I'd never
known that water had a scent. It was disturbing.

Eirani and the others were waiting on the balcony in the atrium of
our building. They had seen me before—as soon as I could receive
visitors, they had frequented my room in the hospital. Still Eirani
rushed down the stairs, faster than I had ever seen her move, fleshy
hips and voluminous bosom wiggling.

"Oh, Muri, you're home!"

I had a feeling that she wanted to give me a hug. People at the
gamra complex didn't hug, and her keihu family didn't hug either, but
she had learned some things from her trip to Earth, including hugs.
Eirani was a *very* hug type of person. She took my other arm, and
helped me up the stairs, which was still quite an exhausting endeavour,
all the while commenting about how thin I was.

It was past lunchtime, she said, but that didn't mean that I
couldn't have any lunch. She had spent most of the morning and also
last night shopping and cooking so that I would get my favourite food.

"It's very good to be back again."

I left out the bit that I wasn't particularly hungry. But I knew I would have to gain some weight and do some strength training, which would fit in well with the recent drive of my team to keep up that alertness and training. I had heard, while I was in hospital, all about how they went out and did night training, but without quite realising how difficult that really was for them.

We came out onto the gallery, where Evi and Telaris stood guard at the door to my apartment. They were normally much more reserved, but their grins showed that they were happy to have me back.

"Now we have something to do," Evi said.

I had no doubt that in my absence my team would have given them something to do, but it would not have been terribly interesting. Things like administration.

We went into the hall.

Everyone was there: Nicha, Devlin, Ynggi, Sheydu, Deyu, Reida, Karana, Ayshada—

He ran up to me, throwing his little arms around my knees.

"You have grown so much!"

Nicha picked him up and held him close to me. He babbled while running both his chubby hands over my almost bald head and pulling my earrings.

Nicha laughed and pulled him away. "Come on, Ayshada, don't hurt Cory. He's just come from the hospital."

Ayshada babbled some words that only his father could understand.

Everyone came to greet me. Deyu and Reida both also looked happy.

Ynggi was more reserved, but his tail would not keep still. "I'm happy that you're back."

Devlin clapped him on the shoulder. "Don't be so shy." And to me: "This young man managed to evict the meili from the roof, and seal up the hole where they were coming in."

Those bat-like creatures had been an issue for a while. "What about your course?" Ynggi had been doing a course in communication and electronics.

Another tail-waggle indicated that he was happy to be asked. "Very well. I got top marks."

"That's great! I'm looking forward to you using your knowledge."

And that was no lie. Pengali excelled in using knowledge in unexpected and inventive ways. I was sure that with spying electronics, that could only be a good thing.

Sheydu greeted me in her usual *I don't want to show any of my emotions* way.

I looked around for—wait . . .

"Where is Veyada?"

"He went into town," Sheydu said in that way that could kill a conversation in a second flat. *Into town* was code for *doing something secret.*

"Anything wrong?" Damn, I hoped not. I was looking forward to some rest, but of course trouble always managed to find me when I was least prepared.

"No." That was a conversation killer as well. *Don't ask.* But then she surprised me by adding, "Just Veyada being Veyada."

Whatever that was supposed to mean. Oh, I knew it meant *something,* but right now my brain was misfiring on all cylinders. Thayu was still holding my arm. The big doors to the balcony in the living room were open, bringing in a breeze that carried the scent of food, of flowers, of the marshland outside, mingling with the overwhelming scent of her.

Blood rushed to my face.

"Sorry." I gently pulled my arm out of her grip.

"Are you all right?"

"Yes, it's just . . ." I blew out a breath. This was going to be *very hard* to get used to.

"Come, there is tea." Eirani said from the door into the living room, where she stood with a trolley full of dishes.

We all sat at the table, and Eirani unloaded a veritable feast of cakes and breads. No red-coded food. I'd have to take a quiet occasion to speak to her about that. I was sure red-coded food would be on my diet now. She'd probably feel slightly betrayed.

Thayu went to shut the doors. I'd always been annoyed at her doing this, but the breeze was actually cold. I'd never felt cold in Barresh.

At this moment, Devlin got up and ran across the room and into the hall. I watched him, because he clearly had been expecting something.

He came back not a moment later, and beckoned me. "Someone wants to talk to you."

Clearly, it was important.

I followed him across the hall into the hub. I hadn't been here for so long, and it felt so familiar. It even smelled familiar—not that I had ever known there was a smell associated with this room. Mostly it had to do with a few empty cups that Devlin had left on the bench next to the central workstation, and maybe there were some empty bowls there as well.

He gestured to me. "Sit here."

By now I was wondering what this was about. I had already talked to my father a few times, and he had told me that he would contact me tomorrow.

Devlin sat at his workstation and pressed a few buttons. The projector sprang into life, displaying the hub's logo, and then he connected to the Exchange.

Devlin said into his earpiece, "He's here now."

He then gave the earpiece to me, got up from his seat and left the room. I sat in the dark waiting for the image to come up.

It did so after a few seconds, and by that time, I already knew that it probably came from Asto, because I could see the coordinates appearing in the bottom of the projection. It was slow because Asto was currently on the other side of the two suns, and the signal had quite a distance to travel.

I had expected Asha, my father-in-law, because he had a tendency to be secretive and spring surprises on me. He was the commander of Asto's air force, and his whereabouts was never advertised. He was also the leader of the Domiri clan, and would probably need me to sign some of those forms that I was supposed to send.

But to my surprise it was not Asha. It was Ezhya himself.

I could honestly not remember the last time I had spoken to him like this. He preferred to come in person or send me short and cryptic messages on my personal account. He was well aware of the fact that anything sent through the Exchange was not exactly secure. He was wary and very careful.

I didn't know whether it was the slow connection or something else, but for a while he just looked at me. To be honest it was quite disconcerting.

And because I hadn't seen him for quite a while, I was never really sure where I stood with him. There was sometimes a level of unease between us that he would laugh away with some kind of joke. Was he my friend or my employer—because Coldi didn't really have friends—or was it something else? Did he expect me to affirm his superiority, or was it all right to look at him because, one time, years ago, he had told me that I could meet his eyes.

I knew he could see me, because his eyes moved as he studied me. He looked at my bare head, over my face, and at my clothing. And he said nothing for an uncomfortably long period.

Finally, he said, "So, you obviously survived."

"Yes. I understand that, for a time, that was under question. But it takes a bit more to kill me. Not even a bottom cleaner can."

He chuckled and I laughed as well, but it wasn't an easy kind of laugh. I was referring of course to the time that my leg had become infected, and I had been besieged by leeches and had needed a blood transfusion, all through my own stupidity.

"It does take a little bit more to kill us," he said.

Coldi put a lot of meaning in their pronouns. It was a very inclusive *us* that he used, a form that I didn't hear very often, and that was frequently used within a family.

He obviously thought that, having Coldi genes, I was part of the Coldi race now. I didn't know that I could feel it, but maybe he could.

I was still trying to make sense of all the strange emotions that awakened in me.

I said, "Is everything all right there? Is there anything you want me to do?"

It was a bit odd that he was officially my employer, but he rarely gave me a specific job to do. I had asked him once. He told me to use my own judgement of what needed doing. As long as I understood that my task was to go into places where he couldn't, and represent his views.

"Yes, everything is all right," he said. "Nimazhu is becoming such a big girl. She is running around the house keeping all my staff busy. Raanu loves her. She takes her out on walks and plays with her all the time."

It was a very strange conversation, talking about the daughters he rarely mentioned. Perhaps he was attempting to ask me, out of genuine concern, if I was all right. The notion of a friendship between unequals was unknown to Coldi. But he probably knew that we humans valued that sort of emotional interaction and that I would appreciate it. Which meant he most likely wanted something from me, and I wasn't sure when he was going to ask.

"Yes, I've heard that they are quite a handful at that age." Ayshada certainly was. I could hear him yell across the hall.

"Have you chosen a name yet?"

There was that naming problem again. I really had to do something about it fairly soon.

"I'm going to deal with it within the next few days. I will notify Asha."

"I would like to know what I need to call you."

"Do you have any suggestions?"

"I would like to call you Rizha."

That shook me a little bit.

In Coldi the letters M and R were sometimes interchangeable. Mizha had been chief coordinator at the time that settlements were planned on Earth. Was there any meaning in his suggestion?

I also felt embarrassed to name myself after such a high-ranking person. I knew that sometimes Coldi parents chose these names because they wanted their children to do well, but it was seen as pretentious. I didn't like pretentious. *He* liked the name?

It was because of Mizha that he had faced a number of problems with Nations of Earth. I could hardly imagine that he would want me to choose a name similar to this man's. Surely he had to be joking.

But I could see no sign of it on his face.

"I will consider all the options very carefully," I said.

He let the subject rest after that. He asked me a few things about the medical procedure and my health and what Lilona had said about travelling to Asto for the initiation ceremony. I hardly felt that he was the person to organise logistics about my trip, but I answered him as best as I could.

It looked like he was about to sign off, without having said anything of significance.

And then he said, "Have you heard anything from Margarethe recently?"

Oh. That was why he had contacted me—he needed to tell her something. I wasn't sure if I wanted to know what it was.

I told him that the last time I had been in contact with her was before I went in to the hospital to have the procedure that went so horribly wrong. So it was probably about a month ago.

"But if you want to get onto Margarethe, you can always contact Amarru, and she will relay the question without any interference from the local media," I said.

"Yes," he said, without further comment.

I suspected that the matter was too sensitive even for the usual channels.

And that worried me even more. For several reasons. Because I had never found out what exactly had happened in those two weeks that Ezhya and Margarethe had been together at Kedras. Both of them had said very little about it. All the worries I had about appropriateness resurfaced. As far as I knew Margarethe still had at least two years of her term to serve as president of Nations of Earth. Ezhya was not a young man, and those in his job did not retire. Chief Coordinators kept serving until the end. When someone at that level in Asto society stepped down, they usually committed suicide, or someone else killed them. It was a harsh and violent world up on the top of the Asto society.

Heart thudding, I suggested, "I can contact her, if you want."

"No, it can wait."

And I knew it couldn't, because otherwise he wouldn't have contacted me. Nor would he have been so casual about it. But he obviously wanted no one else to know.

He signed off in his usual abrupt fashion, and it was only when the connection was cut that I remembered that Margarethe had sent me a message that I could expect Minke Kluysters to turn up somewhere, because they had traced him leaving the planet. But surely Ezhya would care little about that. To him, Minke was just a hustler, a small time politician trying to fight for his attention. I hadn't even briefed Ezhya on exactly how Earth's referendum to join *gamra* was won. It didn't matter.

Ezhya didn't need to know about Minke Kluysters and other Earth-based self-important businessmen.

I was expecting Minke to turn up in Barresh and had already contacted him because he had asked me to help him set up an office. I would deal with that request. I would lead him around and oversee his meetings. It was called *keeping one's enemies close*.

2

____

WELL, THERE WAS an interesting situation straight away. I didn't even get the time to recover and already the mysteries were piling up.

I sat in the hub after he had disconnected, staring into the darkness that really *was* a lot darker than I remembered. I'd always known that Coldi night vision was not good, but somehow had never expected it to be so . . . limited. I could only see the hub console with all of Devlin's empty cups lined up across the top.

The sound of talk and laughter drifted out of the living room. Ayshada was babbling at the top of his voice, making words that meant nothing, to pretend that he was talking, too.

I should go and join them.

I should talk to Thayu about this strange call and what she made of it.

Damn it, I had intended to use this supposedly quiet period to do a few jobs that would bring in some money. Unfortunately my stay in hospital had not done much for my finances and I did not want to ask Ezhya to pay for my decision to employ two new office staff and Ynggi.

But I had *needed* the office staff because of all the local responsibilities that continued to pile up, and I'd wanted Ynggi, because I wanted my household to be varied. I wanted people from different worlds and different clans to be part of it, so that their voices could be heard and understanding gained.

"Are you coming?" Thayu stood at the door, a silhouette backlit by the bright light in the hall.

I pushed myself up from the bench.

Devlin came in from the hall, carrying yet another cup, this one full.

"I'll take care of communication," he said. "You go and join the others."

"Eirani is trying to kill us with food," Thayu said. "You're going to have to come to the table, or she will come in here and drag you out."

I wasn't terribly hungry, but I went with her anyway.

Thayu had not been exaggerating. The selection of food on the table was the most extravagant I had seen for a while.

All the members of my team were sitting around the table.

"Whose birthday is it?" I asked while sitting down. The concept of birthdays was a thing that had become hugely popular in our household. Coldi didn't celebrate birthdays, keihu and Indrahui didn't, either. But all of them understood the concept and enjoyed parties. Moreover, it gave Eirani a reason to break out the special food.

"We have to celebrate that you're home," Eirani said.

I sat down at the table in between Thayu and Nicha, in between their familiar presence and familiar smell. The food was rich, colourful, exquisite. There was nut bread, colourful salads, fruit, smoked fish for Ynggi, lizard eggs, noodles and too many other things to mention. Eirani and the kitchen really had done a lot of work.

For a while, the talk was happy.

Apparently, while I'd been away, Ynggi had turned his downstairs room into a rainforest.

"You should see it," Deyu said. "The plants are growing up the wall and right to the ceiling. It smells of flowers in there."

Ynggi sat at the end of the table, and he blushed, the tip of his tail describing little circles behind him.

"Don't embarrass him," Karana said. She was making an attempt to feed Ayshada, but he was more interested in Ynggi's tail.

Reida snorted. "It was much better before Eirani told him that the ringgit are meant to stay outside."

Everyone laughed, including Ynggi.

I asked where Veyada was, but Nicha assured me that he would be there for dinner.

"What? There is dinner after this?"

I had barely touched the food on my plate. Apart from the fact that my sense of smell was sensitive, my taste was not the same, and what was more, using the tongs that came with the traditional keihu dishes was awkward. I had no idea what was going on with my fine motor skills, but simple tasks like eating and writing felt like torture.

"You have to eat well, Muri," Eirani said. "You're much too thin."

I knew she was right, and struggled with the tongs, never quite getting the grip right.

After watching me struggle for a while Thayu said, quietly, "You are tired, right?"

"No more than usual, but I just had a very strange conversation that disturbs me."

She spoke in a low voice. "That was Ezhya, right?"

"How did you know that?"

"I've spoken to him a few times. He seemed very keen to know how you were doing."

"Did he mention any particular reason for that?"

"He didn't say as much, but I think that in the Aghyrian settlements, here in Barresh and way back in Miran, they tried to do something similar to what you're doing with your body: turn people from Aghyrian into Coldi, because back then some people still viewed being Aghyrian as abomination. They found that the *sheya* instinct was something that was quite affected by changes in the chromosome structure. There seems to be evidence that people actually acquired the instinct after they were treated. I guess he is curious."

"I don't think that applies to me."

"Doesn't it?" She met my eyes. "Why not?"

"Because . . ." I spread my hands. "I haven't noticed any difference in how I relate to you or Nicha."

"I don't know. I would have guessed that you always had a little bit of the instinct. Because I don't think that you would have been able to do as well as you're doing if you didn't understand the instinct."

"Understanding it is not the same as having it."

"No, but understanding it to a certain level definitely requires some kind of affinity with it."

That was a disturbing thought. I had never seen it that way. It took me back to the very first time I'd met Nicha.

I knew that if two Coldi met each other and they had never seen each other before, and there was no precedent for how the two people's ranks related to each other, there was a chance that a fight would break out. Modern Coldi were embarrassed if they came to blows, because they considered the reaction primitive. The fact that they needed to establish if a person they met was superior or subordinate was pathological to them. The *sheya* instinct.

I remembered the very first time I saw Nicha. He had looked at me sideways, and his hand had twitched as if he'd been about to spring. He had never really told me that he'd had a reaction to me, but I had suspected it, because I heard it sometimes happened.

Somehow, he had been much more comfortable since he could admit that he felt subordinate to me.

I had assumed that this was because of something to do with Nicha, not with me.

Then I thought of my strange talk with Ezhya. How intensely he had looked at me. How he had used that very inclusive *us* pronoun.

I asked, "If I had the instinct, would it manifest through a projection?"

Thayu had to think about that. "It usually doesn't, but then again we very rarely talk directly to people who are not already in our association."

That was also true. It was the task of the leader of the association to deal with outsiders. It was the task of the leader to forge a safe path for the others to follow.

Maybe Ezhya had felt something about me as well—he had always displayed a curious interest in me—and wanted to know how the change affected me, whether I had developed the instinct. Throughout history, Coldi society had a record of disdain for people who did not have the instinct. It was not so strong at present, but the Aghyrian movement, its links with the *zeyshi* rogues—who were mostly throwback Aghyrians where the chromosome graft had come undone—was proof of that. Its past treatment of Hedron—people from the Ezmi clan who didn't have the instinct—was evidence of that.

Maybe Ezhya's curiosity about me came because he felt something, and because he couldn't figure me out. Also because if I was Coldi, I would have the right to take his position—having shot his main rival—and he wanted to keep an eye on just how Coldi I was becoming. Because if this treatment made me develop the instinct, then . . . that was a whole minefield I didn't want to get into.

I wasn't Coldi; I hadn't grown up in Athyl. I had no desire whatsoever to challenge Ezhya, but it might just be that this conflict was out of my hands. It wasn't about what I felt, it was about what everyone else felt. If the upper circles in Asto cottoned onto the fact that their leader was weak because he allowed someone they saw as a challenger to live, then . . .

Damn, I didn't even want to think about it.

The door in the hall opened and a moment later Veyada came in. He rushed into the living room and sat down at the table without saying a word. He looked down, not meeting my eyes. His face was red.

He exchanged a look with his mother, but neither of them said anything. Sheydu resumed the conversation she had been having with Reida about some gadget.

I glanced at Thayu. What was that about?

She shrugged in a noncommittal way. I had no doubt I would hear about this later.

After I had eaten as much as I could manage, which wasn't terribly much, I went to our bedroom for a rest. I didn't intend to sleep, but the day had worn me out more than I admitted, and reading up on reports was terribly boring. I didn't notice when the reader slipped from my hand and I fell into blissful sleep.

———

Sometime later in the afternoon, I woke to a knock on my door. I pressed myself up, surprised and feeling woolly.

Devlin came in. "Muri, I am sorry to disturb you, but there has been a lady calling a few times in the last few weeks, and I am not sure what to do about her."

"Which lady?"

"It's that woman who was talking to you before you went into the hospital."

I had to do a mental shift.

That had to be the Mirani wife of Earth-born academic Benton Leck. I vaguely remembered how she had contacted me about having lost contact with her husband, who was on some kind of research trip. I'd actually been annoyed with her, because, while she was worried, she wouldn't give me any indication as to where her husband was and what he was doing there, and I remembered palming her off because of the lack of detail she gave me.

I remembered Sheydu making a cruel joke when I mentioned her to my team. She had said that the man had probably taken off with his mistress. We'd exchanged some lame jokes about it.

Oh man, I really hoped this wasn't something that was going to turn around to bite me in the behind. One of those famous last words occasions where my lame jokes and rudeness while palming her off would be plastered across the media for all to laugh at.

Benton Leck had married into one of the old Endri families of Miran. The woman's name was Aliandra Ilendar—that alone said *everything* about her background. Ilendar was one of the Foundation families, so she came with a lot of attitude. Those families were like the Nations of Earth diplomatic elite, only more established, more entitled and more self-righteous. They generally kept to Miran, but I swore they could give the Aghyrians a run for their money in the arrogance stakes.

The Ilendar family was influential in the Mirani council; they had money and owned a lot of businesses.

For all that Barresh was a shining pearl of a town, it lay inside a small enclave surrounded by the sleeping giant Miran.

Those with influence in Miran were not people to piss off, no matter how entitled their requests seemed. I just hadn't yet figured out what this woman actually wanted from me or why she kept contacting me—wasting our time—if she wasn't going to tell me where her husband was so that I could pass the matter off to the relevant authorities who could find him. If finding him was indeed what she wanted.

When I looked into the matter before, I had found out that she regularly wrote self-important letters to the Barresh Council, complaining about some issue affecting her, like the construction noise from next door, or the times rubbish was collected.

That had been a big factor in my casual dismissal of her. And I was extremely busy, this sort of stuff was not my normal job, and I hadn't been well—

Excuses, excuses.

I hoped I hadn't missed vital clues that this was going to be more important, but something in the back of my mind said that it might just be, and that I was stupid and just as arrogant as the Mirani Endri were said to be.

"Did she give out more information than usual?" I asked him.

"No, but the message came with the seal of the Mirani Council."

Crap, that was just what I needed. They were far too easily offended.

I dragged myself out of bed and followed him to the hub. I looked at the message he had received. It was indeed from Benton Leck's wife, written with the seal of the Mirani Council, with the image of the city of Miran's famous watchtower. As far as logos went, it looked severe and foreboding.

She wanted me to pick up something from a private box somewhere in town. She said that her maid would give me the number and the key. Only to me. She said that there would be payment involved.

The message read,

It is scandalous that nobody in Barresh seems to care except you. The council is rotten to its core. I have been in there so many times and when they see me they always say yes madam yes madam, but I am sure that as soon as I turn my back they laugh at me. Because I am a silly lady.

Well maybe it would've helped if she didn't always go to the council to complain about everything.

My husband is still missing. I have been threatened by people in town. They are high-profile people, too, and I have been forced to leave town while the council did nothing. You probably think I am crazy, but to show you that I'm not, and that my husband has not taken off with another woman, as some have even said, I am prepared to compensate you fairly for your help.

My ears were glowing. This was precisely what we had said, and I had very much been trying to get her off my back.

Nicha came in. His eyes widened as he noticed the logo of the Mirani Council. "Is there a problem?"

I showed him the message.

He snorted. "That woman again?"

"Yeah."

"Why does she keep playing games with you?"

I shrugged. "Because her husband is from Earth, and in the past I have helped people from Earth." I was talking about Robert Davidson, for whom I had gone around to all the residents of Barresh who were from Earth to find out what might have happened to him. I did remember seeing Benton Leck's wife back then, and at some point she must have concluded that I was the go-to person for this sort of thing.

Nicha said, "If she really wants help, she should ask Melissa."

That was Melissa Heyworth, who had been elevated to proper *gamra* delegate after the vote of Earth to join *gamra* went through.

"Melissa is dealing with politics and diplomacy. She has no time to look after individual cases."

"And you do?"

I guessed I didn't, but for some reason I found it hard just to tell people no to their face. No matter how much they annoyed me, people wanted something and the fact that they were asking me often meant that they had nowhere else to turn. If you were a stranger in this town, the local bureaucracy could be very hostile.

I blew out a breath. "I have to admit that I'm not sure how seriously I should take all of her stories."

Nicha snorted. "How about none of them? The woman is crazy, and she just wants attention. We have too much to do to give this any time. You are not well. Find someone else to deal with it."

"She says she will pay fairly, and I believe her on that front. I mean —these Mirani nobles never mention money unless they're happy to part with it."

And Nicha was aware of the fact that we had a bit of an income problem. He also never gave me the usual reply that I got from the others in my association—just ask Ezhya for more—because he understood why I didn't like doing that. Coldi in general cared much more for influence than money, but plenty of people at the *gamra* island thought differently. I didn't want any of my household's ethics brought into question. We needed some independent income and had for some time.

"I guess you want to scope it out," Nicha said, heaving a sigh.

"It seems a fairly easy project."

"You're just out of hospital. You nearly died. Nothing is easy right now."

"Oh, I'm not going into town today to see what she wants."

"Only tomorrow?"

"Yeah, maybe tomorrow."

He rolled his eyes. "I was joking."

"But I'm not. I'll never become stronger if I stay inside and do nothing all day."

"I really wished that you knew how to observe a rest period as Lilona told you to. But I'm guessing I'm holding my hopes too high."

"I feel fine."

"That's what you said last time, in this very room. Then you went into the hall and collapsed on the floor."

3

———

MY DECISION TO GO into town the next day was not met with universal enthusiasm from my team, which was as I had expected.

Thayu told me as much after a restless night. "Why don't you let someone else deal with it? It's not your job to be this woman's personal investigator."

"It's quick to do and will give us some funds. It keeps us in the good books with the people of influence in Miran—"

She raised her hands.

"—Yes, I know you'll say, 'So what? They're only Miran and they're old-fashioned and quaint,' but I care. Who knows when we'll need something from Miran that we can get only because I've been helpful to them in the past?"

Thayu snorted. "Want something from them? They don't even grow mushrooms."

But she was laughing and I laughed as well. One could take this all too seriously. "Look, whatever my reasons, I want the woman off my back. I want to know what she's on about, whether she wants her husband found or not, or whatever it is she wants, and then we can palm her off onto someone else, and maybe get some money and get on with important things."

"Like, how to get you back to health so you can perform the honours to get me pregnant in the first place."

"Watch what you're saying." I lunged for her, but she jumped out of the way. I lunged again, but she jumped further.

"Nope, nope, you'll need to do better than that to catch me. Prove yourself to me, show off all your little swimmers to the medico."

There was that, too. Lilona had said that, before we made another attempt, she wanted to check me out fully. All this meddling into what was supposed to be private was rather tiresome and slightly embarrassing. Especially when somebody poked electrodes to see if particular anatomic functions did their job. But enough about that.

Thayu left the room. I got dressed and went after her.

All the members of my team sat around the dining table for breakfast. Even Evi and Telaris were there.

Ayshada squealed when I came in. He held his arms out, and I picked him up, setting him on my knees. Being Coldi, and a toddler, he didn't yet have the ability to vary his body temperature, and holding him was much like handling a hot water bottle. He didn't feel so warm today, and I wondered if this was because I had a fever or my temperature was permanently going up.

Deyu was showing Karana images of creatures from all over the inhabited worlds. I recognised a picture of my father's llamas. Karana pulled a face. Those things were so temperamental, and Deyu had been the only one who had managed to come close to them.

She flicked to another picture. It was an elephant, a big male with its ears flapping.

"Hey, Veyada, an *elephant,*" Deyu said.

This would normally draw some kind of remark from Veyada, depending on his mood, but he was in discussion with Sheydu and didn't hear her. They were speaking in low voices. Their interactions had held an uncomfortable intensity ever since Veyada had come back from wherever he had been, and I couldn't say that I liked it.

"I'm going for a short trip into town today," I announced.

Everyone around the table fell quiet and watched me. They didn't question my judgement to go into town in front of the others. That was something I had never realised: the dynamics within my association. I told them what I'd decided, and with the exception of Thayu and Nicha, they never questioned.

It was an odd thing, realising this and realising that I had never noticed this before.

Eirani would have questioned my plans, but she had left the room.

I continued, feeling a bit rattled. "We may have a little job to do, and I may ask some of you to assist, but meanwhile, keep doing your regular jobs. Anyone who has time is free to volunteer to come with me."

That's what I would normally say, but it also felt wrong to me. None of them mentioned it, and I wondered if it felt wrong to them, too. Maybe it had always felt wrong to them and it was just me who had become attuned to this.

Or maybe I was just crazy and lingering medical issues were playing games with my brain.

It was awkward; it put a hole right in the place that I'd thought relatively safe from upheaval: my confidence that if I handled the matter in a certain way, my association would understand me.

But nothing was certain anymore, and my confidence lay in shards on the tiled mosaic floor in the hall.

Evi and Telaris volunteered, again because they didn't realise that my *asking* for volunteers was wrong. I should *tell* them.

Blood roaring in my ears, I randomly chose someone. "Reida?"

He looked up. "Yes, of course I'll come." His eyes widened. Was he shocked?

I glanced at Thayu, wondering what I had just done, but she didn't act like she'd noticed anything unusual. My heart was hammering. What was wrong with me?

I spent most of breakfast watching the members of my team interact, nervous, wondering what was different and why.

Veyada and Sheydu were talking about whatever was going on between them. Reida was talking to Nicha. He acted subservient even if his body language didn't clearly show it. How did I know?

I didn't figure it out. Just . . . saw it.

After breakfast Eirani told me that she would help me get ready.

I protested. "That's not really necessary."

"Of course it is. You can't go into town like this."

So I went to the bedroom, and a moment later Eirani came in carrying a basket. Protruding from the top was a soft hairy thing, that looked very much like a—

She set the basket down on the dressing table. "Look, I got this for you." She pulled out the hairy thing. Locks of black hair tumbled down. A wig.

"Oh, no, I'm not wearing that."

"But Muri, you look like a prisoner. Aliandra Ilendar won't think much of you if you turn up like this."

She might well be right, but no. "She is not going to be there. I'm just going to pick up something from the staff."

"They won't think much of you either."

Also true.

"Just try it."

She put the thing on my head. It was hot and itchy. The black hair fell to my shoulders. It was not fake hair, I realised. Coldi hair tended to lose its sheen after while.

"Now have a look at yourself." She turned the chair so I faced the mirror.

Disturbingly, I looked only half as ridiculous as I'd imagined. And even more disturbingly, I barely recognised my own face. The lines in my face had become hard, my eyes sunken, my irises quite dark in this low light. I leaned to the mirror. Yes, my eyes were still blue, but didn't seem as light as they had been.

The skin on my face was soft like a Coldi's.

"Doesn't that look much better?"

I had to admit that it softened my skeleton look. "I'm still not wearing it."

"Why not? You look good like this."

"It's not always about what we look like, but who we are."

She pulled the wig off. "And like this, you look like a sick skeleton that has escaped from prison."

I stared at my mirror image, emaciated, hollow-eyed. I looked like . . . I was transported back in time to when I was six, and my father gently pushed me into a hospital room. It was getting dark outside. I'd come from school and gone to my grandparents who had brought me here.

I couldn't help but stare at the figure on the bed.

That was my mother? What had happened to her silken hair? What had happened to her full cheeks?

She reached out her hands to me.

"Come on, say hello," my father said behind me.

I was too scared to move. She looked like she would break if I touched her.

"Muri?" Eirani's voice shook me back to reality.

"It's all right." I wiped my eyes. "I'm still not wearing it."

Eirani mumbled something about looking like a criminal, but she helped me put on my blue shirt and jacket.

When she had packed up and left the room, I got up and looked at myself in the mirror. Eirani had rather overdone the jewellery, but I let it be. She was determined to make sure that whatever stupid choices she thought I made about my attire, I wouldn't look like a prisoner.

Then I noticed movement in the corner of the mirror. Thayu was standing at the door. How long had she been there?

She came to me and ran her warm hands through the stubble on my head. "What colour do you think it will grow back?"

"Not black," I said.

"No, I think it might be white or grey." She studied the top of my head. "The colour is odd, though."

Her fingers massaged my scalp. The feeling was soothing. I closed my eyes.

"Black looked good on you, though."

I opened my eyes. "Did you see that wig she got?"

"She's been talking about it a bit."

"Do you think I should wear it?"

She shrugged. "You can decide."

Great, now I felt like an arse. Eirani meant well. I should apologise to her. But it only made me more determined not to wear a wig. My mother had worn a wig, in those last days of her illness. Wigs were for sick people.

But we were ready, and met Evi, Telaris and Reida in the hallway.

We left our apartment walked through the hall down the stairs and outside onto the bright and sunny boulevards of the island. People greeted me, and some even asked how I was. I assumed that the news of my stay in hospital was general knowledge.

The trip into town was uneventful.

On the train, I asked Reida about his training. Since his rocky start with us, Reida had doubled down on his learning. He'd taken lessons in formal Coldi, he'd taken an apprenticeship with a company installing security equipment, and then I'd sent him to a specialised training program for listening to and interpreting captured electronic signals. He'd been making little robots and zooming them around the house—much to the delight of Ayshada.

I asked him if there was anything else he aspired to.

"I want to be the best."

"What do you need in order to be the best?"

He looked down. "I would want to go to the spy academy in Athyl." His cheeks coloured.

"Thayu went there. Why don't you ask her how to get in?"

"They will never accept me."

"No, Thayu never said that." She said it would be hard, not impossible. "If you are the best, the most promising student, they will take you, regardless of the fact that you're from the wrong clan." And he definitely was. Reida was a true Asto Ezmi, straight from the *zeyshi* rogues of the Outer Circle. He even had the *zeyshi* tattoos. "Don't be ashamed of where you're from and who you are. Show what you can do. They will accept you."

He was still looking down and didn't seem convinced. I reached out and pushed his chin up until he looked at me. It was a typical Coldi gesture that I had despised when I'd first seen it. But it was not as demeaning as it looked from human eyes. It was a gesture of care and intimacy. A gesture a teacher would make to a student.

"They *will* accept you," I repeated. "Do the work, and they will have no choice. You're good, Reida; you know that."

His cheeks coloured.

We got out of the train at the airport and walked up the hill to the Exchange.

Benton Leck lived in one of the large houses behind the main square, a multi-storey affair that, maybe a hundred years ago, would've belonged to one of the large local families. Maybe a counsellor or some business man with a lot of money. These days those houses were mostly subdivided into smaller units, because few people had huge households anymore, and certainly none lived in one house with all their Pengali domestic workers.

Except it seemed time had passed this house by.

Vines cascaded over the wall, creeping through the gaps between the metal gate and the wall. The gate hung crooked and creaked when

I pushed it open. The pond outside the front door was full of leaves, and clumps of marsh grass had come up in the water. The walls of the house needed painting, and in places the stucco had come off the walls, displaying the bare stone underneath.

We walked across the uneven path up the steps to a dusty porch to the front door.

I knocked.

We waited. Evi and Telaris had remained outside the porch. Reida studied the ceiling of the overhanging balcony. Trying to pick up signs of listening bugs?

Thayu studied the garden, the overgrown garden beds, the unruly bushes that must once have been part of a hedge, the weeds that grew in the cracks in the pavement. It was a riot of green. Insects buzzed from flower to flower, and I bet that the pond would be alive with ringgit at night.

From the other side of the door came the sound of a bolt being drawn back.

The door opened a crack.

In the darkness on the other side I could see movement.

I asked, "This is the house of Benton Leck, isn't it?"

"Oh, it's you," a woman said.

The door opened. The woman was a local, keihu like Eirani. Also like Eirani, she had big hips and an impressive bosom. She wore the grey dress that was often called a "house uniform" and worn by domestic workers. She stepped back to let us in. "Come, quickly."

Thayu, Reida and I went into the house.

I was surprised how musty it smelled inside, as if no one had lived here for years.

The woman preceded us into a large kitchen, where a couple of other people sat around the table, including a young girl and two men and another woman, also dressed in grey.

"He has come about the mistress," the first woman said.

The other adult woman got up from the table. She went to a cupboard against the wall and took something out, which she then gave to me.

It was a key, I presumed the key to the box.

"The mistress said if you come here, to tell you to go there, open the box and she will have put instructions inside."

Why not let the staff give them to me, I had no idea. But the lady always liked making a fuss.

So we left again, picking up Evi and Telaris in the yard.

It seemed rather strange, all these domestic workers living in this grand old and rather neglected house by themselves. Did anyone ever clean up the garden?

The message boxes were in the Courier's Guild building in Fountain Street. The centrepiece of this venerable old building was the giant hall where parcels were processed as well as the hundreds of message boxes that lined the walls. Like the rest of the old city, it had seen very little change in the last hundred years or maybe even longer.

I'd been here plenty of times, but today I noticed things I'd never seen before. Had I ever noticed the smell of the stone floor? Had I noticed the way the coloured window in the ceiling dome cast coloured spots over the floor? Had I noticed that many people here were not local? Had I ever noticed that Kedrasi people had a distinctive smell as well?

The message box that belonged to Benton Leck was one of the smaller ones against the back wall of the hall. I opened the hatch with the key the housekeeper had given us and slid out the tray. There was a letter inside, an old-fashioned handwritten letter.

It was ironic that with all the technology to encrypt electronic data, the most failsafe way to prevent others reading your communication still remained a hard copy. In recent years the Couriers' Guild and the Trader Guild couriers had experienced a increased demand on services everyone thought would have died out by now: hand-delivering hard copy documents.

I put the letter in my pocket and we went back to the tree-lined street.

I stood with my back to a tree trunk when I opened the envelope. I didn't know what I had expected, but I had to admit to being slightly disappointed that there was only a single sheet inside. I unfolded it.

It said,

When you read this I will have left the city. I still haven't heard anything from my husband, but it has simply become impossible for me to stay here any longer. The people who recruited him to work for them are so insistent that they bother me day and night. I will give you a code; come to the Exchange and I will talk to you. If you help me, you will be rewarded.

Thayu had read over my shoulder. "She's playing games with us."

"Either that or she thinks I can be bought."

"You can." She flicked her eyebrows up.

"Yeah, well, not like that. I'm happy to do a small job, but I don't know that we have the time to race all over the place to follow this trail of messages." I was a bit annoyed at this game of cat and mouse, actually. "So we're supposed to go to the Exchange. Obviously she doesn't know that everyone can listen in to Exchange communications. Does that sound like a really stupid idea to you?"

"Yep."

"All right, let's just consider this outing a chance to leave the house. Let's go home. I think we've given her enough attention."

We'd tried, but I wasn't going to play this game. I was still slightly baffled by how Aliandra had been able to hoodwink her staff into thinking the household was under threat, but it was truly not my business how a paranoid woman led her life, and I should be doing different things.

We started walking in the direction of the airport and station.

The issue with Aliandra's husband kept niggling at me, though. I should check the flight registers to see if he had perhaps run back to Earth to escape the woman. If he had done that, I might not even blame him.

But to be honest, I didn't think he was the type. If he was really missing, that was a serious issue, and one that would come back to haunt me if I put her concerns aside too easily.

History was littered with cases where people had dismissed concerns which had later become a huge issue that could have been prevented if the person who'd been warned had taken it seriously.

We turned back in the direction of the airport. I had to admit it was quite nice to be in the street with normal people again, not amongst people who got excited when you moved, who put needles in you to extract or add things, who measured your piss and weighed your shit and would not leave you in peace.

I was going to say something about it to Thayu, but she was busy listening to something in her earpiece.

I had learned to be quiet when she did this, because she would probably be listening to Devlin who had some important security information.

So we walked silently along the tree-lined street. It was midday, and people were going about their normal lives.

The multicoloured lights were again flashing before my eyes, as they tended to do when I was in sunlight and walked in and out of the shadows. There were a lot of shadows in the dappled shade of the trees that lined the street. I thought—I hoped—that whatever ailed my eyes was getting better.

I had to admit that I didn't feel as hot as I normally would at this time of the day.

Thayu stopped suddenly. I went a couple of paces before I realised that she was no longer next to me, turned around and walked back to her. She was looking at her reader.

"What is it?" I asked her.

Usually when the members of my team were doing this, there was some sort of security risk. Someone was following us, or listening to us. But we hadn't done anything that warranted that kind of attention.

"Is anyone spying on us?" I asked.

"Is there ever a time people are not spying on us?" she said.

I guess she was right about that, but usually people in my team did not worry much about the regular background spying that went on, the type of spying that was a security measure as well as a way of independent record keeping.

She showed me the screen. On it, the familiar pattern of dots that showed where listening bugs were, or cameras mounted on buildings, as well as equipment carried by people. The screen showed some dots in the street behind us and in the side street. These dots were in the street rather than in the yards, so they had to be attached to people.

"What's going on?" I asked.

She did not reply. Here eyes were alert. She studied the street and the surrounding houses. I did the same but for the life of me couldn't see anything unusual.

And then I saw a single man, standing straight, at the edge of one of the terraces of the eating-houses that were so common in this part of the city. He stood with his arms by his sides, looking at us like a statue. I could see no weapons on him, and he wore casual clothing, nothing like the uniforms or dark clothing that spies would wear.

I knew him. It was Puck, the Tamerian.

"What is he doing there?" I asked.

"You tell me," Thayu said.

We were looking at him, and he was looking at us, and none of us seemed sure of what to do next.

This continued for a while, and it was rather strange, because I felt that he would like to speak to me, but for some reason did not dare approach us.

"Should I talk to him?" I asked.

"That's your decision."

I was always much better at talking than spying and fights and chases. On the other hand, I'd never been able to get much sense out of Puck, or any Tamerian for that matter. But he had once saved my life, even if he had been ordered to do so.

So I decided to try and find out what he wanted from us.

As I was walking towards him with Thayu following me, she grabbed my arm and said, "Look."

I looked at her screen. The dots that represented the listeners had all come closer.

"It's a trap," she said.

Her hand strayed to her upper arm where she carried her weapon.

"That's a silly kind of trap," I said. "If they really tried to trap us, would they be so open about it? I mean—they know that we use these scanners."

Thayu agreed. "It's a dumb trap, or it's so clever that we don't understand it yet."

It was all very strange, and I wasn't sure what to do. One thing I did know was that I was not up to running or fighting, and I wasn't armed, and had only a few people with me. I didn't want to risk any trouble.

So I just looked at Puck, willing him to come closer.

And after we had stood watching each other for a long time, he did, slowly, with deliberate steps. The way he walked reminded me of my father's dog Fred when he had done something naughty. Subservient.

He stopped a number of paces away from me. The dots on Thayu's screen had not moved.

"Hello, can I help you with something?" I asked him.

He said nothing, but that was not unusual. Tamerians did not communicate easily. You might have to ask a question several times and in several ways to get a reply at all.

So I asked again, "Are you in trouble?"

Now he looked to the side in a kind of shifty way. His forehead gleamed with sweat.

This was strange. I had never known Tamerians to be emotional. They usually did as they were told, no questions asked.

I presumed this meant that he was in some sort of trouble. And he was in emotional turmoil about it that he couldn't express in words.

This brought back to me that we had no idea who commanded these strange men and what sort of orders they received.

I continued, "If you want, you can come to the island, and you will be safe there."

He said a single word, "Surf."

So did he still want me to teach him to surf? "Yes, you can come. I will teach you."

I had no idea if he even understood what I said, but he suddenly turned around and ran off.

Thayu snorted. "What was that all about?"

I spread my hands. "You tell me. Let's go home."

As I said that, the breeze carried an unfamiliar tangy scent, reminiscent of foreign spices.

Thayu frowned at me. "What's that smell?"

I had no idea.

We waited for a bit longer, but he was truly gone, so we continued on our way to the station, leaving the spying people in their positions. For all I knew, they might have been as puzzled about the exchange as we were.

4

———

W E TALKED ABOUT the strange meeting on the way to the station. Thayu asked me to formulate what I thought was so strange about it. Coming from her, the question was odd. She was not the philosophical type but, while I was in hospital, several of my association had attended workshops that dealt with subjects ranging from weapons maintenance to the deep philosophy of the interpretation of behaviour—in relation to spying, I assumed. Strangely enough, they had been far more open about the course material and organisers of the weapons workshops—a private security company in town who had hired a high-ranking *gamra* security head to talk about this—than the philosophical workshops.

Was she testing what she had learned, applying theories? Great, I loved being a guinea pig. But I answered the question. "I thought it was strange how he came to me, as if he were a dog and afraid I would beat him."

"That is subservient behaviour," she said. "It's odd that you're seeing this."

"How could I not? It was extremely obvious."

"Previously, before your treatment, you would not have noticed."

"Yes, I would."

"No, you wouldn't. People, especially Coldi people, act like that all the time. You never noticed any of it, except when it was accompanied by the typical signs and gestures."

"But you saw him. He was just like my father's dog Fred, whimpering and looking up at me, as if he'd stolen sausages from the table."

"Yes, but Puck wasn't whimpering and didn't bow or crawl on his knees and he doesn't have a tail that gives away his feelings, therefore most people would not see it. I see it. You never did, but now you do."

"You're sure?"

"Sure. You never saw it before."

"But he never did any of this—"

"Yes, he did. Tamerians were always like this. They haven't changed. You have."

I had to take her word for it, but I found it very hard to believe. She had not been there when I first spoke to Puck in the hospital when he donated blood. He had not shown any emotion then, I was sure of it.

She continued with her questioning. "What did you think he was doing?"

"I think he was in some kind of trouble. I wonder if he wanted help, but didn't know how to ask for it."

"Why would he want help from you?"

I shrugged. "Because I spoke to him before? Because he saved my life? Because I told him I'd teach him to surf?"

Thayu grinned. "Not everyone is as obsessed with drowning yourself in the ocean as you are."

"It *was* the only thing I mentioned that he reacted to."

"Yes, but did he understand what you were talking about?"

Maybe. Maybe not. Puck remained an enigma.

On the train ride home, Thayu, Reida, Evi and Telaris discussed the significance of the secret observers of the meeting between us and Puck: who they were and why they were there. It appeared that my conversation with Puck had changed Thayu's mind about the surveillance: this was not a routine operation that always went on and served to protect me as much as to gather information about who visited what, where and at what time. That sort of data proved useful if someone challenged you about not having done something.

By the time we arrived at the *gamra* island, the conversation didn't appear to have come to a clear conclusion. The main question was whether the surveillance was about us, or whether we had happened into some situation revolving around Puck.

The train stopped and I filed with the others through the too-dark carriage. Thayu was behind me, but she didn't need to hold me like last time. I even managed to make the step to the platform without stumbling. It was still way too dark for me to make out faces, read signs or notice small obstacles, but I trusted that there were no small obstacles on the platform, and by the time we arrived at the stairs, daylight filtering in from above made the way clearer.

I managed to get to the top of the stairs without help. Progress in little steps. Once, I saved planets. Today, I had trouble walking up a set of stairs.

We came back to the apartment to some sort of commotion at the end of the hallway. Eirani stood at the top of the stairs leading down to the floor with the kitchen and the domestic workers' rooms, yelling at someone. Her voice carried along the hallway to the foyer. ". . . You think that those animals don't bother anyone? This is a house, not a forest. They carry disease, they make noise— What do you mean, something to eat? What's wrong with our food?"

"Ynggi," Thayu said.

I met her eyes. "Do I need to do something about this?"

"Probably not."

But I decided to go anyway. I walked to the end of the corridor. "What's going on?"

Eirani turned around, red-faced. "Oh Muri, you should see his room, he has got a whole rainforest in there."

Ynggi stood at the bottom of the stairs, looking up. His tail was waving from side to side, as Pengali tails did when their owners were agitated. "Cory said that I could make myself at home."

He was one of the few in my household who called me by my name.

"But that does not mean that you can bring the entire forest in here," Eirani said. And then she turned around to me. "You should see his room. It's full of plants and animals and it's such a mess in there. The kitchen is complaining that the ringgit get into the storage and the pantry is infested. We never have problems with them here, thank the heavens, not like in the city."

"Let me have a look."

I went downstairs. Ynggi had insisted his room be down here; he said he wanted to be at ground level because he felt uneasy being away from the garden.

His room was to the right. It had a sliding door into the very small garden, which then went into some bushland, beyond which was a walkway that surrounded the island.

The door in the room was open. The soft warm breeze came in and ruffled the leaves of many plants that stood in neat planter boxes. There were hundreds of them, almost to the extent that nothing else was visible.

I had no idea what he had done with the bed that had been in this room, but I couldn't see it anymore, there was that much vegetation. Judging from Eirani's fuss, I had expected a mess on the floor, but it was quite neat. He had even spread out the rug in between all the pots.

The little bag that he had brought when he came here from the tribe's settlement lay next to the rug. I realised that this was where he slept. Somewhere near the open doors there was a small sound that I recognised as coming from one of the many creatures that lived in the marsh. It was not a ringgit—a crustacean-like creature as big as an adult human hand—but something similar.

"Don't you think this is terrible," Eirani said behind me.

"Well, it's certainly different." I wasn't going to call it terrible, because I thought he had done an admirable job of adjusting the room so that he found it acceptable while keeping it clean.

Eirani was clearly disappointed.

So I asked, "What about the ringgit getting into the kitchen?" Because if that was true, it was a concern.

Eirani preceded me to the kitchen. The cook was sitting in a corner in an easy chair with his feet up onto another chair. I rarely came down here, and he jumped up as soon as he saw me. I told him to stay seated.

He told me that he had found ringgit in the pantry on two separate occasions. One of them was a few days ago, the other much longer ago.

"It's all because of this rainforest next door," Eirani said. "I want it gone. This is a clean house. We keep food in here and want no creatures."

And she looked at me, expecting me to agree with her. I was

already sorry I'd gotten involved. After this morning's episode with the wig, I had probably already squandered some goodwill with her.

I told Eirani not to worry about it, that I would keep an eye on the situation, and that she was not allowed to remove any of Ynggi's plants.

She clearly wasn't happy with this, but I went back upstairs, finding Thayu there, laughing.

"You'll never get her to be happy with that," she said. "Just tell her that's how it is."

"Easy for you to talk."

Thayu and Eirani had had their differences when I first came to live here.

"Yes, easy. You remind her who pays her. You are the boss."

I knew she was right, but Eirani was just . . . different to me, like a mother figure. I didn't like upsetting her.

I was tired of all these little spot fires.

I didn't know what had changed in my household, but I didn't like it. Everyone was so grumpy, although I understood why they wanted to protect me. I just wanted everybody to stop arguing and fussing over me.

I went to my office and pretended to work. But the flashes of light still danced before my eyes, and I found it hard to concentrate while my team was not working well.

I toyed with the idea of contacting Lilona, but what would I say to her? Everyone in my house is grumpy?

On second thought, they had probably all been stressed out about me, and were still reacting to that.

If I was the leader in my household, and the proper head of my association in the proper Coldi way, at least the Coldi members of my household would have felt that they needed to compete with each other for the leadership in case I didn't come back. They would never tell me that there had been disagreements between them, because I was back, and the problem had resolved itself. But maybe, just maybe, that was one of the issues.

Well, damn it.

I breathed out heavily.

Work was not going to happen. I pushed away the documents that I had spent some time looking at and not reading, and left the room.

I would do what I should have done all along. I went to the hub and asked Devlin to call everyone into a meeting.

"Is there a problem?" he asked.

He looked rather surprised. He didn't have the *sheya* instinct and most likely would not have noticed anything amiss with my team. Maybe even he and Evi and Telaris would have provided much-needed stability. And Eirani, too, *not* helped by Ynggi's impression of interior decorating. No wonder *she* was grumpy.

"Just a welcome," I said to Devlin when he raised his eyebrows at me.

"I thought you had already given a welcome yesterday at the table."

"I did pretty lousy job at it," I said. "And this is about work. The other one was about the household."

I sat on the bench and waited. One by one, everyone came in. First Thayu and Nicha, then Reida, Deyu and Sheydu. The latter remained standing around the edge of the room, Sheydu leaning against the cabinet that held the hub projector.

There was one obvious omission.

"Where is Veyada?"

Sheydu didn't know, which was odd.

"He said he wanted to get some training," I said.

He had been talking about how the team skills were sleeping, and that they needed to keep their training up. I knew that he and Sheydu sometimes went to a shooting range.

But by the looks on everyone's faces I could see that this was not the problem.

My heart was hammering. "Then can anyone tell me what is going on?"

No one seemed to want to speak first.

I said, "Does he want to leave? Has he gotten a better job?"

I had feared that this would happen. Veyada was quite young and I still thought that he considered his position with me as a severe demotion after having worked as Ezhya's guard.

Everyone was looking at his mother. Sheydu was never the most talkative of my team. Her contributions to our discussions were always extremely practical or related to some item of tactics.

Her face went red. "I'm not happy with him. I told him that if he wants that woman, he should come out with it and tell you, or let it be. I don't like this hiding secrets and sneaking around back rooms."

"What do you mean? I thought he liked Mereeni, and she is back in Athens." I wasn't even sure that anything happened there.

Sheydu said, "That's what you think."

"Then is she here? In this house?"

"Not in this house. I would never let him do that to you."

"But why? I don't mind her."

But in the faces of the others I saw that they did. Mereeni was from Hedron, and they were traditionally enemies of Asto. They also had a different society that did not rely on the *sheya* instinct which the Ezmi clan of Hedron mostly lacked. They might consider that she wasn't a suitable partner and did not fit in our household.

I think I was beginning to see the problem.

"And where are they?"

Sheydu hesitated a bit more. "In town. He is negotiating."

And then the full situation hit home to me. "She's pregnant."

"Yes."

"When?"

"Not too far off."

Well, what the hell? I looked at Nicha. "Did you know about this?"

"I did." He looked down.

"And you?" I looked at Thayu.

She met my eyes, the expression quite angry. "I did. I don't agree with it. I think she should be with him."

"That's why I told him to leave," Sheydu said.

"That is *not* the only option," Thayu snapped.

Sheydu stuck her chin up. "My loyalty is to Ezhya."

Thayu glared back at her. "Mine, too."

Damn it, here it was. I had always feared that there had been something twisted about members of Ezhya's elite guard falling under Thayu. But as it was, it turned out that Sheydu and Veyada were only with us for as long as it suited Sheydu.

"In this house, we're *all* loyal to Ezhya," I said. I was feeling my way around with my half-arsed understanding of the *sheya* instinct. I didn't *feel* my loyalty; I didn't smell it. I didn't fight when something was not clear. I had no business wading into this conflict, and yet I had no option but to do just that.

I gave them a talk that we were all working for the same goal, most of which was rubbish, but they were too polite to tell me this.

"I have no idea how to do this," I said to Thayu when we both went to our room afterwards. "I want to keep Veyada. I want to keep Sheydu."

"She is the one causing the trouble," Thayu said.

"Did she cause trouble when I wasn't here?"

"She and Veyada had a big fight about Mereeni. When Veyada was here yesterday, that's the first time he's been here for quite some time." She met my eyes. We were standing in front of the small bathroom and the low light from the dusk hit her face side-on. Her eyelashes and eyebrows glittered with their metallic sheen, and the light also made the golden flecks in her eyes glimmer. She blinked. "Please don't leave Mereeni by herself to have a child in a strange place. Don't leave her alone."

Thayu rarely spoke of the time that she had been contracted to have a child for one of her father's enemies, of the time that she had spent pregnant and virtually locked up. Or the fact that she had never seen her son since, and now had no idea where the boy was.

I stroked her cheek. "Don't worry. I have no intention of doing so. We'll find a solution. I don't know what it is yet, but we'll find one."

She smiled at me, and I bent forward. She let me touch the hollow under her ear with my nose and inhale her scent. I could almost feel her warm and soft skin through her clothes. I could feel the soft mounds of her breasts.

She pushed me away, weakly. "Lilona said we must wait." Her voice was low.

I let her go, reluctantly.

Yes. We must wait.

It was almost time for the evening meal, and we went to the living room, where Deyu and Reida were playing a word game.

Sheydu didn't show up for dinner, but Evi and Telaris came in, as well as Ynggi, who brought a handful of little yellow fruit. He set them on the table. "The bushes were good today."

I picked one up—it was firm—and was about to try it, when Ynggi said that you were supposed to add the pulp to hot water. Eirani brought tea, and he demonstrated, to Eirani's horror.

The fruit was extremely bitter, and the flavoured tea left a tingling feeling on my tongue.

Dinner was a rather odd affair.

Deyu talked about the different types of animals she was studying. Apparently the bat-like meili that used to live in the roof were herd animals. They had no obvious social structure in their groups, unlike wolves, which had a clear leader. She mentioned behaviours which were similar across all species, including the species of the human tree. She demonstrated how Ayshada instinctively paid attention to Thayu—who was his aunt—and not to her, from a different clan and not related.

It was an interesting discussion, but it was also very strange.

No one mentioned Sheydu, no one mentioned Veyada.

I missed him.

Thayu and I were about to retire to our room, and were walking through the hall, when we heard Devlin's voice from the hub.

"What? Just outside. . . ? Yes, he did."

He was speaking keihu and the tone of his voice sounded alarmed.

I went into the hub room.

"Muri, security says that they found a body outside the back of the apartment."

"Someone trying to break into the apartment?"

"They didn't say. They said the man is on the walkway."

Thayu and I went into our room, grabbed a jacket and weapons, collected Evi and Telaris at the door. We left the building in the usual way: over the gallery, down the stairs, through the atrium with the trickling waterfall and out the main entrance past the *gamra* uniform shop.

To get to the walkway, we needed to walk past the quay, across the short pier and then onto the walkway.

A couple of *gamra* guards stood gathered around a dark shape on the ground.

We joined them.

The man lay with his face away from us. I walked around to look at him.

It was Puck.

5

————

"WHAT HAPPENED?" I asked the guards. They were the regular *gamra* variety, those ones that Sheydu always complained about as being no good. Sheydu wasn't even here, and I could still hear her voice.

"We don't know that yet," the guard said. He was a tall, beefy man from the local keihu race. *Gamra* provided employment for so many of these young men. "We just found him here. A passerby alerted us."

I looked along the walkway. The marshland stretched into the misty horizon on the right hand side, a low wall ran along the left of the walkway, behind the wall a strip of bushes, and then apartment buildings. Mine was one of them. Light radiated from the windows, edging the bushes in gold. There were no people on the walkway.

"Are there any witnesses?" I asked the guard.

"Our people are just investigating that."

Thayu gave a barely perceptible snort. In the absence of Sheydu's disapproval, she was filling in.

The man wandered away to his colleagues. I had often suspected that their relaxed attitude to us was simply because they knew that my association had extensive security training and we were "one of them", in that we weren't going to do anything stupid like disturb the body that could interfere with their investigations.

I crouched next to the body. I could see no signs of violence, but if he had been shot at close range with a charge gun, there would be none unless his clothes were removed, because only then would you see the burn marks.

"How did he even come to the island?" I asked no one in particular, because one needed a permit to get off the train. It was still possible for people to enter via the water, but even there extensive security systems had been installed recently.

"There are ways," Thayu said.

Of course, there were always ways. But one needed to know them. Had Puck come with a purpose? To kill me?

The guards had met up with Evi and Telaris and stood talking while waving their hands at the buildings and the walkway, likely discussing where the attacker could have come from, or where witnesses could be. A couple of guards were inspecting the surrounding yards and parkland which backed onto the block of apartments next to mine. Thayu and I walked a bit further in the fast-fading light of the dusk. The evening was cloudless and still as it sometimes was in the dry season, and there was a strange bite to the air. I would almost say it was *cold*, but it never got cold in Barresh. Yet, a shiver went over my arms.

"It *is* cold," Thayu said.

These days we only wore our feeders when we went into a *gamra* session. I didn't like the intrusion of someone else's thoughts in my head, and I rarely needed it to know what Thayu was thinking anyway. And she knew my thoughts through subtle signs.

Yes, it was cold, and the smell of the mud hung heavy in the evening air.

Telaris was coming towards us, his footfalls heavy on the boards. "I swear these guards get more incompetent by the day. They have no scans, no results, and no idea what they're doing."

I said, "Or they're not telling us."

Thayu said, "They're not smart enough to keep secrets."

At that moment there was a noise from underneath the boardwalk—some splashing and a male voice, but I couldn't hear what he said.

I walked to the edge of the boardwalk, dropped down to my knees, and looked over the edge.

Ynggi crawled from underneath the boardwalk, with his pants covered in mud.

He jumped up onto the boardwalk, leaving muddy footprints of his bare feet as he came to me.

I asked, "What were you doing down there? How long have you been there?"

"I just went to check this out."

He held something out to me. It was a thin black waterproof folder with a seal lock strip at the top. The satchel was wet and covered in mud, but the seal had kept the moisture out. Tucked away inside it was one of those flat one-use-only readers. I didn't take it out, but I could see the shape and knew what it was.

"How did you know this was here?"

Ynggi said, "I was looking after my plants and I noticed the Tamerian walking around, and then he dropped something to the side of the boards."

"You mean Puck?"

"The one who got shot."

"Did you see who attacked him?"

"No, because I did not pay attention. People are often walking around on these noisy boards and it doesn't bother me anymore. When I saw him bend down, I thought he might just have dropped something, and I didn't think much of it, until I heard the shot."

The area where we stood was not far from where Puck was found.

"Did you hear anyone else after the shot?"

Ynggi wagged his tail—which meant no.

I was trying to picture the situation in my mind. Puck somehow arrives on the island, walks over the boardwalk—to my house perhaps? —it was not exactly a secret where I lived.

Why?

Because he wanted to give me this reader.

When he got close to my house he might have noticed that he was not alone. He might have dropped the satchel under the walkway, and might have tried to run. In vain.

This fitted with my suspicion that he was acting on his own accord, contrary to his orders. This was a very unusual position for a Tamerian to take. The meeting we'd had with him had been very odd.

I turned to Telaris. "Do you have any readings on who the killer is?"

"No, but Devlin may have something."

Thayu said, "My guess: as with most murders committed in the past few years, it was probably nameless Tamerians."

Which meant that they would be virtually untraceable.

I wondered whether we should tell the guards about the reader, but they would probably take it off us, and we wouldn't see it again, let alone find out what was on it. Sheydu would have my head.

So I put the reader in my pocket, and we continued down the walkway, turning left and then left again to go to the other side of our building.

———

When we arrived in the apartment, Nicha met us in the hall. He was carrying Ayshada on his arm.

"What's going on?" he said. "All of a sudden a bunch of you were gone. Ayshada wanted to play."

"Pay! Pay!" Ayshada yelled, raising both his hands above his head and arching his back. Nicha knew that he would sometimes do this, but a less experienced person would have dropped him.

"If you're going to do that, I won't carry you anymore." He set his son on the ground, and Ayshada took off into the living room, squealing.

Nicha rolled his eyes.

I told him about Puck. His eyes widened. "Did you look at this reader yet?"

"No, I was going to do it here, because I want to make a copy and it will probably wipe itself after it has been read once." I preceded him into the hub. "It was really good that Ynggi noticed Puck dropping the satchel over the side of the walkway."

It was not the first time that Ynggi had spotted something that all of us had missed. Yes, I knew that the late-night walkers over the boardwalk annoyed him, but I appreciated him for his sharp ears.

It was as if the people in my household had a sixth sense for when something was up, because Devlin was already looking at images scanned for electronic activity.

He pointed at the projection of the apartment surroundings that the projector displayed. "I can see the charge going off here, but there is no prior record of any use of electronic equipment. I can't even trace how this person came to the walkway."

Puck, too, was untraceable right up until he had been shot.

Devlin took the reader from me and hooked it up to the hub's projector. And then I finally turned it on.

At first I couldn't make much sense of the document that came up.

It was written, of all things, in Mirani, and I didn't have much skill in that language.

Devlin started up the translator, which I knew could produce a reasonably adequate translation of an official document in Mirani.

The document turned out to be some sort of contract. It detailed a period of work, ownership of data, something about a project plan, and payment based on performance.

But it remained painfully vague about the subject of the project. The language was very dry, and full of jargon. Was it some kind of agricultural trial? Was it a commercial project? It spoke of *the project* and *the partici-pants,* but this might be a product of the dry legalese language of a contract and the fact that Mirani put all its power into its great variety of nouns, many of which had exactly the same translation in other languages. So the translation did not do justice to the nuances of the chosen nouns.

I flipped to the very last page where I found a name I recognised in the signatures, even in Mirani script: Benton Leck.

"There." I pointed at it.

There were silent nods all around, and a tail wave from Ynggi. While we were looking at the material, Deyu and Reida had also come into the room.

"He *was* into something shady," I said.

Nicha frowned. "I wonder if that was why Puck came to us when we responded to Aliandra's message."

"You mean, he knew about Aliandra's vague requests to us, and then he came to deliver evidence? What is this document meant to prove? It's vague as hell."

He shrugged. "It's all written in dry legal language. Could mean anything. Sorry, my Mirani is terrible. I don't think that translation tells the whole story, except that Aliandra's husband appears to be involved."

Thayu said, "A *gamra* lawyer should be able to advise."

Yes, and we had such a lawyer.

I didn't know if she made this remark by accident, but Thayu rarely said anything by accident.

A deep silence fell after her remark.

I rose from the bench and managed not to bump into anything in the darkness. "I think it may be time that I go to see Veyada."

"What, now?" Thayu said.

"Yes, ask Eirani to hold dinner until I'm back."

Sheydu gave me a morose look. She stuck her hands in her pockets as if challenging me to say something to her. I walked past, with her gaze burning in the side of my head.

I went to my room to get changed, and not a moment later Thayu came in.

"Thay', I'm not sure if it's such a good idea for you to come. Veyada might be upset if I come with any of you. I was thinking of taking Ynggi. If nothing else, he can help me through the dark spots." Being Pengali, Ynggi's night vision was excellent.

"I agree and, that's not what I wanted to talk about."

I stopped halfway through putting on my jacket. There was an edge in her voice.

"What's the matter? I'm feeling fine. I'll be taking a water taxi."

"No, it's not that either. It's Sheydu. Next time she gives you that look, you can tell her to get out or behave."

I was tempted to ask if she was joking, but nothing in her expression supported that question. Moreover, I *knew* she wasn't joking.

I breathed in.

She put up her finger to silence me before I could speak.

"You know you can't lose control over her. She can't be allowed to dictate what happens in our household. If *you* say that Veyada should come back, that is *your* decision, and your order. She can obey. She can fight him for a position, or she can leave. Those are the options."

As she said that, I knew, as I had known all along but had somehow allowed myself to forget, that a Coldi association was not a group of friends. There was a strict hierarchy. Most of the time, the association functioned as a group of friends, but as soon as trouble arose, the fallback positions would be those that were established in the making of the association.

I stood at the top, Thayu and Nicha were *zhayma*'s under me, Veyada and Sheydu were under Thayu, and Deyu and Reida under Nicha. That structure was set in stone.

I had known that a challenge of some kind would come, because inevitably it always did. I had feared it and hoped I could avoid it. I had hoped that the members of my association would understand that I didn't have the instinct and therefore my association was different, but in hindsight, that was a ridiculous assumption. The association held together because of the instinct.

Coldi associations could be stable for a long time, but inevitably something changed that necessitated a re-alignment.

I had been stupid to assume that this wouldn't happen with mine.

"What should I do? I can't use force against Sheydu."

"You can't?"

"No, because . . ." *She is Sheydu.* I couldn't harm her.

"It is not about her. It's about us as an association. If she can't work with us and can't accept Veyada's choice, then she should get out."

I nodded, feeling resigned. I knew she was right. I still didn't want to act on it. I didn't want to lose either Veyada or Sheydu.

"Sheydu is someone who will test the boundaries. How else do you think she got as far as Ezhya's personal guard? She's not huge and strong like Natanu. She's *old*, she's past her peak. She has nothing to lose. She will keep pushing and taking liberties, and I can push back at her, but I need your help."

I opened my mouth—

"No, don't say anything about not having the *sheya* instinct. You do handsomely, and it's high time you supported your decision to join the Domiri clan with some strong leadership so that everyone knows where they stand."

She was always complaining that I wasn't firm enough, that I let Sheydu too loose. According to her, the two youngsters were given far too much freedom, and Sheydu talked nonsense into their heads.

Yes, I knew Thayu was right. She was always right.

Putting it into practice, however, was much harder.

I went back into the hall, where Ynggi was waiting.

As usual after Sheydu gave me one of her looks, she made herself scarce.

"That's typical," Thayu said.

"I'll see her some other time."

"See her now. The delay is what she wants. She always does this. She upsets you, and then runs away, because you let her get away with it. She undermines your leadership."

"Tomorrow. I need to go now, or it will be too late."

She blew out a breath. She went into the dining room shaking her head, and I joined Ynggi, who had to be the only member of my team who was not grumpy.

I needed to talk about something else, so on our way out of the building, I asked him about my planned survey of the coastline. The Thousand Island tribe lived in the tribal lands south of Barresh. His presence with me opened doors to my team that were closed to many. The local Pengali were from the Washing Stones tribe, and they were held down by their long history of exploitation by the keihu people. It was not long ago that if a Pengali wanted to work as domestic servant in the city, they had to cut off their tail, presumably because "Pengali use tails to steal things". That barbaric treatment set the scene for the lack of mutual respect between Pengali and keihu and the fact that most Pengali still worked simple jobs and were considered "unreliable".

The Thousand Island Pengali were very different even if for the sole reason that the tribal boundaries kept them out of the city. I'd had to move a lot of bureaucracy with the Pengali office in order to make Ynggi a resident, and probably the only reason that I'd been successful was that I didn't live in the city proper. The Thousand Island tribe was a lot friendlier to Coldi visitors and dealt commercially with Asto directly. The tribe, and those even further to the south, were much more likely to want to host me, as I was a representative of Ezhya. Ynggi was well connected.

The driver of the boat that turned up at the jetty was, of course, from the rival Washing Stones tribe. I could see that because the skin on his arms bore grey-white zebra stripes. Ynggi, like most Thousand Island Pengali, had giraffe-patterned skin.

The driver gave Ynggi a nervous look, as if he expected to be stabbed in the back if he turned away from us.

We sat on the benches, next to each other, close to the front of the boat.

I asked Ynggi if he had any trouble since coming to the house, especially since I hadn't been there for such a long time.

"No more than that the woman complains about my room."

"Don't mind Eirani. She always complains about everything, but she doesn't really mean it."

"That is the trouble with people saying things they don't mean. I don't always understand."

It was a known fact that Pengali had a knack for being clear about what they wanted with politeness as an afterthought. They were not particularly polite, in every possible way. But I hated how so many of them were subservient. They were the proud people. Especially those from the Thousand Islands tribe.

On a night like this, I doubly appreciated the Pengali. With my recent poor eyesight, I could see almost nothing in the night, but the Pengali had excellent night vision, and the driver had no trouble finding his way through the many channels and shallows of the marshland. The trip was quick.

He dropped us off at the jetty next to the station. We walked up into the town through Market Street, where most of the guesthouses were.

Thayu had told me in which one Mereeni was staying. Ynggi offered to stay in the forecourt. I told him that I had no problem if he wanted to come, but he said that the guesthouse's staff might. Of course they were mostly Washing Stones Pengali, and though Ynggi had a permit to come into the city, this was private property and they might object to him coming inside.

I walked up the steps, clenching my fists against my sides.

The future of our team depended on this.

As soon as I came into the courtyard I could see Veyada and Mereeni sitting at a table in the corner. The table between them contained some empty plates and glasses. They were talking, and holding hands under the table.

I hadn't seen Mereeni since we were in Athens. She had ditched her official *gamra* uniform and wore a loose-fitting tunic. One so rarely saw pregnant Coldi women in the street that I stared for an impolitely long time at the rounding of her stomach under that tunic, and the two pronounced mounds of her breasts. Coldi women did not grow breasts until they became pregnant, and they took a number of years to shrink back to nothing after birth.

I was looking at what Thayu would look like.

How long before Mereeni gave birth?

She and Veyada were deep in an argument, as usual, but in the middle of it, he reached out and touched her cheek. His mouth curved into a rare Coldi smile, his eyes smiled. His face radiated happiness.

This was terrible.

In the time that I had seen them together they had always been fighting, arguing over something or other, and I had the impression that they hated each other's guts.

Had he felt it necessary to put on that behaviour as an act?

I wanted to disappear, slink into the shadows. Maybe it would be best if I left them alone.

But then Veyada saw me. He jumped up from the table and came across the courtyard. He bent his head and let his hands hang down both sides of his body, palms facing backwards, in the subservient position.

"Don't be ridiculous," I said to him in a low voice.

"I'm sorry." He let his head hang further.

He knew that I hated it when he displayed this behaviour. I had told him many times not to do it. But it was a very strong instinct that was impossible to kill. I could even feel that he thought it was the right thing to do. Maybe it was; I didn't know anymore. I was on thin ice, and spring was coming. Soon, the ice would crack and swallow me. I had no idea what I was doing with this situation. Everything I said felt wrong.

I looked past Veyada to Mereeni, who was watching intently.

I said, "Let's talk."

We went to the table, where a waitress quickly came to collect the empty plates.

I ordered some drinks and waited until the waitress had gone before starting.

"This has been going on since our visit to the Nations of Earth court?" I looked from one to the other.

Veyada nodded.

"So all these arguments you had in the foyer of our accommodation were just for show?"

"We do discuss a lot."

Discuss? At times it had sounded like they were about to murder each other.

He gave a sheepish grin.

"So while you were fighting during the day, you were doing a different kind of fight at night?"

He gave me a sharp look. "Oh no, I would never do that . . . only when I was clear that you wouldn't have a problem with it."

"And it was good?"

Veyada looked cute when he blushed. I knew him as one of the most reliable and even-tempered people in my team, and this was an odd situation.

"Yes, it was good," Mereeni said.

She was an ideal lawyer, straight to the point, no bullshit, not unlike Sheydu. Maybe that was why he was attracted to her, because she was like his mother; and maybe that was why Sheydu didn't like her, because she viewed Mereeni as competition.

"I'm sorry," Veyada said again. "I'm just—" He spread his hands. "—not getting any younger, and you start thinking about what you want to leave behind. And then along comes someone special, someone you lie awake at night thinking about."

"Yeah." I knew what that felt like.

"I just knew in one instant that I wanted her child. Not anyone's child. Only hers."

"So when is it happening?"

"Soon. That's why she came here. So I can be with her."

"What then?"

"That depends on you."

"As far as I'm concerned, I see no problem. Nicha brought Xinanu into our household and didn't ask my permission. I didn't like her. No one liked her, not even Nicha. We all know that Ayshada is going to create problems for us in the future, because he is from the Azimi clan. They will make claims on him and his loyalty. But I think that Ayshada is an asset, because one needs to keep one's enemies close."

That was something Veyada always used to say to me.

He looked down at the table. "This is different."

"I can't see why."

"My mother and I were part of the Inner Circle, the highest section of society. The fact that my choice of partner is one from a long-standing enemy of Asto is unforgivable to her. I can't stay in this association while she thinks this way."

"Not even when I tell her that she should?"

"She is too old to change her opinions."

"I'm trying anyway."

Veyada reached out and put his hand over mine. "I appreciate it." His voice sounded hoarse. "I want to see you get big and strong. I want to know what colour your hair is going to grow back. I want to see you become a member of the Domiri clan. I want to see Thayu become a mother."

Yes, I wanted all those things, too.

"I will try," I said. "It may take me a while." Then I dug in my pocket. "This is only one of the reasons I came to see you. We have stumbled into a bit of a situation. Do you remember Puck?"

He said he vaguely remembered me talking about a Tamerian, and I told him everything that happened. "To make a long story short, I would like you to have a look at this document. It seems it is some kind of contract of work, but I can't really draw any other conclusions from it. It's in Mirani and the translation is not terribly good. I need someone with legal knowledge to look over it."

"I would be happy to do that. I always am."

I heard between the lines that he found it quite hard being out here without having much to do except relax in the many bathhouses until the child was born and his enforced holiday would come to an end—and then he might be out of a job and in need of a new *zhayma*. That was, if I couldn't persuade his mother to accept him again. I was beginning to see Thayu's point. Sheydu was the problem.

So I gave him a copy of the document, with the assumption that I would come back a few days later to talk to him about it.

———

On the way back home, sitting in the boat with Ynggi and the driver at the wheel, I felt as black as the night that we travelled through.

At a normal time I would have appreciated the warm air and a beautiful night which was surprisingly clear. I could see the stars above and I could see Asto, pink and bright on the horizon. It would soon sink below.

I didn't want to lose Veyada. I didn't want to lose Sheydu. Was this the beginning of the end?

When we got to the island, Ynggi and I walked across the jetty into the building and upstairs without speaking a word.

Evi and Telaris stood at the door, their faces grim. They had known me for quite a while, and I guessed that they could tell I wasn't happy.

I was about to go through the doorway when Evi held me back.

He towered over me, imposing, with his skin so black that it acquired a green sheen. Lately, his hair had started to lighten. Not visibly grey, but less intensely bronze.

His moss green eyes were intense. "Do you remember that time that I had a black moment? That I did something so terrible that it is today still unspeakable?"

I nodded. How could I forget?

We had been in the underground settlement of his archenemy Romi Tanaqan, who had settled in Ethiopia, and was building a secret society there. Evi and Telaris' sister had been killed by this man. Back then, he'd been young and angry, and all he wanted was revenge, to the detriment of the job he did for me. After he had so gruesomely shot his enemy, he asked to be released from my team because he let emotions get the better of him.

I had refused, because the very fact that he realised that he had done something wrong meant that he would be more valuable to me.

"When something goes wrong, that makes you stronger," he said.

I knew that, but it was hard to hear when you were in the middle of it.

"Use something for distraction," he said. "Give the team something to do, something to keep themselves busy and occupy their minds so that we can work together rather than fight."

"Thank you." I put my hand on his shoulder and squeezed it briefly. Then I went inside.

It was quiet in the hall. I couldn't see anyone in the living room. The light was on, and the table set for dinner, but no one had turned up yet. Ynggi made for his room to get changed. I went to check the faint glow in the hub room, but not even Devlin was present.

I went into the room and sat on the bench. A couple of lights flickered softly in front of me, but it didn't look like anything important was being received. This was probably why Devlin had gone to his room, or had gone to the kitchen to have dinner. He would be back later for another shift.

I opened the news channel and scrolled aimlessly through the news. While I had been in the hospital, I had plenty of time to look at the news, and the irony was that it must have been the most boring period for news in history. I'd had to contend with the silly rumours about wars that were no longer news, that had been going on for so long that no one wanted to know about them any more.

I wasn't in the mood for news either. I didn't know what to do about this problem with Veyada. If he stayed away long enough, I would need to replace him. I didn't want to do that, because if I did that it would seem permanent to everyone.

I already missed him terribly.

There was something to be said for the advice Evi had given me. Give the team something to do.

But *gamra* wouldn't sit for a few weeks, and even then, the next session would discuss nothing that I had a great amount of involvement with.

But on second thought, that thing we could do had been obvious all the time: we should help Benton Leck's wife.

A small sound came from the hallway, and a moment later Thayu entered the room.

She crossed the floor wordlessly and sat down next to me on the bench. I'd still left a news item open. Something about a delegate who had double-crossed his partner. These kinds of stories were part of the daily news cycle.

"I didn't think you were interested in that sort of gossip," she said.

"I'm not," I said. "I was looking for something to distract me."

"How did it go?" she asked. "Did you see Veyada?"

"Yes. I gave him the document. He will look at it."

She snorted. "How was your talk with Veyada? Seriously, you're just as bad as Sheydu."

"He's finding it difficult. They're very much in love and she is very pregnant."

"Yes. I saw them."

"I'm going to try talking to Sheydu."

"How?"

"I don't know yet. But first, I've made a decision. We have to do something. Screw waiting for a reason. Let's go to Miran to see what Benton Leck's wife has to say."

6

———————

FOR ALL THAT IT was the neighbouring country, there was quite a lot of preparation to be done for us to go to Miran. Miran—which took up most of the main continent on Ceren —had always been a strange place, setting itself up under the illusion of seclusion, with the idea that it could control who entered the country based on political opinions they held. Its history was extensive and violent.

Some time ago, it had spent most of a century sliding into a cruel dictatorship, which held traditional values above all else. Through most of history, the nation had been the main competitor for Asto: Asto's nemesis, its main rival. It had been ridiculed in *gamra*, and had been the subject of books and books full of detailed economic sanctions.

Miran had turned quiet in recent times. It had fallen into a deep hole since the defeat of the dictatorship and had spent most of the last hundred years working themselves out of the hole. But some things they seemed unable to change. Traditional values were still enormously important. The capital—also called Miran—was still in the hands of the rich Endri nobles.

Mostly, Miran was a place of history. Therefore, it was no surprise that an academic linguist and historian like Benton Leck had married a woman from the upper rungs of that society. The Ilendar family was one of the five Foundation families. Aliandra Ilendar could probably trace her ancestry back four or five millennia, and the city's history would be littered with names of her ancestors.

Despite periods in which they had left the city—or even the planet—the five founding families of Miran had as strong a bond with their history as ever.

All of which was to say that Miran was peculiar.

Visiting it meant a fair bit of bureaucracy. In addition to the usual checks of who visited and what their record was, they liked to know what they came to Miran to do. Apparently "sightseeing" wasn't an acceptable reason. One might be forgiven to think that they really didn't want people to visit. This was the impression I always got.

And so, despite living in a tiny enclave surrounded by the giant nation of Miran, I could count the times that I'd officially crossed the border on the fingers on one hand.

While I busied myself getting all the appropriate permits—with extra ones because Miran had a specific dislike for Coldi people— Eirani was busy getting all the clothing ready. It was winter, and although Miran, like Barresh, was almost on the equator, it was also at an elevation of about six thousand metres, and pretty damn cold.

Over the next day, the pile of bags grew in the hallway, the usual place where we accumulated these things. I worked in the living room, and could see everything that happened in the hall.

Ayshada found the pile of bags amusing, even though we had told him a hundred times on every occasion that he was not allowed to jump on our luggage. But he squealed and jumped anyway. No one seemed to mind because his laughter made us happy.

Nicha had made the decision that instead of hiring a tutor, he was going to send Karana to some teaching courses, so that she could start teaching him to read and write when the time came.

She was at one of those lessons right now, and there was no one in the house to rein in the enthusiastic youngster. It was a game for him, running away when Eirani came into the hall, hiding when one of us came, and scurrying at incredible speed if Sheydu came.

But not even Sheydu could bring herself to give him a slap on the backside, which I suspected was going to be the only thing that would make him stop jumping, if only for five minutes.

And then Ynggi came upstairs. Ayshada went nuts, showing off his climbing skills. Watching Ynggi climb up the side of the house to evict the noisy and smelly roosting *meili* from the roof cavity had convinced Ayshada that climbing was useful, and that tails were good for climbing. He was most upset that he had no tail, but was determined to do as best he could without one.

Karana—a good girl, but honestly too gentle—had no hope of controlling him once Ynggi was there, because Ynggi was Ayshada's hero.

That morning, Ynggi had caught a fish off the boardwalk in front of his room, and he had given Ayshada a piece. Now all Ayshada wanted was to catch fish. He used the Pengali word for it, too.

And because Ynggi and Ayshada would both stay here while we went to Miran, I suspected that the bond between the two would only become stronger.

Nicha brought his pack into the hall and all of a sudden Ayshada was gone. The foyer went suspiciously quiet for a while, until Ayshada came into the hallway dragging one of his father's travel bags over the ground, because it was too heavy and the handles were too long for him to carry it properly. He couldn't lift the bag onto the pile of luggage, so he pushed it next to the pile, and this made the bag tip over and all the toys spill out over the floor.

Sheydu came into the hallway to dump her bag on the pile, her face looking empty and morose. She gave Ayshada a look that could kill, and I remembered Thayu's warning about Sheydu. I knew Thayu was right, but couldn't bring myself to have this major confrontation just before we were about to leave.

"We'll only be gone for two days," I said, when she glanced into the living room and saw me there.

She gave me a sideways look, but didn't say anything. I held out hope—probably futile—that she would speak to me about her future with us and her relationship with Veyada, but it wasn't going to happen today.

Sheydu aside, most people seemed happy to be doing something.

Deyu came into the hall all rugged up in a fur coat with fur-lined hood, and knee-high fur-lined boots.

"I'm ready," she declared, looking into the living room.

"I can see that. Make sure you don't die of heat stroke before we leave."

She sat down on the little bench that had been in the hall since I took over the apartment from the previous owner, but that was rarely used. I had never understood its true purpose. Maybe this previous owner liked to leave his guests waiting in the hall.

Deyu flicked through a couple of screens on her reader. From a distance I spotted the outlines of big, bison-like hairy animals. They were called tiyuk, and the herds used to be the major source of meat and clothing in Miran.

"I don't know that we'll see any of those," I called out to her.

"It is winter. It says here that in winter the herders bring the animals down into the valleys. That they bring them to market and then sell the wool and pelts."

She was probably right about that. But, to be fair, Mirani tiyuk herders were not in the forefront of my mind.

We were ready. I had my permits, I had the tickets, and everyone else had collected the gear. I sent Benton Leck's wife a special message through a courier to expect our visit.

Then it was time to go.

Ayshada wasn't happy when he discovered that he was not coming. I wondered about that. Coldi tended to include children in their activities from a much younger age. When trained well, they were usually much better behaved than human children, and they learnt quickly. Maybe we should start to include him, especially since he was going to be such an important bridge between two rival clans.

First, of course, we had to take everything to the airport. I had asked Devlin to get us a water taxi, because the idea of carrying all that gear on the train was just too daunting.

A driver with a town buggy met us at the jetty, and took us the short distance to the airport.

We were using a commercial shuttle, and had to go through all the regular boarding procedures.

I could have hired a private shuttle, but I knew that Miran preferred everyone to come on the commercial flights. The shuttle was a medium-sized Hedron-built craft with mixed crew. It was packed and, because it was winter, everyone carried big jackets and cloaks and boots in the cabin. To say that you could barely move was no overstatement.

Finally, we were off.

The craft took off over the water, made a sharp turn back inland,

and flew in an easterly direction. We passed over the marshlands that were iconic of Barresh. In recent years, the city had expanded to include more artificial islands like the one that held the *gamra* headquarters. Because the city lay on low-lying islands in a tidal delta, most of these islands were set on posts that elevated them above the water. A few of the modules were even set on floating pontoons that went up and down with the water level.

From the air the city looked like a vast interconnected network of little hubs, linked to each other with train lines. It was morning, and sunlight glinted on the water. Here and there mist still hung in the shadows. The city was surrounded by fields of green, mostly with floating lilies that provided the bulbs that were the staple food of the city. There are also groves of megon trees standing with their trunks in the water. Little boats were out on the channels, catching fish and hauling in nets. Bigger boats took produce from the fields to the city.

In the distance I could see the rainforest-covered point which marked the boundary to the home territory of the Thousand Island tribe. I spotted Ynggi looking at it too. I wondered if he felt homesick at all.

The craft continued to climb. It crossed the cliffs of the escarpment, one of the most amazing views in all the inhabited worlds. Along the rainforest-lined coast were several outcrops where steam rose from the ground. At a little inlet, a big waterfall tumbled down the escarpment. The forest at the base of the waterfall was the home of the Washing Stones tribe. The boulders at the bottom of the waterfall were called the washing stones—in the twisted way Pengali conjugated their verbs, washing stones were stones being washed, not stones for doing one's laundry.

The view of the rainforest on top of the escarpment was clear, and this was quite unusual. Usually the rainforest was shrouded in mist. But today we could see the rills and valleys covered in verdant green.

The official border between Barresh and Miran lay somewhere here. No one really cared exactly where it was, because no one lived down there. The rainforest was full of insects and leech like creatures that were not particularly friendly to people, and it had served as a useful buffer between traditional-minded Miran and tiny, rogue, entrepreneurial Barresh for many centuries. I didn't expect that to change. Ceren was an underpopulated world where unforgiving wilderness reigned.

The craft climbed, and the forest grew sparse. Eventually we came to a clear line, as if cut by a giant lawn mower, where the trees stopped and green fields started. This was the territory of Bendara, Miran's agricultural powerhouse.

From now on we flew over a lot of fields with little towns between them. There were roads and train lines and occasionally you could even see a vehicle move.

The craft climbed and climbed. Green pastures gave way to rocky terrain and then the occasional snow patch.

But it was now getting dark very quickly, because the craft was going east.

I tried to sleep a bit, but it was quite uncomfortable in the narrow seats. Also, it was apparently not possible to keep the cabin temperature at a level where everyone was comfortable. Most people had come in thick winter clothing, but I found it simply too cold in the cabin.

"Join the club," Thayu said.

She had taken out her winter jacket, and draped it over the top of her. She looked at me over the furred rim of the hood.

Chills had become part of my life. In fact, I hadn't felt hot at any time since waking up in the hospital. I'd put it down to the hospital being temperature controlled, and the fact that it was the dry season, so naturally the night temperatures were slightly lower than in the wet season.

But I wondered how much of it was because I had changed. And I was still changing.

Nicha and some of the others had no trouble sleeping in their cramped seats. I had always been jealous of his ability to sleep anywhere. I stared into the darkness outside the window, seeing nothing except the faint light of the two minuscule moons on snowy slopes. I remembered that light being much brighter, but that would forever be a memory. I guess I could be lucky that I still saw some stars.

Eventually it started to get light and the pilot announced that we were about to arrive. People stirred, Nicha woke up and Reida commented that he couldn't see much down there.

But the craft was obviously coming closer to the ground. I could make out the snowy slopes and rocky outcrops. The tips of the tallest mountains came closer and we started to descend between them.

There were absolutely no trees anywhere, a landscape as hostile as ever. I had always been baffled by why people had chosen to settle here. Most of the world of Ceren was covered in ice, and in fact just the two coastlines and a small section of the middle of the continent were green.

The city came into view. It lay on a mountain pass, in between two giants of mountains. The ancient part of the city was a jumble of houses surrounded by a wall. I could see the famous watchtower poking from among the jumble. We'd be staying in a guesthouse there and Aliandra's house was there.

The newer sections of the city had been built outside the wall, some on the bank of a little creek, from which I knew the city got crayfish and some of its water, and others further afield.

By now all the passengers were looking out the windows, because it was rare they could glimpse the coastline from here all the way out to the eastern Kesilu Sea.

The craft flew low over the snowfields and put down at the airport, which lay on the western side of the city.

The pilot told us to get out quickly. The craft was going to go back to Barresh straight away.

So while we collected all our bags that we had taken into the cabin, the engines kept running, sending vibrations through the floor of the craft.

The door opened, sending biting cold air into the cabin.

People started moving towards the exit.

When I made it to the top of the ramp, the first thing that struck me was the noise. The craft had the engines running at full blast—without the engine fans engaged, of course—and the airport staff had brought out two huge air cannons that directed hot air at the engines. I had heard that they did this, and apparently it was the only way these craft could come to a place as cold as this.

My team got together in a group.

The Coldi members of the team were all looking around at a landscape more alien than they had ever experienced. Thayu had been to

Miran before, but only in summer, when the fields that surrounded the city were green.

"It's all so white," Deyu said.

"This is the place Asto invaded to get food?" Reida asked.

He had been reading about the history as part of an education goal that I had set him, because, since we had returned from Earth, we had each made goals to improve ourselves. His was to gain general knowledge that he so lacked after having grown up in the wilds of Athyl's Outer Circle and the *zeyshi* warrens.

I was going to answer his question about Miran's vast agricultural capital, and that he'd slept through the part of our flight where we flew over the Bendara agricultural area, but a couple of customs officers were coming towards us and needed to see all our permits. They were not particularly happy with the Coldi make-up of my team, and asked us no end of questions. I suspected they didn't trust my designation as a full delegate of *gamra*, probably because I looked as if I had spent time in jail.

They got hung up on the fact that Sheydu had worked in the Inner Circle for Ezhya Palayi—they had clearly done their research on her.

Sheydu made matters worse by questioning the officers' need to have this information. "Really, we have no interest in staying here."

At this point Thayu shot her a look like daggers, and when we were finally allowed to follow the other passengers—by this time the new passengers were already walking towards the craft from the building—I spotted Thayu exchanging some stern words with Sheydu.

I missed Veyada.

7

———————

W E FOUND THE HOUSE where Benton Leck's wife lived in the old part of the city, within the city walls. It was a two-storey house in the traditional style of the Endri noble class of Miran. The main part of the house had two floors and, over the years, single-storey extensions had been built onto the sides. The front door was at the veranda, two steps up from the yard, which was covered in nothing except snow. The path had been cleared from the gate to the steps.

We had decided that Thayu and I would go inside, and that the rest of the team would keep an eye out in the street.

The intrusive security at the airport made me quite nervous, and I wanted to make sure we were not being followed. I swear, if one was not paranoid before coming here, this place quickly turned you paranoid.

Thayu and I walked up the steps to the front door. I dropped the knocker on the wooden surface, wondering how far that wood would have come, because the closest trees were probably at the bottom of the giant cliffs to the east of the city, and that was still a good distance away.

After a while, the door was opened by a red cheeked woman wearing an apron. She said something in Mirani that I didn't catch, but I mentioned Aliandra's name, and she nodded profusely and gestured for us to come into the hall.

It was dark once the door shut. Thayu and I stood in a small foyer, just off the main hall, where people took off their coats and left their shoes. A coat stand almost collapsed with fur cloaks and against the wall stood a rack with house shoes.

A door opened in the hall, and Aliandra herself came out. She was not a tall woman, for an Endri, and was quite thin. She wore her white hair in a bun at the back of her head. It looked severe against her dark dress with long sleeves and lace collar.

"I am glad that you could make it," she said. "Take off your things and come into the living room, where it is warm. Find any pair of house shoes that fit you. Would you like some tea?"

Tea at Mirani Endri families houses was somewhat of an institution, I had heard.

We took off our coats and boots, and each found a pair of slippers on the shoe rack—mine were fluffy and dark brown—and followed her into the living room.

With its heavy dark wooden table and cabinets and velvet-covered chairs, the room reminded me of when I was little and we used to go to historical museums of people who came to New Zealand in the eighteen hundreds.

A couple of heavy couches stood around a low table whose wooden polished surface reflected the flames from the fire in the hearth. Glass-fronted cabinets with the family's fine tableware and shelves full of heavy books lined the walls. Against the wall opposite the door stood a low cabinet with drawers, and above on the wall hung a huge portrait of a man with elfin-like, near-white hair, draped over a magnificent fur cloak fastened with a gold buckle. With its elaborate —if faded—frame, I assumed this man to be the family's founder.

Thayu looked around, her expression astonished, as if she wanted to say, *People really have houses like this?*

Aliandra bade us to sit on the chairs near the hearth, which radiated a pleasant amount of heat. Despite my thick coat, my hands had gone numb and my toes were not much better.

Aliandra sat opposite us. She studied my face.

"I did hear about your health problems," she said.

There was a whole world of undercurrent in that simple word *problems*. They were not problems. I'd undergone a medical procedure, and she would know that.

"Thank you for your concern," I said. "I am fine."

I wasn't going to elaborate on the subject any more than necessary. As open as Coldi were about various bodily functions, the Mirani did not speak of them.

"Tell us about your husband," I said.

A young woman had come in carrying a tray with cups, a teapot and various plates with cakes and biscuits. She was one of the other people who lived in Miran—the Nikala, or common people, who were more sturdy, shorter than the Endri, and tended to have curly or even frizzy hair. You sometimes saw them in Barresh working on building sites. They were strong, reliable workers and many had done very well for themselves.

The servant woman gave both me and Thayu a startled look.

Aliandra did not speak until the woman was out of the room. "You have to excuse the staff. They do not often see people like you in the house."

People like you meaning Coldi people and people who looked like they had served time in jail?

She continued into the uneasy silence. "You probably wonder why I am no longer at my house in Barresh."

"There is no need to explain. I can imagine that the house is very big and quite lonely if you're there by yourself." I remembered the state of the house's yard. It seemed to me that her commitment to Barresh must already have waned, and she probably had all kinds of reasons to return here.

She held up a finger. "No, young man. I was frightened."

"Your staff mentioned that, too. Frightened of what? Was anyone threatening you?"

"*Anyone?* How about *everyone?*"

I did my best not to sigh or roll my eyes. We were into conspiracy theories again. "You could have gone to—"

"—The guards? I did. They laughed in my face."

Yes, well, fancy that. I suspected that her constant barrage of strange complaints might have had something to do with that, but I wasn't here to lecture someone who should know better on ways to stay on the good side of the guards. "Tell me what happened, then."

She sat back in her chair. "When my husband left, I didn't know much about the project that he was working on. I knew he was contacted by a man in Barresh who wanted him to do some linguistic studies. He said he'd be paid well, and that he would be away for about two weeks."

"This was a Mirani man?"

"No. Why would you think that?"

"The contract was in Mirani."

"What contract?"

"The contract of work that was filed with the Exchange's legal branch."

She frowned. "I've never seen such a contract." She sounded bristled. "Anyway, when my husband left, he told me that he couldn't say where he was going, and that he would not be able to contact me much while he was gone. I didn't like it, but I knew his research meant a lot to him, so I didn't protest too much. After all, his project did need money." She picked up her tea and took a sip. "He left and sent me updates every few days. But two weeks went by and I heard nothing. And I continued to hear nothing for a long time. No, young man, don't tell me that I should have contacted the authorities, because I did. The trouble was that no one took me seriously. I had no documents that showed where he had gone. People laughed at me. They even told me in my face that he'd probably taken up with a mistress who was less annoying than I am."

For a noble lady of her age, her voice was fierce, and her eyes burned with anger. Her finger went up again. "My husband would never do that."

"Tell us what you do know, then. Do you know anything about this man who hired him? Why did he contact your husband? What is the project about?"

"It's a long story. My husband had an idea. It was a vast and ambitious project to tie together all the linguistic backgrounds of all the people of *gamra*. From looking at language and type of communication, one should be able to tell where people came from just by the words and gestures they use to communicate."

"Like the Human Tree project?"

"Like that, but for language." Her face twitched. Was that distaste I saw? "But you know it is always hard to get people interested in things that they can't sell, or can't touch. They'll pay for an industry that produces things. They won't pay for people who deal in ideas. It's been like that since the beginning of history, and I'm hearing the same things from all over the inhabited worlds. My husband had a grand idea, but no one wanted to fund it. So he wanted to do some extra side projects so that he could get some money."

Wasn't it always about money? But oo—er, I could sense a bitter rivalry under the surface. Between the Barresh Hospital and the linguists? Between linguists and medical science? Or just between Lilona and Benton Leck? Or . . .

Aliandra continued, "He got a few projects, but they were a lot of work, and didn't end up making him a lot of money. Of course, we were fine; it was not like we were going to be beggars or anything."

Judging by the size of the house, that certainly did not seem to be the case. But, unless I was mistaken, researchers worked in teams and were employed by institutions and governments, like the hospital, like councils, like the Trader Guild, or *gamra* even. Why was Benton Leck trying to go it alone?

"The problem was that my husband needed research staff, and these people don't do work for the love of it. So he needed a lot more money. And then this stranger came to him." She hesitated.

I wondered why.

"I have to say that my husband really didn't trust him right from the start. And I even told him that if he didn't trust this man, he shouldn't work with him. But then he said the money was just too good to be true."

"And I guess too good to be true probably proved the truth, right?"

"Well, I don't know. He was told by this man that he was not supposed to talk about the project because it was going to be so controversial. But when the results were published, my husband would have academics and people with funding beating down his door. He didn't really care so much about that, but this man did offer to pay him a lot so he went along with it."

"Did you ever find out what the project was?"

"He said something about finding out about communication. That certain groups of people communicated in a way that we didn't yet understand, and that there might be a big lesson to be learned in studying these things."

I was beginning to have a bad feeling about this, because Tamerians did not communicate well. And having failed to produce a group of people who were effective communicators, the creators of Tamerians had just wasted a lot of money and effort. Their project, slated to be the producers of a superhuman race, had failed miserably, because the people could not communicate, or no one knew how to communicate with them. They listened to orders but they did not seem to have any opinions of their own, or did not know how to share them. Put a linguist on that for a measly salary, probably quite a lot for the linguist, and try to solve that problem.

Then give the linguist the license to publish the results and gain credibility for the project all over the inhabited worlds. It was one way to subvert the original project. Tamerians were meant to be superhumans. The project to produce them failed, and this was an attempt at rescuing it.

Maybe.

"Did he show any other details of the project?"

"He was not allowed to talk about where it was, where he was going or even for how long. I was told that I would be able to contact him through a messaging service."

"Messaging?"

"Well, yes, it was kind of similar to the Exchange, but different."

I gave Thayu a concerned look. We had known that these secretive people had different ways of communicating. That there were satellites out there in deep space that were used by them specifically to communicate only with each other. I had asked Asha to take out some of them that were watching Earth, because we could pinpoint their position, but space was incredibly big and it would be impossible, now and forever into the future, to take out all of them. At some point, *gamra* would have to come to terms with the fact that there would be networks other than the Exchange that people used to communicate and travel.

"And did you use their messaging system?"

"I did. I got some messages from him, but after a while they stopped."

"Did he ever drop any hints about where he was?"

"No, but he complained that it was cold, and also the last message was quite disturbing. Wait I'll show it to you."

She rose from her chair, and went to a cupboard against the back wall. She pulled out something in a folder that she only opened when she sat down again. Inside lay a flat reader, similar to what we had obtained from Puck. I looked at Thayu, and I saw that she was thinking the same thing. *Tamer.*

Aliandra tried to turn the reader on, but the screen remained black.

I told her, "That is because it is one-use-only."

She gave me an alarmed look. "But I swear the message was there."

"Yes, we got one of those devices, too, but they tend to self-destruct after they have been read."

Her eyes widened.

"Do you remember what it said?" Thayu said.

"He was worried about not being able to talk to the people who had hired him. He said he was at the research base by himself, no one had visited for a while, he felt isolated, and he wasn't sure if this message would reach me. That was the last I heard."

I exchanged another look with Thayu. She gave a tiny nod. Yes, she agreed with our dropping the façade of casual interest. This was serious.

I said, "Look, I'm sorry for not having taken you seriously."

She stared at me. "But you *have* taken me seriously. You're just about the only one."

"Not as seriously as I should have. But I'm going to need everything you've got."

"Are you going to find him?"

"I don't know. If he's where I think he might be, then it won't be easy at all. But I'll pass it on to people who will be able to look into it."

And the only people who could do that were the Asto military, because Tamer had no Exchange, and failing an Exchange node, the only way to reach Tamer was through the military sling. Which meant that Benton Leck had signed up with the only other people who could reach Tamer: those who used Aghyrian technology to circumvent the Exchange, and I'd long suspected that they were still active in Barresh, and on Earth as well.

"I'm going to need to know who the man was who hired your husband. Do you know that?"

"You're going to think that I'm a silly woman, but I don't know his name. I work with artists, and I don't have time to track all my husband's contacts. I don't want to. I *trust* him." Her fierce eyes met mine. The irises were pale blue. "But I do know this: the man who hired my husband has a company that hires out people for all kinds of jobs. He is probably just an intermediary. His office is in town next to that new shop that sells all those modern gadgets."

Sure enough, Jasper Carlson.

Not only that, he was the owner of poor Puck, who had been trying to tell me something.

My heart skipped a beat, and then another one.

It could, of course, just be that Jasper acted as intermediary, because that was his business, but in combination with what had happened to Puck? And that contract on his reader?

I took my reader out of my pocket and turned it on. Aliandra watched me, suspiciously, sipping her tea.

"We obtained this document that mentions your husband." I turned the reader to her.

Thayu and I watched while she read.

Two women were talking elsewhere in the house. The only sound in the room was the soft popping of the fire.

Aliandra finished reading, nodded and pushed the reader back to me. "It's not very specific."

"Is it like the way they communicated with your husband?"

"Exactly like it."

"We're having a lawyer look over it." Veyada. Ouch. "So what did you do when you didn't hear from your husband?"

"I wanted to know where my husband was. I was worried, so I went to this man's business. I didn't even get to see him, only people in the office, and most of them refused to answer any questions. They told me I had to make appointments and then cancelled those appointments at the last moment. They weren't interested in talking to me, they only made those appointments to keep me off their backs. And then people started harassing me."

She left a dramatic pause. "People were hanging around the gate outside, and they would send me abusive messages. Someone emptied the garbage bin on my porch. And at night people would throw things in through the windows. They would harass my staff when they left. And I was just too scared to be in that big house by myself without anyone who could help me."

At this point, I felt deeply ashamed of my prejudice. I had thought of her as a crazy woman, one of these people who sees ghosts in every corner and complains about every little thing. And she might still be a bit of a nutcase, and that, sadly had led to people ignoring her, in the same shameful way I had done.

Some people were their own worst enemies, but some other people would do well to can their judgement. Yeah, I wasn't proud of myself right then.

I told her that we would look into it. Obviously I couldn't promise her anything about her husband's wellbeing and could only offer her sympathy for her suffering.

Our meeting was over, and it was time to go to our accommodation. The change in time zone had left me feeling very tired, and it was mid-afternoon. Early enough to go to bed, right?

Thayu and I walked through the yard. My breath steamed in the cold dry air.

"I don't like the sound of this," Thayu said.

"No. Me neither."

"What can we do?"

I shrugged. "Without Ezhya's approval, nothing." Tamer was not a *gamra* world and had no Exchange. In order to get there we'd need to use Asto's military sling. If we decided to go there. And I didn't feel a strong desire to do so.

I'd wait until we had advice from Veyada and until I could discuss this with the others.

But when Thayu and I arrived in the street outside the Ilendar house, my team was not there. Well, that was interesting.

"Over there," Thayu said.

I looked downhill, where she pointed. The street opened out into some kind of square, with structures that looked like pens or market stalls.

I checked my reader, and I had indeed received a message from Sheydu that they were going in that direction, sent while we were inside.

So we wandered down the street.

I told Thayu of my suspicions that Tamer was involved. She agreed.

"This big conflict has been in the background ever since we

started working together," Thayu said. "It's the establishment against the new people, who think they can do everything better. It's Asto against the other inhabited worlds. Whether they are Amoro Renkati, the Aghyrians, Tamerians or the Pretoria Cartel, they all want one thing: a world without rules and one where an alternate version of the Exchange exists that they can control. They might be slightly different people, but they're all linked. They don't want *gamra,* they hate Asto, and they think the answer to all their problems is to let crime fester, calling it *business.* I don't think anything *gamra* does can solve it. I don't think anything Ezhya does can stop it. At some point, we're going to have to make deals with these people."

I agreed with everything she said. "Keeping one's enemies in one's association."

"Precisely."

I looked at her. Thayu did not often make political statements, but when she did, they were profound.

She was right, of course. *Gamra* would have to deal with the situation at some point.

I was glad that particular calibre of negotiations was out of my hands.

We arrived at the market, a jumble of tents and temporary pens filled with groups of big hairy creatures that grumbled and snorted.

"What are those things?" Thayu asked, her eyes wide.

"Tiyuk." The Mirani highland pack animals that had been used by people to negotiate the highland passes for thousands of years.

"They're huge."

They were. All of the creatures, barring the young ones, were taller than me. They stood placidly in the pens, awaiting their fate, a jumble of shaggy hairy bodies. With the fencing and the animals' long matted fur disturbing our view, it was even hard to tell which end was the head and which the tail.

They rumbled and hummed and blew out noisy breaths.

Thayu said, "Urgh. They stink."

That, too.

We found the rest of the team soon enough standing at a pen which contained about ten huge hairy individuals.

Both Sheydu and Reida watched, their hands in their pockets and their hoods pulled over their heads as far as possible without totally blocking their vision. While we were inside, clouds had rolled in. It had started snowing a little bit, and they did not look impressed with the situation.

But Deyu had pushed down her hood, and one of the animals was nosing her jacket through the fence. The nose was black and wet, covered in bits of straw. The animal's eyes were golden brown, mournful, with long eyelashes—reportedly to keep out snow. It had long ears which drooped down both sides of its head like a lop-eared rabbit's ears.

She rubbed its furry head with her gloved hands, scratching between the ears and ducking out of the way of its tongue.

"See, he likes me."

I wasn't sure how she determined the animal was he, but it was certainly big enough, and the two sets of horns on its head looked quite menacing.

Deyu continued, "I read this amazing story last night. It was about someone who had travelled with these herds for a long time. They go up into the mountains so high that the air is so thin that you can barely breathe. But these animals are so well adapted they have no trouble with thin air. They eat lichen and moss that grows on the mountainside, and if they can't get the moss off the rocks, they just eat the rocks and poop out the stones. There is almost nothing up there except snow, and still big animals like this can survive. They talk to each other with the low rumbles that you can hear. And their herders can imitate the sounds and talk to them in return."

She made a kind of humming sound, and to my surprise, the animal responded.

"What does that mean?"

"I have no idea." And she laughed.

8

———————

FROM THE ANIMAL MARKETS, we walked into the city centre to find our accommodation, an apartment close to the centre of the city, in one of the city's old dark stone buildings with small windows. I had heard that at one time there used to be no glass inside these windows, and I was glad that I did not live in that time, because I was frozen solid even from walking the short distance from the livestock markets.

The guesthouse catered to visiting business people, reflected in the quiet air of professionalism of the foyer and reception area. The keys to the apartment we had booked already lay waiting for us, and checking in was so efficient that we didn't even have the time to look at the numerous historical artefacts that were displayed in glass-fronted cabinets around the room.

We went up the stairs and came out into a central hallway with three doors to the bedrooms. Straight ahead was a living area with some couches around the hearth. Deyu and Reida immediately took up spots closest by the fire. The couch got Sheydu's approval. She looked rather tired to me. The standoff with her son had to eat at her. She never said so, but I was sure that she loved Veyada.

Wan grey light fell into a small, narrow window which looked out over the street. Golden light radiated from shop windows, where people browsed wares and looked at the displays in the windows.

Nicha suggested that he get some food for us.

That was a good idea, because we were all quite hungry.

I went to get changed into something a little bit more comfortable than the super thick jacket, while Reida threw some fire bricks into the hearth, and the resulting spark of flames led to squeals of laughter from Deyu, because neither of them had any experience with fire. You could not light fires in Barresh because of the fire-retardant properties of the megon-nut oil that hung in the air; and on Asto there was no need for fires. For Reida and Deyu, fire provided an endless source of entertainment.

Nicha came back, his arms full of wrapped parcels that spread a wonderful smell through the apartment. He unloaded his loot onto the table, and unwrapped it all until there was all this wonderful food sitting in the middle of a mess of scraps of paper.

"I was always led to believe that Mirani food was horrible," Nicha said.

That was the anecdote, but obviously things had improved a lot. There was fresh bread, and different types of stews and breadsticks, and stewed fruit, and different types of beans. There was also a bit of fish for me and Reida. I thought of Ynggi and how he would be having fun with Ayshada in my apartment, and of Veyada, who loved fish.

We all found room around the table, sitting on the hairy rug.

Deyu was a bit dismayed to find that the rug was in fact the pelt of a tiyuk. "They're such beautiful creatures."

"That is what people use these animals for," I said. "Blankets, rugs and clothing. Nothing grows up here, so they can't grow any fibres."

"But yet they can use wool. They don't need to kill the creature."

"This is an agricultural society. They use animals, they don't keep them as pets."

Of course the horses and the llamas she had liked at my father's house had been pets. Also, the majority of Coldi didn't eat the meat of vertebrate animals.

Eventually, the discussion turned to the situation at hand. I told them about our meeting with Aliandra Ilendar.

"The situation is quite a bit more dangerous than I assumed," I said.

They all looked at me, a circle of serious faces around the table, now bathed in a bluish glow from the dusk.

Nicha said, "So this is all still related to the whole situation with Robert Davidson?"

"We never solved this part of it," I said. "We always knew there was a line from the Pretoria Cartel going to Tamer. We could never investigate exactly where it went and who was there to receive it."

"But why would an academic get involved in that?"

"This is my theory: it is well known that Tamerians are very poor communicators. I think Benton Leck was contracted to try and teach them how to speak to others. I think the creators of Tamerians knew that their project was a failure. Benton Leck is trying to rescue it."

"Who are the creators of Tamerians?" Reida asked.

"That's a very good question. I think they're related to some people in the Pretoria Cartel. I think they might be related to the group we knew as Amoro Renkati. I think they could include some Aghyrians from the Aghyrian compound in Barresh. I think Jasper Carlson is in contact with them. But it's all speculation. They're on Tamer, and we have as much access to Tamer as those people have to *gamra* networks."

"Less than that," Sheydu said, her tone dark. "*Gamra* security is as transparent as a window. With no glass."

No one said anything for a while.

And then Sheydu said, "I see. I guess it does make sense after all."

"So what do we do with this information?" Nicha said.

I replied, "There is only one thing we can do. Go home, tell someone at *gamra* and then get on with our jobs."

"That doesn't sound like you."

"I don't know what else we could do. We have no means of getting to Tamer short of begging Asha if we can use the military sling, and I really don't see what we can do there. If this is indeed the place where they make Tamerians, then they'll have a gun-crazy ready-made army. There are only seven of us—six without Veyada—eight counting Evi and Telaris."

"Asha should bomb the lot of them out of existence," Sheydu said, her arms crossed over her chest. "That will solve all the problems."

"You can't bomb everything."

"You absolutely can if they don't listen, if they threaten the peace."

"Still, that's not for us to decide."

"If not for us, who will decide? Because no one has done anything about this festering issue in the last ten years."

Whoa, I had no idea why she needed to dig in about this. I decided to let the subject rest.

"What is even at Tamer?" asked Reida. "Why do they get so hung up about a frozen ice ball?"

Deyu pulled up the details about the world and they did indeed look very uninviting. Tamer consisted mostly of ice, frozen oceans, mountains and glaciers. Apparently the geological history indicated that it had once orbited closer to the sun, and used to have oceans and plants.

The information recorded no electronic signature anywhere on the surface, which meant that there were no settlements where people lived. The world's description included some vague information about wildlife, though. One line mentioned the existence of megafauna, but there was no further information about the type.

"Hmm, looks really riveting," Reida said.

"Good place to hide," Thayu said.

I said, "I would have expected some electronic signature to show up, unless the bases or whatever facilities they use for making Tamerians are in orbit."

Deyu said, "This type of scan is probably not sensitive enough to detect small amounts of radiation. Also remember that, since there is no Exchange node, we're looking at data that's over thirty years old. This is *visual* data, from telescopes."

True. And smart. That was Deyu. Meticulous as hell. I was so used to having the instantaneous communication provided by the Exchange.

We finished all the food, talk turned to lighter subjects, and after a while we all went to our rooms. The shuttle home would not leave until the next morning.

When I went into the room I shared with Thayu, she was standing in front of the window, looking out into the street.

She turned around when I shut the door, and smiled at me.

"Look, it's snowing," she said.

It was, too. Tiny flakes drifted down in the glow of the streetlights.

"Do you want to go for a walk? I wouldn't mind going to see some of this amazing place."

"It's going to be cold," I warned her.

"Yes, but that adds to the charm, doesn't it?"

I kind of agreed with her. I had never seen, in person, some of the things that people went to see when they came to this city.

So I went to my pack and dug out all the cold-weather gear I had brought. We put on our boots, we put on long coats, we put on our gloves, and we laughed at each other because we looked so silly.

"I feel like one of these bar game people," Thayu said.

And we both laughed, because in the more seedy bars of Barresh, people played a game where somebody put on as many layers of clothes as possible, and then others would bid for this person to take everything off. The highest bid of course would be for the final layer.

When we left the room, we found Deyu and Reida still sitting by the fire. The sound of an angry voice drifted through the door of one of the other rooms.

I frowned at Deyu. "What's going on?"

"I think she's talking to Veyada," Thayu said.

That remark hit me, because I still missed him terribly, and I wondered how our team was going to function without him. Just when things seemed all right, it turned out they weren't.

I said, "Do you want me to go and talk to her?"

"I don't know," Deyu said. Sometimes when asked a direct question she would still crawl back into her shell of poor confidence.

"You'd probably get your head bitten off," Reida said.

That was probably as good in assessment as any, so I decided to leave it until Sheydu sounded a little less angry, and Thayu and I left the apartment. We went down through a dark staircase where it smelled of wet stone.

"We do need to sort something out about this," I said to Thayu when we were in the street.

"Yes. I told you so."

I thought she was going to say more, but she didn't, at least not for a while. We walked between the shoppers in the glow of light that came through the shop windows. It was a kind of surreal experience, and I remembered that once when I was little, probably about nine, my father had taken me to a Christmas market someplace in Germany. It had been snowing, and coming from New Zealand, I had not seen much snow, except as dirty white patches on mountains. Snow on the ground was special. I remembered looking at the imprints of my own little boots.

"What would you do about Veyada? I know I'm supposed to know this, but I've never faced anything like this before."

She smiled. "You are so good at playing helpless."

"I *am* kind of helpless. I can't fall back on an instinct, like you. I don't want to screw this up. I don't want to lose Veyada. I don't even want to lose Sheydu, even if she is being difficult."

"Everyone would like to see Veyada stay. He brings much knowledge to the team, and he is very even-tempered."

That was my assessment of Veyada. Other than that, I had only recently realised that it was his judgement I appreciated the most in difficult decisions.

"Wait—did you just tell me to let Sheydu go?"

"She's probably ready to step back. She can't keep going forever."

"Where would she go? I'm happy to keep her around. I don't want her to feel homeless."

What *did* Coldi do when they retired? At least I knew for a fact that most spent their last years with their families. But Veyada was Sheydu's family.

"She will have a plan."

I didn't like that. I felt that if she left, she would be lost, and would probably disappear somewhere and then not much later we would hear that she had died. I remembered how shocked I had been to find out about the hidden secret of Asto's society: that people high up in the hierarchy went underground and killed themselves. That this was an acceptable outcome.

All right, I would accept that, if the team judged that Sheydu should leave. I had sort of expected this for a while, because the two of them had come from such a high station before joining my association, but I would never want her suicide on my conscience.

Never.

And something else. The team did not make this decision. Only I could.

So, what? Tell Sheydu that she had to leave and hear that she'd killed herself a few days later?

Never.

My chest constricted with that thought as I walked next to Thayu in this winter wonderland.

The street opened out into the famous town Square of Miran. We entered from downhill, between the shops and the commercial district. Across the snow-covered expanse in front of us was the government building, with a broad set of steps leading up to the main entrance. In the middle of the square, looking abandoned and poorly lit, stood the Foundation monument. This was one of the oldest surviving human artefacts on the planet.

After the meteorite strike on Asto, three ships had fled. Two had come to Ceren: one with residents from a spiritual group, who had come to Barresh. The other had been from upper government and their craft had more or less crash-landed in the Mirani mountains in heavy mist. They had run afoul of people who lived in these highlands, people who were acclimatised to the cold and thin air and who had evolved to be able to climb up and down steep ravines to find mushrooms to eat. To say that they had been very unhappy with these invaders in their territory would be an understatement.

After a particularly bloody confrontation, the Aghyrian newcomers had packed up everything and had come down to the mountain pass where the city currently lay. After a number of years, the native people came to join them, during a particularly difficult time, and they signed the famed Foundation agreement. This monument, with its five pillars that used to support a roof that had long since fallen down, was built in honour of that agreement. Foundation was the Mirani constitution. Foundation was written in Mirani law. Foundation was their religion.

The monument had long been neglected, but as the Human Tree project in Barresh gained importance, something started more than a hundred years ago in Barresh by the founder of the Aghyrian society Daya Ezmi, so did the interest in Mirani history increase. Because the Mirani Endri were pure-blood Aghyrians, directly descended from the refugees from Asto. These days a chamber underneath the monument held a register where people could go to check their ancestry.

The entrance to this chamber was through the gates of the government building. I'd heard that the chamber was open day and night, and so we walked through the gates. By now it was starting to snow quite heavily, and our boots left deep footprints in the freshly fallen snow.

A golden glow of light came from the entrance, a little triangular building that stuck up out of the snow. The door slid open when we came close, and in the hallway, a guard asked to take our coats. A little booth blew hot air to dry our shoes.

With that done, we descended the sloping pathway underneath the pavement of the square.

The walls were made from hewn stone. This section of the monument was quite new, because the chamber had not been reopened until quite recently.

At the bottom we came out in a plain stone chamber. It had five walls to mirror the five corners of the monument above. In the middle of the chamber stood a table with a glass top. When you went close up to it, you could see into its depths.

Thayu chuckled. "They have a galaxy in there."

I looked. She was right. A miniature galaxy floated in the dark space under the glass.

Inside the table must be some kind of holo projector that produced these images, although I could not see how it was done.

Around the edges of the table were panels with instructions about how to operate the equipment. You had to go to a little recess in the table where you inserted your finger, and a machine would scan it.

Thayu put her thumb in, and I could see a blue light tracing the outline of her skin.

The image inside the table changed. It showed a tree structure, with branches. Most of the tree was white, but one line through it, trailing back to the trunk, was blue. Thayu's ancestry was no surprise. She descended directly from one of the thirty-six clans on Asto.

"Now it's your turn," she said.

I went to the little recess in the table and put my thumb in.

The blue light traced my finger. It was a little bit warm and tickled.

Then the tree came up. There were no coloured lines on it at all. The image flickered and then disappeared.

And then the tree came up again. Now it displayed a couple of blue lines, but they did not join up.

Some of them were clearly related to Thayu's, and others were way over to the other side of the tree. Another short blue line went right into the trunk of the tree.

I chuckled, feeling uneasy. "Well whatever the hell you make of that?"

Thayu looked a bit disturbed. She pointed to the trunk. "This part is the Aghyrian heritage that all humans share." She pointed at the part at the other side of the tree. "This part is your birth heritage from Earth. And the part on the other side is your new Coldi blood."

Here was the evidence that my genes had really changed, if I needed any more evidence. I stared at the graphic with the three disjointed sections. I guessed that the projection had flickered because the program didn't know how to deal with someone like me.

"That's interesting," said a male voice behind us.

It was a Mirani man, and I hadn't seen him come in.

He was one of those elfin-like Endri people, like Aliandra Ilendar, tall and willowy with long near-white hair. There were not many of these people left; most of them had pure Aghyrian blood, and they suffered quite a bit of inbreeding. I wondered where his lines on the tree would be.

"Do you work here?" I asked him.

"I do. I presume you're visitors?"

"I'm a patient of Lilona Shrakar's."

His face showed comprehension. "Have you had gene treatment?"

"Just coming through it now."

He nodded. "That explains that strange phenomenon." He gestured to the disjointed branches of the tree.

"Do you work with her, too?"

"We correspond on occasion." I sensed a "but" underneath the surface. "The human tree is a very big project and many people work on it."

"Have you heard of an academic called Benton Leck?"

"I have indeed. He comes here a fair bit. His wife is a local."

"Does he work for the project?"

"Not directly, but he's a collaborator."

"What is his task?"

"He has shown us some very interesting aspects: that the different people on these different branches don't just have different instincts, they have different ways of communicating. You should be able to trace not just the way you look, but also the way you feel and behave through this. Anyway, I was about to go home. Nice to see interest from people outside Miran. Have a nice day."

He left through the corridor up the ground level.

It had been a while since I'd removed my finger from the recess, and the projection had flipped back to showing a slowly-revolving galaxy.

Just for interest's sake, I put my thumb back in the recess.

This time, the tree did not flicker. It now showed an almost complete path from the trunk to the branches, all of them Coldi.

What the. . . ?

"Look at this," I said.

Thayu was reading some of the panels on the wall, but she joined me.

"That's completely different from how it was before."

We waited until the tree turned into a galaxy again, and I put my other thumb in. It showed a fragmented line again, but less Earth heritage than Coldi. Even as we watched, one of the lines winked out and flipped to the Coldi side.

Well . . . that was . . . strange. Disturbing.

9

———

WE WENT BACK HOME next day. It was a long journey, and while I watched the landscape slide under me, I worried that we were wasting time on things that were ultimately not going to be in our influence to control. I worried what Ezhya was going to say about this. I was also wondering what Veyada had found while we were away.

It was evening when we arrived in Barresh, and the day was winding down.

I felt much stronger so we decided to forego the lengthy process of finding a water taxi and caught the train back.

In the carriage, we attracted some strange looks from our fellow passengers. Why would people travel with furs and high boots?

If I had expected to come home to a quiet evening, however, we were mistaken.

As soon as we opened the door, Ayshada ran cross the hall, and threw himself at his father.

He had come from the hub, where most of my team who'd stayed behind had gathered.

Not just Devlin and Ynggi, but also Evi and Telaris and some of the people from downstairs. Also, Melissa, the new *gamra* delegate, was there.

"There they are," Devlin said.

They all turned to the door, with the bluish light from the hub silvering their faces.

I asked, "What's going on here?"

"I asked Melissa to come so that we could translate some things," Devlin said.

"Things?" I sat down at the bench, and looked at the projection that was displayed in mid-air. It was a news item from one of the more sensational news services on Earth.

It mentioned some kind of gathering of what they called alien people in Cairo. These news services could never be accused of being too diplomatic.

I asked Devlin and Melissa why they thought this meeting was significant, and Melissa said, "Amarru alerted us that this was happening, and warned us to be on the lookout. There have been rumours that, since the election turned out in our favour, some people unhappy with that have been organising themselves either to leave Earth together, or to establish enclaves of sanctity. Unfortunately, this includes a lot of the Zhori mafia, who were all too happy back when the Exchange had no teeth to chase up their smuggling."

"So, what? Are they planning to come here? They'll just face the same problems."

"That is what we don't know. But since the areas previously controlled by the Pretoria Cartel were opened up, there has been a lot of material coming out that such cells of resistance in fact exist, and that they are planning to take action. We don't know what that action is. Word is that some of the Zhori leaders have already left and have started to investigate a place where they can be safe."

"Why would they come to Barresh?"

"They wouldn't, necessarily, but leaving Earth is definitely an option, so we need to keep an eye on it."

Yes, it was, and I had not discounted the possibility.

Truth was that since the election was won, we'd lived in a strange vacuum between campaigning and Earth finally getting its act together and sending people to help Melissa.

"How are things going with the preparation?" I asked her. When we spoke, these days, I almost always spoke Coldi to her. Not only had she grown up in a half-Coldi family, but I was ashamed to say that my knowledge of official terms in Isla was slipping.

"Slow. We've got an office for the Earth delegation, but we need apartments. I've got a couple of people lined up, but some will need training. Amarru is providing it, but it all takes time."

Yes, it did. I'd used the time while the bureaucracy slowly churned for my treatment, but a lot of others had not been sitting still.

"Is this Zhori activity something that concerns you a lot?"

"I guess we could always expect the hardcore mafia element to want to move *somewhere* they can continue to ply their trade. They'll try to avoid the laws for as long as they can. Seriously, good luck to the organisation that lands the unenviable task of pulling the Sudanese solar glider industry into line."

We both laughed. We knew the sort of mess that was, with Indrahui interests—and their vile life-debt systems—threaded all through the local economy.

Then Melissa's face turned serious. "It did not worry me overly. As you know, my family has strong bonds with the Zhori clan."

Yes, I knew. Her half-brother Klaus Messner was Zhori. He was a spy for Amarru, and she had her loyalties deep within that clan.

"You said it *did* not worry you. But now it does?"

"Yes. Some parts of it, at least. It seems our dear friend Mr Kluysters has become involved."

"Why do you think that?"

"He's left Earth."

"I heard that, too. I'm not sure that it has anything to do with the Zhori."

Melissa switched to Isla. "You're not sure? Cory, the man is vile. He puts on this veneer of sophistication, but you know what he did behind the scenes. You were there and you saw it. You know they were basically trying to resurrect the dead—no, don't give me any of that 'He didn't know' bullshit. *Of course* he knew. It was his whole point in hanging onto that company. He *wanted* to sell Sandowne Pharmaceuticals for a long time, and kept it just so that it could provide a cover for this vile trade."

I blew out a breath. When Melissa went like this, there was little opportunity for discussion. She loved scandals and political stirring. "I met Minke Kluysters. Look, I'm not trying to excuse him. I don't believe he knew exactly what was happening—"

"You let yourself be hoodwinked!"

"Listen to me. He asked to see Ezhya, and I managed to deflect that request—"

"Good job. As if Ezhya would be interested in seeing a criminal like that."

"He would."

Melissa stared at me. Her mouth fell open and closed again.

"Ezhya is no angel. I am no angel. Minke Kluysters is no angel."

Melissa snorted. "You can say that again. That man is—"

"I don't think Minke Kluysters knew what was going on in that shed that—yes—technically lay on his own land. He didn't know the full detail, because he's not interested in that kind of stuff. He's tasted power. Real power, not of the slow and political kind, but the type of power that is traded between very influential and wealthy people behind closed doors. And that type of power is exactly the type that Ezhya is interested in. He watches with bemusement as the *gamra* assembly takes years to decide what he would simply order to be done. He likes *gamra,* because it affords Asto power without the need for spending any military effort in maintaining it. But when there is a disruption, like we saw with the Pretoria Cartel, rest assured that he is interested in investigating who is behind it, because if by chance the focus of power shifted away from *gamra,* he would want to be in the front seat of whatever came to replace it. Minke Kluysters is playing a lot of games and moving a lot of mountains and, yes, sometimes flattening groups of people who get in his way. A while ago, I contacted him about the office he wanted to establish in Barresh. If I don't help him, someone else will. I have some ideas who this someone else may be, and to be honest, I don't want those people anywhere near him, so I've extended the invitation myself. He hasn't replied yet."

She stared at me. "Damn it, Cory, do you know you scare me sometimes?"

"That has been said before."

"All this just when we're working towards a more peaceful world."

"The ultimate peaceful society is a utopia. Society is always in a state of flux. We've just added to a huge flux by getting Earth to join *gamra.* Think about it. Asto is *gamra*'s biggest world. Earth will be the second biggest. Many people feel scared for all kinds of reasons. We can't expect all of them to play happy families. As soon as things are too quiet and the ruling party gets complacent, something happens to upset it. I learned that on my very first day of employment."

"I was there, remember?"

I did remember, and I also remembered how vicious and opinionated she had been back then, working for Flash Newspoint. I had never understood Nations of Earth's decision to appoint her in my place, but we were stuck with it now, and it looked like she was going to be the formal *gamra* delegate for Earth for the foreseeable future.

Melissa pushed herself up from the bench. "I better go home now. I'll let you recover from your trip. You're probably still tired." She glanced at my hair. "It *is* turning a very interesting colour, though."

After she had left, Thayu came in. She told me that Veyada had sent a report about the contract and that she put it on the reader that was in my office.

I asked her, "Thay', is there anything strange going on with my hair?"

She came to me and studied my hair. She turned on the light on her reader, and had a closer look. "It's like . . . it's turning gold."

"Gold?"

"Like Evi and Telaris'."

They had bronze hair, but whenever I watched them through the UV-protection lenses, their hair was more yellow.

I leaned into her, feeling her warmth behind me. Damn it, how long did Lilona say we had to wait?

I pushed myself up from the bench. "I better have a look at what Veyada says."

In the hall, I met Eirani, who informed me that she would bring refreshments soon.

It was quiet and dark in the hallway. I had obviously not been the only person to feel tired. And, to be honest, I would rather have gone to bed, too. Especially if the bed had Thayu in it.

I opened the door to the office, where it was dark. Faint light radiated from outside—and someone stood in front of the window.

I gasped.

The person turned around. "I figured you would come in here."

Sheydu.

Time to face the music.

I went to stand next to her, and we said nothing for a while. I was waiting for her to start. While I looked out into the darkness of the marshlands, I suddenly knew how I was going to approach this.

Eventually, she said, "So you spoke to him, did you?"

"Yes, I did."

"What did he have to say for himself?"

"I would actually like to speak about something else."

She turned to me.

"I would like you to tell me why you decided to have Veyada, and what prompted your decision."

"That's a very long time ago."

"Yes, I realise that, but I would like to hear it anyway. I can imagine that the same decisions that you made in those days affect him right now."

She leaned on the windowsill in silence, her typical reaction to a situation that she was not comfortable talking about. She would be happy to talk about tactics or weapons, but found it hard to talk about herself.

"Well, it seemed like something everyone in my position did: get a child for yourself, an heir."

"You made sure that he was male?" That wasn't supposed to happen, but I knew it did anyway.

"I did. Not much point raising a child for the Vonayi clan."

Coldi children took their clan from the parent of the opposite sex —so Veyada's father was from the elite Vonayi clan. That was interesting.

"And all that time that you have worked together with him, you have felt nothing for your son?"

She said nothing for a while. Obviously, she did.

"You work pretty well together, so I can't imagine that the current situation does you any good."

"I've got my loyalty to Ezhya." Her voice was harsh. "I can't, with any kind of twisting of my mind, think how it's going to be a good thing to associate with the Ezmi clan from Hedron. They've been ridiculing us for years."

This was an important issue for her and for my team. I had to be careful addressing it. "It is my philosophy to do as Veyada himself always tells me. He says to keep your enemies close. He says to keep your bugs in as many homes as possible."

That was a Coldi proverb.

She gave a small snort. "There are times that the proverbs are right and times that they are wrong. In the case of Hedron, I don't think we can apply the same rules."

"But what if I said that Mereeni was mainly aligned with the Athens Exchange? She is from Hedron, so does not have the *sheya* instinct."

"You can believe that if you want."

"You don't?"

"No."

"She does have the instinct?"

"Why do you think it is that she and Veyada argue all the time?"

Was it, really? I stared at her, but in the darkness I couldn't see her face.

But I knew she was right, and I should have realised this. Because Mereeni was Coldi, if she truly hadn't possessed the instinct, Veyada would have ignored her. But they had pretty much argued since they met, sizing each other up, trying to best each other, until they had come to the conclusion that they were *zhaymas,* equals, and it was a better idea to jump into bed with each other.

"But I don't understand. You encouraged them."

"That was before I realised he was serious about her. Nothing wrong with a few contacts here and there, but . . ."

"So, if she has the instinct, where do her loyalties lie?"

"That is a very good question, isn't it? In a society like Hedron where the instinct is actively repressed, how does it behave?" She let a dramatic pause lapse. "I did a bit of research. She went to the Leadership school of the Hedron Mines. Only their brightest go there. She studied law at Kedras and went to work for Amarru. Those are her networks. Hedron—which is not friendly to us—and Amarru."

"Amarru is friendly to us."

"Is she?"

My heart skipped a beat. "Is she not?"

But I remembered several times that I'd felt uneasy with Amarru's level of control over communication on Earth. All those electronic recording devices that had been secretly built into computer chips. I'd asked her about it, and she had been evasive until she could no longer deny it. I had pressured her to negotiate with

Margarethe. She had negotiated with Margarethe, not with me, or *us*.

Sheydu said, "The conflict on Earth about joining *gamra* was not between the ineffective Nations of Earth and whoever they fancied were their political opponents. Nations of Earth would not have cared one way or another whether Earth joined. *Gamra* would not have cared whether Earth joined. The conflict was between Amarru, who wanted Earth to join, and the Pretoria Cartel, who did not. Ezhya was merely watching. He would have accepted either result."

Damn it, she was right.

And damn it, I remembered a time when I'd seen Amarru behave subserviently to Ezhya—and I had told her to grow some guts. But I'd missed the signs. Ezhya and Amarru did not get along. At all. Maybe Amarru had been Ezhya's rival in Taysha's network, and Taysha had tried to topple Ezhya. He had failed, leaving Amarru stranded, and she might now be trying to strengthen her ties with the Azimi clan, who held the position of Asto's representative with *gamra*.

Even thinking about it made my head hurt.

"So . . . why do you think Veyada ignored the implications of this relationship?"

"I have no idea. It may have been a misjudgement, but he refuses to talk to me."

"That sounds very much unlike Veyada."

She gave a barely audible snort.

Yes, Sheydu, you're going to have to find a better story for what went wrong. Veyada does not refuse to talk to people.

I breathed out. "I highly appreciate both of you." Hell, I owed a lot of my recent success to the presence of both of them in my association. "I'm committed to making sure Veyada returns. I will be happy to accept Mereeni as well."

Another snort.

"You may have noticed that it has been my aim to gather a team that's as varied as possible. This is why we have people from different clans. It's why we have Devlin. It's why I have Ynggi in our household. And Evi and Telaris. I'm happy to add Mereeni to the team."

"Having her is a break in my loyalty. I can't have someone in this house who has loyalty to Amarru and be loyal to Ezhya. Not unless I am not in Ezhya's network, and I'm unwilling to cut that contact."

Where did I fit in terms of the instinct I didn't have? I considered myself as someone loyal to Ezhya, but, on the other hand, I didn't jump when he wanted me to. I *challenged* him sometimes. I was not a model of what a loyal citizen was like.

Ezhya liked to walk on the sharp edges of acceptability. He toyed with people, and he was attracted by people who stepped outside what he considered obedient behaviour.

Sheydu turned to the door. "Whatever happens, I remain completely loyal to you," she said from the darkness of the room. "Tell me what you want done, and I'll do it."

She rolled the door aside—letting in the glow of light from the hallway—and left.

Well, that hadn't gone as I had expected. Not at all.

Damn, I really didn't know what I was doing. And we still had no resolution. Sheydu didn't really expect me to speak up and fire her, did she?

I leaned my elbows on the desk and put my hands over my face.

After sitting like that for a while, I dragged my reader to me to look at the document Veyada had sent me.

It was quite long, and included a copy of the original contract as well as his interpretation of the law.

Veyada's interpretation of the contract between the employer named as Genetic Services and Benton Leck was summed up by a single word that he'd added at the top in big letters: exploitative.

I read over all the comments. In short, the contract was full of problems. It was not clear how long it would be for, how much it paid and when it ended. Veyada had made strong comments about requirements of secrecy about the project.

At the bottom he had said, *This document is an instrument of slavery.*

10

———

VEYADA'S INFORMATION turned out to be the most frustrating ever. His interpretation suggested to me that Benton Leck had likely walked into some kind of trap that might have been designed to get him to work cheaply on turning the investment into making Tamerians into a useful venture, but we could do nothing about it unless I applied for assistance from Asto's army.

And I didn't know that anything in the case was serious enough to warrant that type of action. I was sure that "I have a bad feeling about this" didn't qualify as serious enough. But I *did* have a bad feeling about it.

Over the next few days, I could do nothing except attempt to go back to work.

A *gamra* sitting was coming up, in which the arrangements for Melissa's office and the arrival of other Earth delegates were going to be discussed. These were important issues, because the placing of delegates' accommodation meant a lot about *gamra*'s perception of the importance of the member entity. Maybe the authorities wanted to give Melissa a much better office, but since no new members had joined for many years, they had simply run out of available space. The game then became about who to evict from where.

After years of having lived in apartments around the edge of the island, Melissa was learning the new power of her position, and insisted that she be given an office next to the Asto delegation, which was in the hands of Ayanu Azimi. As someone familiar with Coldi relationships, I saw an immediate problem in that location, because of Melissa's ties to the Earth branch of the Zhori clan.

The disconnect between Ezhya and Amarru went right through what should be a unified Coldi front.

I should do something to bridge that gap. But I found that I had trouble concentrating.

I tried to combat the feeling of lethargy by accompanying Reida and Deyu to their training. We did shooting practice, but also strength training, a program run by the Barresh city guards. My association had started this program after we came back from Earth.

But when we were doing the training, I kept thinking about Veyada, and how this was his initiative, and how nothing had been sorted and everyone kept skating around the issue of Mereeni.

Part of me hoped that I could postpone action until we'd received the message that the child had been born, and that Veyada could come back to live with us and all would be as it had been before, as with Nicha and Ayshada.

But I also knew that it wasn't going to happen. For one, I had never caught Nicha saying anything good about Ayshada's mother Xinanu. She had taken advantage of him and he had bought her out.

This time, things weren't going to be as simple. Veyada and Mereeni intended to maintain their relationship.

I also spent a lot of time in my office staring at Thayu's list of names that I needed to choose from before we went to Asto for the ceremony. Fortunately, a date for that visit had not yet been set, but it was coming up. I expected to hear from Asha any day now. I was actually surprised that we hadn't heard from him yet.

None of the names really appealed to me, so I requested my own copy of the register of available names. And then spent a lot of time staring at that, too.

A few other things happened in that time that were significant.

Apparently, when he made the translation for me, Veyada had also contacted the Exchange about Benton Leck's contract. They had a service where such things could be filed and not be altered, so that the original text of the document could be referred to in the future if a dispute arose. I didn't know this, but he obviously did.

The writers of the contract hadn't filed the document, but Benton Leck had.

The Exchange notified me that the contract was definitely sent from Tamer, and even managed to get me some coordinates on the planet's surface.

Armed with this information, I went back to Devlin's projection of the planet, and tried to determine where this location was. But the details of the surface of the planet were not sufficiently known to show me anything useful. Besides—why did location matter on a ball of ice?

The work did, however, reveal the existence of a satellite that no one had been aware of. There were many such satellites around the inhabited planets, including Earth and Ceren. This particular one was located near Tamer.

Then I asked Devlin to check the Exchange for any communication coming from that satellite—since we now knew of its existence and knew where to look—and there was rather a lot of it. I asked for a data dump and received a couple of rather large files in my account— and all they proved was that the satellite was active thirty years ago.

Damn it. I kept forgetting that we only had this instant communication through the Exchange.

I looked at the data anyway.

A quick glance at it revealed a lot of code. I called in Thayu and Reida and Sheydu, who specialised in decoding of secret messages, but we weren't even sure if it was a secret or legitimate message or maybe some automated process spitting out ancient gibberish long after its builders had gone. Space had that quality of turning a well-built device into a perpetuum mobile, still functioning long after the demise of its makers. Relatively intact Aghyrian satellites were still out there, spitting out information that could only be read by machines destroyed over fifty thousand years ago. Go figure.

But still, settlement on Tamer wasn't that old, as far as I knew, so the satellite was likely to be fairly recent. But at least thirty years old, at which time Amoro Renkati might have been active with their alternate Exchange, which was picked up only when they decided to start killing people with the technology.

Overall, I started to like this convergence of events less and less. A missing academic, and an onerous employment contract brought to us by a Tamerian who had grown a conscience and been killed for it.

I needed . . . to make some decisions.

I could ignore this issue and play it into the court of the authorities as "not my problem", but in the past, issues to do with Tamerians *had* been my problem, especially when Earth was also involved. And it was involved, however tenuously, through Benton Leck. I didn't think anyone in the *gamra* assembly would see the need to investigate, or maybe they did, but a request would get lost in the vast bureaucracy, somewhere between the thousand-year project that involved bringing peace to Indrahui and the negotiations of who really owned Exchange nodes: *gamra* or the locality where the node was located.

This was where my lack of a clear work contract bothered me. Ezhya paid for me, but as employer, he never told me what to do, he just assumed that I knew what he wanted and I would go and do it without his involvement.

I *thought* I did what he wanted—at least he didn't protest—but know for certain? No, far from that.

Looking at this strange issue from the perspective of Ezhya, would he want me to investigate? He was curious about Tamer, so from that standpoint he did, for sure. But did he want it enough for me to place my joining of the Domiri clan even further back?

I had no idea.

I needed some advice.

But Thayu would just tell me to look after myself. Nicha would be cynical and ask me what it was going to contribute to the team.

Over those few days, I realised that this was an issue for which they were not in a position to advise me. This was *my* problem, and I needed to make this decision, because that was inherent in my position as leader of the association.

The only person who could help me was someone ranked higher.

So I randomly chose three Coldi names from the list: Rizha—as Ezhya suggested—Mesheya, because Thayu liked it, even if I was not a fan, and Teya, because it happened to be the last name on the list. I still felt really ambivalent about the whole renaming thing and hadn't found a name in Thayu's list that made me think "Hell, yeah!" Just the idea that someone had died so that I could use the name was weird.

Anyway, I had now picked some potential names—and now had an excuse to contact Asha and ask his opinion.

Maybe I should not have been surprised that he was out of range at a location unknown.

I asked Thayu what she thought about it, and she responded with a laconic, "If he wants to talk to you, a message will reach him anyway, and he will contact you in return."

Thayu, being Thayu, was completely correct in this.

That same evening, after we had just finished dinner, Devlin came running into the living room, saying that I was wanted immediately.

I followed him to the hub.

The projection displayed the *gamra* logo, because Asha was on sound only, probably because he was aboard one of Asto's military ships. I also noticed how the locality window, normally displayed in the bottom right of the projection, was empty.

The threat of Asto's military was always present, like a crocodile under the surface of the water, watching and waiting.

Devlin left the room.

"I'm here," I said, while looping the earpiece over my ear.

"What did you find out about that woman?" he asked.

It took me a while to realise which woman he was talking about: Aliandra Ilendar. Because he would never be caught asking such a polite question as "How are you?" now would he?

"We went to visit her, and her story seems genuine."

In older days, I would have wondered how he knew about this, but now I just wondered why he was asking me about her.

The line crackled for a bit. The lag was really quite terrible, worse even than when I had first started this job. I figured he was probably quite far away. If my suspicion was correct, he would probably be looking at the world that we had been talking about: Tamer. He would be using the military sling to communicate with me. Hence the lag, hence the lack of a visual channel.

"Did she tell you who hired him?" No names mentioned, as usual.

"In a roundabout way." I wasn't sure how much he would appreciate me telling him on the line, because although his part of the communication might be shielded, it still went through the Exchange for the short distance between the Barresh Exchange node and my house.

There was no need of reminding him of that fact.

"Is it who we think it is?"

"I think it might be." Well, I hoped he was thinking about Jasper Carlson, but come to think of it, I could only hope that he was clued up on the things we discovered on Earth during the election. I did assume that he had been in command of the craft we ordered to destroy the Tamerian satellite that orbited Earth or he knew about the connection with the Pretoria Cartel.

He said, "We must talk."

"I think that might be a good idea."

"Expect some news soon."

And that was it. He signed off, and if I hadn't already had a couple of these really strange discussions with him before, I would now be feeling extremely pissed off.

But I had learnt to read between what he said, and I figured he would probably be sending some sort of craft to pick me up and take me to . . . wherever.

Tamer? Really?

What did he expect we could do there?

Thayu came into the doorway and gave me a puzzled look. I think she knew who I had been talking to.

She crossed the floor and sat down next to me in the faint glow of the control panel's many blinking lights.

Damn, I had intended to ask Asha about names, and had not even gotten the chance to do so.

A moment later, Nicha came into the hub as well. If they didn't have a sixth sense, they had very good hearing or good surveillance.

He also sat down.

"I think we have just received an order to go to Tamer," I said.

Neither of them protested, and that, more than anything unsettled me. They had been expecting this.

Thayu and Nicha would be in contact with their father, and they might even have a better idea than I did what this was all about.

"Do you know more about this?" I asked her.

There was a slight hesitation as they both looked at each other.

"Not that much," Thayu said. "All I know is that those data that you got from the Exchange, from that satellite, suggested that something is happening at Tamer."

"Any data from Tamer would be thirty years old."

"Normally, yes, but the wake suggests it is not."

I had learned all about the Exchange wake when we first learned of the Aghyrian ship. Whenever something was sent through an Exchange node, it produced a wake through space, and this contained information that could not be encrypted, and that frequently leaked information from the main message. It was how we'd been able to discern information about the Aghyrian ship: because of the massive wake it produced when it jumped.

"But I don't understand how that works? Does visual data like you get from a telescope have a wake?"

"It doesn't. But this does. Clearly, we've intercepted some data that happened to be destined for Barresh that they sent with their Exchange system into their uncovered territory."

"So what is this thing that's going on?"

"There is a lot of vehicular activity, that's all we know. It's too far away, and Asto's ships can't come any closer than they already are. They're taking utmost care not to be discovered."

Well, that confirmed my suspicion about Asha's locality.

Thayu continued, "It could be that they have been producing a lot of Tamerians and are now shipping out a giant army, although I am not quite sure what they would do with it. Tamerians are only good at following orders. They may be strong and fight well, but as superhumans, they're failures. Maybe they're now doing other things at Tamer, like producing more ships."

"So this is where we come in? We're supposed to go and find this academic as an excuse for finding out what is going on. Sounds like a dangerous mission, to go somewhere not even the Asto military wants to go."

"It is dangerous, and they can go there, but not without consequences. We can say we come to rescue the academic. He's from Earth, so that will give us an excuse for why you are involved."

"But hang on, if they're producing armies or craft, then does he expect us to go in there with just a small group? Are we meant to survive this?"

"If we weren't, we would have found out about it much sooner. I know you don't think much of my relationship with my father, but his loyalty is very strong."

I had little choice. The train had been set in motion the moment we showed interest in Benton Leck, and these were the games played by high-ranking men on Asto.

All I could do was to make sure that we were well prepared.

"Our association is unbalanced. I would really like to take Veyada," I said.

"Any progress on talking to Sheydu yet?"

"It's quite a bit more complicated than I imagined, as I'm sure you realise. I have thought about it. And I still think that Mereeni would be a good addition to our team."

"Haven't you heard any of Sheydu's objections?"

"I have, but I have a vision that I want to include as many people from as many different groups in this household as possible. Imagine if I could hand Ezhya a link of friendship with the world of Hedron."

I could see her think. There had been such relationships in the past, but because most Coldi from Hedron didn't have the *sheya* instinct, it was always going to be hard.

I continued, "It's possible, and it has happened before. One of Ezhya's predecessors had a long-lasting relationship with the heiress of the Hedron Mines. They even had a son."

"Yes, and Daya Ezmi was the biggest brat in the history of all of humanity."

"Don't let anyone in town hear that."

"We're not in town and he *was* the biggest brat in history."

It was true, and yet Daya Ezmi was considered one of the most influential people in recent history, up there with captain of the Aghyrian ship Kando Luczon. Daya had pulled Barresh out of its backwards mindset, he had staved off the extinction of the Aghyrian race and was the originator of the human tree project. He had paid for the hospital, and the Exchange. People in Barresh spoke of him like a god. Moreover, he was the main source of the Aghyrian money, having left the Aghyrian community his stake in the Hedron mines at the time of his death about fifty years ago.

"I want to try this, because I believe in it. Maybe I'm a brat, too, but I'll try to be a good brat."

"You're not a brat."

"Some people might think differently." Like Minke Kluysters, like Kando Luczon. "Ezhya is brilliant and dangerous. Amarru is brilliant and dangerous. Direct connections to both will make us stronger."

"I hope you're right."

"I think I am. I think it will be important, for us as well as the future generation, to heal this rift between sections of the Palayi and Azimi clans. I don't want Ayshada to feel like this is not his home."

I met Thayu's eyes, and realised something important. Ultimately, I couldn't get anyone to sort this out for me, and I couldn't wait for time to sort it out. I needed a complete team if we were to go to Tamer. If there was going to be a confrontation, then so be it.

I pushed myself up from the bench and went into the hall.

The living room was empty.

While I'd talked to Asha, people finished dinner.

So I went to Sheydu's room, feeling clammy with nerves.

She was sitting by the window, looking out over the marshland in the last rays of daylight. She looked up when I came in, but said nothing.

"I guess you know why I'm here," I said.

She made a small sound. I came into the room and sat down opposite her. I was a little bit disturbed by how old her face looked when side-lit by the glow from the window.

She said, "Yes, I know that it's time for me to retire. I've had a good run of life."

"Why do you think I should ask that?"

"But you were going to, weren't you?"

"If that is the only way you can see out of this problem, but I would like you to reconsider working with Veyada."

She shook her head. "Once the links are broken there is no way back. I know you don't want me around."

"I do want you around."

"No, you don't. You may appreciate my knowledge, but you get annoyed at my stubborn ways. You want to do something big and daring with this group, and I want to be safe. I am too old and curmudgeonly for new ideas. Just invite him back, invite her too, if that's what you want." There was an edge in her voice.

"You're disappointed?"

She shrugged. "I had hoped that my son would get a great position in society."

"But he did. He's a damn fine lawyer and he worked directly under Ezhya. What more do you want?"

"Yes, but I didn't see it. I wanted more and I wanted to push him. But I've come to realise that I am the thing that holds him back. I need to step away and let him shine at what he does best. I need to leave."

My mind filled with horror. This was the situation where the older Coldi people just vanished and killed themselves just to be out of the way and to be saved from embarrassment.

"Can you at least stay with us? I wouldn't want anything to happen to you."

She met my eyes in an understanding look. She had been there when we visited the *zeyshi* burrow where Risha killed himself after his attempt to take Ezhya's position failed.

She knew what I meant.

I wasn't sure I could see Sheydu as a doting grandmother, but it wouldn't be the first time that she surprised me.

She pressed her lips together. "I'll consider it. If you're worried, you're not going to get rid of me just yet. Just do your job and get back into the team."

"But what are you going to do?"

"I'll just go and stay in town for a bit."

Well, *that* was one hell of an unsatisfactory reply. Coldi did *not* just "stay in town", not by themselves at least.

She waved her hand. "Go. I'm not going anywhere. I said I remain loyal to you. None of that changes."

It was awkward, heart-wrenching, leaving the room. I felt very much like I would like to hug her, but one did not hug Sheydu.

I felt weak, like a failure, because, unlike what Thayu had told me, I had not been the one to formally fire her. I wasn't even sure that she *was* fired, or what she would do "in town".

Proper Coldi would breeze through the inevitable alignment of associations, but I was just a stupid human pretending to be Coldi, and I knew nothing, and the thought of harm coming to Sheydu frankly made my eyes prick.

And that would never do.

11

─────────

I WAS SURPRISED by how shaken I felt when leaving the room.

Considering the severity of the situation, the talk had gone well. There had been no fighting, not even verbally. Sheydu had simply agreed to step aside. She had even assured me that she wasn't going to harm herself. This outcome was the best I could have hoped for, but why did I feel so bad about it?

I went into our bedroom, where it was dark.

There was a little alcove with a washbasin just inside the door.

I splashed water on my face, looking at the deep shadows in the haggard expression on my face. When had I become so *old?*

Eirani was right. I looked—and felt—terrible.

Who was I to think that I could solve any kind of problem in this state?

The door slats rattled as the door rolled aside, and Thayu came in. I could see her in the mirror.

She stopped. We met each other's eyes via the mirror.

Then she came into the alcove and put her hands on my shoulders. I raised my hand to caress her fingers.

For a while, we said nothing. I didn't need to tell her what had happened.

"It is best this way," she said. "Left to fester, these conflicts always get worse. Rogue members of associations have been known to become aggressive to their former association."

I guessed I did not want Sheydu to become aggressive. She knew far too much about explosives. Would she really do that?

"Yes, but it's . . ." I let out a heavy breath. My voice felt unsteady. Hell, *I* felt unsteady. These few days, since coming from the hospital, had been string of emotional upheavals.

I was exhausted from pretending that I had everything under control. The reality was that I had nothing under control, and never had. My association relied on instincts I could never share.

"It is not an easy thing when an association readjusts." Thayu's voice was soft. "When it becomes clear that one of the people does not benefit the group as a whole, that is always a painful situation. It is not simply a matter of putting someone else in that position. The person who leaves has their ties linked up with the association, and those ties will never be severed. We can draw comfort from knowing that they will never use those ties against us, but it can also be a problem later. Anyone at Asto, and especially someone in the higher circles, goes through multiple phases and moves in and out of multiple associations. The links accumulate. The older you get, the more acquaintances you accumulate, and the more enemies."

"I feel *very* old."

While she caressed my shoulder, I realised something else that I had never given much thought: Coldi did not often form emotional bonds with people with whom they had children, unless that person was also in the association. Coldi did not marry because they got life-long bonds from associations.

I leaned into Thayu, enveloped by her female scent. Before I had the treatment, I had been aware of that scent, but it had never seeped into my very soul like this. My heart sped up, my cheeks glowed, my breath became faster and deeper so that I could drink that scent like honey.

She continued stroking my shoulder, and I had to force myself not to turn around, pick her up and carry her to the bed. In my addled mind, I was strong enough to do this, strong enough to rip off her clothes.

Lilona said wait.

Yes. We must be good and wait. I might just be strong enough again to lift Ayshada, but I could forget about Thayu.

I whispered, "I want you."

"Yes, I want you, too."

"I can't wait."

"We must wait. It will be good."

I turned to her, breathing the scent of her skin. I blew out a breath in the intimate hollow under her ear.

She gasped. "You've become so warm."

"I feel like I have a fever from being too close to you."

She pushed me away, gently. "Don't. Or I won't be able to stop. Let's contact Veyada."

We went to the hub, holding hands while we walked down the hallway. I'd never held hands in this way anywhere other than when we visited New Zealand.

It was dark in the hub and Devlin was nowhere to be seen. But I knew how to use it.

Veyada, however, did not reply either. I thought that he might be at the hospital with Mereeni.

Thayu scoffed when I told her that. "You really don't know much about Coldi customs regarding birth and children."

"I don't, and I don't think that Xinanu was a good example."

"She was a disgrace. She said she organised everything, but she didn't, only so that she could blame Nicha for failing her."

In Barresh, I had heard it was common for Coldi women to hire a room in a birth clinic.

Coldi births didn't often require medical intervention and women with larger homes usually set up a hammock at home. I had also learned that it was a mark of respect for the woman that the father of the child assisted in some way, and that not doing so was a mark on his reputation.

"I don't know that Mereeni is that close to giving birth yet."

And I trusted a woman's word of experience.

"What about I offer him a comfortable place so that he doesn't have to hire a room?"

Thayu gave me a sharp look. "You keep insisting that you don't understand Coldi customs, but you understand well enough."

"I guess we learned from Xinanu."

Far too many things had gone wrong there. She had an exploitative personality, but we could have managed the situation much better. *I* should have managed it better, but I hadn't understood that it was partially my task, and also we'd been busy saving the galaxy.

I wrote a long message to Veyada, that he was welcome back and that his mother had agreed to leave. My feelings about the mother-son bond still tripped me up. I was trying so very hard to see it in a way that this was normal, and that the fact that Sheydu left didn't mean that she would break off contact with her son. On the other hand, I wasn't even sure that Veyada would want to hear about this. He'd know in his own way what had happened and deal with it in the way that only Veyada could: calm and rational.

But damn, I was rattled to the core.

I went to bed long after Thayu.

I was tired, but as soon as I lay down, my mind started churning.

It really wasn't a good idea to race off to Tamer in our current state. Even if he came back, there was no way I could expect Veyada to come. If we went, I'd have to take others to make up for Veyada's absence, because our association would be lopsided. If there were any Coldi people nearby—and there would be if Asha sent transport—then the risk was that they would fall in with us in the same way Veyada and Sheydu had.

And I'd heard Sheydu rummaging in her room which suggested that she was packing her things. I did not want any more upheavals.

I wanted peace and quiet to return. I wanted to feel strong and healthy again.

———

It was mid-morning the next day when I sat working in the living room.

Ayshada and Karana sat on the rug, playing a word game. All of a sudden, Ayshada sat up, all alertness, looking into the hall.

He called out, "'ada!" and ran into the hall.

I followed.

Veyada and Mereeni stood inside the door. Ayshada had ambushed Veyada by holding him around his knees, as far as he could reach. That signified how I felt about it, as well.

Veyada was back.

Mereeni stood behind him, looking rather quiet. With her well-advanced pregnancy, she was no longer wearing her exchange uniform, and this made me think of all the things she'd had to give up to be here. There might even be someone at the Exchange, like Amarru, who was not happy about this.

"You came," I said to Veyada. It was a bit awkward.

"I got your message." He looked down, as I knew was utterly appropriate at this moment. "Thank you. We'll be happy to accept."

It also felt utterly appropriate to touch him lightly on the shoulder, and reassert our relationship. That symbol of dominance and subservience had turned into a gesture of comfort, of knowing where we stood, and that we could count on each other.

It felt right, if disturbing. I had always hated any of my team acting subservient. Was I beginning to understand the function?

Thayu came in from the other side of the hall.

She and Mereeni looked at each other.

I watched, ready to spring, not that I knew what I'd do if a fight erupted.

It was my guess that Mereeni had been told at Hedron that to perform a subservient greeting was out of the question. Thayu probably wasn't sure whether to expect it. Or demand it, since Mereeni was going to take Sheydu's place.

I held my breath.

Then Mereeni bent her head.

Phew.

Thayu gently touched her shoulder and then put her hand on Mereeni's rounded stomach.

Mereeni touched Thayu's hand. A strand of her curly hair had escaped from her ponytail and hung down her ear. She wore Veyada's earring with the green stone of the Palayi clan. He wore one of hers, the amber of the Ezmi clan.

I felt ashamed. We should have been there for the ceremony. I would probably have been in the hospital, but someone from our household should have been there.

There was much to be repaired.

Right now, I loved Thayu so much it hurt. She was ready to do this experiment with me.

I spotted Sheydu walking through the far end of the corridor, slinking into the shadows. She carried a pack that was no bigger than the one she took on trips. In all that time she had lived with me, she had never accumulated anything she could not carry. That, more than anything, probably told the story.

I wanted to go up to her for a hug, but she would probably snap at me. I had to let it be, because out of all of my team, she was the only one who could not be controlled.

Then I thought that it might even have been the intention of Natanu, who had been at the head of Ezhya's guard association, to get rid of the pair for that reason. So yes, coming to me had been a demotion for Veyada, but it had nothing to do with him.

Letting Sheydu go was the right decision, even if it was a painful one.

I hoped she would be all right. I hoped Veyada would be fine with it. I wished—no, I should stop obsessing over this. It was done. We should move on.

There was much to be done.

Veyada rearranged his room, and I told Mereeni to order the things she needed to turn the spare bathroom into a birth room. Thayu took special interest in this. None of this had been done for Xinanu. My household's relationship with her had been poisoned from the beginning, and it wasn't just her fault. That was one of the first tasks I should do once I was officially in the Domiri clan: to apologise officially to the head of Xinanu's Azimi clan.

Veyada told me that he wouldn't go with us to Tamer if Asha's transport turned up soon and I told him that I didn't want him to come even if Asha let us wait long enough for the child to have been born. "You should be with her. This is a time in your life you will never be able to repeat."

He told me to take Ynggi instead.

"Ynggi? But he'll have to wear clothes and shoes."

"He has many qualities that the team will appreciate, even if they're very different from mine."

True. Also, we might have a greater use for Ynggi's skills than for a lawyer.

———

There were a lot of preparations to be made, even if Tamer was not an officially inhabited world and we didn't need permits. We did need a lot of cold weather gear.

We also needed weapons that could deal with the cold. We would need those weapons, even if only because Deyu found that some sources classified the native fauna as hostile.

I also needed to decide who to take. When I asked Ynggi if he would like to come, he asked me if there was fish on Tamer.

Was there? I had no idea.

"There might be," Deyu said. "We know that there are large animals, and I can't see what they could possibly eat except smaller animals. Some might live in water."

We'd had endless discussions about what exactly constituted a "fish". In Isla, a fish was a creature with gills and a certain body structure. In keihu, a fish was a particular type of vertebrate that could not live on land. By their definition, a marsh eel was not a fish. But according to Pengali, anything that lived in water was a fish.

"Beisili are a fish," Ynggi said.

I would classify them as a reptile.

"Well, if you use that definition, there will be fish," Deyu said. "There will be creatures that live in water."

"Then I will come. I will pack my things." He rose and walked to the door before turning around and pointing at me with his tail. "Luggage."

Yes. Indeed. I needed to get Eirani to fashion him suitable clothes for a very cold climate.

After he had left, I looked at Deyu. "If the large creatures eat the smaller creatures, what do the smaller creatures eat?"

Deyu shrugged. "The large creatures, after they've died? Something that grows in places where we can't see it? They might eat stones like the tiyuk in Miran. Or they eat each other?"

"Sounds riveting," Thayu said from the door.

I met her eyes. Yes, we both remembered our excursion to the Thousand Islands to find Robert Davidson and our run-ins with beisili. That trip was going to seem like a holiday compared to this one.

———

Again, the pile of things in the hall grew, and Eirani was very unhappy that I was leaving again. She had envisaged feeding me every hour of the day.

"I don't understand why you're leaving again, Muri. You are not even fully recovered."

"I feel much stronger now, but thank you, Eirani. I'll be fine."

"But I don't even know where you're going, and it's hard to get everything you want. Those snow blankets you asked me to get are not available anywhere in town."

We ended up buying a whole pile of second-hand cold weather gear from a Mirani shop in town.

Evi and Telaris brought out their winter gear.

Deyu got out the winter jacket that she bought in Miran. Reida brought a whole box of electronic gear.

I asked Eirani to get a tailor in town to adapt a suit for Ynggi because he was too small and if adult snow gear was hard to get in Barresh, it was nothing compared to suits in children's sizes that were not in garish colours.

Thayu and I spent much of the two days that it took us to prepare walking and exercising, so that I could gain as much strength as possible. I felt a lot better physically, although mentally I was still confused by strange behaviours and scents. One day I ended up in a wrestling match with Reida and was astonished that he had to put in a real effort to defeat me.

My hair grew a tiny bit longer every day. It made a gold fuzz over my head.

I continued to have problems with my fine motor skills until Veyada, at the shooting range, made an odd suggestion.

"Why don't you try using the weapon in your other hand?"

"My *right* hand? That makes no sense."

I had been left-handed since birth. All Coldi were left-handed. That was one thing I had not expected to change now I was becoming more Coldi.

But he was right, the weapon felt more secure in my right hand. After a few misses, I was able to hit the target, too.

What about other things? Eating? That was easier, too. Writing? I tried, and that felt too weird.

I spotted Thayu and Veyada exchange a worried look when Veyada told her about our adventure at the shooting range.

"There *are* right-handed Coldi," Veyada said.

"Do you know any except the one we both know?"

Veyada didn't.

And the one we knew? Ezhya, of course. Damn it, what was happening to me?

———

Deyu and I talked a lot about Puck and why he would have disobeyed his fellows. I was wondering if it had anything to do with the fact that he gave me his blood. Sadly, we couldn't ask him anymore, and I doubted he would have been able to answer anyway.

On the evening of the third day, I received a cryptic message from Asha that a ship was ready. An order like this from Asha usually meant that he wanted us to jump straight away, so we collected all the gear in the hall onto a trolley.

Veyada and Mereeni watched us from the hall, with the members of the domestic staff who were staying here.

Ayshada had protested a bit when he realised that Nicha was leaving, but now he was sitting on Veyada's arm, and they looked like such a happy little family. Father, mother and young child awaiting the arrival of another sibling.

Veyada's absence left Thayu in a strange situation of not having anyone under her, while Nicha had Reida and Deyu, but it should not be too big a problem. It was not the first time that we didn't take the entire team. Nicha had taken quite a few breaks when Ayshada was born.

So we left the apartment, Thayu and I, Nicha, Evi and Telaris, Ynggi, and Deyu and Reida. It was a mixed company with many different talents.

The ship Asha had sent was the typical unmarked type that the Asto military liked to use. It stood in the quiet side of the airport, furthest from the fence, between the tarmac and the path where we came up from the station. It came with a pilot and two crew, both of whom wore dark clothing typical of the Asto army. They were quiet and efficient, and didn't ask us any questions but simply loaded our gear on board.

I had no idea how many of us they expected, but they didn't protest at the size of the party. The cabin was big enough for all of us, anyway. There were five rows of seats, and a door in the back where I assumed a second room to be.

The craft was a normal Asto-made model not suited for cold weather, but we wouldn't be using this craft to go to Tamer anyway. It was a shuttle, and we'd be going somewhere in orbit.

Contrary to all the military craft I had flown on, the shuttle had a few windows, and Ynggi insisted on sitting next to one. He carried his fur coat over his arm. He'd grown very attached to it and resisted any suggestions that he might put it with our other luggage. It would be cold, he had heard, and he was going to be prepared.

Reida and Deyu sat on the other side of the aisle from him, Nicha sat behind us, Evi and Telaris were still at the door to the pilot's compartment, and Thayu and I sat in the first row.

It was a bit strange travelling without Sheydu and her array of explosives.

I had asked Veyada if he had heard from his mother, and he had said that she was in town and had rented a warehouse. That was an interesting development.

"Do you know what she's doing?" I asked him.

"She hasn't told me, but if I had to guess, it would be that she wanted to set up a security training business. She always complains that procedures here are so bad."

That made sense, and it made me feel a little bit better. Sheydu planned to go into teaching. Yet, was that a good thing for her to do? Sheydu had as much patience as a ringgit in mating season. She'd have no patience for dumb students.

But the decision had been made. It was out of my hands.

When we had all taken our positions and were strapped in, the craft left. The flight crew didn't tell us where we were going, but I presumed that they would take us to some kind of military installation and from there to the military sling.

I was also reminded that I didn't like space travel very much, at least not the kind that involved weightlessness and being cooped up in a tin can. At least it wasn't as hot as I remembered it being inside these military ships from previous trips.

Through the small window, I could see Barresh rapidly vanishing, as more of the rugged coastline, the offshore islands and the ocean came into view. Then the endless forests and the mountains and the ice caps of the main continent.

Reida and Deyu were quiet. Reida kept looking at the crewmember who stayed in the cabin with us as if he expected the woman to pounce on him any moment.

I had no idea what people in the Outer Circle thought of the military. Signing up was not an option for anything further down than Fifth Circle, so the military was an elite force that was far removed from the lives that Deyu and Reida had led in the Eighth and Outer Circles.

They could not join, they knew no one who was in the military, and the military ignored them.

For a long time, I had never understood how Coldi people knew with such certainty what position another person held, but it was becoming obvious to me. It was in the way they dressed, in the way they interacted when meeting each other. Reida and Deyu kept quiet when faced with military, because there were no lines of loyalty or any connection between them.

The craft rose and rose. There was nothing except our seat belts to keep us from floating around the cabin.

I'd had the foresight to take some medication, but my stomach started feeling queasy anyway.

I looked at Thayu, who didn't suffer any of my discomfort. "Do you know how far we're going?" Just in case lunch was going to make a reappearance, I wanted to be prepared.

Thayu said. "They'll be waiting outside the limit of the range of the Exchange node."

Yes, this would be true. Asto military did not want to be seen by sources open to the public.

I tried to see, over the pilots' shoulders, if there was some kind of point of light ahead, but whenever I caught a glimpse of the screen in front of the pilots, it displayed only blackness.

Before too long, the craft turned, and in the dizzying view through the window the arc of the planet slid past, the beautiful blue marble floating in the darkness of space.

The pilots now seemed busier than before, so I assumed that we were almost there. Wherever "there" might be.

After a short while, a rectangle of light came into view on the pilots' viewscreen. It grew in size, and features that surrounded it materialised out of the darkness. Grey metal walls showing the degradation from long-term exposure to space. A hatch and some sensors, an antenna and some tubes attached to the outer hull. This was one big ship.

We entered the docking space not too much later.

The pilot's screen showed the inside of the hall which contained a lot of other craft, each slotted into a bay along the walls. Mechanical arms reached out, grabbed hold of the craft and hoisted it up into an empty bay against the wall. I had seen this type of arrangement when I went to the big space station that was in orbit around Asto.

The door opened and the familiar, metallic hot air wafted in.

We had returned to some form of gravity. Were we in a ship or a space station? I didn't know there were any stations in orbit around Ceren.

A walkway extended from the gallery along the side of the hall to the ship. The female crewmember was the first to leave the cabin. She crouched at the entrance of the craft to fasten the walkway.

We gathered all our things, but one of the pilots said that people would be on board to collect our possessions.

I was the first of our team to leave the craft. Thayu and Nicha walked behind me, as was customary and proper for an association to venture into an unknown environment: the leader first, then the second, then the people underneath.

The walkway led to the gallery, into a frenzy of activity from people in overalls clambering up and down the sides of the hall. The air was filled with mechanical noise and the hot smell of ozone produced by the tools. There was some gravity, but it wasn't a lot. I was reminded of some of the places in Midway Space Station where, because of the locality in the station, gravity was lower than Earth standard. We used to go to play there as children, and then the adults would find us and we'd get into all sorts of trouble.

A couple of people arrived to assist in unloading our luggage from the craft.

Ahead on the gallery, a sliding door opened, and someone stepped out. Someone I had seen many times before, and I had expected to see at some point, but not just yet.

Asha Domiri. In his full pink uniform.

I got a curt nod, and he said, "Come with me."

Coldi tended to be abrupt and rude, but he took this to an entirely new level.

He didn't even pretend to be interested in my new appearance. No comment about my hair or questions about how I felt. Not a word of greeting to his children.

I glanced at Thayu, and she nodded. "Go. I'll look after what needs to be done."

So I followed Asha through the doorway. It was a lift cubicle.

While we were standing there, and the lift was taking us down, his dark eyes studied me.

I was never clear what to say to him. Anything personal you said fell into a hole, but then you would find out later that it hadn't, because after a long time of deliberation, he would come out with a profoundly personal remark. Like asking me to join his clan. That had surprised me, back then. I'd been convinced that he thought I was dirt.

Heck, it still surprised me.

"Did you get the coordinates?" he asked.

For a moment, I wondered what coordinates he was talking about, then I realised that he must be talking about the coordinates on Tamer, where the communication from Benton Leck had come from.

"I just got them from the Exchange. They're available to all," I said.

"We don't have access to that channel here," he said. "We can only listen into conversations. And we are very careful about not interrupting any of the regular communication. It is better to do it this way —not that we can't get the information, but we don't want to go places we shouldn't be when there is no need."

Different rules to different people and all.

So I took out my reader, and I gave him the coordinates.

He studied the screen for a while.

"I can see why there is such a tremendous advantage for people to hide on this terrible world," he said. "It is shrouded in a strong magnetic field, and the weather is terrible, with very high cloud cover over most of the world for most of the time. We don't really have a clear view of the world from our position, and we can't come as close as we want to. There are virtually no recognisable features on the world. It is full of mountains and frozen lakes and glaciers. It would not be hard to detect spots of warmth that indicate activity of people, if it wasn't for the fact that there are also volcanic outlets, and it is very hard to see which is which in scans. The magnetic field makes any form of communication very difficult, and any off-world transmissions need to be tightly focused. In short, it is very hard to listen in on what these people do if you have no idea whereabouts on the planet they are."

All of which, I guessed, was a roundabout way of saying we had no clue what was happening and where people were.

He put up my coordinates and overlaid them on a projection of the planet that he produced from his reader.

It looked like the ice world of Tamer was floating over his hand. He twisted it around as you would a globe by touching it with his finger and moving it. There was a small yellow dot on the surface.

"I guess this is where my coordinates are?"

"That would be correct."

He said nothing for a while and studied the little globe of light.

The lift rumbled and shook, and seemed to change direction yet again.

Then it slowed.

The doors opened.

The ice ball projection vanished.

We were in a large hall, where a lot of people were sitting at workstations facing screens. There were also screens all around the walls of the room, displaying graphs and lines and trajectories.

In the middle of the room, a circle of seats surrounded a circular bench.

I was surprised that he would take me to the command centre, but that was what it looked like.

He put his reader down on the circular bench, and invited me to sit.

A couple of other people came to join us. I suspected these were technical crew, and secretaries, because none of them looked at me or Asha.

They all wore crisp uniforms, all of them the same shade of desert pink, but most of the jackets were much emptier than Asha's.

He touched the screen on his reader, and the same projection of the planet came up again into the air in the middle of the circular bench. That was why it was designed like this. It was not a command centre as much as a seminar room.

"We have a location," Asha said, sounding important.

I wondered if this was really news or if he was putting on the show for my benefit.

He turned to me. His dark eyes met mine. He had never shown any sign of wanting me to show subservience to him.

"As far as we have been able to track, there is only one main location where there is some kind of base or settlement on the surface, it is the only place where craft visit. Most of the time there is too much cloud cover, and we cannot get close enough to get a clear picture of the world."

He moved his finger as if to turn the projection around, and the globe in the middle rotated, so that the little yellow dot was facing me. It was in a location slightly north of the equator, in a jagged mountain range.

"We're going to send you there."

I nodded. I had expected that.

"But there is something you need to know."

He gave me an intense look. Here was the trouble.

He didn't speak immediately, but zoomed out the projection. With a touch of his finger, the image changed. The planet—now much smaller in the projection—became a ball surrounded by filaments of green. I guessed this was a depiction of the electromagnetic field around the planet.

"Tamer is a world with an iron core and molten interior. It has a strong magnetic field."

"Yes." I was familiar with that.

"Now look here." He pointed at a spot where the filaments of whatever it was that the green threads represented bent aside. He hit the screen on his reader and the image started moving. The little bubble of deflected threads of green moved around the planet. "See this?"

"What is it?"

"We can't tell, but it's big enough that we have a suspicion."

"It's very big. Does Tamer have moons?"

"It does. But they're insubstantial lumps of rock and ice."

True. Something like this would be caused by . . . an artificial object. A chill went over me. "That's their main network node, isn't it?"

"We think so, yes."

All right, so the expedition had just jumped a whole level of seriousness.

"Does that mean they'll be able to detect who comes close to the world?"

"We're not sure that it does. If it functions like a regular Exchange node, then an unmarked unidentified craft could come quite close."

"Not that close."

"Close enough to fire a weapon."

Oh no, oh no, oh no. "I don't think that would be wise. At least not until the end of our visit."

"Granted, but I've instructed my crew that I want it taken out anyway."

"Before we go down to the world?"

"After."

"But there may not be time."

"They will make time. Those are my instructions." And that was a final statement. We were here by the grace of the Asto military. They had agreed to take us, but they would also decide which other steps would be taken.

Well, wasn't that great. There went my hope to get in and out without being noticed.

Asha took me back to the others.

They had waited in a room at the gallery, close to where the craft was docked.

The room itself was comfortable, with soft couches and a food dispenser, but the door was locked. When I came in, Ynggi stood near the door, reading some instruction on the wall. Deyu and Reida leaned against the wall, both sipping from a cup, and Evi and Telaris had been sitting on the couch, but jumped up as soon as the door opened, and an expression of relief came to their faces when they saw me.

Only Thayu and Nicha looked at ease, with Nicha giving his father a small nod.

Deyu held out a cup to me. "Manazhu?"

I would never say no to that. I took the cup from her, sipping from the bitter dark green liquid.

Asha gestured for me and Thayu to come to the gallery. We stood in a small group just outside the door to the room while, all around us, the activity of maintenance and refuelling crews in the arrival hall continued.

"A name," he said in his usual abrupt fashion. "I need a name so I can plan the ceremony. I also suggest that you reserve names for the child."

What? Were we supposed to pick out names for a child that hadn't even been conceived?

"It's a competitive business. Don't wait, or the good names will be gone."

"I'm open for suggestions." Other than if a name resembled that of a successful person, I was baffled as to what constituted a good name.

"Aveya."

"For me?"

"Yes. It's good and strong, and different enough that it doesn't sound like anyone else important. Because *you* are not like any of them."

Well, that was . . . "Thank you. I'll definitely consider it."

"Not consider it. Aveya. I've always wanted to use that name for a son. Except I got a daughter, and got to use another favourite name on her. It's served her well. Aveya, because you're worthy of that name."

I glanced at Thayu. She shrugged. I hadn't liked the suggestions she had picked out, nor Ezhya's suggestion. I guess I could live with Aveya.

"All right."

Well, that was that problem settled.

"Good. Then I will arrange the ceremony. Pick a name for the child and let me know next time I speak to you. Now let me arrange your transfer."

He turned around and was gone.

Thayu and I looked at each other.

"Aveya," she said.

"I have to admit, his way of solving problems is growing on me."

"Yes," she said. "You should do this more often. Make a decision. Don't ask for opinions, tell all of us what we're going to do."

Well, yes, that was easier said than done.

12

HAYU AND I went back into the room with the others.

In the absence of further information we could only wait. I gathered that Asha didn't expect to let us wait very long, or he would have provided us with beds.

A soldier did turn up, however, with a trolley of food. When he took the lid off the tray and revealed the closely packed square containers covered with lids, I remembered these meals from the two weeks I'd spent aboard a military ship on the way to Asto. Even the smell was the same. Apparently rations hadn't gotten any more interesting in the intervening time.

I thanked the man, and he left the room.

Ynggi lifted the corner of the lid on one of the containers. He sniffed the steam that came out and recoiled.

"I think you'll need to be careful which ones you eat," I said. "The green-coded food will be labelled."

That was true, and he found some containers with grey lids. He wanted to know if any of them contained fish.

I laughed. "Coldi don't eat meat, certainly not purists like the military."

Did they even have fish on Asto, he wanted to know, and Deyu said that they did, but that they were poisonous because the ocean was poisonous. And while she said this, she pulled up the lid to one of the red-coded containers. The smell that came from the mushrooms within was heavenly.

I put down the container with the bland puree I had been about to eat and went back to the remaining containers on the trolley.

"What are you doing?" Thayu asked.

"I have to have some of what Deyu has."

"It's red-coded."

"I know. I have to have some."

"But it will—"

"It's not a matter for debate. I have to have some." That smell was driving me insane.

Deyu held the container out to me. I picked a mushroom out of the sauce.

I remembered trying a tiny bit of red-coded food when I still lived in Athens, before I met Nicha. I remembered how it burned. I didn't care.

I put the mushroom in my mouth. The taste exploded on my tongue and spread through my mouth. The warmth of it seeped through my body.

I became aware that everyone was looking at me, faces concerned.

"I'm fine." I held my hands up. "Lilona suggested that I might want to eat some red-coded food."

In fact, my reaction suggested that I *needed* it. I went in search of a container with mushrooms and ate half of it before deciding that, for the time being, I'd probably eaten enough poison. It would have killed me a few months ago.

Afterwards, I lazed on the couch, watching Reida and Deyu tap into the room's control panel to retrieve information about the ship. That was Sheydu's training at work right there.

Reida informed me that this was not a space station, but a very large ship with a rotating residential section. The ship was idle at the moment and had only been fired up for two short bursts of activity that fell under "engine maintenance" in the past year. I knew the signs: this was a permanent spy base watching Ceren. The fact that Asha allowed us in here probably meant that he didn't mind if we found out, or even wanted us to know.

A bit later, another crewmember came to deliver a stack of grey jumpsuits. She ignored Reida and Deyu with their electronics by the door, still trying to hack into the ship's systems, and dumped the stack of fabric onto the table in the middle of the room.

"You need to put these on," she said.

She glanced at Reida and Deyu, but still ignored their activity, even if she had to walk around them leaving the room. Apparently this information-gathering by our team was perfectly fine.

Ynggi took a suit off the stack. The legs dragged on the floor even when he held it up with his arms stretched.

"I think I'll take that one," Evi said, reaching over Ynggi's shoulder.

The next suit was smaller, so Thayu took that.

We debated whether we needed to take off our regular clothes, but decided against it. After all, Tamer was going to be cold.

While I pulled on the suit, which was made from thick, rigid fabric, I realised that even the Coldi, who were a relatively uniform group of people—having been created artificially from thirty-six couples—would have to deal with increasing variability. There were studies that showed that the Coldi genetic pool was getting ever wider. The variation was not limited to those with the *sheya* instinct and those without. The Hedron Coldi were distinctly different, and so were the Zhori who lived in central and southern Africa. There were women as tall and broad as Deyu, and men agile and slender like Reida, and institutions like the armed forces would need to cater to different shapes and abilities.

Variety. That lay at the basis of Coldi fears of change.

Ynggi had gotten to the bottom of the pile, and the only suits left were still much too big for him, so he had to roll up his sleeves and trouser legs. The suit had no provision for his tail either, so he had folded it along his body, and the tip, with the little white tuft at the end, stuck out of the suit's neck ring. It moved constantly, as if a rat lived in the suit.

Evi and Telaris complained that the suits were hot, but fortunately someone else turned up soon after to take us to the next step of the process.

In order to use the sling, we would need to be a considerable distance from any kind of world. The sling produced a lot of radiation and light. It was supposed to be a secret installation, and allowing the output to be seen from the surface of the planet was not the way that the Asto forces liked to operate.

In short: we needed to travel to the sling first.

This we did in a special fast shuttle that was going to cover, in two days, a distance that would normally take weeks. The craft was more engine than cabin and had space for just ten people. Those people were meant to travel in pressurised couches—hence the suits. The couches contained inflatable cushions that would put pressure against our bodies to compensate for very high levels of acceleration.

I asked about the craft's pilots, and was told there weren't any.

Well, that wasn't particularly encouraging.

But no one else appeared to have a problem with it, so I pulled my head in and went along with the procedure.

We had to lie on the couches. An assistant stuck a number of sensors on our skin. An infusor band went around my wrist. Then the assistant hit a button and the suit inflated. It was so tight in the capsule that I couldn't even move my head.

Thayu was in the couch next to me, but I couldn't see her.

We must be about to leave, because a hum had started up and had risen into an annoying whine typical of idling engines.

Then the assistant slotted capsules of medicines into the infusor. One to slow my metabolism, one to keep my temperature low, one to make me sleepy.

A cold feeling spread from my arm with that last one. I didn't even see him leave the room.

Two days was not a very long time when you slept through it.

The first thing I noticed was that people were talking around me. A crewmember came to free me from the restrictive confines of the couch.

The door to the craft was already open, and Evi and Telaris were helping the crew move our luggage out.

Out was a long and narrow docking space, occupied only by one other ship: a strangely-shaped square thing that was unlike any of the regular Asto-built craft.

The door stood open, and light spilled over the ramp. People moved inside.

Thayu laughed. "It's like a flying field station."

According to Nicha, installations like this stood all around Beratha where Thayu had grown up, especially where a lot of exercises took place.

Once we were inside, the field station part became evident. We came into a comfortable-looking living area, where a glass door led to the control cabin. There were two pilots and a crewmember. Because there were three of them, they were obviously a complete single layer association with one person at the top and two zhayma's underneath the leader. I found myself wanting to know who the leader was, because I'd have to address this person. This was the military where this sort of thing was done properly.

They were busy, and the assistant who had come into the craft with us told me that we'd be introduced to the crew later.

"Will these people go to Tamer with us?" I asked.

"Yes, they will, but they will take care of the craft. That is their responsibility. As you may appreciate, this type of craft is not that easy to fly, but very comfortable to use as a field base."

Yes to both statements. I couldn't imagine that a square thing like this flew well, but it did have a lot of space inside.

"The crew's responsibility is the craft. There is no need for you to worry about any of the operations. You tell them what your plans are, and they will operate within that understanding."

Clearly an independent association, and one that had been ordered by Asha to take out the alternate Exchange node at Tamer.

From the living area, a hallway ran the length of the craft. We passed two doors to what looked like bedrooms with hammocks.

We were directed that way into a room that held another set of travel couches. I remembered these, because I had also used them the previous time I had used the sling.

The assistant told us that we had a limited time window in which we could depart. It needed to be planned so that the anomaly was on the other side of the planet from where we arrived.

So we had to rush and quickly strap into our seats. I was also given a feeder, and I suspected that meant that there were more facts I needed to know.

Last time I had made this journey just with Thayu. This time, the whole team was going.

The seats were like easy lounge chairs, with seatbelts and the familiar heavy gel-filled blanket. When the assistant arranged the blanket over me, the sticky heaviness of it brought back memories. This blanket was not exactly the same as the last time, which also made it clear that they had been working very hard on this technology.

Reida and Deyu were slightly alarmed by the proceedings. Ynggi seem to be enjoying himself. I had not noticed that he had any trouble with travel sickness and his Pengali curiosity knew no bounds.

After we were all strapped in, the crew left the cabin and shut the door, and the lights turned off. Only a couple of pinpricks of light remained, and the air inside was stifling, although I could hear it rushing from a vent.

The floor of the craft vibrated. I sensed motion, although I couldn't say in which direction. Thuds and thumps went through the hull of the ship, and I assumed that meant we were leaving the docking hall.

After a little while, a projection spun into the air in the middle of the cabin.

It showed Asha, as if he were standing in the middle of the cabin. Next to me, Ynggi gasped.

"There are a few more things that you should know before you arrive at your destination," he said.

I had not expected any different. Was there ever a time when he had told me the full story in our first encounter?

"It is true that there has been a heightened level of activity in the area where your coordinates are. We have also been able to track some of this activity back to its origins. There is a surprising range of localities where communication or traffic is coming from."

"Communication or traffic?"

"It's hard to tell from this distance."

Yet he said he had ships close enough to hit the node? Sometimes I really didn't want to know the extent of Asto-built weaponry.

"Is there any indication what they're communicating about?" I felt that I was coming to yet another one of these points where something major would be revealed that changed my understanding.

"Nothing terribly obvious. The communication seems to revolve around a decision which will be made or needs to be made or, as some are saying, is forced to be made."

"About what?"

"About a program. It's not easy to follow."

"Are they communicating in Mirani?" It had enough noun and verb forms to baffle everyone except those immediately familiar with both the language and the subject matter.

"No. Much of the communication is in the language of your home world."

My heart jumped. "Mine?"

"Yes, that is possible, isn't it?"

I blew out. Possible, certainly, but . . . "Who would be there from Earth?"

But I already knew the answer to that. They would be people from the Pretoria Cartel or others related to those people. Perhaps ties with the Zhori mafia, or other elements that had been involved with the—damn, the Tamerians that we had found were being made in South Africa. Not terribly successfully, but they were good enough at killing people and nobody cared if they died.

Were these people producing an entire army on Tamer? Was that why they needed Benton Leck to figure out how to best communicate with these Tamerians?

That was taking the threat up two extra levels.

I blew out another breath. "Do you know where the Tamerians come from?"

"There is one location on the planet. We're not clear on what happens there or of the occupancies of the craft that we can sometimes observe going in and out. It's easier to detect their communication."

True. "There is only one settlement on Tamer?"

"From what we can tell, it seems so. Or if there are more, they're closely related. We're sending you there to investigate. Your cover is that you will try to find the missing academic. Your team has already found the data we have on this locality."

Did they? Oh, he was talking about Reida and Deyu's probing.

"The ship's crew have our latest data on the terrain and the ship has survival kits, plenty of fuel and emergency beacons. If you fire them, someone will come. There will be a lot of trouble, but someone *will* come. I guarantee that. I would strongly prefer if you did not do this too lightly."

With that, he signed off.

Well, damn, I'd wanted to ask him if he still planned to take out the local rogue Exchange node.

I was left looking into the darkness, wondering if any of the members of my team had heard his words.

"Thayu?" I tried reaching her through the feeder.

She had already figured what I wanted to ask. "No. None of us heard what he said. I trust it was illuminating."

"Yes, it was. I'll talk to you about it later."

By now the craft was burning a lot of speed. I was pressed sideways into my seat, and the gel blanket that lay over the top of me stopped me pushing into the side of the chair.

Another projection spun into the air. This one informed us of our speed, of the time until transfer, and other details which I didn't get. Reida understood, and so did Nicha. They spoke for a bit about technical details, but soon the acceleration of the craft became too much for talking to be comfortable.

Ynggi on my other side appeared to be asleep, or maybe he had already passed out.

A huge white flash ripped me of all my vision. It took quite a while for my eyes to discern the inside of the cabin again. Everything was separated into rainbow colours that slowly merged until they overlapped again.

The craft was still moving, but now it was losing speed and I was pressed into the other side of the chair. After a while, the light in the cabin came on again. A sign in the middle of the projection said that it was all right for us to move about.

I pushed the gel-filled blanket off me. The rush of cold air on my sweaty skin made me shiver.

Everyone was getting out of their seats. Except there wasn't much "getting up" because we were still in zero gravity.

Ynggi discovered this too late, and he floated through the cabin, hitting the wall on the other side.

Evi and Telaris laughed.

"I hope there will be something to eat soon," Reida said.

Yes, I was a bit hungry too.

Nicha floated to the door and opened the door to the cabin. A bright glow of light came in from outside.

"Wait, let me go first."

We still hadn't formally met the crew.

I pulled myself along the handgrips through a corridor that led to the living area. In the bedrooms, the hammocks drifted about aimlessly.

The light in the living room was still low. The glow from the instruments and the pilots' screens filtered through the glass partition.

All three crewmembers were in this area: two men, one woman. They wore uniforms, all of them with the stars on the sleeve that meant they were flight personnel. They hadn't yet noticed me, but as I came in, one of the men turned around.

He met my eyes. And stiffened.

Uh-oh.

The *sheya* reaction. Meeting someone from an association who was in no way related to yours. This was the pathological need to establish who was superior before he knew how to relate to me.

The man came to the door.

"Keep back," I said to Nicha behind me.

"No, are you crazy?" Thayu said.

Then Nicha added in a louder voice, "He is not familiar with the instinct."

But Nicha's position in my association was as my second, and communication between unfamiliar associations went only through the association leaders. That was me, and that was this man. If he wanted to sort this out, I could not avoid it.

If he wanted a fight—he did.

He opened the glass door, pushed off and shot into the low light of the living area.

In passing, he lunged for my arm, but I pulled myself towards one of the seats. He turned around, but I had done this zero-g wrestling before, and managed to stop him by clamping my legs around his waist. We both slammed into the wall. My shoulder collided with a handgrip, which I then used to hold myself while twisting my body sideways so I pinned him to the wall.

Threat deflected.

He relaxed and looked down, letting his hands sink past his sides, palms back.

My heart still hammering, I touched his shoulder, noting his earrings. Yellow. Lingui. "What is your name?"

"Yana. My seconds are Taleyu and Rixya."

They also performed the subservient greeting. Both were Lingui as well. Many in the Lingui clan were pilots and couriers. Maybe that was why I had no connections with them.

I turned to my team and introduced them.

Then Yana spoke about the ship and the facilities. Yes, there was food on board and he showed Reida the cupboards where he could find the packets, how to add water and cook it.

The two pilots had gone back to their work. I should ask him when and how he planned to destroy the Exchange node. I didn't expect an answer, but the replies would be telling, anyway.

"You can come into the control room," Yana said to me. "Just stay at the back, so we can still do our work."

He indicated a bench to the left hand side of the cabin.

I anchored myself on the zero-g seat. The air inside the cabin was uncomfortably warm, even more so than in the rest of the craft.

The two pilots were busy looking at instruments and studying screens. The few screens in front of them looked like windows, but I knew they were not. Likely, this control centre was not even at the very front of the craft.

After I had been sitting there for a while, the male pilot Rixya turned to me.

He gestured. "Have a look."

I detached myself from the seat, and floated towards the control panel. I caught myself at the back of the pilot seat, where both of them were strapped in.

On one of the screens that faced the pilots, I could see what I presumed was a real-time visible light projection from the front of the craft.

It showed a stark black background with a few pinpricks of light. In the middle hung the arc of a light blue planet, with a thick haze of atmosphere around it.

"Is that Tamer?" I asked.

"It is."

The side of the planet I could see was almost entirely covered in a giant swirling mass of cloud. I searched the area around the planet.

"Where is this anomaly at the moment?"

He pulled out another screen, one with the familiar green lines. Well, except there was a lot more detail to be seen this close up. The object, whatever it was, left a trail all around the planet, which was strongest where it had just passed and weakest just before it was about to orbit past again. The focus of the green lines was almost on the other side of the planet.

"What's that bright light over there?" I pointed.

"Tamer has a couple of moons. They're insignificant, made out of ice, and are not big enough to worry about."

From our position, the planet was almost backlit by the sun, a pale arc of blue where sunlight was diffused by the atmosphere. The planet itself was shrouded in darkness and did not show any of its already sparse features.

"Where is the locality we are going to?"

He was about to answer, when Taleyu, his co-pilot suddenly stiffened. "Look at this."

Rixya turned around. "What's up?"

"We got a warning on the proximity."

"Give me the scan." Every bit of conversational tone was gone from his voice.

The pretty picture of the planet disappeared to make way for a much more utilitarian picture of a beam tracking through space. It showed up little blips of colour, and Taleyu pointed to one of them.

"What is it?" Rixya asked.

"I don't know. It's triggering the alarm."

Something on the control panel started to make little beeping noises.

Taleyu said, "Shut it off."

The beeping stopped, but then it started again.

"Another one?" Yana's voice sounded concerned.

He pulled out a panel from the wall. "Turn around a bit so I can get a fix on them."

I was astonished. "You're going to shoot?"

Taleyu turned around to me. "Don't worry about it. There is a lot of ice in this area. We want to avoid a collision, so we'll get rid of it."

But another alarm started blaring. This one definitely got a lot of attention.

Rixya immediately turned to another screen, and pressed a button.

"I've lost contact with the base," Taleyu said.

"Fire the engine."

Taleyu worked at the panel for a bit. Then she said, "It's not responding."

Rixya said, "I'll start up the long-range engine, just to get us out of here."

No one said anything for a while.

Taleyu worked at the controls. I couldn't tell if Rixya had any success with the long-range engines, but I heard nothing. He didn't seem concerned, though.

Yana studied the screen while directing a beam through the panel in his hands.

And Yana said simply, "There."

One of the screens zoomed in. On it there was a star field and another one of those tiny moons. But in the middle of the screen was an area of darkness.

"What the hell is that?" Taleyu asked. "The anomaly is on the other side of the sun."

"It's massive," Yana said. He had let the panel slip from his hands. It floated through the cabin, tethered by the lead that attached it to the main controls.

We all stared at the screen. I was beginning to get a very suspicious feeling about this, because I had seen this before.

I said in a low voice, "I think . . ." My heart was thudding. "I think we have found the Aghyrian ship."

"That's impossible. They have no electronic signature," Taleyu said. "Previously, we could trace them across the galaxy."

"They were using their engine."

"Yes, but a ship this size would still emit a lot of traceable signatures." She sounded like she thought I couldn't possibly know anything about this subject.

Rixya said, "I agree. This is a piece of space junk."

"A very big piece," Yana said. "What would it be? Because if it was a base used by people here, there would definitely be a signature."

"You have not seen this ship before," I said. "They have technology you have never dreamed of."

"Every piece of equipment leaves a signature," Rixya said, his tone definite. "No shielding is that perfect."

"Then restart the engine and get us out of here."

Thayu gave me a sideways glance. I probably shouldn't have said that, because Coldi were direct but seldom sarcastic, especially these military types who were far too convinced that they were right.

But with each moment that our engine remained unresponsive, I was more certain that this was, in fact, the same ship I had visited before.

The shuttle made a slow turn, and the planet and the sun slid from view.

Everyone in the cabin was looking intently into the darkness on the visual viewscreen.

Taleyu said, "I can't restart the engine. We are being pulled in by them."

Yana ordered, "Prepare defence."

Whatever good that would do.

I spoke softly to Thayu. "Go back and warn the others in the team. Get weapons ready, in case we need to fight."

I got up from the bench and floated to the door to the living area, where my team had made short work of a selection of packaged food.

"What's happening?" Reida said, his eyes wide.

"It's not good," Nicha said.

"No." I pulled myself down into a seat. "We're going to pay a visit to our old friend Kando Luczon. They're pulling us in."

13

———

WE COULD DO NOTHING. The dark shape was pulling us in, taking up an ever increasing proportion of the viewscreen.

Ahead, the dark maw of the entrance became ever bigger.

No one in the cabin spoke, but they all stared at how the faint light from our craft lit a small patch on the huge dark structure, the matte black hull that was pitted and scarred and that bore hatches and protuberances the purpose of which I could only guess.

The shuttle drifted into the darkness of the giant docking hall. All engines had cut out a while ago. I'd told the crew that this happened the previous time we'd encountered this ship. I'd told them how big the hall was, but they were still gaping at the screen.

The pilots now had all the view screens on camera view. A small alarm beeped at the control panel.

"What's that?" Yana asked. He was nervous, clutching the controls to the long-range cannons in his hands. I presumed that his military training would mean nothing would go off accidentally, but wondered whether his threshold for firing was much lower than ours.

Damn, I didn't like coming here with these highly-strung military people.

"There is some kind of object to our right," Taleyu said.

I said, "They're landing platforms suspended in mid-air."

The last time we had been in this hall, we had been forced down onto one of those platforms, and then Captain Kando Luczon and his party had come to us. He had walked on an invisible walkway in mid-air.

Nobody spoke as the ship slowly drifted. While the engines were off and the operations of the craft reduced, we still had internal power. Rixya tried several different types of camera scans in different wavelengths. The infrared was "interesting" according to Thayu: a plain dark-grey screen, without any features. I wondered aloud what it meant.

"They're either well-shielded or the ship is dead," she said.

Rixya turned a switch.

It was as if a shockwave went through the cabin.

Ynggi clamped his hands over his ears. "It's so loud!"

I didn't hear anything, but I could *feel* it, in my stomach.

The screen facing the pilots had changed to a monochrome light-green and black, and it displayed outlines of the vast hall.

Thayu next to me made a small sound of surprise. "You actually have this sonar technology installed on the ship?"

"It's a new gadget for precision navigation. I agree it's very uncom-fortable."

"Do you have any control of the ship yet?" I asked the pilots.

"No."

The control panel displays on all the instruments went dead.

Still the craft was drifting down slowly. With the sonar scanner, we could now see the floating platforms that surrounded us. There were too many to count, at least fifty or sixty, maybe even a hundred. There was no sign of what held them up. Some of them even contained small aircraft, many of them capable of flying in atmosphere, judging by the design.

The floor of the hall was coming closer. It was mostly empty, except for box-like things spaced out in even intervals. Were they power stations? Toolboxes?

The shuttle drifted down and settled on the floor with a small bump.

The sonar went dead. The light in the cabin went off.

"Hmm," Taleyu said in the darkness. "I guess they didn't like the noise either."

"The outside air is safe," Rixya said.

Thayu made a light with a nifty little device that she had strapped to her jacket.

Deyu and Reida got up. This was easy, because the ship had gravity. Deyu put on her jacket. She strapped her arm bracket with the gun on the outside. A second gun went on her belt.

The light from Thayu's lamp showed Deyu's outline in stark relief. I remembered the shy adolescent she had come to us as. She had turned into a formidable fighter, trained by Sheydu. Because of her clan—Omi—Deyu automatically assumed that she was the lowest in the rankings. She didn't waste time with power games. She went and did the work.

She opened the door with one hand, while holding her gun in her other hand. The doors to the craft were locked and armed, and you couldn't open them with one hand, so Reida helped her. The panel beeped, the mechanism zoomed, and the door opened.

The air that wafted into the cabin was fresh and smelled slightly dusty.

Deyu leaned outside.

"Can you see anything?" I asked her.

This was when Kando Luczon had approached on my previous visit.

"Nope." Her voice echoed in the huge hall. "Whoa. Did you hear that? It's really echoey in here."

She pulled herself back inside. "It looks safe."

We all got up and collected weapons.

I called a brief team meeting. We would go in to explore, we would stay together, and we would make no effort to be quiet in case the ship's residents thought we were hostile. We would try to attract their attention without making so much noise that we couldn't hear their presence.

The crew still maintained that the ship was dead, and nothing I could say countered their opinion. We'd seen far too many pieces of equipment still in operation long after their makers had passed on. They wanted us to locate the device that, in the absence of crew, continued to attract ships that came too close.

Or at least that was their theory.

The shuttle had little power, and the ramp wouldn't operate, so the crew had to extend it manually.

They would stay with the aircraft while we went into the ship. I was glad of it, because they were far too keen, for my liking, to use weapons.

Thayu handed them little devices that would allow them to stay in contact with us, although how far into the ship that would continue to work was a question. I tucked mine into the space between my under-shirt and my skin just above the belt. The receiver had a little rubbery pad on the back, that became sticky when connected with the skin. It was similar to the feeders which we couldn't use here of course.

We left the shuttle one by one, jumping the last part from the ramp onto the floor of the hall. The floor was made from metal, and each person landed with a thump that echoed through the hall. If there was someone aboard this ship, that would definitely get their attention. A thick layer of dust covered the floor as far as I could see, a soft grey carpet that showed no sign of recent disturbance.

As when I had come here before, I experienced a sense of desola-tion. The ship might be very powerful, but there were no people here to operate it. Those people were in the big hall upstairs, asleep in pods.

When all of us were out of the shuttle, we tested our communica-tion devices, found that they worked, and then walked across the floor in the direction where some people had spotted an opening on the sonar scan. But it was now far too dark to see the sides of the hall.

Several of us carried lights, but in the vastness of the hall, they produced no more than mere pinpricks.

Ynggi insisted going first. He was the only one who could see well enough in low light.

I followed the little waving tip of his tail, listening to the utter silence around us. Our footsteps were muffled in the layer of dust.

After a while we came to the wall. I had feared that we would be faced with closed doors, but there was an opening into a low ceilinged corridor.

In the corridor it was even darker than in the hall. Now all of us used the lights on our readers to see where we were going. I followed Ynggi's tail, through the clouds of dust he disturbed. It was fine and light grey and lay in a soft carpet evenly distributed over the floor.

A door on the left hand side of the corridor stood open. Ynggi and Telaris stopped, directing the glow of their lights inside.

"Have a look?" Ynggi asked. His voice sounded muffled in here, damped through thick layers of dust.

"Why not?"

The door led into some sort of a equipment room, with unusual devices on benches all covered in layers of dust.

"I don't like this place," Deyu said. "It's dead. It's like we would find the ghosts of dead people here."

Coldi rarely spoke of supernatural beings except in the sense of death. They spoke of echoes of the dead.

Reida stood near the door, studying the inscriptions on the wall panels.

The Aghyrian language had two written versions. One of them was a traditional style of script with characters for syllables. The other, which was the official language, used hieroglyphs that were often little stylised pictures that together formed words.

This official version would be used for signs on walls and instructions, much like signs for public services and amenities on Earth. But the system was far, far more extensive. It was a written language in its own right, and the Aghyrians of the past were extremely fond of writing on walls. Even the old caves near the landing place of one of their ships in Barresh were full of these engravings, telling stories of how they arrived and how to grow crops in their new hostile land, and giving details of astronomy and the laws of their new community.

Of course one needed a proper linguist to understand what it meant.

A linguist. Maybe the ship *was* dead, and maybe people needed Benton to translate these signs. I didn't know that I would have chosen him to do it, since there were a lot of true-blood Aghyrians available who had a greater knowledge. They didn't use the official language anymore. In fact I understood that the Aghyrian language itself had been rescued from the brink of death, and that there were still arguments over how to pronounce certain letter combinations. When Daya Ezmi had started the revival of the Aghyrian community a hundred years ago, Aghyrian had been a dead language.

But maybe there were some reasons that whoever hired Benton Leck couldn't hire those Aghyrians. Maybe we would find Benton Leck here in the ship.

I wondered where the ship's crew had gone and why they weren't here to meet us.

We continued down the corridor.

Ynggi and Telaris went first, because their night vision was so much better. Evi was at the back to make sure that nothing approached us from behind.

After a while, Ynggi stopped. "Do you hear that?"

We listened. All I could hear was the beating of my own heart.

I was glad when Nicha said, "I can't hear anything unusual."

"Air is coming out of the holes in the ceiling."

Yes, now I noticed it too. Air circulation meant that the ship was not dead.

Reida said, "Maybe they've just parked the ship in orbit and have gone down to the planet."

Nicha said, "I don't think people who have lived for hundreds of years on a ship would elect to just leave it and go down to the planet."

"Not of their own will," Thayu said, her voice dark.

That was another thought.

"Hey," Ynggi said at the front of the group.

"What's going on?" Reida asked.

"It stops here."

He was right. The corridor stopped abruptly at a sheer metal wall.

"Then what is the point of this corridor?" Deyu said. "It doesn't appear to be going anywhere."

She directed the light up the wall. There was no ceiling, but the corridor turned into a shaft. A stale waft of air drifted down from the darkness above.

"Wow, that goes up a long way," Ynggi said.

Then I remembered something. At my previous visit, I had been through a hallway just like this one, which ended in a sheer metal wall, and you continued on by simply walking up the wall. There was a gravity field inside the wall.

I walked around the members of my group, who were clustered in front of the metal wall, and touched the metal. It was warm, and my hand felt heavy, as if it stuck onto the metal.

I leaned my elbow against the wall, and got the same sensation, and then put my foot flat against the wall.

Whoa, that was . . . strange. I waved my hands to stop myself falling.

Then I moved my other leg closer until my knee touched the wall, slowly leaned forward, or whatever direction it was, against the metal wall and then suddenly I was sitting on the wall, looking at the members of my team sideways.

Deyu gasped and pointed. "Look at that."

The others looked. Eyes widened.

"How did you do that?" Deyu asked.

"You just climb up the wall. Try it."

Ynggi was the first to try. He leaned against the wall, touched it with his tail, and then ran up a few steps. He stopped a few paces above me and laughed. "This is fun!"

One by one, the others tried, too.

With a bit of stumbling, they all managed to follow me onto the wall. I shuffled on my knees for a bit, but after a little while gained enough confidence to walk straight up the wall into the shaft. I remembered it now. This was how we had done it last time, but I had been with Kando Luczon and the Aghyrians, which had included Lilona. I refused to believe that the ship was abandoned, and no doubt somewhere up in a control room some of the ship's inhabitants were laughing about our efforts. Maybe it was a test. Maybe it was a trap.

The shaft—which turned into another low-ceilinged corridor when one walked up the wall—continued up for a little while before opening up into a huge void. If I remembered correctly, we now came out in the giant circular central hall of the ship. We reached the lip of the shaft and looked into the giant empty space.

"Whoa," Reida said, and his voice echoed in the darkness.

Only a few pinpricks of light penetrated the gloom, and they were not strong enough to show us the entire hall. It was hard even to judge how far the lights were.

"What now?" Telaris asked.

I said, "I think we can walk along the walls. If we are in the place that I remember, this is a large globe-shaped space. There is no gravity in the middle, but you can walk along the walls."

Ynggi dropped to his knees and edged one hand and his tail over the lip of the shaft. He turned around and lowered one leg, and then the other, and then he sat on his knees as if he'd been glued to the wall. It was very disorienting.

We clambered over the confusing, vertigo-inducing edge where the direction of gravity changed, and walked into the hall.

The floor was round and the weak light from our devices reached what looked like the banks of sleeping pods that I had seen on my previous visit. There had been people inside, in stasis. I was sure that during my previous visit, the pods themselves had issued light from within. Now they were all dark.

I reached the bank of pods, and put my hands on the glass. It was cold. I used the light from my reader to look in through the transparent cover. The pod was empty, allowing me to see a gel-filled bed and a couple of loose leads that lay in the space where the occupant's head would have been.

I checked the next pod. It was empty, too.

"Do you remember all the people who were in here?" I asked Thayu who had come up behind me.

"Yes. Where are they all?"

"I guess they've been woken up and taken away."

"But they're not in the ship." Her voice went dead in the huge space. She looked around at the vastness of the hall with walls which were far out of the reach of our little lights. Last time there had been light in this hall, because I remembered seeing how big it was. There was no gravity in the middle, and in order to move from one side to the next you could just float through, or float indefinitely if you missed where you were going.

Now it was dark, and all the lights were off.

"Is there anyone here?" I called out.

My voice faded in the huge space.

I was beginning to fear that the shuttle's crew were right. The ship was dead. Because surely someone should have come to us by now? Even if just to defend their ship.

What would have possessed people who lived on the ship for over 400 years to abandon it like this?

Especially if the planet below was covered in ice, offered no food, and we could detect no signs of life.

Maybe their contact with us gave them some horrible disease and they all died, said a little voice inside my head.

It was not a helpful thing to be thinking about when we were here, alone in this giant hall, and our shuttle was helpless and unable to leave.

We continued walking along the side of the hall. A lot of it was taken up with equipment and pods. We found that some pods were still occupied, but all the lights on the panels were off. The transparent covers were cold. Did this mean that the occupants were dead like mummies inside?

Ynggi led the way. He seemed to know where he wanted to go, since he could hear and see far more than we could. We passed several passageways that led away from the main hall, but he kept going. Looking back in the direction where I thought we had come in, I saw only blackness. I had no idea how to get back. Walking on the floor, ceiling or walls of this ship was immensely disorienting. We relied on Ynggi and his amazing night vision.

After a while, we came to another passageway that looked just like others we had passed.

Ynggi got to his knees and looked over the lip of the passage. I had no idea why he chose this one.

I sat down next to him and looked into the sheer darkness as well. Except it wasn't completely dark.

Golden light radiated from the end of the hallway, revealing a wall and the interior of a room.

"There is activity there," he said.

Damn it. Had he heard or seen something where none of us had a hope to detect any light or sound? "Can you see anyone moving?"

"No, but I can hear them."

I couldn't hear anything, and I didn't think anyone else in our team could either. Ynggi clambered over the lip of the passage, pushed himself to his feet and led us into the passage.

We walked more silently this time, because if there were people there, we didn't want to give them the impression that we were hostile.

After a while, the passage opened out into a larger room where it was warmer than it had been in the hall or the passage. There had to be people close by, because lights were on at a work station in the corner, and a jacket hung over a chair.

"Is anyone here?" I called again.

We waited for a while, but our reply was the continued silence.

Several members of my team had their hands on their weapons. If this captain wanted to pull any tricks on us, we were prepared.

"We come in peace," I said.

Again, there was no reply.

I glanced at Thayu, and she was looking around, her dark eyes searching the room for danger. Whoever had left the jacket had to know that we were here. Reida had a scanner out, but whenever I could see the screen, it displayed nothing except a straight blue line. The room contained nothing that triggered a reading.

Ynggi led the way across the room, between several workstations —most of which were off—to another door.

He seemed quite certain of himself, and since his hearing was obviously much better than any of ours—probably all ours combined—I was happy to have him in the lead.

He went through the doorway, into a passage where the walls consisted of control panels with lights and instructions in hieroglyphs, which led into a residential area with couches and tables.

He stopped a few paces into this room. He held up his finger, and his tail.

I knew it meant *listen*.

Now I could hear it, too: it was a kind of whimpering sound, like an abandoned puppy.

I raised my eyebrows at Ynggi, and he made a gesture with his tail that I thought meant careful.

Behind me, Thayu and Nicha took their weapons from their arm brackets.

"I come in peace," I said, in clear words. Last time, some people aboard the ship had spoken Coldi.

Aghyrians had an amazing capability to learn languages, and during their interaction with us a few years ago, they would have picked up all the available literature that would teach them the modern languages of the settled worlds. They'd had a few years to learn, and they liked learning things.

The whimpering stopped.

I continued, "We are not here to conquer or do any harm. You can come out now. Slowly show yourself, holding your hands in the air. Don't point any weapons at us, because we are armed."

We waited.

The only sound was the air hissing out of vents high in the walls.

We waited.

I gestured at Ynggi to move aside, and let Thayu, Nicha and Deyu into the room, their weapons drawn.

I pulled my gun from its bracket and followed them.

The room contained a table, couches and comfortable chairs, making it the most inhabited place I'd seen in the ship. A couple of lights burned along the walls, with the indirect light casting a warm orange glow through the room.

Thayu and Nicha ran straight for one of the couches, jumped over it, and lunged at someone behind the backrest, who let out a loud squeal.

Nicha pulled this person up by the front of the shirt. It was a man, protesting loudly.

I crossed the floor. "Stop, stop."

Nicha set the man on his feet.

He looked wide-eyed at us.

He was an adult Aghyrian, probably in his middle age, and at least a head taller than Nicha, but there was not a gram of muscle on him. His arms, pale-skinned, looked thin enough that I could break them with my bare hands.

His cheeks were hollow, his eyes sunken. His lips trembled.

"Can you speak?" I asked him. "Do you understand me?"

"Yes, yes."

I gestured for Thayu and Nicha to step back. They did, but kept their guns trained on him.

"Who are you and what are you doing here?"

"Jayten. Jayten Kolari." He held his hands up, looking nervously at the guns. "Please. We need help. We are trapped here. I tried to wake my people, but we have no power, and they cannot be woken. Many are dead. Hostile people watch us from space, and threaten us, even if we are peaceful. We just want a place to live, and are tired of fleeing."

14

J AYTEN TOLD US that since Lilona had stayed behind in Barresh, and the captain had made himself so unpopular that the ship had been banished from all *gamra* worlds, never to return to inhabited space, there had been a lot of problems aboard.

For the many years that they travelled, the captain had reigned unchallenged, not because he was such a good leader, but because what he did was sensible, and the ship had a goal.

But once the goal—to return to their home planet—had been reached and they had found their home world occupied by the Coldi, things started to unravel.

From the moment the ship had left, a good number of the Aghyrians had held up the ideal of returning to Asto. They had designed their journey with the sole purpose of bridging the fifty thousand years needed to return their home planet to liveable condition. They had slowed time aboard the ship by pushing close to lightspeed and by performing certain types of anpar jumps.

They knew how many years had passed on Asto and that the climate would be getting back to liveable, yet had never considered that there would be people who had lived on Asto all of that time, and who did not know that some of the original inhabitants had survived.

After the ship had been told to leave by us, some people aboard the ship wanted to make an agreement with one of the non-*gamra* inhabited worlds, and find a place to settle. The idea of living in space was wearing thin.

They had been shown pictures of what their home world of Asto used to look like, and wanted to return to a place like that. Some of them even accepted the fact that their original home world was now owned by different people.

But the captain wanted none of it. And he had a couple of powerful allies.

"He was going to lead us on a never ending quest to find the perfect world where he could rule for ever. He had a list of requirements. Most importantly, the inhabitants needed to be intelligent, but not too intelligent. They needed to be thankful for what he brought them, because he didn't think the people of *gamra* appreciated us enough."

Nice story, but I wasn't buying it as the whole truth. Everything we had seen from Lilona pointed to the fact that, though the people aboard this ship might have a lot of knowledge, they were also incapable of detecting emotional nuances in people outside their fellow ship-bound Aghyrians. I didn't think they were interested in what *gamra,* or anyone else for that matter, thought of them.

But I decided to play along with it, and poke him a bit more. "So when the captain couldn't find a suitable world with suitable people, he gave instructions to produce a new artificial race just like someone had once produced the people who are today the Coldi?" And I gestured briefly at Thayu, Nicha, Deyu and Reida, all of whom could kill this pathetic Aghyrian with the single press of a button. I was surprised by the depth of my hatred that resurfaced.

He frowned at me. "A new artificial race?"

"Because he didn't like what the Coldi had become, he decided to try again?"

He gave me a blank look. "I know there was some exchange of information, but I have no idea who received it or why. I'm not the captain and the captain makes decisions without consulting us."

"Can I talk to the captain, then?"

His face became sad. "You can't. Our captain has lived for a very long time. He is not well, and went in search of treatment down to the world."

Oh, really? He went to an ice ball with no discernible habitation, while the Aghyrian ship and its information were the source of the most advanced medical knowledge in the inhabited world?

To me, it was starting to look like there had been a substantial disagreement and part of the group had been banished or had fled to the planet.

"How many people are on board this ship now?"

"Didn't you see them?"

"No, I haven't seen anyone except you."

"Then come."

He walked to the door, past the members of my team. I followed him into the hallway with the control panels, and then into the big hall.

"Here," he said, making a broad gesture at the vast space.

"I did see those people, but they're asleep."

"These are the crew members."

"What about the empty and dark pods?"

His expression went sad again. "These people have been in stasis for a very, very long time. Many of them beyond their capability to live. It is not very good for a human body to be treated like this. We tried to revive a lot of them, but the material we had to work with was simply too deteriorated for them to live."

"*We?*"

"Myself, and . . . the others."

"Where are those others? Can I meet them?"

"I will ask."

He sounded hesitant.

"Are they all right? I haven't seen any other people who are awake since we came here."

I was still struggling to figure out how much of this was an act. Maybe he was truly alone here in this big ship. Maybe there was some sort of problem with the health of the ship. Maybe the captain had already known this the previous time when he turned up. They had come back to us not because they wanted their planet back, but because they had run out of places to live, including their own ship. They called these ships *generation ships* but how much did we know about how much plants and animals—including people—could be inbred until the population was no longer viable? Four hundred years had passed aboard the ship. That was a long time to keep a population healthy.

I tried another angle. "So who are these people that your captain went to visit down on the planet?"

"I don't know very much about them. The captain keeps information to himself."

Sadly, that was true and I did not disbelieve him.

"All I know is that the captain gave them some tasks to do, and gradually they assumed more authority and started taking over work from us. I think the captain wanted this work to be done on the planet so that he could fix the defective sequences in our genome. But I think the people he got to do this work had different ideas about it. They were greedy or hungry for power, and wanted to use the technology in a different way."

"And that was the technology to make new people?"

"You can do many different things with it."

"Has the ship been here for most of that time since you left our system?"

"Yes, because our ship needs a lot of maintenance, and there is no one who can do it so we must do it ourselves, but there is too much work, so we must take a long time. The ship is old and tired."

"Why didn't the captain simply ask us for help?"

I was sure that many people would have loved to help these space travellers, especially with the lure of hearing of what lay beyond our galaxy.

"Because the captain thought that all your methods were inferior. He was stubborn. Many of us disagreed. This is why we are in the state that you see us today."

I wondered if we had been wrong. During my previous visit, I had thought the ship was quietly sleeping, waiting to be woken up, but now I saw a more likely truth: they were not about to wake up, they were about to die.

"But one thing I don't understand. You went to a different galaxy. If you had that capability, why bother coming back here?"

He actually winced when I asked him that. And then he said nothing for a while. Oh, how I wished I could hear what he was thinking. Was he genuinely as naive as he pretended to be, or was this all an act?

Finally, he continued, "It is not easy to talk about; and, also, I was born on the ship when most of this had already been going on for many years. Yes, we went to another galaxy. We had a lot going for us there. There was a world we found that was not so different from any of the worlds here. But there was a way that people integrated with the natural life. It is hard to describe when an organism grows on you and becomes part of you. We call it *senkai*. It is when the organism benefits you and it starts to influence your thinking. Its thinking becomes part of you. The captain was very much against this. He believes in purity, and did not want to compromise in order to survive better on our new world. It was clear that the people who did undergo this symbiosis did far better, were smarter and lived longer than any of the people who did not. But he was stubborn. Not just that, he wanted to rule in his own world as he always had on the ship. Coming to a liveable planet was a bad thing for him, because people had options other than to follow his commands. And the young ones, especially, did not care for his old-fashioned ways. He got angry and called in the people who could not refuse his orders because their families were indebted to him. He managed to get only half the number of people required to fill the ship, but he thought that would be enough. He made a lot of heroic speeches, claiming that we were going to retake the old world, and be rulers of the universe. And then when we got here, he was overwhelmed by the size of your society, despite the fact that his generation had done all the colonisation. It was as if he had expected your people to be waiting for our return and have followed none of their own initiatives. He flew into a rage that the knowledge you used to build your Exchange was all ours, and we dared not contradict him, but no one could turn back the clock. Several of us tried to talk to him, to make him see sense, that we were only a few in comparison to all of you, and that we could never hope to win a war if it came to that. But he insisted on flexing his muscles, and pretending to be a lot more than he was, and a lot more than we were: a small population in deep trouble."

Whether or not his story was entirely true, the anger I had always felt for captain Kando Luczon resurfaced.

How Jayten had described him was exactly how I'd experienced him. This man had to be one of the most selfish bastards in the history of the universe. He did not allow refugees onto his ship when a meteorite was about to strike Asto, he did not help any of the refugees after the event, he left the survivors to fend for themselves, and just took off out of the galaxy. And then he exploited the people who chose or were conscripted to travel with him, and tried to stop them from leading happy lives, just so that he could rule somewhere.

Yet, the story of how Jayten came to be here alone still didn't add up. But I didn't press it. I was sure we'd hear the truth of it later.

I had to admit I felt sorry for him. To be here in this giant ship with all these sleeping and half dead people had to be pretty creepy. Even if he was not alone, this ship was big enough for a crew of only a few people to spend almost all their time alone, when they just covered the maintenance work that needed to be done.

I told him that if he could let us go, we would go down to the planet and find his captain for him. I told him that we had come to look for someone's husband and that this was not a mission sanctioned by *gamra*.

"It must be a pretty influential woman if she can inspire you to travel this far to find her partner."

"She is."

I was not sure what he meant with that strange statement, but I knew very little about the society of the Aghyrians on the ship. Lilona had never said much about it, except I had the impression—between the lines—that she had been a personal slave, potentially sexually, to the captain, controlled through the implant in her arm that she'd had the courage to rip out. My stomach still churned when I thought about that.

He said, "If I turned off the shields and the navigation guiding, you could leave. I wouldn't want to leave them off for long, because there are enemies out there, and we are far too few to defend ourselves. But I could turn them off and let you leave. If you went down to the planet, I could tell you where the people are."

"What would you want us to do?"

"I want enough of our crew to come back to operate this ship. I want to hand myself and the crew and the ship over to you, so that both our societies get the benefits from working together."

"We can do that. If you let us go."

"All right."

I asked him for any information about locations on the planet. He took us to another control room off to the side, where a giant projector displayed a 3-D image of the planet below.

The images we had from the Exchange were nowhere near as detailed.

The surface consisted of rugged mountain ranges covered in snow, huge glaciers running down into ice lakes, and jagged mountains of ice.

"The base is across the mountain range in this valley."

He enlarged the image to show the area. The lake looked more like a plain of ice to me. It was neither smooth nor liquid. The mountain range consisted of jagged peaks.

I could see the building of the base only when he pointed it out to me. It was set into the mountain, half buried in the snow. The surface of the valley looked quite smooth, but the white plain probably consisted of treacherous powdery snow.

Next to me, Thayu shuddered. We had brought our temperature retaining suits and the gear we bought in Miran, but I wasn't sure if that kind of material would even be suitable for a climate like this.

"What's that?" Deyu asked. She was pointing at a dark spot in the mountainside that had, for want of a better word, a couple of tracks coming out of it.

"There is some fauna," Jayten said.

Yes, I had heard about some big animals living on Tamer.

"What kind of fauna?" Deyu asked.

"They are about twice the height of a person, they appear to dig for something in the ground to eat, but we're not quite sure what they find. They walk on four legs, they have protuberances along their heads and backs. We are unaware that they have been named. They walk around in groups of about ten or twelve. Sometimes you can see small ones with them."

"Do they show any interest in the buildings?"

"We have not seen that they do, but we rarely see any activity outside these buildings."

"Are they aggressive?"

But he could not be expected to know that. Most likely he was not even aware of the concept of a predator or an aggressive animal.

We copied the maps from him, and he told us that we could rest while he retrieved supplies for us. He took us to a kind of dorm room down another shaft—I started to think this was the Aghyrian concept for stairs.

The air in the room smelled musty and stale. There were ten beds, and a thick layer of dust had gathered on the cover of each.

I asked Jayten how long we would have to stay here, and he answered in a time measurement that meant nothing to me. Apparently the shield needed a while to come down.

I asked him if we could speak to the shuttle in the hall. He said that our communication did not work inside the ship—something we knew already.

He also promised he would do his best to get ready as quickly as possible.

When he had left, Thayu, Evi and Reida walked around the room checking for bugs. They found a suspicious spot, and pulled out a panel in the ceiling with some device behind it. They couldn't be sure what it did, but they pulled it loose and disabled it anyway before they declared the room safe to speak.

"I don't like this," Thayu said.

No, neither of us did.

Nicha said, "It seems really strange, that he is sitting here by himself, in charge of this huge ship, not doing anything. It seems oddly passive. If he was really so desperate for his captain to come back, wouldn't he wake up some of his fellows?"

Reida said, "Yes, especially since he is in charge of all this technology. He even has aircraft. And he's lived on the ship all his life so it's not as if he doesn't know how to use it."

That was true, especially since the ship was said to have an array of unknown powerful weapons. So was he really as much as a victim as he made out to be?

I said, "I'm wondering if there has been some kind of mutiny and he's been abandoned by the others."

"I've seen no signs of a struggle," Thayu said. And she was hypersensitive to this sort of thing. While I had listened to Jayten's story, she would've been looking around checking out signs that he may or may not have been telling the truth.

"So, what do you think he's hiding?"

"The obvious thing would be that he is here with purpose, which is probably to put us off guard or make us think that things are not as they are."

We all agreed on that front.

To the question what we should do about it, my team were happy to play along for a bit, letting him believe that we believed him. If that got us down to the planet, it suited us.

We looked around the room. Apart from the beds, it contained a table and chairs, and a cupboard, which turned out to be some kind of washing cubicle. You stepped in and water and steam came out from everywhere, complete with some type of soap and after a few minutes, it turned off and blew hot air to dry you.

After I had tried the strange contraption, I came back into the main room and found Thayu, Deyu, Evi and Telaris studying some panel on the wall. Thayu had her reader out.

"What are you looking at?"

"There is some sort of text panel on here. I'm trying to figure out what it says."

I came to stand behind them.

Thayu turned around to me. "You smell strange."

"It's the detergent in the washing cubicle."

Telaris was running his finger along a panel of hieroglyphs on the wall while looking at his reader. "It says here to read this from right to left, and the first one means careful."

I joined in the game of puzzles, and we figured out that the instructions covered an emergency procedure. It seemed natural that the ship would have these.

The beds were quite comfortable, filled with some kind of gel that made them both hard to the touch and soft at the same time. When you lay down, the blankets extended automatically from the sides.

I was just wondering what the ship people had for food, when Jayten came into the room with a trolley, filled with a number of containers.

"Retrieving the supplies I want to give you is going to take a while, and so is powering down the shield, so you will need some food. I think you should all be able to eat these."

He handed out bowls and explained to us what all the various items were. I was not surprised to see that the people in the ship grew a lot of their food. I remembered that, when I had lived on a space station, people said that we should all eat artificial food, but things like salad and small tomatoes, eggs and small animals like chickens and fish were popular. People's emotions were tied to planets, no matter where they lived.

Jayten told us that, by his understanding, the dark green leaves and the orange fruit grew on plants that had originally come from Asto. Likely these plants were the only ones still in existence in the universe. It felt like sacrilege to eat them.

There were also cubes of protein, which were clearly artificial.

I asked him if they kept any animals.

"I understand there used to be animals on the ship, but there haven't been any in my lifetime. We have all their genetic material in storage, but there are simply too few of us to maintain a healthy population of animals."

I made the mistake of wondering what the cubes were made of. Mostly, on Midway, these sorts of things would be made from recycled material, which was a euphemism for rubbish. Also, on Midway, these sorts of cubes would not be fed to people, only to livestock.

I politely tried a cube—it tasted bland—but declined any more. I didn't trust him, and I didn't like this situation.

I asked, "So you've made the entire journey back here eating only this?"

"Yes, because the captain could not find a full crew, as I said. But I must go and check on the shield. Make sure that you rest."

I debated asking him to bring some food to the pilots, but decided against. The shuttle was our way out, and I did not want to give him the opportunity of planting a listening device on board. The shuttle was self-contained and had plenty of supplies.

After he left, and we spent some more time wondering what was going on.

"The food was quite good," Telaris said.

"Did you think so?" Nicha said.

"Not all of us grow up being able to afford expensive food."

"It is quite similar to the types of food that people eat in space stations," Thayu said. "The leaves are easy to grow, the small fruit probably grows on a small plant or a vine that doesn't take up too much space, and the cubes can be made artificially."

"What do you think they're made of?" I asked her.

She gave me an understanding look. "How much time have you spent living in a closed environment?"

I told the team of the brief time in my youth spent at Midway space station and the long haul space flights to get there.

Deyu raised her eyebrows. "Seriously? Do people still do those sorts of things?"

"They did until they decided to join *gamra*." I understood that the first commercial shuttles would start operating from Earth fairly soon.

And then I wondered what would happen to old ships like the ones I had travelled on to Midway and Taurus and Mars.

We decided that the option to rest was an attractive one as we were in what would normally be the night anyway.

It was a strange kind of night. Probably the strangest I had spent anywhere. We were surrounded by the unknown technology of the giant ship. I wasn't sure whether it was really as much of a lame duck as Jayten suggested. It might be that they were spying on us. It might even be that he was stealing our genetic material. There was no way of knowing.

After a long and restless period, Jayten returned with yet more food. He brought us a kind of porridge that seemed clearly plant based. We had explained to him yesterday that Coldi didn't eat animal based food.

We asked him if we could be returned to the shuttle.

He seemed surprised by the question. "If I want you to go down to the planet, how else could you go?"

"I just wanted to make sure. You could have your own ways. I noticed there were shuttles in the hall."

He laughed. "Those have not been touched in my lifetime."

That was fast becoming his reply to everything. But in short, the shields were down, he had the supplies ready and we were allowed to go back to the shuttle. He even took us there.

As it turned out, the way we had come here was not the shortest one. A passage led from the residential quarters into another passageway that went straight to the arrival hall.

This particular passage looked a lot more well-used. There was no dust anywhere, and the rooms that were on either side—at least the ones that we could see into—were clean and the equipment inside all appeared operational.

I had to admit that I was glad to see the shuttle again, and that it sat exactly as we had left it, except the pilots had pulled up the ramp and shut the door, so as not to be surprised by any intruders.

Next to the shuttle stood a stack of crates.

Jayten lifted the top one off and opened the lid. He took out a couple of sections of metal strips and wired and slotted them together, forming a construction on thin metal legs. From the bottom of the box he retrieved a rectangular unit with a screen on top. There were slots in the sides for the metal legs and plugs for the wires.

When he finished it, the thing kind of looked like a giant spider, about knee-high. It had six legs, and the box that held the panel was its body. He sat it on top of the pile of crates.

Then he gave me another device, which you could wear like a watch. He strapped it around my wrist.

"Move your hand."

I did.

The spider crawled to the edge of the crate.

"Oops. Better not make it fall off."

"Try making it fall."

I made a more violent movement with my hand. The thing leapt into the air and landed safely on the ground.

By now my skin under the wristband was getting warm.

I loosened it. "Is it supposed to be warm?"

"It is how it obeys you. It reads your intentions."

Great. Another feeder type of device.

"This little device will crawl into small spaces and dangerous places where you don't want to go. I figure that you might be able to use it when you're down there."

"Thank you."

We took the box and the controllers with us, but I was careful to keep the watch away from my skin.

By now, I noticed that our communication with the shuttle was working again, and I trusted that my team contacted them about what was going to happen. The pilots were extending the ramp.

"I'm going to leave you here," Jayten said. "In order for your ship to leave this hall, I need to be up in the control room."

I thanked him, still not sure what to think. For the time being, it looked like he was really going to let us go.

When the ramp was extended, Yana came out. "What's in these crates?"

"Supplies, supposedly."

Deyu wedged the lid off. Inside, we found packets with dried food. She pulled a face. "Urgh, that smells."

It did smell, but in a pungent, not spoiled way. Like when you went into a domestic supply shop in Barresh for the first time, and were hit in the face with the concentrated scent of megon oil.

People of the Aghyrian branch of the human tree had sensitive noses. Aghyrians did, Coldi did. Being locked up inside a giant tin can for four hundred years might even have heightened the importance of smell for the Aghyrians.

In another crate we found a burner with what we thought were canisters of fuel. A large crate contained parts for a small vehicle and yet another small electronic parts that—according to Reida—would probably make a receiver that was powered by whatever was in the metal canisters that were really heavy.

"Do we load all this?" Yana asked.

Thayu walked around with her scanner. The line on the screen that indicated electronic activity remained flat. "It's probably safe," she said.

The crates sat on a platform that turned out to have wheels, so we pushed it up the ramp into the shuttle's cargo hold.

We all boarded, and dropped into a seat.

Through the glass wall that separated us from the pilots, I could see that the control panel lit up. A moment later, the hum of the engines vibrated through the floor. Then the lights in hall outside went on and showed us the huge dimensions of it.

"Holy crap," Deyu said.

Yes, indeed. This was a giant. A sleeping giant maybe, but a dangerous giant nevertheless.

15

ON OUR WAY IN, we had seen only a small section of this huge hall, but when Jayten turned on the light, all of it became visible.

The pilot turned on the outside viewscreens, and all of us just gaped at the huge size.

"There must have been an entire town in here," Telaris said.

The hall went up many floors, with galleries along all the levels. The floating platforms occupied mostly the sides of the hall. Some were empty, some contained small aircraft.

The ones we passed were all covered in a grey layer of dust.

"Look, they move aside," Deyu said.

It was true. As our aircraft slowly moved through the hall, the platforms drifted aside.

Behind me, Thayu, Evi and Reida had sprung into action. The fact that Jayten had turned off the shields meant that they could probe the ship's systems. Scanned information was already scrolling over Thayu's reader screen. They'd get their hands on whatever they could grab.

The exit of the hall lay ahead, a rectangular opening that seemed to lead straight into space.

It was still a type of airlock, only an invisible one. The craft went through it slowly and while we were in the opening, the pilots' instruments went blank.

And then the ship spat us out. We drifted in its massive shadow.

The vast shape of the ship stretched beyond view above and below us. The outside of the hull was grey, pitted where debris had struck it in space.

It was so big that I could actually see its shadow as a very faint dot tracking over the clouds that covered the planet below.

"I'm very glad to be out of there," Nicha said.

"Yeah," Thayu said.

Everyone agreed.

"I really don't understand what he's doing up there."

"I don't believe he's there by himself," Deyu said. She leaned over to show me her reader. On it was a picture of some sort of scan. It showed the outlines of the ship with a couple of lighter spots.

"What is that?"

"There is activity in those areas."

"Does that mean there are other people?"

"Most likely, although it could also mean engine activity."

I had suspected that, but for now, there was not much point worrying about it. We were on our way to the planet, and whatever we might find there. It just illustrated that we should not trust Jayten on these matters, which we already knew.

Jayten had provided the pilots with detailed data of the surface, which they had fed into the navigation systems.

In order to go down to where we needed to go, we needed to complete one and a half orbits of the planet.

Yana said, "That brings us past the anomaly that is still disturbing the magnetic field. We can check out if it really is an Exchange node, with your permission."

"Would it be safe to come close?"

"We'll stay at more than a safe distance."

It sounded like a good idea to me, so I gave that permission.

Then I sat back and let the crew do their work. In order to pass closer to the anomaly, they needed to change our course, and certain trajectories and speeds needed to be recalculated.

Deyu, Thayu and Reida were also busy.

I sat back in my seat and tried to doze, but I could never sleep on transport, so I observed the members of my team through half-closed eyes. I wondered how Veyada was coping without us, and if the child had been born yet. I wondered what Sheydu was doing and if I'd ever see her again. I wondered—

Ynggi gave a squeak. His tail went right over his head.

"What is it—?"

All the instruments in front of the pilots lit up. An alarm went off. Rixya and Taleyu sprang into action.

A couple of viewscreens went dark. Lights flashed on a couple of the side panels.

The floor of the craft vibrated.

"What's going on?" My hands gripped the armrests so tightly that my fingers hurt.

"I don't know," Thayu said. "My guess is that something upset the instruments."

She was trying to sound calm, but I could hear the worry through her voice.

"Something? Like, what? The Aghyrian ship shot at us?"

But right now, that question was much less important than the one about how we were going to survive this.

Another screen turned off. Warning lights flashed.

"Status on navigation," Yana said.

Taleyu said, "Stable for now, slowly declining in line with descent to the planet. Nothing unexpected."

Rixya said, "I don't have external input at all. The system is idle while waiting."

"Stop that process."

Rixya nodded and used the controls.

The pilots appeared calm, but I spotted Rixya quickly wiping his face.

We were now going down fast, and the craft was shuddering. Damn, were we meant to survive this?

The outside screen showed a projection of a map. Yana pointed. Taleyu nodded, businesslike, her lips pressed together.

They were trying to put us down as close to the base as possible.

We dived into the atmosphere. The craft shook and rumbled. From where I sat, I could see a temperature warning light on the controls. The craft would be built for this, but everything felt very shaky right now.

Then we were through.

With a clang, the wings extended from the sides. A mist of air trailed from the wing tips.

Reida sat frozen in his seat, his eyes wide.

When we entered the cloud mass, visibility outside was reduced to zero. We drifted through a white-grey soup that rushed past the side of the craft. The pilots enlarged the map that Jayten had given us.

Warning lights still flashed at the control panel. We would just have to hope that the information was correct, because there was no visibility. We might simply fly into the side of a mountain if the maps were wrong, and they easily could be. They could even be wrong on purpose. Maybe Jayten let us go so that he could shoot at us. Maybe he wanted us to disappear. Maybe that was what happened to Benton Leck, too.

My mind ran away with possibilities, each more horrific than the next.

The craft bumped and jumped through the clouds.

"It's very windy," Nicha said.

Very helpful, thanks, Nich'.

The craft shot out from under the clouds, in a landscape that was grey and monotonous, with jagged mountains and a thick cover of snow.

Underneath us was the white plain that looked quite even, but that was probably treacherous.

We came closer and closer, flying low over sharp mountain peaks.

The craft flew low over a snowy field.

"Brace for landing," Yana said. The glass partition door was closed, and his voice was tinny through a loudspeaker.

The craft went lower and lower but lost little speed. This was going to be rough—like, really rough. Normally, a shuttle would slow right down and use the downward jets to land gently on the surface. But it appeared the downward jets weren't working.

The craft juddered when it first hit the snow and jumped back up. The seat belt bit into my shoulders. Then it hit the snow again and slid on its belly, bumping and rattling all the way.

Eventually, the craft settled and came to a stop.

The engines whined at a lower and lower pitch and then fell quiet.

"Phew," Reida said.

I unclamped my hands from the armrests of my seat. My heart was thudding like crazy. I could be mad, but I guessed this was one of the closest shaves with death I'd had.

Rixya drew his hands over his face.

"That was close," Nicha said.

When I got up from my seat, I could feel the floor wobble. "Whoa. Is it safe to move?"

"The substrate is not very even," Yana said. "We'll go outside and secure the craft. We'll have to be careful when we leave the cabin."

He sounded shaken.

I didn't ask what had happened. I was sure we'd hear more about it soon enough, but for now I doubted they knew themselves.

The light was on in the pilot compartment, but half the instrument panel had gone dark.

While we undid our harnesses and blew out heavy breaths of relief, Yana put on a suit and went into the cargo hold. A click and a few beeps indicated that the outer door had opened. A cold draft of air came in, even if the cargo hold was at the back of the craft and the door between the cabin and the hold was closed.

The closing of the outer door was followed by some clunking noises outside.

Then Yana came back inside. His cheeks were red. "It's extremely cold out there. There is a lot of snow."

Yes, that figured. "Do you still have an outside viewscreen?"

"One or two. Whatever hit us out there fried the rest. We need to make sure the central command module is not damaged. I put the feet out, so the craft should be stable now, and we can assess the damage."

Rixya and Taleyu had already started doing that, and it looked like it would be a lengthy process, so we gathered in the living area to discuss what our next steps would be.

The maps that Jayten had given us matched with the terrain that we saw through the rotating camera that fed into the viewscreen. There was a mountain in the right position, and a valley in another, and we trusted that the peaks we could see to our right were really the top of a lower ridge and there was another valley on the other side.

But we could not see any signs of the base that was supposed to be here.

"We'll have to go out and check it for ourselves," Evi said.

We would have to do that tomorrow, because we needed to plan this out properly, but right now, we might be able to explore the vicinity of the craft.

The air's vital statistics were good, although there was a rather high component of sulphur, presumably from the world's volcanic activity. The heat scan showed a volcanic vein that ran close to the surface, from the shore of the ice that lay at the bottom of the slope where the craft stood to the valley on the other side of the peaks to our right. When I turned the camera in that direction, I could see a hole in the ice at the shoreline where wisps of steam rose into the air.

Volcanic springs meant energy, and we might well need it to recharge the craft's engines, since sunlight would be sporadic at best.

We retrieved our cold weather gear from the luggage compartment and spent some time sorting it all out. The boots and jackets and tracking gear took a while to put on, especially since we were unused to it.

It was mid-morning, local time, so we had at least a few hours to investigate. The days on Tamer were rather short, and the cloud cover would not help us. It was already quite dark down here, and there might be bad weather ahead.

We decided to use the luggage compartment door as entry and exit. It was easier to control the temperature in the main cabin that way, and—even though no one else thought of this—keeping snow boots quarantined in there would keep the main cabin from becoming wet.

We were ready.

Nicha opened the door.

A blast of cold air laced with snowflakes came in. Standing at the front, Reida copped the full blast of it. He swore.

Deyu pulled the hood of her jacket over her eyes, jumped out, and disappeared up to her waist in the snow. It was loose and powdery and it was hard for her to find solid footing. She flailed around and eventually Reida pulled her back onto the steps of the shuttle.

The entire hillside was covered in loose snow like this.

Well, I guessed that would hamper our plans somewhat.

"We need to make snowshoes," I said.

Then I had to explain to the team what snowshoes were, which reminded me of how I'd spoken of skiing to Puck.

Poor Puck.

Yes, it did look like skiing could be a handy skill here.

Did we have anything to make makeshift snowshoes or skis?

Ynggi and Nicha went into the tools and maintenance section of the compartment. I wanted to come, but there was only room for two people, especially when wearing lots of cold weather gear.

"How about we use this?" Reida asked.

He held up the little drone that Jayten had given us. I had noticed that he'd been fiddling with it on our trip down.

It no longer looked like a spider, but he had attached big flanges to either side to resemble wings.

"I don't quite like the way that thing is controlled," I said. "You don't know what it records and where it sends its material."

"No, I didn't like it either. Don't trust it if you don't understand it."

That was something Sheydu would say, and yes, I missed her a lot on this trip. Her practical, no-nonsense advice would have been invaluable.

"Therefore, I changed the machine a bit," Reida continued. He pulled one of the flanges until it was fully extended. It was a wing.

"It flies?"

"Yes, I figured that's faster and more useful to us. I used the engine from the drone that we shot down on Earth."

That was when my father had driven us to the airport, and we had spotted a drone following us. That technology was probably Sudanese and before that from Indrahui, and Reida had applied his inventive *zeyshi* Coldi mind to making it do what he wanted so that he could use it in South Africa. Now he had whipped up this machine in little time. He was getting to be *really* good at this kind of stuff.

He explained that he had attached his own controller to it, so that he knew exactly what data was being sent where. I could hear echoes of Sheydu in everything he said.

He climbed down steps and carefully put the thing on top of the snow. It was light enough not to sink. He sat down, took his reader, and turned on the engine with a soft purr.

The drone skated over the snow for a bit until it took flight. It went up the hill, a little black speck against the grey, snow-laden sky, turned around and came back down.

"Test flight." There was a broad grin on his face. Reida knew when he had done well. He switched on the camera, and a view from the underside of the drone came up on his screen.

"I'm impressed," Nicha a said. "Sheydu taught you well."

We looked around the area surrounding the shuttle using the little machine, while standing in the entrance to the cargo hold, while the wind bit in our faces.

The ridge that we could see from our position consisted of a number of extremely sharp rocky peaks. They were like thorns in the landscape, and it would be hard to find a way through.

"There is a path," Deyu said, looking over Reida's shoulder at his screen. She pointed. "There."

He investigated that particular area. "Am I mistaken, or does it look like those are tracks?"

He brought the drone closer again, and from what we could see, it looked like Deyu might be right. Jayten had said something about fauna. I was wondering when we were going to run into these animals.

The valley on the other side of the ridge consisted of a gently sloping plain that led to the base of a steep cliff. That cliff lead up to the taller mountain. There was a gorge on the far end but no sign of a river or glacier going through.

In fact if there was any such thing as liquid water on this planet, there would be signs of erosion on the rocks.

I concluded that because of the jagged peaks, all these rocks were volcanic, and the ice had done little to alter their appearance. It was a geologically young landscape.

The gorge was not made by a river. It was a cleft in the landscape, where some geological feature had caused a break in the rock. There was evidence of volcanic activity, because a plume of steam rose from the ground at the base of the cliff. We could even see a small pool where the snow had melted.

Lots of tracks in the snow surrounded the pond, but we saw no sign of whatever made those tracks. The track of trampled snow went from the pond through another gorge which led straight to the lakeside. The snow in that area was disturbed, and there were dark areas. I couldn't see what they were, but I suspected they could be animal droppings.

The area was geologically spectacular, but not particularly interesting for the reason we were investigating it.

Reida took the drone back over the ridge in the direction of our shuttle. He started investigating the mountainside a bit further from where we were.

All of a sudden, a flash lit the landscape.

"What was that?" Deyu said.

None of us could answer that, of course.

"I thought it came from around the corner," Reida said.

A rocky outcrop limited our view in that direction.

So he sent the drone to investigate. The sky looked dark in that direction.

Was there such a thing as lightning in a snowstorm?

On the other side of the outcrop we discovered a structure in the landscape that was definitely artificial: a square building which looked like a bunker, set into the side of the slope with most of the structure under the ground. A light flashed on one of the walls.

As we watched with the drone, a slit opened in the concrete wall, spilling bright light onto the greyness of the snow.

"Call it back or land it," I told Reida.

He put the drone down on a flat piece of land at the top of the outcrop.

The door to the bunker opened wider. The strip of light grew, and from somewhere within fell long shadows across the snow. What made those shadows? They were moving.

They were . . . people, marching in rows, now coming out of the opening. An army.

For a moment, I was afraid that they were coming to check us out, but they marched from the opening down the slope to the lake.

"Are those Tamerians?" Thayu asked.

"I guess they are."

The whole army marched in perfect rows, following one another into the valley. They didn't take any notice of the drone.

But by now the army was so far onto the lake that they also came into view of the shuttle's outside cameras.

They marched on, oblivious to our presence, over the frozen water of the lake.

"Where are they going?" Thayu said.

No one knew.

We watched them in amazement. Reida increased the magnification on the drone's camera until we could see the—quite blurry— details of individuals. The army consisted of men with a familiar stocky build and olive skin. Their faces were slightly different, but they were all Tamerians like Puck.

The army marched into the middle of the lake, and then stopped and marched back again. They didn't take any notice of our shuttle, which they should be able to see from where they were.

They marched on and on, back in the direction of the concrete bunker.

But while the army came closer to the shore, they wandered onto ice thinned by the presence of the volcanic spring in the lakeshore.

A section of ice cracked under their weight, causing a good number of men to slide into the water.

The surface of the water bubbled and churned. Reida focused on the area. The light was poor and the maximum magnification further reduced the quality of the image. Was there really something under the ice that picked off the soldiers as they scrambled to safety? Few made it, most disappeared under the ice.

Occasionally, a piece of an animal, a fin, a part of a head, stuck out of the water.

Ynggi watched with all of his Pengali alertness. "See? There are fish."

"I guess so," I said. "I'm not sure that these are fish you want to try and catch."

But I feared that to Ynggi, *all* fish were game.

The rest of the army marched on, oblivious to what had happened.

We watched, stunned into silence, as they marched up the shore back to the bunker. The door shut as soon as they were inside.

"Well," Thayu said. "That was interesting."

Interesting indeed.

16

INTERESTING WAS A WAY of putting it.

The big question of course was what was the point of this strange performance, and did no one notice that a bunch of soldiers had just been eaten by something that lived under the ice? What were they even doing there?

Not that any of us could answer those questions.

We decided that we had seen enough, and needed to digest what we had seen and look at all the data that the drone had collected. We needed a plan and we needed to make our snowshoes before we could venture out of the craft.

So we shut the door, let warm air flood back into the cargo hold and took off all our winter gear again.

It felt a bit ridiculous, not having gone anywhere, but we had definitely needed the warm clothes, because my feet and hands were as cold as ice. Thayu's cheeks were uncharacteristically red. It was disturbingly attractive.

She gave me a mischievous look. The breeze carried her alluring, very female scent past me.

Oh boy, was it a pity that we were cooped up in this tin can. Or maybe it wasn't a pity, because we were supposed to wait, right?

We came back into the cabin to find that the crew were still busy. They had moved aside the glass partition that separated the cockpit from the passenger seating during flight. They had turned around the

seats so that they stood in a more living room like style. They had
pulled out a table, which they had covered in instruments and electronics. Some panels on the sides and the control module were open. I
took that as a good sign. At least they weren't digging around in the
engine compartment.

I sat down, watching them work.

It was warm in the cabin, and for once I did not complain.

Thayu joined me on the couch with two cups of the dark green
coffee-like *manazhu*. She gave one to me. Its tangy smell rose from the
steaming surface.

We drank in companionable silence while watching the others.

Telaris and Nicha set about constructing snowshoes with lengths
of carbon material that they had located in the maintenance
compartment.

Meanwhile Deyu and Reida sat on one of the other couches. They
pulled out all the data that the drone had collected.

From what I could tell, it had gathered a lot more than just visible
light.

Their heat map, for example, showed the outline of the base
clearly in the mountainside. There was more of the building in the
mountain than outside it, and I suspected that they used the volcanic
vents for heating.

Only a small part of it stuck up out of the snow. Our most detailed
magnification of the building suggested that there might be windows
looking out over the lake from the top floor.

Another scan showed a lot of footprints over the ice, as if this
army marched across it more. There were no signs of other disasters
that had befallen the marchers. Then again, it was so cold that the
surface would freeze right back up again. We also found a number of
perfect parallel lines up the hillside on the other side of the base. We
puzzled over what they could be until we realised that the army must
march up the hill in the same formation every day and use the same
tracks.

A well-worn track from the lakeshore up the mountainside on our
side of the lake had a much more natural appearance. The narrow
path was well worn where it went through the gorge, but the tracks
dispersed when they reached the open field. They were animal tracks.

I took the maps that we had received from Jayten, and overlaid the material Reida had collected onto it. The features matched perfectly. The hot air vent at the lakeshore was exactly where it should be, and so was the one in the cleft in the mountain behind us.

Other than the tracks made by the army, there were no signs of how people reached the base. To be honest, it looked semi-deserted. Was this the area where the Exchange had detected increased activity? In that case, I wasn't sure I wanted to know what the rest of the planet was like.

I became aware that the crew had stopped their work. Rixya and Taleyu had gone to the kitchen to make drinks, and Yana joined us.

"What is the news?" I asked, but I could tell by his drawn face that the situation was serious.

He breathed in heavily. "Not good. We are not sure what happened up there. I hate to insinuate that the Aghyrian ship fired at us, but something of the kind was triggered by our course change. The command module is busted."

My heart jumped. Did that mean that they had just landed us on manual? I would have expected a lot more frantic activity in the control room. But then again, these people were trained professionals who would calmly do their jobs under stress. If the craft went down in an irretrievable nosedive, they would calmly do their jobs until they hit the planet. Because they were military.

Well, damn. "I thought you had a spare command module."

"We do, but we can't seem to get it to work. Probably some of the connections are fried, too, but it's too cold for us to take the engine apart without doing much more damage to it."

"What can you do?"

"Several things. We can take parts of the engine out from the inside, but it will require us to power it down completely, and it means we're completely stuck for at least five days. We lose all agility."

"The craft can fly?"

"It can, but we have no navigation, so it's not advisable. Of course we have no Exchange and communication either so we're not going anywhere major. But it can fly. Of course, it won't function optimally, so flying will do damage to the engine, so it's not advisable for long distances."

"The other options?"

"We can trigger the alarm. But it will draw lots of attention to us, so it's not advisable until we've completed as much of our mission as possible, and the turning up of Asto military craft is likely to raise the ire of that big ship out there, and whatever else is watching this world. I can't guarantee that it won't lead to armed conflict. In fact, I would guess that it likely will, with all consequences."

Double damn. That put us in a hard spot.

"So what do you suggest?"

"I would prefer to 'borrow' a command module or failing that, an entire ship, if we can locate one."

And it didn't look like the base had an airfield at all.

"Anything else?"

"Yes. Since we took a hit up there, it is highly likely that the people who are in charge of this world know that we are here."

"How long do we have before someone turns up?"

But nobody could be expected to know the answer to that.

We couldn't do anything now. It was getting dark, and the wind whipped snow against the outside of the craft.

We sat around the table, making a plan.

First we would have to go to that base to see if we could find anything we could use, and if we could locate the craft that the Exchange had spotted coming to Tamer.

Since, even if we had snowshoes, there was no chance that we could easily walk to the building—let alone get inside—we figured that it would be easiest to stick to the existing animal track. Rather than wade through the deep snow on the mountainside, we would go up and walk through the canyon to the lakeside. It came out much closer to the building. We would wait until the army came out and try to sneak in with them. If they took no notice that their comrades fell through the ice, then they might not notice that a few extra people joined them, either.

"While you're gone, we will de-power and test the engine and fix problems. When you come back with the module—"

I asked, "Wouldn't it be easier to simply take a whole craft, as you said?"

"In theory, yes, but in practice, since they don't appear to be using the Exchange, they may not even be Exchange-enabled in the sense that we understand it. I prefer to go with the module."

Although that was clearly the most fiddly option.

Yana decided that Rixya would accompany us, because he knew what to look for and how to safely remove it.

They did give an assessment of our resources to survive in the craft. We had enough energy, and could always recharge at the hot water springs, although getting the array of energy pearls down to the waterfront would be an issue, so they preferred not to have to do it.

Survival was not going to be an issue, although it would if hostile people turned up. The craft itself had limited defensive capabilities, the crew were all armed, and there was a heavy-duty cannon in the cargo hold, but it needed to be assembled.

Yana asked me if they should do that, and I said that I thought it would be a good idea; so they retrieved a large crate from the cargo hold. They spent most of the evening putting the weapon together, under the watchful eye of Reida who found it very interesting and had probably never been this close to such a sophisticated piece of weaponry.

Having assembled this weapon, it meant that someone had to guard it, and so we lugged the thing back to the cargo hold, where we placed it in front of the door. Rixya set up a fold-up bed next to it, as he was going to take the first shift.

The rest of us went into the rooms with the bunks.

I tossed and turned through most of the night. I hadn't slept in one of these hammocks for a while and found it annoying that it swayed whenever I moved.

The wind whistled around the outside of the craft and, every now and then, a gust would be so strong that the craft wobbled a tiny bit.

————

I must have fallen asleep, because I woke up to people moving about. It was still very dark in the room where I had slept, but Thayu and Nicha's hammocks were empty.

I found them in the living area, making breakfast.

The light in the cabin was low, mainly from the single outside viewscreen that was in operation. Through it, the view of the landscape was grey. I didn't recognise any of the features since everything was covered in a fresh layer of snow. In fact, it was still snowing.

Were we going to go out in that?

Breakfast was typical Coldi fare. There were not many Coldi dishes that did not contain mushrooms. These ones were reconstituted from dried rations of course.

Ynggi, Evi and Telaris had to eat the bland, floury stuff.

In yesterday's overview, Yana had not mentioned food in the equation that determined how long we could stay here, so I assumed they had plenty aboard the ship.

I was well aware that these were mushrooms I had never been able to eat, the kind that made your eyes water if you took as much as a single lick. I had never done more than experienced that sharp, biting feeling that made your tongue numb. That sensation was gone. Proof, if I needed any, that my body was still changing.

Rixya joined us for breakfast, while Taleyu went to sit with the cannon. It seemed to be protocol that when the weapon was live someone had to attend it.

Rixya said that the night had been quiet. He had not noticed any activity, near the base or otherwise.

When we finished breakfast, it was time to try out our snowshoes and see if we could find anything useful about the surroundings. I thought we could check out the hot water vent to see if we could use it for anything.

We put all our cold weather gear back on and went back into the cargo hold, after having secured the door to the cabin to keep the warm air inside. Taleyu turned off the gun's control panel and slotted a strip into it, presumably so that it wouldn't go off accidentally while we walked past.

When Reida opened the door, a flurry of snowflakes came in. The wind whistled around the craft's protuberances. Eddies of snow blew in corners and very soon we might not even have to cover the craft with snow because it was happening by itself.

We strapped the constructions of slats under our shoes. I had told Nicha to put some varnish on the bottom to make them smoother so that we would be able to ski through the snow.

I was game to try first. I jumped out of the craft into the snow. It was loose and powdery but, wearing the snow shoes, I only sank in to my ankles. That was a good sign.

I helped Nicha out, and then Evi. Deyu and Reida and Ynggi wanted to come as well.

Telaris would stay with the craft, because he was still processing the scans from Reida's drone.

I made sure that everyone was all right, and slowly started up the hillside. It had been a very long time since I had done any cross-country skiing and it took me a while to get the hang of walking with these things.

The air was biting cold, so I pulled the shawl over my face.

I regretted not taking any snow glasses, because the cold made my eyes water. I made sure that I kept an eye on the locating device which told me where the shuttle was, because after we had gone a few steps up the hill, I couldn't see it any more.

I could just see Nicha and Deyu, Reida and Ynggi behind me. Ynggi mainly because his tail kept waving about to keep his balance. He also complained that his tail was cold. We were going to have to make some sort of glove for it. I had thought that he could just keep it under his jacket, but the reality was that Pengali used their tails for balance and that having it constrained under a jacket severely hampered the owner. So we'd better not stay out here too long, because I didn't want Ynggi's tail to suffer frostbite.

After a while, I reached the rocky spikes at the top of the ridge. They were just as sharp as they looked from a distance, jagged spikes of volcanic basalt. And if we hadn't known that there was a path between them, we would never have found it. But I knew it was to the left, so I turned that way and struggled along the mountain peak against the blizzard.

I found the path through. The wind had erased all evidence that anyone or anything had ever been here. I waited for Nicha and the others to catch up with me. They were not as handy with the snowshoes.

The wind howled between the rocky spikes at the top of the ridge.

I peered down the mountainside. The mist and drifting snow obscured my view of the shuttle. The other members of the group emerged from the storm like grey silhouettes covered in snowflakes.

Reida and Deyu were laughing. Apparently Reida had fallen and he was entirely covered in snow. Ynggi was laughing, too. The typical Pengali snorts came from within his big hood. At least someone had fun.

I led the way through the narrow passage between the spikes, pushing against the wind.

After a short distance, we came out to the valley on the other side. This was supposed to be a snowy slope gently undulating to the bottom of the next section of mountain. That was also the location of the cleft where the smoke rose from the ground. But we couldn't see any of it because of the weather. The whole area was shrouded in mist and drifting snow.

Nicha stood with his hands in his pockets and his face hidden deep within his shawl.

"Amazing view," he said.

Thayu came up behind him, just as another squall of wind blew a cloud of snow in our faces. Deyu and Reida had also come through and for some reason that escaped me, Reida took off, skiing down the hillside at incredible speed.

"Hey! What are you doing?" Deyu took off after him.

"Come back here," I called, but my words were blown away by the wind.

I couldn't see them anymore. Well, damn. I hadn't planned on going much further in this weather.

I made sure that we were all together, and then slowly set off down the hill, following the tracks made by Reida and Deyu. I slipped and fell, sliding a short distance before I could stop myself.

Ouch.

I dug in the snow, and my glove met pure ice.

Now I understood why Reida had suddenly taken off. The layer of powdery snow over the ice was very slippery, and it was hard to stop ourselves sliding down.

It was because the snow melted from underneath, due to the volcanic vent here.

We made our way down the slope very slowly, following the tracks made by Reida and Deyu.

I called out a few times, but the wind made so much noise that I would have been surprised had anyone heard me.

I had to stop several times to check our location according to my reader, and I had to make sure that I didn't drop it, because my hands were cold and the gloves were very awkward; and if it fell, I might not be able to find it in the snow.

It became impossible to see where they had gone, because the wind erased the tracks immediately after we passed.

The cliff wall loomed out of the mist. The wind was not so strong here, but the snow was quite deep in places.

We reached the bottom of the valley, with the pond issuing steam into the air.

The snow had recently been disturbed in a lot of places. Dark spots marked the whiteness.

My heart jumped.

That looked like . . .

Sickness rose in my stomach when I skied closer. Yes, the patches were dark red in the snow.

I called out, "Nicha!"

He came to me. "Is that . . ."

I took off my glove and picked up some of the red-stained snow.

Thayu and Evi had pulled out weapons. They squinted into the mist.

The snow had a faint earthy scent. The stains appeared to have come from underneath. Nicha kicked a lump in the snow. It burst open, spraying rust-red fluid all over the snow.

"Well, what the hell is that?"

Ynggi held a clump of snow to his nose. "It's a plant, or a fungus."

I blew out a breath. For a moment there, it had really looked like someone had been murdered and torn to pieces here.

But that still left two questions: where were Deyu and Reida? And why had they kicked open the lumps in the snow?

"The tracks continue there," Ynggi said.

He was right. The tracks made by the skis continued on the other side of the pond.

We walked around the pond through the slushy, slippery snow.

The direction of the wind was such that the clouds of steam from the pond blew into the gorge, making it really hard to see.

I called, "Deyu, Reida, are you there?"

There was no reply.

We advanced into the gorge, following the tracks in the snow. I went in front, keeping my hand on the gun in my pocket.

Thayu and Evi had their weapons out as well.

The light was low in here, and the sheer grey walls seemed like they could collapse on us any moment.

The snow was very deep in places here, and whirled about with the wind. It had started snowing more heavily, or the loose snow was being blown into the gorge from higher up the mountain.

The gorge opened up into a field of snow-covered boulders.

"Where to now?" I asked.

A feeling of despair crept up on me. The weather was really too bad to keep searching for much longer. I was getting really cold, and if I felt this way, I hated to think what Nicha and Thayu felt.

And Reida and Deyu.

Damn it.

"This way," Ynggi said. He pointed with his tail and then grabbed his tail and tucked it back under his jacket.

I couldn't tell how he knew where to go, but Pengali were good at tracking so I trusted him.

Nicha and Thayu went ahead. It was hard going because the snow was very deep in the spaces between the boulders, and the wind blew snow into our faces.

Then out of the snowstorm, above the roar and whistle of the wind, came another sound.

Nicha and I stopped, eyeing each other. I saw the question in his eyes. *What was that?*

I called, "Thayu, stop."

She ducked behind one of the boulders.

A person came out of the whirling snow, struggling through the powdery drifts.

"We're here!" Nicha yelled.

The person must have heard him because the silhouette came in our direction. Thayu reached out a hand and hauled him through the snow behind the rock where she stood. Him, because it was Reida.

"Where is Deyu?" Thayu asked.

"Back there," Reida said, pointing to where he had come from.

"What happened?" I asked Reida.

"I hit this slope back there and those slides are so slippery that I just took off." He panted. "I didn't know how to stop. I went all the way down the hill and I fell into really slippery stuff near the hot water spring. Deyu shot past me, but I don't know that she saw me. I tried to call her but she didn't reply. And then I managed to get out of the slush and ran after her, but I ran into these giant *creatures*."

"Creatures?" I'd heard of native fauna on Tamer, but no one knew much about it.

"Yeah, they're big and hairy and they have *horns* on their heads and back. Many horns."

"Did they threaten you?"

"I didn't hang around to wait."

"Where are these creatures?"

"Over there." He pointed into the snow and mist. I couldn't see anything.

"What about Deyu. Did you see where she went?"

He shook his head. His eyes were wide. Deyu was his *zhayma*. I was unsure what sort of relationship they had, but it was common for *zhayma*s to share a comforting sexual relationship. Losing a *zhayma* was everyone's nightmare.

Evi grabbed his heavy-duty gun. "We'll go and find her."

But no one moved.

We knew we'd been defeated.

The way ahead was covered in deep powdery snow that was almost impossible to walk through. Visibility was no more than a couple of metres. The wind blew up whirling clouds of white fluff that bit into exposed skin.

I was cold. Everyone was cold. There were big animals out there.

I started, "I think we should go back to the shuttle and explore the area with the drone. We may have better equipment, too, and we could—"

"Wait." Nicha unclipped his gun from his arm bracket and raised it.

We looked in the direction he pointed.

From the shadows in between a couple of jagged rocks came a shaggy animal. It held its head close to the ground, horns poised. It was followed by another one and another.

They had long hairy pelts, matted into dreadlocks, which trailed over the snow. A set of horns grew from their shoulder blades, and the backs and sides were protected by a shieldlike growth, like a rhinoceros. In fact the whole animal was a bit like a rhinoceros, only much taller. And a lot hairier.

The animals came slowly up the hill towards us.

"There is another group," Nicha said.

These animals were a bit further down the hill, and they were using their horns to open mounds of snow, and eating what was inside. Here was my answer to what had happened to the lumps of snow near the hot water spring.

"They don't look very aggressive," Nicha said.

But I wondered what the horns and plates on their backs were for. Reida said, "Look."

We looked where he was pointing. Another group of animals was coming up the hill. And someone in a thick fur coat sat on the top of the first one.

"Its Deyu."

It was true. She sat on the back of a giant animal with horns as long as my arm. Its fur was black and glossy.

The animal slowly ambled to where we stood, followed by a couple of others, and came to a stop. Deyu slid off, using the shoulder horns to hold on.

When she came towards us, the animal followed, blowing steam out of its nostrils.

"They're quite peaceful," she said.

Reida gave her a doubtful look. They definitely did not *look* peaceful.

Deyu patted the animal on the shield. "They like to sit in the sunlight, and collect warmth with this plate on their backs. When there is no sun, they like to wallow in hot water. When you sit on the plate, especially someone Coldi like me, they like it, because we're warm."

"I am not too much of a fan of those horns," Reida said.

"They use them to dig for food."

One of the animals demonstrated just that when it started digging into a mound and uncovering the orange stuff. A few other animals joined it, trampling the red juice that squirted up into the snow until it looked like someone had been murdered.

"Come on, try riding them," Deyu said. She grabbed the animal's horns and swung herself up.

Reida was the first one to try. I think that after his adventures with a horse in New Zealand, he was still trying to impress us by how well he could handle animals. But Deyu was pretty much a natural in all the ways he was not.

The animal shook its shaggy head, and though those horns might not be for defending itself, they were certainly quite sharp. He retreated.

"No, not like that," Deyu said. "Touch the shield first. They like warmth."

Reida reached out and patted the shield. "It feels like . . . it's soft."

The animal leaned into him.

Then he grabbed the horns and got as far as swinging himself onto the animal's back, before the animal shook itself and he flew off into the snow.

Everyone laughed.

Deyu was right, the creatures were quite peaceful and completely unafraid of people.

We all got close. They liked being touched on the shields on their backs, which felt like rubber.

They even followed us for a bit when we went back in the direction of the shuttle. We had established that yes, it was possible to get to the lakeshore by going up the mountain and then walking through the gorge, following in the steps of these animals from one hot spring to another.

17

———

THE ANIMALS FOLLOWED US all the way back to the shuttle.

At some point, Deyu climbed back onto the big animal—I decided it was one of the leaders of the herd.

I had a try at riding one, too.

My animal was smaller and lighter in colour. When I heaved myself onto the back, holding on by the horns as Deyu said, the animal's ears twitched up and sideways. Because of the shaggy fur, I had not noticed the ears, but they had very long ears, like a lop-eared rabbit, only the size of the animal made the ears as long as my forearm.

"I think they may use their ears for communicating," Deyu said.

Nicha had to try riding, too. Thayu was more cautious, but she lifted Ynggi up to sit with Nicha so that he wouldn't keep sinking in the snow. Ynggi tucked his tail in between his back and Nicha's front.

It was surprisingly nice to sit on this creature. The shield was like a saddle, soft and comfortable. I sank into it a bit and it moulded around my body. It was black, possibly to gather as much warmth as possible. The animal's many sets of horns made a swaying fence before me. The feet were broad and hairy, with no sign of hooves or nails. The creature walked like a camel, moving both legs on the same side. This swaying effect made it a very effective snowplough.

Seeing us sit comfortably even enticed Thayu to climb onto one of the creatures. She seemed a bit skittish when the animal tossed its head, but soon relaxed.

Since they did not have a name, we decided to call them *neshi*, from *neshya*, which was a Coldi word for a type of heavy armoured vehicle that the army used to traverse hostile terrain. On Asto, that was mostly deep sandy desert drifts, but it would work in snow, too.

Evi walked ahead and led the column through the narrow pass between the rocky spikes on the ridge and then down the hillside to the shuttle. It was easier for him to walk through the snow, because he was much taller than everyone else. We were now backtracking the path we had made ourselves.

The cargo door of the shuttle opened. Rixya sat behind the big gun.

Oh, damn.

I waved. The gun barrel lowered. Rixya got up.

Yana and Taleyu joined him at the door, staring at us and our hairy companions. Even Telaris came from inside the cabin.

"We have found a way to go down to the lake," I called out to them when we were closer. "We're just picking up some things."

Picking up meant that Telaris would come, and Rixya as well, because he wanted to scout out for something that would allow him to repair the shuttle. Telaris went back inside and came out quickly wearing his thick jacket, boots and his giant gun slung across his back.

He tossed a pack into the snow and went back into the main cabin to get another pack.

Then he brought out a box. "Anyone hungry? We should take some food."

He was right, and he tossed a handful of rations to each person, and we stuffed them into our pockets or bags. Reida wanted his drone, so he took it apart into a couple of pieces and found a bag to carry it, and the charger.

Rixya was the last to be ready. He jumped down with two packs, and waded through the snow to where we waited with the herd. He and Telaris were also hesitant to get onto any of the animals, so they walked ahead with Evi. Telaris gave his pack to Reida to carry on one of the animals, but Rixya insisted on carrying his own. I wondered why he needed two packs and what was in them.

He had not been the most talkative sort, probably constrained by the military version of the *sheya* instinct, which I had heard was particularly strong in the armed forces. If I wanted to talk to him, I needed to go through Yana. Yet Yana couldn't go with us because leaving two *zhayma*s in charge could lead to problems.

I thought I was beginning to understand. I didn't *think* my absence in the hospital earlier had caused Thayu and Nicha to fight, but that was the way an association worked. Someone had to be in charge. If there was no one, the void led to problems.

First we went back up the hill, through the passage between the spiky rocks; then we turned left into the gorge, where we found the path trampled by the *neshi* herds.

As we already knew, it led straight to the hot water vent at the shore of the lake.

The herd had passed here many times in the recent past, and the ground consisted of solid trampled snow. The one thing that could be said about these animals was that they were not particularly fast. Evi, Telaris and Rixya walked ahead, and the *neshi* barely kept up. It was a bit boring, sitting here in single file between two sheer rock walls.

Nicha, in front of me, dug out a food ration and unwrapped it. That was a good idea.

I had ended up with one Coldi ration and one Aghyrian package. I knew the Coldi ration contained a block of protein and crisp mushrooms. It was fairly boring, but filling.

I unwrapped the Aghyrian packet. Inside I found a block that consisted of compressed, cream-coloured granules. I sniffed it. Oo—er. That was a mistake. A pungent smell reminiscent of strong cheese hit me in the face. I took a small bite. It was salty, and creamy, and stuck to my tongue.

It tasted better than it smelled.

I took another bite, but then decided I couldn't eat something that smelled like that, rewrapped it and stuck it back in my pocket for another time when I was really desperate.

I broke my Coldi ration in half and ate that instead.

The gorge opened out into a gentle slope. We couldn't see the shuttle from here because it was behind a rocky outcrop.

The column of animals slowly walked down to the Lake Shore, led by Evi, Telaris and Rixya. I wriggled my reader out of the pocket of my jacket to check the time. It seemed like we had been in these mountains all day.

While I was trying to read the screen with eyes watering from cold, a sound echoed from the ridge behind us like a hoarse cry.

All animals in the herd raised their ears straight up. They stopped walking and listened. Heads went up and turned around.

"What was that?" Thayu asked.

I wasn't sure if I wanted to take a guess.

Evi had gone a little distance before he realised that the herd was no longer following him. He turned around—and the front of the group broke into a run down the mountain. They charged past Evi, Telaris and Rixya.

The sound came again.

I turned around to look at what could possibly have made that noise up on the mountain ridge, but I could see nothing because of the mist.

But the herd started running. The big animals ran like camels, and produced a swaying motion that made it very hard to stay on their backs. I dug both my hands into the shaggy fur, but my hands were cold and numb and I bumped around without having any control.

The screeches were getting louder. Next to me Thayu was holding on for dear life, bent over the animal's back.

Nicha's animal ran past us, charging through deep snow, throwing up white clouds on its way to the shore.

I looked over my shoulder, and spotted a huge shape on the mountainside, walking on two feet like a giant bird, but much, much bigger. The muscles rippled under the leathery skin, the long tail whipped from side to side, lashing through the snow. The snout came to a sharp point, the mouth was open, with rows of long, needle-like teeth. The bulging yellow eyes roved.

It had the shape of a chicken, it ran like an ostrich, and looked like a lizard. It resembled some kind of dinosaur, and it was fast.

The others had seen it too. Ynggi's tail escaped from his jacket and snapped an alarmed warning.

Others drew their weapons.

Our poor herd of *neshi* had little chance. They stopped running and formed a tight circle, all the animals pressed together with their heads—and their horns—facing outwards, like a fortress wall.

Those of us who were riding the animals ended up inside the circle. My animal stood wedged between the others. Its flanks were moving with fast breaths, and it kept tossing its head. I had pulled up my legs so that they didn't get caught between the animals' flanks.

Thayu had done the same.

The animals were snorting and pushing and jostling.

Evi had gotten caught up in the middle of the circle and managed to stop himself getting squashed by climbing onto the hairy backsides, but Telaris and Rixya were caught outside.

Telaris unslung the big gun from his shoulder. The dinosaur was ripping down the mountainside and I knew Telaris would not have the time to set up the weapon and charge it.

Both Evi and Nicha fired at the same time from inside our fortress of horns. The charges both hit the dinosaur in the chest, engulfing it in a web of crackling light like lightning. It slowed briefly, and then opened its mouth. It let out a roar and a gout of fire.

Holy crap. A fire-spewing dragon.

Nicha aimed again, but Deyu yelled, "Stop! It likes the heat. That's why it's following us!"

She was right.

But the brief distraction had given Telaris the time to charge. He fired the big gun. A crackling beam of light sizzled through the air. Telaris did not miss.

The creature toppled and went down in the snow with a thud that made the ground shake.

Phew.

I blew out a breath.

But then light crackled over the animal's carcass. Fire bloomed from its belly, quickly engulfed the rest of the body. With a massive fireball, it exploded.

A spray of snow, flaming debris and burning pieces of meat flew into the air, and rained down on us, with sickening thuds where chunks of meat landed.

The air filled with a distinctly petrochemical smell.

I wiped a sticky piece of meat off my sleeve. It was already half-frozen.

Holy crap.

"Everyone all right?" I asked.

"This creature stinks." Telaris wiped his face. He'd copped the full blast.

"You did the job," I said. I hated to think of the alternative. If these creatures had reserves of rocket fuel in their stomachs, they were walking bombs.

Ynggi's tail snapped.

And Deyu said, "There!"

She pointed.

Two more dinosaurs came running down the hill.

We had no time to make decisions, the decision was made for us.

As one, our column of pack animals, cumbersome and heavy as they looked, broke the circle, and barrelled at full speed down the hillside in the direction of the frozen lake. I held onto the fur of my animal for dear life. All I could see was Thayu bumping around on the back of her animal in front of me, and Evi hanging onto the back of another animal, mostly being dragged through the snow.

I didn't know if everyone was with us. I didn't know if Telaris was safe.

The animals at the front of the column reached the shoreline, and ran onto the ice. I prepared to jump off and swim, or rescue others, but the ice held for now.

Then they slowed down, but kept walking.

I checked, and everyone was present. Nicha, Reida and Deyu on their animals, Rixya and Telaris walking while he fiddled with his gun.

"It's damaged or wet," he said. "It won't work."

Rixya was trying to help him.

I didn't mind that the gun didn't work. I wasn't sure if it was such a good idea to conjure giant fireballs on the ice or anywhere close to it.

The ice cracked under our weight, but did not break.

The dinosaurs stopped at the shoreline. One of them tried the ice but it made a big creaking sound, and it sank through to its knees. It pulled itself out and clambered back onto the shore.

The herd of *neshi* continued to walk further away from the shore. The ice protested under their weight. The loud pops of growing cracks echoed through the valley.

"It's going to break," Thayu said. Her eyes were wide. Coldi hated water. They hated ice.

We held our breath.

But the ice held.

These lumbering pack animals knew how to avoid this big predator. Likely, they had done this many times before.

At the shoreline, both dinosaurs had turned around and started gobbling up pieces of the carcass of the animal Telaris had shot.

They showed no sign of intending to leave.

But I really wanted to get off this treacherous ice. I kept seeing how the army had marched across and how many of them had fallen into the freezing water. The wind had long since erased their footsteps so we could not see which route was unsafe.

From where we were in the middle of the lake, I could see the shuttle on the hillside in the distance.

There was no reception and we could not reach them unless we set off an emergency beacon. But everyone including the big ship out there, including the base on the lakeshore, would be able to hear it, and, more importantly, trace where the signal went. We could only do that in a very dire emergency.

It was *cold* out here. The biting wind blew loose snow over the grey surface of the ice.

We dismounted and walked between the animals, out of the wind. The ice was slippery, especially with the powdery snow over the top.

The *neshi* did not slip because of their fur-covered feet. They continued at a steady pace in a long line.

All we could do was hope that this dinosaur got tired of playing the game before it got dark.

We got the *neshi* to stop briefly so we could eat something, but it was a miserable meal, and none of us were very hungry.

Telaris had pulled a side panel off the gun, and he and Evi were fiddling inside, shutting the panel, turning it on. I could see on their faces that they hadn't had much success.

Something knocked the ice from below. I could feel the vibration of it through my feet.

Ynggi jumped up. "What was that?"

I said, "I have no idea what lives under there, and I'm not sure I want to."

We continued walking around, keeping ourselves warm, wondering if maybe we should go to the far shore of the lake, because we were too close to the base and the dinosaurs would attack us as soon as we came in their direction. They might even make it onto the ice. They might melt the ice. They might break it and drown all of us. Dangerous as it was to shoot them, we didn't even have the big gun anymore to defend ourselves.

"Look, there!" Reida said.

A blue light had flashed on the outside of the bunker. The door opened and light spilled out. As they had yesterday, rows of men marched out, in the direction of the lake.

Great.

Now we were caught in the open with two ferocious dinosaurs and the marching army.

The army showed no sign of having seen us, but then again, I doubted they would break ranks for us, if even half their comrades sinking into the water hadn't upset them.

When they came closer, there was only one place to hide: behind the animals.

The army seemed completely oblivious to us.

But they might be collecting information for whoever lived in that bunker.

I wanted to be close to the entrance of the building, so that we could sneak in with the army when they returned.

The dinosaurs had lost interest in us and appeared to have cleaned up the remains of their comrade. They had gone to the water's edge and were rolling in the steaming mud of the hot spring.

We weren't too far from the entrance, so we slowly started moving in that direction.

But after a short distance the dinosaurs rediscovered us. They had stopped rolling in the mud, and one tried to claw its way onto the ice. This was causing the ice to crack and crumble.

"What is the chance that if we leave these *neshi* here, it would go after them?" I said.

"I think they're equally likely to come after us," Deyu said. "They have learned that we—and our weapons—are a source of warmth."

And warmth was what drove creatures' actions on this ice ball of a world.

"We'll try anyway. We can't sit here and wait until it decides it's had enough of us."

We judged the distance to the bunker.

Could we run that far if necessary?

The marching army had turned around and was on its way back.

We had to do something.

So we took all our packs off the animals' backs. One of the dinosaurs was half in the water, trying to get onto the ice. The other stood in shallow water, pawing the mud. Occasionally, it put its snout in the water and blew out through its nostrils. This resulted in steaming froth.

The ice was cracking alarmingly, especially as the dinosaur was stirring up hot water. More and more steam rose from the hot spring.

We shouldered our packs and walked quickly away from the herd.

The *neshi* were not naturally fast walkers, but they followed us at a slower pace.

The army was coming closer, and still showed no signs of being interested in us at all. We were out in the open and, if they were going to do anything, they would have done so long ago.

"Come on let's go for it," I said.

We walked as fast as we could, I went first, Thayu and Nicha behind me, and the rest following.

Ynggi was one of the last ones. He had to run, his tail swinging free of his jacket.

It must have been the tail that captured the dinosaur's interest, and it made its way onto the ice, shaking water off its skin and coming in our direction.

The *neshi* herd—in between us and the dinosaur—broke into a run, also in our direction, but the ice was quite thin here, and cracked alarmingly.

"Quick!" I yelled.

You never had to spur a Coldi person to run quicker. All of them were much faster than I was, and overtook me. We were almost at the shore. Where the water met the land, the ice was really thin, more like slush. Thayu and Evi waded through the knee-deep slippery slush, reaching the shoreline safely. Ynggi and I were quite slow compared to the others, and the herd was catching up with us, chased by the dinosaur.

The ice cracked under my feet. Water bubbled up from the cracks, making the ice even more slippery.

Reida at the shoreline had taken out his gun. He was firing full blast at the dinosaur.

Deyu had taken her gun out, too, but she did something else: she fired at the ice. Each time the charge hit the ice, a flash bloomed out from the spot, turning ice to water under the dinosaurs feet.

It sank, scattering chunks of ice.

The dinosaur threshed in the water, and a few of the *neshi* slid in as well.

The army of Tamerians had arrived, but as I had half-expected, they did nothing. A couple of the soldiers even marched right into the water, without looking. It was a cesspool of frothing water and panicked creatures, with water rising between the cracks in the ice underfoot.

Ynggi was quite slow, because he was so small, so I grabbed him by the back of the coat and dragged him the remaining distance to the shore. Behind us a wail erupted.

A huge thing came out from under the water, threshing and fighting with the dinosaur. The water became murky with mud and blood.

The *neshi* bellowed and screamed. The dinosaur thrashed. The creature's head came out of the water. It was smooth like a snake's head, pale grey with scales like a fish. Long fins ran down each side of the neck. It grabbed the dinosaur with its fanged teeth. The dinosaur roared and clawed over the creature's snout. It let go of the dinosaur, which landed in the water with a huge splash. The water creature lunged again, biting into the dinosaur's leg with enough force that I could hear bones crack.

The dinosaur limply disappeared under the water and the water creature went down with it. A few of the *neshi* managed to scramble back onto the ice. They ambled off towards the shore, wet and bedraggled.

Ynggi and I reached the shoreline safely, but shaken, cold and wet.

The army of Tamerians had reached us, and instead of marching on, they had stopped, forming a half-circle around us.

Their faces were like wax in the cold light, their eyes like empty holes. Their faces barely moved, their heavy brows locked in a perpetual frown.

Most of the soldiers were very similar, without distinctions on their dark uniforms, and those uniforms were absolutely inadequate for the weather.

None of them said anything.

"Can you take us to your leader?" I said.

There was no reaction from the wall of silent faces. At least twenty of them had gathered around us, while the others waited behind, with no indication that they were curious—or even human, for that matter.

I mimicked being cold, but they did not react. I mimicked eating, because maybe we might find some sympathy.

But they just stared at me.

"Please, we have news about Puck."

At the mention of the name, their faces lost the blank expression. They glanced at each other, frowning.

"Puck," I repeated. "He came to us and lived in our town. I was going to teach him to surf." I wasn't going to go into the fact that Puck had been killed by his own people.

Now one of the men said, "Surf."

He said the word in the same dead voice that Puck also used.

A second one repeated it.

But another one raised his weapon.

Immediately Reida, Nicha and Thayu grabbed their weapons.

"Whoa, stop, stop!" I lifted my hands. "We come here in peace. We have lost someone. His name is Benton Leck."

This name elicited more frowns and confused looks.

I continued, "We are friends of his."

It was unlikely that Tamerians would understand the concept of the word friend, but I was out of ideas. How did one communicate with people who didn't even understand the concept of eating?

I blundered on, "Take us to your leader."

"Leader," one man repeated, and another echoed him.

"Leader."

Without a word, they turned around and started off in the direction of the bunker.

18

THAYU AND I GLANCED at each other, and then looked at Nicha.

What the hell? Did this mean that we could come with them?

The other Tamerians followed the first ones, ignoring us. They returned to marching in their straight lines, with serious faces, and acting as if we weren't there.

I called out, "Come on, let's go."

I stepped into line with the rear part of the army. Thayu came with me, followed by the others.

The Tamerians did not even acknowledge us. They didn't try to stop us either.

From close up, the bunker looked even more forbidding than it had in the view from the drone.

The wall that faced the frozen lake was quite high, and although there were windows, as we had seen, they were at least two or three floors off the ground. The door that slid open was itself more than two floors tall. It stood open now, and resembled a dark maw.

Maybe, at some point, vehicles came out of this entrance. It was certainly big enough, although I couldn't see where these vehicles would go, unless they used the frozen lake for something, like taking off. But there were no tracks. Did this place have a summer where the lake was free of ice? If so, would you want to sail a boat on it, knowing the size of those creatures that lived in the water?

We followed the soldiers inside a huge dark hall where it was hard to see the ceiling.

All the soldiers arranged themselves in the middle, in a grid pattern with straight lines. There had to be more than a hundred of them.

None of them said a word.

The big sliding door closed with a soft zoom and then a final thud that echoed through the hall.

Light came on in the ceiling, a blue-green hue that washed out any cheerful colours. It reminded me a bit of the old-fashioned pearl lights in Barresh, which produced the same kind of dead, greenish light. These days, those cheap pearls were only used as streetlights.

The hall was bare. There was nothing on the concrete walls, nothing on the floor, no furniture, no doors. Except for the door we had just come through, the only way out of the hall was through a low-ceilinged corridor in the far wall.

The soldiers just stood there, waiting silently.

I wasn't sure what we should do, whether someone would turn up or we would be stopped if we went into the corridor.

Then the sound of footsteps echoed from this passage.

A moment later, an old man came into the hall. He was quite tall, most of his head was bald, and the little ring of hair that surrounded his head was white. He wore a dark-coloured robe with, underneath, a vest that was made from the skin of an animal. He also wore fur boots and a thick woollen shawl.

His eyes met mine, and his face cleared.

"You came."

The man was Benton Leck, academic from Barresh. More gaunt and thin than I remembered, but otherwise looking healthy.

"Were you expecting us?" I asked.

"My equipment is quite poor upstairs," he said. "But I did send my wife a message that I know she received. I was hoping that she would make enough of a fuss that someone would come. It seems she has. She's very good at creating fuss." He smiled. "But do come upstairs, out of this dreadfully cold hall."

He turned around and was about to go into the corridor, when he seemed to remember something.

He stepped aside, and called out to the army, "Go upstairs first. Then dinner."

And then he added to us, "Step aside for a bit while they pass. They are not the smartest."

"We've noticed."

I was keen to quiz him on what he knew about the Tamerians.

The army marched through the corridor, the air heavy with the sound of so many footsteps. None of them spoke, none of them looked aside.

By my guess, there were at least a hundred soldiers in the group.

They walked through the corridor and up the stairwell at the end.

We followed them, albeit at a slower pace, because Benton did not walk very well.

"Are you well?" I asked him.

"The cold messes with my arthritis. The food here is very monotonous. I guess I could be healthier."

"How long have you been here?"

"I'll tell you all about it when we get upstairs. I need something warm." And to be honest, walking with us seemed to take all of his breath.

We got to the broad staircase and walked up painfully slowly. The stairs led into a large dining hall, where some soldiers already sat at rows of tables and some filed in after whatever happened "upstairs". Apart from the tables, the hall was as bare and featureless as the passage and entry hall downstairs.

It was incredible how such a large group of people could be so silent. All the people I could see were Tamerians, and all were male.

Each of the soldiers faced a plate and a cup. A couple of soldiers were walking through the aisles with a trolley that contained a large pot. One of them would get a plate, and the other would put a spoonful of glop on it. The soldiers who had received their food started eating. Most of them appeared to finish quickly, and continued staring at their plates. I wondered if this was all they received.

"Come." Benton Leck set off through the aisle that led through the middle of the hall.

We came past the trolley and I glanced into the pot. Whatever the stuff was inside, it didn't look terribly appetising: a pale kind of porridge, like very watery mashed potatoes.

"That's standard fare for the army," Benton Leck said. "We will have something better."

"It doesn't look like they get a lot of food," I said.

"Don't worry, it's incredibly nutritious. If you were to eat what they're getting, you'd feel so full, you'd be ill."

We reached the other side of the hall, where he took us through a door into a smaller room, which was much more homely and comfortable.

This room was also where the windows were. A couch sat in the corner, and a couple of chairs were arranged around a bowl that looked like a gas burner, where cheerful flames leaped into the air. Warmth seeped through the room.

A tray with covered bowls stood on the low table that faced the couch.

"Sit down."

We did, and Benton Leck pulled another chair closer.

This chair had been facing the window, through which we could see the last pale glimmers of daylight over the mountains that lay on the other side of the frozen lake.

"Could you see us coming through here?" I asked.

"I could."

He took the lids off the bowls on the table. Inside was some kind of stew, as well as something that looked like protein cubes. He put out bowls on the table and spooned some of both mixtures into each of them.

I wasn't game to ask what was in the stew.

"I'm afraid the fare is not of the standard that you're used to," he said. "It's nutritious, and that's about all that can be said in favour of it."

I tried a bit. It tasted bland and floury.

For a while, we all ate. The members of my team had been quiet since we arrived here, but they were all alert and each looking out for the things that were their expertise. Thayu glanced at the ceiling and corners of the room for listening equipment; Ynggi sat with his head cocked, listening out for sounds elsewhere in the building. Deyu studied the furry rug on the floor. Reida had put a scanner on the seat next to him, with a map of the building displayed on the screen. He'd made that while walking through.

"Are you alone here?" I asked.

"I am. Sometimes other people visit, but I have not seen anyone for a long time."

"Other people?"

He looked out the window, where the light was almost gone. I could see his face in the reflection of the glass.

"I was not very smart, and I made a big mistake," he said, his voice low. "I thought this project would be interesting."

"Your wife told me that your employer was going to pay you quite a lot of money."

"Well, as you can see, money is not everything. There is not much use for money in a place like this." He chuckled. "Maybe, if I ever get out of here."

"You don't sound hopeful. We have every intention of getting out of here, so all you need to do is follow us."

He chuckled again. "You don't know these people and, besides, I'm an old man."

"Rest assured, getting you out of here is one of the main reasons we're here. We're not leaving without you."

He gave me a sad, droopy-eyed look that, to be honest, shook me. Maybe it was because he was very old—at least in his late seventies if not older—and his eyes were naturally droopy and watery and lack of exposure to sunlight had made his skin waxy and almost transparent. My father was old but his face was a lot more bronzed and healthy-looking, if probably also more wrinkled. But they were *good* wrinkles. They were wrinkles of happy experiences, of time spent on his boat and walking the dog and fixing up the community's solar plant with Erith and their friends.

This man was . . . I didn't know. Ancient. Vulnerable. He unnerved me.

"So, tell us how you got here." Back to comfortable ground.

"I barely even know where to start," he said. "I made so many bad choices. I was offered a position with the human tree project. But somehow I got it into my mind that I was going to be the lost stepchild, and that my research would not receive the attention it deserved. So I decided to strike out on my own, and make my own project, the language tree. This was a number of years ago, before all of this happened."

He gestured at the room in general.

"So when did you first come into contact with the people you're working for now, and who are they?"

"I'm coming to that." He picked up his cup and sipped from his tea. His hand trembled.

"I was quite attracted to the money. I think it is pretty much a universal truth that the humanity sciences are the poor stepchild of science in general, and they never attract quite as much interest. It's as if people feel that the information your research gives them is not worth very much. It is much more lucrative to be in the medical sciences or engineering, for example. If you can make a different type of engine, or cure a particular disease, you'll get plenty of funding. Whereas we just talk about languages or how people feel, and people don't think that's terribly important."

A lot of bitterness in those few sentences. "So you thought that you were going to be a second rate part of the human tree project?"

"Something like that. I also have to admit that some of the people in it rub me the wrong way. I know that's a wrong thing to say, and we should all be professional and objective, but life is hardly like that."

He looked away when he said this, and I strongly suspected that this involved Lilona and maybe even me. Out of all the people from Earth who lived in Barresh, Benton Leck was one of the ones I'd had the least contact with. Maybe he thought that I didn't like him. The truth was that I didn't have much contact with any of the other people from Earth either, save Melissa, and that was only because she lived on the island. I didn't need Melissa, I didn't even like her terribly much, and I didn't need contact with expats from Earth in the first place.

"But I am glad that you've come," he said. "Really glad. I hope you understand that."

"Do continue." This whole preamble was starting to feel like a bunch of excuses for something terrible that he was about to tell us.

"So, while I was looking for funds, someone came to me."

"Jasper Carlson?"

His cheeks went red. "How do you know that?"

"The Exchange leaves all kinds of trails. One of our team is a lawyer, and he knows exactly where contracts are stored and how to retrieve them."

He gave us a startled look, as if he had not realised this.

"I didn't know anything about the Tamerian project," he said. He sounded defensive.

"You should have asked."

"Yes, but I was quite desperate. They said it would be explained once I got here."

"So you signed a work contract while you had no idea what you were supposed to do?"

"Well, I signed the contract, which was for gathering information about the language tree, I would give the information to my employers, and I would be able to write about it. As you will understand, this was most important to me, as an academic."

"The publication?"

"Yes. You're not an academic so you wouldn't know, but an academic career falls or stands with what you publish and how many people reference your work. If you ask for funding, that is the first thing they will ask."

Ah, I saw. And I guessed he had neglected this aspect and had been working on his little projects and it wasn't important until he wanted to work on a big project, his magnum opus, and for reasons of rivalry or personality issues, needed to strike out on his own.

"How did you end up here?"

He gave me a shifty look. "What do you mean?"

"Quite literally: how did you get here? I know there's no way to come here through the Exchange. How did you come here? Who are these people who paid for your work?"

"I have sworn not to talk about it. Please, don't ask me, because they will harm my wife if I tell you."

"Your wife has gone back to Miran."

His eyebrows—white and with rogue bristly hairs—flicked up. "Has she?"

"Yes. Does that surprise you? She was worried about her safety and went to stay with her family."

"Did anything happen to her?"

"She is fine."

He blew out a breath. "I tried to contact her, but I realised they were listening in and nothing is secret. I couldn't tell her to get help."

"She got it anyway."

"But you're stuck here with me. After I started working on this project, they abandoned me."

"And the project, I guess, is that you were asked to try to communicate with Tamerians?"

"Something like that. They tried to make superhumans, but while Tamerians are strong and have a lot of advantages in a fight, the main flaw of Tamerians is that they don't communicate well. Some say that this is by design, because they didn't want people to challenge their orders. But if you take away the capacity to challenge orders—the capacity to think independently—the result is that Tamerians don't seem to think and communicate at all. I was hired to find out how they communicate."

"Hired, by whom?"

"Look, I already said that I can't talk too much about it. I've tried to disable the listening devices that I knew existed in this building, but there will be many others. I want to see my wife again." His cheeks coloured.

All right, let's take a step back. "Where do the Tamerians come from?"

"Most of the ones you see in this building were already here when I arrived. Supposedly, they're elite troops, but if they really are, heaven help us for the rest of the army."

He was deflecting my question, ever so smartly. "Were they made, or born or what?"

"I have never seen that facility. Sometimes they bring new ones, but they're always adults. I don't know if children exist."

"Are they made in orbit?"

"In orbit? What do you mean?"

"There could be a station." Or just a giant ship, for that matter.

"I know nothing about that."

That was quite definite in a way that meant this was something else he didn't want to talk about or genuinely didn't know. I didn't want to antagonise him, so I changed the subject.

"Have you found how they communicate?"

"They seem to use very subtle body language. They don't use sound at all."

"Has anyone tested their hearing?" Deyu said.

That was an interesting thought. But no, at least Puck could hear. I could also not imagine how superhumans could be deaf.

Benton Leck said, "A lot of their communication is so subtle that it's hard for us to pick up. One of them will catch up and then the others all follow for whatever reason."

"Are these leaders always the same people?" Deyu asked.

"No, I looked at that angle, but I can't see any patterns in their behaviour."

"Except that they march onto the ice every day," I said.

"There has to be a reason that they do that," Deyu said. "They've been told, or do it out of habit, or there is some other reason."

Benton Leck frowned at her.

I introduced her. "This is Deyu Omi, a member of my association. She has a particular interest in the behaviour of animals."

"Is she a scientist?"

"No, but she has a lot of practical knowledge."

His expression remained suspicious. I knew that in many circles on Asto, the Omi clan was not highly regarded. They were workers, mostly lived in the vast Eighth Circle sleeper cities of Athyl and did not often make it to other worlds.

It was a sign of Nicha's brilliance that he had picked both her and Reida to come and join our team. I had asked him to think outside the usual box, and he certainly had done that. Both the youngsters were developing into very fine people indeed, and I would defend Deyu against these arrogant attitudes.

"Go ahead, Deyu, and tell him what you discovered about the behaviour of the *neshi*."

Benton Leck frowned. "Neshi?"

"That's what we decided to call those hairy herbivores, because they're kind of like armoured vehicles."

"They're smarter than you think."

"We discovered that."

And then I had Deyu tell him about their behaviour, how they used their long ears to communicate and how they were attracted to heat and how they could be used to transport people from one side to the other without the use of noisy vehicles.

His interest picked up when she was speaking, but when she finished, he asked no questions.

So I asked him, "In your experience, can the Tamerians be used in similar fashion? Is there anything in particular that motivates them to do something?"

"If there is, I have not discovered it."

"But you certainly have a vocabulary of words they use and their meaning?"

"I do, but it is very short."

"Can you show us?"

He got up from his seat, and went to the bed in the corner, where there was a small pile of books. He pulled out an old-fashioned book with dog-eared pages which he gave to me.

On the first page, Benton had drawn a crude representation of the typical Tamerian: male, squat, with a heavy brow. He noted that most had dark hair and an olive skin.

"It's a few pages in," he said to me.

I leafed through another few pages of notes about Tamerian behaviour—mostly about their lack of verbal communication, and found the list.

I gestured for Deyu to sit next to me.

She joined me on the couch, a comfortable warm presence in an otherwise quite chilly room. It had started snowing outside, and the wind lashed snowflakes against the window. Many of them did not even melt, but slid down the glass and settled on the windowsill.

The list was only two pages long.

I looked for the word Puck and surf, but I didn't see them on the list. Instead it contained words like "come" and "see", and other really simple commands, including the word "dinner" which he had used downstairs when we first came in.

I asked him, "Are you sure that these are words that they use to communicate?"

He looked at me, kind of offended. "These are words they understand. They don't use any words if I don't ask them."

"Would you say that these are words that you taught them?"

"Of course they are. Have you heard them speak voluntarily? They speak because we ask them a question."

My mind went back to when I had first met Puck, when I had been in the hospital and he had donated his blood. Rather, he had been told to donate his blood. By Jasper Carlson?

I had asked him questions and he had given single-word replies. He had repeated parts of my speech. Had he cottoned onto the word "surf" because he had picked it out of what was for him an unintelligible mush of my words?

He had mentioned the word "ski" as well. I had put it in his mouth. Likely, Jasper had called him "Puck" and likely, he had learned to associate the word with "name".

"So your task was to understand their communication. But that is not an easy task."

"It's an impossible task." He shook his head. "I am a professor of linguistics. I cannot talk to people who don't talk. They don't seem to comprehend any communication. It seems like whatever you say disappears into a black hole. They barely acknowledge that you've said anything. I didn't realise how bad it was until I got here. But by that time of course the people who supported me in the project had already gone. The project was to immerse myself with these men for a while so that I could learn the language and understand how they communicated. That's how I always studied many different types of people. These Tamerians don't seem to communicate at all. They go out every day, they march over the lake, and then they come back. Sometimes a new batch of them arrives, and sometimes others leave. They don't make friendships and don't seem happy or sad when people arrive or leave."

I said, "Yet there are some instances where I have communicated with them."

"You have?" His eyebrows flicked up. "Yes, sometimes I have thought so, too. Sometimes I will say something and there will be a slight reaction. But I can never get any further."

"There was a Tamerian called Puck in Barresh," I said. "I have spoken to him, and he expressed an interest in learning to surf."

Benton Leck laughed. "You're serious?"

"Well, that is what I have been able to figure out. He mentioned surfing when I met him later. And when I mentioned his name just outside the building here, the Tamerians seemed to notice us and seemed to recognise his name. They stopped marching, and they allowed us to come inside when we mentioned Puck."

"That would be a first," Benton Leck said. "I think they simply allowed you to come with them. I don't know why they stopped. Half of them can drown in the lake on any of those trips, yet I have never seen any of them stop to look or try to rescue their fellows."

I glanced at the window, and realised the horror of what he must see every day when scores of men fell through the ice and were eaten alive by whatever monster lived in the depths of the lake.

We had seen the same theme often, of Tamerians completely abandoning their stricken mates. They did not come back to avenge their fellows, either.

If someone told them to shoot their fellows, they did. Like they did to Puck.

I asked, "Are they even human?"

"That is a very good question, isn't it? While not listening to their absent communication, I've had lots of time to ponder that and write philosophical pieces on what it means to be human."

"And what is your conclusion?"

"In some parts, they're human, in some parts, they're not. Mostly not."

I continued, "So, from the point of view of the creators, the Tamerian project is an utter failure. They tried to make superhumans, but they're not human. Yes, they have people who will obey, but no one is quite sure how to communicate orders. Tamerians have been made not to object to orders, but in doing so, all their initiative has been stripped as well. What then did the creators want you to do? Salvage their project? Have they now decided that it's a loss and abandoned you here?"

"That pretty much sums it up."

"Then why don't you still want to speak of who your employers are?"

"Because I still need to get out of here, don't I? And my wife is still at risk." His cheeks coloured.

"We're in the same boat. We can help if you can help us. We have a vehicle, but it's not operational. We need a new control module or, likely, need to 'borrow' someone else's transport. What equipment do you have here? Rixya here is tech crew and he will be able to assess if there's anything we can use. Just tell us what you have."

He hesitated. "I'm not a technical person."

"But vehicles arrive at this base, do they not? The big doors downstairs can let them into the building?"

"Oh, those doors haven't been used for that since I've been here."

"But how do people arrive here, then?"

"By air. They land on the roof."

That was something, finally. "Are there any aircraft here?"

"Look, I'll show you around tomorrow. It's dark now, anyway. I'll show you to the guest quarters that are as comfortable as it gets."

19

———

HE TOOK US OUT of the room, back through the short passage through the main doors.

In the big hall, the men had finished their dinner. A few men were collecting empty bowls. In the absence of any other sound, the clattering of bowls against each other sounded really loud.

It was cold here compared to the comfortable living room with the fire. Our breath steamed in the air, but the cold didn't appear to bother the men. I wondered what they had eaten, because a peculiar scent—resembling that of vinegar—hung in the hall.

We went out the door at the back of the hall into a dark narrow corridor. It was possibly even colder here, and there was virtually no light. I just hoped that the floor was even.

I said, "It's very dark in these places, even in the hall."

"They don't need much light to see," Benton Leck said. "Tamerians have excellent night vision."

I had already known that. In most of our dealings with Tamerians, they had done their jobs at night, when they were clearly at an advantage compared to my Coldi association, and that now included myself.

I sometimes got a feeling that the designers of Tamerians had overcompensated for the supposed failures of the Coldi and poor night vision was one of those things.

At the end of the corridor we came to a broad staircase that went up into a landing. There, Benton Leck opened a door to an apartment.

A fire burned in the hearth, and a few chairs stood around it on a carpet of fur. Deyu knelt and ran a hand through the fur. She looked at me. This was obviously fur from the *neshi*.

The apartment had no windows, and I guessed we were now in the part of the building that was dug into the mountainside.

Benton Leck said, "You'll be comfortable here, at least until you realise that there is no way out." He kept harping on about that.

"We have no intention of letting that stop us."

"You don't realise how dangerous it is out there."

"We do. We just came from there."

"This world looks dead, but around every corner, behind every rock and every layer of snow hide things that will kill you. Believe me, you are so much better staying safely indoors."

"Have you tried to escape?"

He spread his hands. "Where would I go? They're watching us from Dorell on the other side of the mountain ridge."

That was interesting. Jayten had said nothing to us about two bases. "What sort of place is that? Have you been there?"

"Everyone comes in through Dorell. How did you come in if you didn't know about Dorell?" He frowned at us.

"Wait." I took a deep breath as I realised the implications of what he said. "So, this Dorell uses the satellite out there in orbit as an alternate Exchange node, and it transports ships as well as communication?"

"I guess. I don't know anything about it. We just came normally, in a ship, from Barresh, just as one travels to other worlds."

"Tamer is not on the Exchange network and is not part of *gamra*."

Benton Leck gave me a disturbed look. "But they told me . . ."

"It doesn't matter what they told you. These people will not openly admit this anyway. You went outside the Exchange network."

"You're sure? But then how did you get here?"

"We used Asto's military sling, the one that everyone knows about but won't acknowledge the existence of."

His frown deepened.

I didn't understand why he, supposedly an academic, didn't know anything about this. But then again, Coldi had a term for this. There were people called *ichi*, who travelled to other worlds and were aware of all the between-world politics, and there were *ata-ichi*, people who preferred to live on one world and stay there. People at *gamra* were *ichi*; people like Eirani and my father were *ata-ichi*. Not that they didn't travel at all, but they liked to focus their energy locally.

I guessed we should have known that the alternate "dark" network that *gamra* had been fighting against for many years already existed, and that with help from the Aghyrian ship—which *gamra* had helpfully banished from inhabited space—this development had been given a boost.

And we were now in *their* space, and looking at the results of *their* network.

And Benton Leck had not even noticed anything unusual.

Another deep breath. "So, they made you swear that you wouldn't talk about who they are. But do you understand what these people are doing? Do you understand *what* they are? Do you know what is out there, watching us?"

He gave me a blank look.

"This is about the continual challenge to build a second Exchange network, one that allows shady people to circumvent the rules of the current Exchange. No, we did not come through Dorell, and we have seen the giant Aghyrian ship that watches from orbit." The ship that had tried to mislead us into believing that this was the main base, with the assumption that we would become stuck here as well, helped along by their firing at our ship as we left.

Oh, I was right not to have trusted Jayten.

"Well . . . well, even if I knew and believed what you say, what am I supposed to do? I'm just someone contracted for a job."

"But we are here now, and we're going to do something, because they know we're here, and I have no doubt they realise that we used the Asto military sling to get here. And they know Asto's army is waiting out there. And if they're smart they want to avoid a confrontation with that army, so they probably won't wait too long before they do something about us being here, and we want to leave before that happens."

Another disturbed look.

If he heard an implied threat in those words, then that might have been my intention. I was still trying to decide whether he was naive or trying to make me believe that he was. For one, why would he sign a work contract that didn't even spell out who he would be working for?

Was it really as simple as a need for money, as his wife had said?

Benton Leck gestured at the room. "Anyway, this room is comfortable and warm and you can stay here while you try to get your shuttle repaired."

Never mind that it was impossible to repair the unit that needed replacing.

Oh, how he liked to divert the conversation to comfortable topics.

He showed us the bedrooms that were to the side of the main living room. The apartment appeared well prepared, if a little unused. It was cold in there and smelled musty, and I couldn't see anything inside the bedrooms until he had made a light. None of the rooms had windows, and the only way out appeared to be through the main door.

"You should be comfortable here," Benton Leck said. "When you go down the stairs at the end of the hallway, you'll find a bathroom. It's rather lavish, although it looks a bit grim. It's safe—I've used it a few times. But, to be honest, it creeps me out a bit. Nothing is going to harm you there, but it's just, you know, creepy. But safe. I'll come back in the morning with breakfast and then we can talk further. I'll leave the door open, because I don't want you to think that I'm locking you up; but just so you know, the men can be quite volatile if they find you in a place where they don't expect you. They may look dumb, but they're not harmless."

I nodded. I knew.

And then he left us.

As soon as the door shut, the first thing that Thayu and Reida did was pull out their electronic equipment. They needed to check for bugs.

I let them walk around, holding their scanners up and checking all the corners and cupboards.

I wondered if there was a way to make some tea. I looked around, but there was no kitchen.

We were also going to have an issue with beds, because there were only eight and we needed nine. I guessed I could share a bed with Thayu, but . . . that wasn't going to end well.

I glanced at her backside while she walked through the apartment. Like a cat, I had called her when I first met her. Seeing her around had become a comfortable thing for me . . . until I was told that I wasn't allowed to touch her.

No, sharing a bed with her would not end happily, or at least not from the point of view of our promise to Lilona.

Thayu had finished a scan of the apartment, and found nothing in the way of bugs. My team never liked it when this happened, because it rarely meant that there were none. It just meant the bugs were of a type or in a place where the scanning didn't pick them up.

Thayu gestured *bathroom*.

This was code for us to gather in the least likely place where listening equipment would be successful. Even if a bathroom was bugged, the quality of the sound was hollow and echoey and it was easy to create additional sound that distorted the recording.

A meeting in the bathroom had become standard practice for us, but both Rixya and Ynggi looked a little puzzled.

We went down the stairs, a dark circular staircase of plain stone. I was curious about this creepy place.

Benton Leck had told us how the lights worked, so we turned on the one in the stairwell, and then the next one, but the greenish glow did little to dispel the gloom.

Towards the bottom of the stairs, I could smell the water. I could smell the dank mustiness of algae on stone.

We came out in a low-ceilinged room, where the smell of water was overwhelming. From somewhere within the darkness came the sound of water trickling into a pond.

Telaris turned on a light.

The room held a sizeable underground pool, filled with steaming water.

I could see what Benton Leck meant about grim. The entire room was made from dark stone: the edges of the basin, the benches around it, even the plain decorative feature that held the light. The ceiling was low. The place resembled something out of an old horror movie, and the coating of black algae on vertical surfaces did little to dispel that old, abandoned feel.

I went to the water and put a hand in. It was very warm.

"Presuming nothing lives in here, this should be a nice place to warm up."

I knew what I had said as soon as words left my mouth. Thayu gave me a mischievous look and all the feelings that I wasn't supposed to have yet rushed back to me.

My cheeks glowed.

She flicked up her eyebrows and I could almost hear her say, "Lilona said to wait."

Well, tough. I had this feeling that in this matter, Lilona might not have the last word.

The team gathered around the trickling water inlet, sitting down on the pool's edge and nearby bench, while Reida walked around with his scanner. He found nothing that concerned him.

I started, "So, what do we all think?"

"At least half of what he says is nonsense," Reida said.

Nods. We all agreed with that.

Nicha said, "Whatever is going on at that other base, that's where we want to be."

Again, there were nods all around. Reida brought up the graphic we had obtained from Jayten, which clearly showed the building of this base, but nothing in the valley to the north.

"Dorell, huh?" Deyu said, and she searched for the name. Only one reference came up. Marcus Dorell, freedom fighter for the Western Liberation Army in New California.

That was a coincidence, right?

On the other hand, probably not. Marcus was South African by birth and had moved to northern America specifically to fight, and had lost his citizenship over breaking the imposed sanctions to the area.

This was disturbing.

Imagine how bad it would have been had the no vote won the referendum on Earth.

I showed Thayu the information, and glanced at the soft skin in her neck while she read. She nodded, giving me a concerned look.

I said, "Jayten probably sent us here so that we can be occupied with this strange situation here and hopefully not be able to get to the other base."

Nicha snorted. "He didn't count on us having Deyu."

"She's our secret weapon," Thayu said.

Deyu's cheeks turned red.

I continued. "I think we should try to get out of here as soon as possible, but we have a number of issues. We don't know the way, we can't contact Yana and Taleyu back in the shuttle, and we don't know that Benton Leck will let us go."

"He will," Thayu said, with that typical finality that carried an implied threat. "I have a feeling that he has a lot more control over this army than he lets on. He's a linguist, he studied their communication, he's lived here with them for a while. When we first came in, he told them to get dinner. I think we may need to apply a bit of pressure to him and he will change his story. Something doesn't add up. He seems too naive."

Much as I hated to admit it, I agreed. I didn't think Benton Leck had told us the entire story, either.

"That army worries me," Nicha said.

More nods. We all knew how dangerous Tamerians could be. These ones seemed more obtuse than any we had met before, but I very much doubted that they were harmless.

I looked at Rixya. "Is there anything in particular that the Asto army knows about Tamerians?"

He rattled off, "Their command structure is unclear, probably internal. They don't display the behaviour of normal armed forces; they don't appear to give orders to each other and are probably more like individual contractors. They receive their orders electronically, and they usually possess electronic augmentations that give them superior fighting skills."

"Do they communicate through implants?"

"We have never found any sending abilities in equipment retrieved from Tamerians."

Retrieved. What a clinical way to say something so horrid.

He continued, "They appear to be the blunt end of a hammer, the part that hits the wall. Their orders go one way, and the individuals are disposable."

Coming from the mouth of what I already thought was a society of a high degree of disposability, this was quite astonishing. If even Coldi thought that Tamerians were disposable, they must be super-disposable.

I asked, "Do you know anything about how or where they are produced?"

"We've generally assumed that it is here at Tamer—"

"Or in orbit?"

"Yes, or in orbit. We cannot get our hands on precise data, but we perform a process called heat balance. The only thing we can find out about their transport and communication is through emitted radiation. That does not just cover transmissions or Exchange wakes. A body emits radiation. By looking at a ship, we can measure how many people are on board by the amount of heat it emits. By looking at a single place of arrival and departure, we can make a guess of the decline or accrual of population through the balance of people coming in versus the number of people going out."

Occasionally, I got a glimpse of just how silent and scary the Asto army could be. This was one of those times.

"Tamer's balance usually runs deep into the negative, meaning more people leave than come here. This is the basis for our assumption that Tamerians are produced here. But lately, the balance has started shifting into a more neutral territory."

And this was clearly the thing that had triggered the army's and Ezhya's interest in Tamer.

"This Dorell is where we need to be," I said.

Nods all around. Clearly.

Thayu double-checked, but it really wasn't on any of the maps that Jayten had given us.

"Over the next ridge, huh?" She enlarged that area.

The ridge was sharp and tall, like the one behind the shuttle. Geologically, this area looked like a substrate made from layers of volcanic stone, and tipped on its side by further volcanic activity. The world looked young, with not much erosion.

"Look, there is another *neshi* track," Deyu said.

She was right.

A track led between the rocky spikes, across the ridge into the next valley.

That valley was wider than this one—ideal for landing large cargo craft—and it widened out to what seemed to be the shore of a frozen ocean.

We peered at the projection but could see no evidence of habitation.

"I can send the drone over the ridge to look," Reida said. "It's not that far, and if there is activity, we should be able to see it from up there."

That was an excellent idea. "What do you need?"

"Go outside to release the drone. I can do everything else from here as long as I have reception."

"Would you do it in the dark?"

"Preferably not, but if it's the only time we have, we may need to take it."

"We don't know how long we'll be stuck here."

"Not long," Thayu said. "I also suggest that having a look in the dark makes it easier to see a settlement if there is one. There is quite likely to be light. Right now, all we want to know is whether the settlement exists, and its approximate location."

That was true.

That left the next question: "Where can we release the drone?"

My team was never idle. While Benton Leck had led us through the building, Reida had made a scan of the building's likely layout. The section above the corridor on the other side of the hall contained smaller rooms, which they suggested could be dorms, so we agreed to stay away from that area.

But the floor above us contained several large rooms which registered electronic signatures, according to Thayu; and, what was more, it looked like there was only one floor above us. Although it did suggest that even part of that floor was set into the mountain. But according to Benton Leck, aircraft landed on the roof, so there was definitely some open space, and presumably also a way to get up there.

We put our warm gear back on.

It was also extremely dark in the building, and rather than fiddling with the light on the walls as Benton Leck had shown us, we decided to use the lights on our readers.

I did wonder why Benton Leck had left the door open but in the same breath warned us about the Tamerians. There seemed to be a couple of tangled-up messages in there. If he hadn't wanted us to explore, he'd have found some excuse to lock the door. If he didn't mind us exploring, maybe he did want to get out of here. Or maybe he left the door open because he was curious to see what we would do— or give him an excuse to set the army on us. That was a disturbing thought.

The corridor was quite long and dank, and it smelt very humid in here.

We found a staircase halfway down, hidden behind a door that looked like there was a normal room beyond.

The staircase led to a corridor on the top floor, which looked very much like the one on the ground floor. There were a couple of doors to the side, but opening them was a challenge. Each door had a panel to the side, with some buttons that would probably take a security code to get in.

Reida consulted his map to determine which rooms were still in the mountain and which had a proper roof.

"You don't need all that equipment," Ynggi said. "You can hear the wind around the building. You can't hear it back there."

Reida and Nicha gaped at each other, wide-eyed. None of us heard anything.

Evi said, "Thank goodness for Ynggi, I guess."

Thayu and Reida spent some time trying to decode the panel on a nearby door, but they ended up frying it and pulling it out of the wall. This still didn't open the door, but at least it disabled the mechanism that kept it shut. Moving the giant stone door in its track on the floor required three people. I felt up to helping them, and Nicha said, "You know that you have become much stronger?"

"I'm still as weak as a baby."

And to demonstrate I grabbed his arm, and he pushed back at me. He had trouble pushing my arm back.

"Come on, Nich', you're just putting it on to make me feel good."

"No, I mean it, you have become much stronger. It must be the Coldi genes."

Like my eyes had changed and my hair was changing, the rest of my body followed.

There were no mirrors in this building.

I balled my fist and pushed up my sleeve, looking at the muscles in my arms. I didn't see anything unusual, but I had felt quite well in the last few days, which I had attributed to the lower gravity.

The air inside the room was warm and smelled of earth. It didn't look promising for finding a way to get onto the roof, but there might just be another door here.

Against the wall inside the door was another panel, which Thayu did manage to get to work. The text next to the buttons was in a language I had never seen, but we pressed one, and the fans came on.

We pressed another, and the room flooded with bright glow, and we could see all the plants, in pots that stood in rows on raised mesh. They were plain old ordinary potatoes.

Well that was something I hadn't expected. This confirmed my niggling feeling: that elements on Earth—those who had almost made us lose the referendum—had quite a strong presence in this project.

The air was heavy with the smell of soil. Another row of bays contained cabbages. Against the back wall stood a row of large vats that issued a strong smell of vinegar. I lifted the lid of one, finding shredded cabbage inside.

Sauerkraut.

That's what I had smelled in the hall.

We also found a corner where tomato plants grew. I remembered from living at Midway Space Station how we always got small tomatoes with every meal because they were easy and quick to grow.

Evi was fond of tomatoes and collected a pocket full of different ones.

The room was huge and took up all the space along the right hand side of the corridor. But we didn't find a way to get to the roof.

On the opposite side of the corridor was another door protected by an electronic lock.

While Thayu and Reida tried to open it, I couldn't help but think back to the cellar of horrors that we had found in the game park in South Africa. Parts of human bodies in storage, x-rays of people with electronic parts inside their bodies, aquariums with live organs. Sooner or later, we were going to run into the place where the Tamerians were made, and it was going to be just as disturbing as the discovery in that cellar.

But when Thayu pushed open the door, the room turned out to contain the heaters and air purification and recycling equipment. A room off the side contained a room filled with medical equipment. There were treatment tables, equipment with leads and pads that could be placed on the skin—I guessed—but I had no idea what else it would be for. Not sure I wanted to know either, considering what we'd seen in South Africa.

But whatever was done here, this room did not provide access to the roof.

The corridor ended in a blank wall. There were no further doors, which was odd, because why have a corridor that doesn't lead to anything?

"Over here," Ynggi said.

With his dark-sensitive eyes, he had spotted a number of rungs set into the wall. Thayu directed her light to the ceiling. There was a hatch.

Emergency exit?

Evi climbed up and pushed the trapdoor. "It's stuck."

"Try opening the hatch," Ynggi said.

Evidently, he was the only one who could see a hatch, so he climbed up using only some of the rungs and cracks in the wall, as well as his tail. He almost hung upside down on the hatch, while Evi retreated.

He did something that sounded like shoving metal over metal.

"There."

He let himself drop from the ceiling, turning around and landing on all fours with a soft thump, like a cat.

Evi pushed the hatch. It creaked open.

"Whoa!"

Evi climbed out and disappeared into the darkness.

A blast of cold air came in.

"It looks like this is the roof."

Excellent.

"It's really cold up here."

That was not so excellent.

Reida climbed up and I followed him.

Evi had not lied about the temperature. An icy cold wind blasted me in the face, but it was not snowing and to my surprise I could even see patches of clear sky in between clouds edged in moonlight.

Reida knelt on the ground, putting together the drone while Evi held up the light for him.

Thayu came up behind me. "It's so cold." Her breath steamed in the light of Reida's screen.

"Wait downstairs if you want."

But that was not Thayu's style. She knelt next to Reida, helped him roll out three screens and attach them to each other. Deyu arrived as well and the three of them checked the camera and the engine on the drone. I hoped no one heard the whining sound it made.

Then Thayu took the drone to the edge of the roof, and let it go.

The whine of the engine vanished in the night.

I went back to Reida who had navigation modules up on the screen. It displayed a model of the surrounding valley. Deyu pointed at a little glowing dot on the screen, on the hillside on our side of the frozen lake.

"That's the shuttle."

It comforted me that the lights were so clearly visible in this otherwise barren landscape. It meant Yana and Taleyu were fine. It meant that if there was any light in the next valley, we would see it, too.

The drone climbed and climbed. The hillside was quite steep. There was supposed to be a *neshi* track here, but it was far too dark to see it, so I looked at the 3D map instead.

"What's that?" Thayu asked, pointing at the dark screen from the camera projector.

At first, I couldn't see anything, but then dark jagged outlines materialised against a slightly lighter sky. The glow got brighter and brighter until the drone came over the edge of the ridge and the screen went white.

"Whoa!" Reida turned down the sensitivity.

Out of the whiteness materialised a bright glowing dome. Next to it stood a low building, and in front of it was a brightly-lit square patch of snow with dark shapes.

"Those are aircraft?" Thayu said.

There were, too, quite a lot of them.

Reida zoomed in to the view, and now we could see them quite clearly, and even spotted people walking between them. A surprising number of people, actually. What were they all doing there?

"Right," I said. "That's where we're going tomorrow."

We returned to the apartment, where Telaris and Reida busied themselves with lighting the fire in the bowl in the middle of the living area.

We all gathered around to watch their efforts.

During our investigation of the agricultural chamber, Evi and Ynggi had collected a variety of little tomatoes. Ynggi in particular had all his pockets full of them. He expressed his dismay at the absence of fish.

"No wonder the army doesn't look healthy. No meat. No fish. No thinking food."

"You don't think they look healthy?"

"There is no life in them," he said. "I see these men in Barresh. They are stupid and never say anything, but they look good and are strong. People tell them *move this pile of stones* and they go and move it."

Ynggi emptied out his pockets on the table. Little tomatoes of all colours rolled over the surface and some bounced onto the floor.

"What are these things?" Rixya asked.

"*Tomatoes*," Thayu said, using the Isla word.

Rixya picked up an orange one, rolling it between thumb and forefinger.

Ynggi was right that people used Tamerians like that in Barresh, and we had become used to their presence.

In the beginning they had mostly done dirty jobs, like kill people, but at some point, and I didn't remember when, that had changed. They were strong, reliable workers. They moved stuff, they dug holes, but they were too non-communicative to work as guards.

We made a plan for tomorrow while working our way through the collection of tomatoes. We'd all go to the next valley. Hopefully, we'd find some *neshi* to ride, but if not, it wasn't too far so we'd use the track. We'd make sure that we all carried weapons. Once we were in the valley, Rixya and Telaris would try to steal the required part from one of the aircraft there. Rixya said that he recognised some of the models. Alternatively, they would steal the whole aircraft, but only if there was no time to remove the part, since taking the whole aircraft was obviously going to attract a lot more attention.

The rest of us would try to find out what was happening at the base, or try to distract attention from Rixya and Telaris' activity if that proved necessary.

After we finished the tomatoes and the plan, people started going to bed.

We had an important day tomorrow, and if there was anything I had learned about Coldi and snow, it was that it made them very tired.

But Thayu and I still had to share the same bed, and that was going to be a real problem, because ever since she'd given me that look earlier in the evening, I'd felt hot whenever she looked at me.

So I told her to go to bed, and that I was going for another swim, hoping that she'd fall asleep before I came back up.

I quietly made my way through the living room and down the stairs. The water was as still as a mirror, reflecting the ugly stone struts on the side of the hall. Steam rose lazily from the surface.

I took off my clothes and let myself slip into the warm water.

But it was very quiet here, and Benton Leck's comment that he found it creepy made me nervous as well. Also, I was tired. I might be getting better, but I didn't quite feel up to my old self, and I knew we'd need our rest for the next day, maybe even longer.

I climbed back out of the pool, put my clothes back on. I didn't bother with my shoes, although the stone underfoot was ice cold.

I didn't bother turning on the lights in the stairwell either. I knew where the steps were.

Except in that pitch darkness, my knee hit something soft.

Something that took in a sharp breath.

Something that smelled like . . .

"Thay'?"

She ran her hands through my hair by way of reply.

I climbed up two more steps so that we were at the same height.

I bent over her shoulder, and breathed the scent in the hollow under her ear.

She ran her hands down both sides of my hips and up over my back to my shoulder blades.

"It's cold in here." Her voice held a deep, hoarse resonance. I didn't need to see the blush on her cheeks or her watering eyes to know that she was close to flushing.

I could smell the sweet scent of it. Blood rushed to my cheeks and ears and other places.

"I am . . . I never smelled you like this."

"You have never flushed before."

"Do Coldi men flush as well? I never heard that." But I knew it was true, and I knew I had been trying to fight it ever since I'd come home from the hospital.

"It's the best-kept secret of all. You're like a virgin adolescent boy who discovers one more function of his body."

"A virgin?"

She laughed a deep resonant laugh. "Like a virgin wanting to taste the fruit. Here is the fruit, come eat it."

"Do you think this is a good idea?"

"I think it is an excellent idea. Catch me."

And she was gone down the stairs.

A moment later, a big splash echoed through the pool room.

I rubbed my hands over the stubble on my head. I felt hot. My skin was hot. My cheeks glowed. Other parts of me . . . were painfully ready to perform their duty.

I decided what the heck. I was fighting a losing battle with my own newly awakened hormones.

Catch her, I did.

We broke our promise to Lilona resoundingly. And regretted none of it.

20

I HAD TO ADMIT that I slept really well after that.

We'd had some strange and tiring nights, and trying not to think about Thayu while smelling her next to me had been more distracting than I'd admit.

Whatever happened now was out of our hands. I could relax, it was warm next to her, and I fell into a deep sleep.

I woke up when Thayu stirred next to me.

It was pitch dark in the room, but she leaned over to grab her reader and made a light. In this windowless bunker, it was impossible to know the time. My reader said it was early morning, but I didn't trust that the timing schedule I had set up on my reader according to Tamer's day length worked properly.

"What is it?" I asked.

The sound of rustling bedding meant that others were also waking up.

"There is someone in the living area," Thayu said.

We went into the living room, and found Ynggi standing next to the fire bowl, where the remains of last night's fire still emitted a soft glow.

"Did you hear something, too?" he asked.

"Yes," Thayu said. "There was someone in the apartment, but that must have been you—"

"No." He shook his head, his eyes wide. His tail also waved *no* behind him. "There is a sound outside, an engine."

We listened.

"I can't hear anything," Thayu said.

No, I couldn't hear anything either.

Ynggi said, "It's gone now. It was coming close."

"An aircraft?" I asked.

"Could be."

"Did it land here?"

"It flew over there and then over there." He pointed with his tail to different corners of the room.

I felt cold. "They've come to look for us."

Behind us, Rixya said, "I have to get back to the shuttle and help defend it."

"Come on, let's go," I called. I could smell food somewhere in the building. With a bit of luck we could grab a quick breakfast and be on our way.

Thayu came in, wearing her outdoor gear, which included two layers of suits that snugly fitted her figure like a wetsuit.

She met my eyes, and a barely perceptible smile crossed her face.

Damn, I loved that woman.

I'd been told that Coldi women often knew the next day that they were pregnant. She had told me on previous occasions, but had not said anything this morning. I wasn't sure what it meant. Hopefully that our adventure in the pool last night had no further consequences, we could wait two weeks before she was able to flush again and do the proper thing by Lilona by having all the tests first. Because "I couldn't control my urges" was going to sound so terribly mature as excuse.

But it had been good last night. Very good.

The door to the apartment opened, letting in Benton Leck.

He greeted us with a cheery, "Did you sleep well?" And then he looked around, frowning at our clothing. "What's happening?"

"We'd like to have a quick bite to eat and then we're going."

"Going? Where to?"

"We have our crew to worry about. Was there an aircraft flying over just now?"

He gave me a bewildered look. "It's not impossible, but it would be strange, because I haven't seen anyone for days. I definitely didn't hear anything. I think you must have been mistaken. The wind makes a lot of noise."

No, it wasn't the wind. Ynggi's ears were never wrong.

He continued on, "If you want something to eat, breakfast is being served. I usually eat breakfast with the men. It's quite nutritious."

We picked up all our things and went with him into the big hall, where all the soldiers sat at the tables. The only sound in the room was that of spoons in bowls and of the rattling of the serving trolleys. None of the men spoke, yet I could *feel* their presence in the room.

They all looked in our direction, and turned their heads as we walked past. Most of them had dark eyes, utterly without expression. Their blank facial expression was one of the things that made them so scary. Were they people? Were they machines? The ones we'd seen on Earth were more machine than human in body, but men like these ones had few mechanical augmentations—we knew that from the Tamerians that had been killed and studied by various authorities in Barresh.

Yet they didn't act like people.

Benton Leck took us to a small corner of one of the tables, where a number of chairs had been left unoccupied.

There was not enough space for all of us at the end of the table, so some of the soldiers needed to move aside. Rather than find different seats on other tables, they bunched together. So—something told them that they'd rather stay with their comrades than spread out over tables. They were drawn to each other. That meant they had to communicate in some way.

"What is that smell?" Deyu asked in a low voice.

Yes, I smelled it, too, that kind of sour scent that reminded me of sauerkraut. Last night, that could have been explained by the content of their bowls, but there wasn't anything in those bowls yet.

We all sat down, and a Tamerian came to bring us breakfast. It consisted of a bowl with yellowish glop that looked and tasted like mashed potato with a lot of cream. It didn't smell sour at all.

The men further down the table attacked the glop as if they hadn't eaten anything in days. Benton Leck had told us that it was very nutritious, but clearly the rations were on the stingy side.

Deyu sat across the table from me. I met her eyes and she frowned and glanced aside to where the men were eating their porridge. I could swear that she was thinking about this. Thinking and coming to a brilliant conclusion, as Deyu often did.

"I was going to show you around today," Benton Leck said. "I haven't forgotten. If you come with me when we've finished here, I will make some tea and you can explain what you want."

"Actually, there has been a change in plan, because we're going to leave today."

"Leave?" He seemed surprised.

"Yes. There are some craft searching this area—"

"I don't know why you think that. They would have told me."

"We know. At any rate, we are on a strict time schedule and we're leaving."

"But what about me? What am I supposed to do?"

"I suggest that if you want to see your wife again, you come with us, because I cannot guarantee what will happen when we get to the other side of this ridge."

He gave me a shocked look. "Do you think you can just walk from here to Dorell?"

"Well, It doesn't look like you have any kind of transport. We came here by walking, and I understand that the people in the main base might not agree with our arrival, so it's best that we keep ourselves out of view for as long as possible."

He stared at me. I could see his throat move. I wished I could get into his brain to figure out what, if anything, he was still hiding from us.

"So, I suggest that you let us know about any type of information you have, or if you have any items that can be useful to us."

"I don't have anything. I don't even know much about Dorell. I never spent much time there. I just know that it's dangerous out there. I've already told you. You've seen the wild beasts that live out there. They're much bigger and faster and stronger than we are. Those big predators that run on two legs, you can't shoot them or they will explode in fire."

"I assure you, we already know that. We can handle it."

By that time, most of us had finished our breakfast, and Ynggi was looking around nervously.

"Is anything wrong?" I asked him.

"The sound, it has returned."

I did my best to listen, but that was just too much noise in the room to hear anything.

I asked him, "What are you hearing? The same as before?"

"Engines, more than one of them."

We were wasting our time here. We were never going to get anything from Benton Leck because either he knew nothing, was determined not to share it, or had instructions to keep us here as long as possible. I pushed myself up from the bench and said to the team, "Come on, get your things. Quickly. We leave now."

Benton Leck continued his protest, but I was not going to listen to him anymore. I realised we might have to force him to come, because I couldn't face his wife to tell her that we found her husband, but left him on Tamer.

We picked up our things and left the dining hall, with Benton Leck running after us through the corridor, still trying to change our minds.

"But you can't just leave. It is dangerous out there. You will die."

He was getting so desperate that he pulled my jacket. I stopped and turned around, yanking the jacket from his hands.

"Listen. You can come with us as I already said. I understand that you have limitations because of your age. We can handle that. But we are not staying here. There are aircraft flying around outside, and we're not going to wait until they've landed."

"They might be friendly."

"Out here? I very much doubt it." I continued walking.

We arrived in the empty foyer hall, where our footsteps sounded hollow.

"But the door doesn't open unless I tell it to."

"Then you had better open it for us."

"You don't understand."

"Well since you have shown no inclination to explain to us, I think we will use our own methods."

Before Benton Leck could protest, Evi balanced to the big gun on his shoulder and fired at the door. It exploded outwards in a ball of flames.

A blast of cold air came in. It wasn't snowing yet, but it looked like it might start any minute. We had better hurry up.

Benton Leck stared at the gaping hole where the door had been, mouth open. "What have you done? Now they will definitely come here to check it out."

"I repeat: They are already looking for us and our craft. I very strongly suggest that you come with us. This is your one chance to get out of here. We are not coming back."

We walked out of the building. The snow was fresh and powdery. The path we had made yesterday when coming from the lakeside to the base was almost invisible under fresh snow. But we knew where we were going, and the *neshi* trail going up the other side of the valley was visible as a slight dip in the white surface.

The *neshi* were nowhere to be seen, so we shouldered our packs. Benton Leck came after us, running through the snow.

"Listen to me. You can't leave, because the soldiers won't let you. I'm warning you now, because I can talk about it outside the building. These soldiers are programmed to keep me here and to keep you here. They'll come after you if you venture too far away. I know; I tried. It's best not to resist, because they will kill you. Look, they're already coming."

I looked.

The entire army of Tamerian soldiers had come into the broken entrance of the base.

Evi and Telaris immediately unslung their guns. Thayu, Reida, Deyu and Rixya reached for theirs.

The Tamerians ran out into the snow.

I reached for my gun, too, but we needed another trick. A giant dinosaur, or a hole to open up under their feet. There were far too many of them for us to fight.

Benton Leck's voice rose to a squeal. "See what you've done? I tried to tell you this all along."

"Well, it looks like now might be the time to use what you've learned about their communication."

"I told you I can't communicate with them, at least not very well. What you saw is about the extent of it. I could only figure out how to tell them to march over the lake, and then hope that, gradually, enough of them would disappear so I could escape."

What the hell . . . "So *you* were doing this to them?"

I stared into his pale, waxen-skinned face. I didn't know whether to feel horror or sympathy. Tamerians weren't really people in the normal sense of the word, but the image of men falling through the ice and their colleagues completely ignoring them would not leave me. How could anyone do that to living creatures, even if they weren't human? That was . . . disgusting. I had no other word for it.

The soldiers surrounded us, a wall of solid muscle. I didn't know that any of them were armed. It probably didn't make any difference whether they were on not. There were hundreds of them, and we were only few. We could shoot a good many of them, but there would always be more.

Benton Leck was hiding behind Evi and Telaris who held their weapons raised, but they also realised that as soon as they started shooting, that would be the end of us.

We only had one option: Use whatever little we knew of Tamerians to confuse or scare them.

"We're doing this for Puck!" I called out.

Whatever they thought Puck meant. Whatever result it would have.

Deyu joined me in shouting, "Think about Puck. We're doing this for Puck."

"There is no point," Benton Leck said. "They won't listen to you."

His voice was almost drowned out by Reida, who shouted, "Puck, Puck."

This was going to go badly, and I sure as hell wasn't going to give up without a fight. I reached in my pocket for my gun—and my fingers met the wrapping of the half-eaten Aghyrian ration I still carried in there.

And I had an idea. Whatever it was that Tamerians wanted, the fare inside the base was pretty poor. If they were given food, they ate very quickly, so they must be hungry. Every creature reacted to the prospect of food. The Tamerians understood the word "dinner".

Deyu was still shouting, "Puck, Puck."

She waved her arms. But the effect of whatever Puck meant to them had worn off.

I closed my hand around the half-eaten ration. I unwrapped it and waved it in the air. "We're going to get food for all of you. Dinner! More dinner than you can ever eat."

The men stopped. Shoulders relaxed. Some men retreated. I'd been wrong about their facial expressions. Their faces cleared. They showed interest and curiosity. A couple of them clearly *sniffed* the air. Urgh, yeah, that package really smelled bad.

I also realised that when we had met them first on the ice, it might have been the smell from the ration in my pocket that had made them stop .

I addressed them, speaking slowly. "You are hungry and have been treated badly. We will find food for you. Please help us go to the other base. Please help your leader pack his things."

To my great surprise, the men turned around and went back into the base. Benton Leck ran after them.

"Do we wait or go?" Nicha asked.

"I can hear the engine," Ynggi said.

The temptation to run off and get a head start was great. But no. "I'm worried that Dorell will have surveillance and that it will be guarded. It might be easier to enter in the company of a local. Also, those craft have been flying about since this morning. I think that when the command module was fried, it had two effects: it killed our navigation, but it also stopped others from being able to track us. I presume Yana and Taleyu have taken steps to hide the shuttle."

Rixya was nodding.

I continued, "They seem to be safe for now, because scouts have obviously not found the shuttle. It's up to us to get what they need and return to them safely. I think we have a better chance if we bring—"

"—An army," Reida said.

He was looking at the entrance of the base.

Benton Leck had come out again, wearing a thick, Mirani-style cloak. But he was not alone. The entire army was with him, in various degrees of preparation. Some wore jackets or coats, but others didn't. Some carried weapons and others had packs.

"Right. An army." If it was indeed their intention to come.

And as we found out, it was.

"They follow me everywhere I go," Benton Leck said. "I told you I can't leave without them."

The men lined up behind him, a wall of solemn faces.

I exchanged glances with Thayu and Nicha.

Thayu signalled with her gloved hand *let it be*. Nicha signalled his agreement.

"Dinner?" I asked the men.

A few of them nodded ever so slightly.

Right. Dinner, it was. No pressure, Mr Wilson.

We couldn't afford to waste any more time on this.

Besides, it might be advantageous to be able to hide in an army.

We continued up the slope on the north side of the valley, slowly, because Benton Leck didn't walk fast.

Unfortunately, no *neshi* were in sight, but the snow held off and we didn't have much distance to be covered.

I sped up a little so that I walked alone with the members of my team.

"So, the Tamerians do react to the attraction of food," I said.

"I'm not sure that is indeed the case," Deyu said. Her voice was not loud, but carried a strange intensity.

I remembered the way she had looked at me across the table in the dining hall. "Do you have an idea?"

"I do. But it's only an idea, mind."

"Let us know. It's not like we've got a lot to do until we've crossed this mountain."

"Well, I thought like this." Deyu spread her gloved hands.

All the members of my team came in closer, including Rixya who, after a bit of adjustment, appeared to fit the team well.

"Most types of humans are visual creatures. They react to bright, bold colours, but they are terrible at seeing in the dark and their hearing is so-so. We Coldi rely less on sight. Our perception of colour is not very good. I know because Cory keeps complaining about colours we can't see and how combinations don't match."

Nicha laughed.

"Our night vision is terrible, but we have a pretty good nose. Now Indrahui people have really good eyesight and their ears are excellent."

Telaris said, "That's so that we can keep tabs on what you're up to."

"Nah," Evi said. "Who'd want to know that?"

More laughter.

Deyu turned to Ynggi. "Now, Pengali have excellent night vision, but they get blinded during the day."

"That's because you're supposed to be asleep then," Ynggi said.

Deyu continued, "They use smell, sound and touch quite a bit because they are nocturnal."

I was wondering where she was going with this.

"Tamerians do not appear to use sound. They can see well enough but don't appear to use their faces to communicate emotions. They can learn to use words, but they don't use them to communicate with each other. There is, however, a sense that none of the human types use very much for communication."

I knew—and it was brilliant, and it fitted perfectly with my experiences from this morning. It even fitted with why the Tamerians had been distracted by me holding up the half-eaten package of food.

"Smell," I said.

"Yes," Deyu said. "I think they use smell. A few times when we've come close to Tamerians, especially groups of them, like in the dining hall, or when they've been very stressed, like Puck, I've noticed a strange smell."

And damn it, she was right about that.

"Likely, they have a really good nose." Deyu turned to me. "Like Fred finds where other dogs have been, and like your *police* uses dogs to find missing people."

Damn it, Deyu. That woman was worth her weight in gold.

"Is it really as simple as that?" Nicha wanted to know. "The Tamerians followed us because they were hungry and they have a strong sense of smell so they could smell the food in your pocket? Is there really more to it than that?"

"It's a theory, I agree. Most creatures react most strongly to simple impulses," Deyu said.

I glanced at Thayu, who was biting her lip to stop herself laughing.

React most strongly to simple impulses. Well, yes. Clearly. Her cheeks glowed.

"I don't get it," Rixya said. "You're talking about smell as communication. Apart from detecting things, can anyone actually communicate something with a smell?"

"The way Nicha farts, he definitely does," Reida said.

And when we all stopped laughing, Deyu said, "He's right, you know. Communication goes both ways."

"Believe me, you don't have to tell us that," Reida said. "When he farts, we clear out."

And then we all laughed again.

Nicha said, "But if I fart, what is that going to mean to a Tamerian?"

That was a good question, and one that none of us could answer. But the smell of food definitely did something. I checked over my shoulder, but the army still followed. Two men walked on either side of Benton Leck, helping him up the steep incline.

One might be forgiven to think that he was their leader and that they were following him, but if Deyu was right, it was all about something smelly in my pocket.

21

———

THE PATH BECAME really steep. We had to walk in single file and could no longer talk to each other. The wind picked up, and it was my guess that it wouldn't be long before we were either in the mist or it would start snowing, probably both.

Deep within the hood of my jacket, while watching Evi's back in front of me, I had plenty of time to think about what Deyu had said. It fitted disturbingly well with our experience of the Tamerians.

But that still left the question: what was the point? And why had Benton Leck not discovered this in the time he'd been here?

I would have to ask him.

Right now, he was still struggling up the hillside, moving ever slower than we did. I'd have to call a halt when we came to a sheltered spot. The top of the ridge wasn't far away.

We were just getting to the part where rocks poked through the snow when the clouds rolled in and took away our view of the valley behind us. We could no longer see the frozen lake or the building nestled in the hillside. We could no longer see the hillside where the shuttle stood hidden under the snow.

It became much harder to see the path, as well, and progress slowed, because Reida needed to check his maps to see if we were still going in the right direction.

More disturbingly, I could no longer see Benton Leck and the Tamerians.

Where could we stop for a bit so that he could catch up? Not for his sake but ours. I didn't trust that man at all.

When we came to the ridge, visibility was nearly zero. Biting wind hit us in the face, laced with snowflakes sharp as icicles. Most of the rock spikes were narrow, offering no shelter to a group the size of ours.

The other side was much more exposed.

The upside of this was that snow didn't collect in deep drifts and it was easier to walk, if also much colder.

Evi and Telaris stopped.

"What's wrong?" I called. My words were almost carried away on the wind.

Evi pointed a gloved hand.

A group of round, snow-covered lumps lay in the snow behind a rocky outcrop ahead. As we watched, one tossed its head and produced a low moan.

Neshi.

Deyu pushed between us and approached them slowly. Big shaggy heads turned. Wads of snow fell off their horns. One animal blew out a cloud of steam.

She was right in that they were unafraid of us, but they still looked impressive with their multiple sets of horns. Protection against the big dinosaurs?

Deyu inched closer. They seemed a little nervous, but let her come close enough to touch the shield on their backs. Once she had done that, they allowed her to step between the animals. I still thought it was amazing how Deyu did this so fearlessly and managed to get the animals to do what she wanted. One of the creatures followed her. She brought it to us, and Reida climbed on its back.

By now, Benton Leck turned up. With his long-haired cloak he almost resembled a *neshi*.

"The worst is over," I said to him.

"Do you really think so? These people can control that whole army with the press of one button. When they see us coming, they can send commands to the army and there is nothing we can do about it."

"There is no reception here."

"Maybe not up here, but there definitely will be when we get further down."

He had a point there and I could think of only one way to prevent trouble: somewhere on that slope, we should run ahead while we still had the advantage.

Deyu came with the next *neshi*. Thayu climbed onto it.

While she walked past me on her animal, I gestured to her *I want to talk with you*.

She gestured back, *careful*. Of what, she didn't say, but I judged it likely that she also didn't trust Benton Leck. Something was up with him. If these people paid so much for his work and he had lived with the Tamerians for months, he *had* to have discovered more about their communication.

When Deyu brought the next *neshi*, I showed Benton Leck where to put his feet, and I helped him up. His face looked haggard inside the depths of his hood.

"I have to ride at the back," he said. "The army will follow me."

The Tamerians stood behind him on the path, a solid wall of dark-clothed men, their hoods, hair and shoulders dotted with snow. To be frank, they looked miserable. Some of the men didn't even have a proper coat. No one was going to tell me that they weren't cold.

"Dinner," I said, taking the half-eaten ration out of my pocket and showing them. "I promise."

Damn, someone was going to have to draw up a set of regulations about how these men should be treated, even if they weren't entirely human.

After a short break, we continued on, pushing into the biting wind.

We used the same formation as before: Nicha shared an animal with Ynggi, and Evi, Telaris and Rixya walked at the front of the column.

Telaris did give Reida—immediately behind him—his big gun, and Reida beamed with pride.

Last night, Reida's drone would have flown in this area, but now we couldn't even see a short distance into the valley for the mist and drifting snow. Who knew if they might be waiting for us?

We were going directly against the wind, and Deyu in front of me was the only shelter. I checked Thayu behind me. She displayed her *I hate this* face.

Yeah, I don't think any of us liked it. Did clothing that was warm enough in this sort of weather truly exist?

The going was slow as the animals stepped carefully. They knew the way.

The wind whistled between the sharp rocks, producing a variety of whistling and groaning sounds.

On a few occasions, I thought I heard something that was not the sheer force of nature trying to bend these rocks, but any snatch of sound—was that the whine of an engine?—was soon swallowed by the howling of the wind.

Ynggi, who rode with Nicha, turned around, watching the sky.

Was I crazy, or was there really something going on? We'd seen plenty of activity here when spying with the drone last night.

I didn't want to go down to the valley and find ourselves unpleasantly surprised by a much bigger operation than we had expected. I had no idea what the Tamerians would do. Did my promise of food mean they would follow us, or would they bail at the first sight of any of their comrades?

I wanted to ask Ynggi, but he was in front of Deyu. A couple of Tamerians had come down and walked alongside the column. I wanted to ask Benton Leck, whose sense of hearing was similar to mine, but he was at the very end of the column.

I turned around.

Benton Leck was just coming around the corner where the path swung around a rocky outcrop. He was looking at the screen of his reader. As soon as he came into my view, and he noticed that I was watching him, he put the reader into his pocket.

Holy crap.

I called out, "Stop."

Evi and Reida at the front of the column didn't hear me, so I yelled a bit louder.

Evi stopped and Nicha stopped and Deyu had to stop as well. The *neshi* bunched together, grumbling and snorting.

"What's going on?" Thayu asked.

I gestured at Benton Leck. "He's got something in his pocket."

My animal did not want to turn around, so I slid off, and ploughed through the snow to the end of the column. Benton Leck saw me coming. He jumped off as well. He landed awkwardly in the snow, lost his footing and slid sideways. A bank of loose snow stopped him sliding further into the valley, but instead of getting up, he was rummaging in his pocket, and I would've bet that he had some sort of weapon in there.

Thankfully, Thayu and Reida saw this, and jumped off as well. Both of them waded through the snow, and pushed Benton onto his back. He yelled out.

"Help me, help me."

But it was already too late. Thayu held his arms and Reida was rummaging through his pockets.

I kept an eye on the Tamerians, but coming with Benton Leck was not the same as protecting him.

Reida found an object in his pockets, which he handed to me: a metal cylinder about the length of my hand. It felt solid and surprisingly heavy. It had a nozzle at the top with a button.

"What did you intend to do with this?" I asked him.

"That is just a single charge to defend myself in case of a robbery. I used it in Miran and forgot it was still in my pocket." He was pale and shivering.

"I've never seen anything like this before."

"I swear I'm telling the truth."

Reida found his reader which he handed to me as well. The screen displayed some text in Mirani.

"What's this?"

"A letter from my wife. Please, I worry about her a lot."

My knowledge of Mirani was rudimentary, but it was enough. "If you so desperately need to apologise to *your wife* for not being able to stop us, might it just be that 'your wife' is in that base down there?"

I took out my gun.

Benton Leck's eyes widened. "Are you going to. . . ?"

I dialled the strength of the charge right back.

"No, no, please, I'll do what you say—"

—I placed the tip of the barrel against the screen and discharged the gun.

He blew out a breath.

"A trick I learned from my security. It won't be misused against us

anymore. I don't like discharging on people. It's messy. But I will do it
if necessary."

"No, no, that won't be necessary." His voice was high.

I noticed how Thayu straightened next to me and drew her
weapon. She was looking up the mountainside behind us.

The Tamerians had come closer. And they were no longer passive.

"What did you do? Send them a code so that they would obey
you?" Holy crap.

We were in the middle of a snowstorm, couldn't see anything, and
had no way to go. This was the worst possible situation.

Reida hauled Benton Leck to this feet. He flung the man over the
neshi shield, vaulted up himself and gave the animal a good slap on the
neck. It took off, half-running, half-sliding, down the hill.

We ran to ours. The animals were skittish. The ears went up and
flipped sideways and went up again.

I jumped onto my animal and it took off after Reida. The slope
was steep and the animal slid on all fours, using its hairy feet as sleds.

I lost sight of the rest of the team. I lost sight of Reida. The snow
was so heavy that I needed to pull my hood over my eyes and concentrate on just holding on. Thick mist made the light featureless and
grey.

After a while, the slope evened out, and the animal went back to
walking.

To my relief, Reida was there, and Nicha and Ynggi arrived not
much later, followed by Thayu and Deyu.

We peered into the snowdrift up the mountain. The tracks we had
made sliding down were already being covered. Where were Evi,
Telaris and Rixya?

They had no animals to ride, and could not descend as quickly.
They had the best weapons, but they also had an entire army to deal
with.

I strained my ears for the sound of weapon discharges, but the
wind made too much noise. Discharges were never loud anyway.

I hoped they were all right.

How had this job turned from finding someone's husband to such
a harebrained mission? All the equipment we used in situations like
this didn't work. Had we become too reliant on the Exchange
network? It showed how helpless we were without it.

And this mission had never been about Aliandra's husband. We'd been looking for an excuse to come here. Well, now we were here, and we were damn well going to get out of here, too, and that meant everyone who had come with us.

We gathered in a small group in a snow-covered gully. Our animals were covered in snow; our coats, our gloves, any strands of hair that stuck out under our hoods were encrusted with it. Heavens, poor Ynggi's tail had icicles hanging from the tuft of hair at the tip.

"We need to go for the bold option," I said. "They obviously really don't want us to reach the base, so I think we should make an utmost effort to get there. We have nothing to lose and nothing to defend. Let's forget trying to sneak around removing parts from aircraft. We'll take the whole thing. Deyu, you're the pilot. Pick one that you like. Reida will help you break in. Thayu, Nicha and I are going to ask this poor excuse for a human being to introduce us to his masters."

Benton Leck chose to remain quiet, still hanging over Reida's animal. He pushed himself into a sitting position, and Reida let him. I debated having him tied up, but there was nothing an old man was going to do in this climate. Besides, if he really wanted to see his wife again, he had better stick with us.

We had to keep moving or we'd freeze to death. We could do nothing about Evi and Telaris. They were capable of defending them-selves—I repeated that a few times to myself. Besides, Rixya had the emergency beacon. They would be fine.

The weather was getting worse. Drifts of snow blew into my face, and the clouds descended until we were in a grey mist. I had to stick close behind Deyu or I couldn't see her anymore.

All of a sudden, she stopped.

My animal stopped next to hers. She was looking at something on her reader.

"There are people around," she said, showing me the screen. It displayed a mush of grey with some lighter spots.

"Do they know we're here?"

"If we can see them, they can see us. Likely, they're using their local Exchange satellite and they know far more about us than we know about them."

"They're not attacking us."

"No, they're not."

"They don't look like they're getting ready to stop us."

She shrugged. "I don't know." I heard *this would be Sheydu's job* in her words.

"How far are we from the base?"

She enlarged the view, and the dome we'd seen last night appeared as a blazing half-globe in the top left hand corner of the screen.

"Not that far?" I said.

"Not terribly close either. These people are either a patrol, or—"

"They're not doing typical patrol things," Thayu said, coming up on Deyu's other side.

"Or what?" I asked.

"Or they're also watching the base," Deyu continued.

I interpreted the meaning of that statement. "They could be friendly to us."

"They could be. I also think it is quite likely that they've followed our path from the moment we entered the valley, or maybe even before."

"So what should we do?"

She met my eyes from under the icicle-rimmed edge of her hood. "Well, we can't go back."

True enough.

She took her biggest gun out of its bracket and nudged her animal forward. Ours followed, staying closely behind.

Deyu kept a close watch on her screen, and whenever I glimpsed the glowing surface, I didn't think the white dots moved. Maybe—but that was more wishful thinking—maybe they were *neshi*.

But no.

We came out from between two snow-covered rocks and a single figure stood on the path. I couldn't see if the person was armed, but he or she did not wear fur, being dressed instead in some kind of helmet and a sleek jacket, and a waistband with equipment. The person was also disturbingly tall.

Crap. Aghyrians.

Deyu, Reida, Thayu and Nicha had all drawn their weapons.

"Who are you?" Nicha asked.

The person came closer, holding out both hands to show that this was not an armed conflict. Under the helmet was a female face, with startlingly green eyes. Her expression was calm and in control but also wary. The weaponry on her belt—wow. I caught Reida looking at it. I sincerely hoped not to have to deal with it. Strangely enough, she also carried a dagger.

"We're happy to talk," I said.

Deyu and Reida lowered their weapons ever so slightly. She had made no attempt at touching any of the equipment on her belt. She could probably control it with her mind.

"Why are you here?" Her voice was clear, but she said the words in a mechanical way, as if reading from a script.

"We're looking for transport off this world. Do you have any?" Preferably any that didn't go back to the ship.

"We are but few." In that same mechanical way. I had a feeling she was reading from a translation.

"Why are you here and not inside?"

"My leader, he will talk to you."

Deyu gestured, *You go. We will keep watch.*

Thayu and I slid off our animals and followed her along a snowy path. Around a corner, a temporary shelter had been built, jammed under an overhanging rock.

The front of it consisted of a number of panels that looked like they might be inflatable and bulged outwards with the pressure of air. Warm air, too, because the snow melted where it hit the material and steam rose from the surface.

The woman opened a door, letting us into a tiny hallway where we took off our boots and coats.

When she opened the door to the main room, I was surprised by its size. This was a fairly sizeable cave.

Inside the room, we found three more people, all of them Aghyrians. They greeted our guide and us with solemn nods. They were a woman and two men, all of them in middle age. Did they even have young people aboard that ship?

"You arrived," said the oldest of the group, a man in a uniform that reminded me a lot of the clothes Lilona had worn when we first saw her. He wore his elfin-like white hair in a ponytail at the back of his head. He gestured at a chair which, when I sat down, was definitely some kind of blow-up thing, if comfortable.

"You seem to know more about me than I know of you," I said. "Are you from the Aghyrian ship?"

An uncertain look passed between them.

Then the oldest man said, "Yes, we are. I'm Sarlin, assistant captain of Rakhshya."

That was the first time I'd heard the ship referred to by name.

"We were up there. We spoke to Jayten Kolari."

His hostile look disturbed me. "Jayten is a traitor."

"Yes, he is. He sent us to the wrong place. He gave us maps that didn't have this base marked. He gave us a drone, but we rebuilt it so that it doesn't use any of your technology so it's not as easy for him to listen in."

He breathed out through flaring nostrils.

"We want our freedom."

"Like Lilona?"

His eyes widened. "Do you know her?"

"I see her quite a bit."

"She is my sister." His eyes were haunted.

I would have judged him much older than she was. "Jayten told us how, when you had settled on a new world, the captain had forced you to board the ship and return with him."

"Yes, he did. But Jayten is one of the captain's stooges. He should not be talking like this."

"He told us that the captain went down for medical treatment."

"Jayten is a liar."

"He also said that some people in the ship wanted to settle on a world and wanted to work for *gamra*."

"Did he really say that? The traitor. Yes, that is true, but it's more than 'some people'. It's most of the crew. But the captain controls us and he will not let us go. Here." He pushed up the sleeve of his jacket and showed vivid red scars in the same place where Lilona had ripped out the implant that controlled her. I felt sick when I remembered that.

"So what are you doing here?"

"The captain is in the building. He is talking to people from many different kinds of worlds. He needs certain things to keep the ship alive. He wants people and supplies. We have left the ship because we're sick of chasing everywhere and being forced to stay in the bad atmosphere while not having enough people to fix everything that breaks. We're sick of the captain making promises and then lying to everyone. He has done that for as long as I remember. He makes promises, doesn't deliver, makes more promises and then when it goes wrong it's all someone else's fault. Yet people still believe him. When we left your world, he ordered another batch of crew to be woken up. They still believe him, but they're our brothers and sisters. We are here to free them. We're here to get our ship back. We're here to stop him. There is only one way to end this tyranny."

He didn't need to say what he meant.

22

———————

I **TOLD SARLIN** and the other Aghyrians only what I felt safe sharing, although the group's intentions seemed genuine enough. At my mention of Benton Leck being with the group waiting outside, Sarlin let out a low hiss.

He said in a low growl, "The academic also works for the captain. He will not come in here."

Well, that was something I didn't know, and yes, that was why he had to keep his employer a secret. Jasper Carlson was a middleman, not for the Pretoria Cartel, although they might be involved, too, but for Kando Luczon.

Awesome.

"Whatever we plan to do next, we must do it quickly," I said. "Some members of our team were separated from our party and they are in the company of an army of Tamerians."

Another low hiss. "All of them?"

"A whole army. I don't know if any stayed behind."

"They're likely come to the defence of the base. We've kept a siege for days."

I now remembered all the people I had seen at the airport last night. I'd wondered what they were doing there. Keeping watch, as it turned out.

"All right," he said. "If the army is coming from over the mountain ridge, we're not going to be safe here for long. We need to leave. We get one chance to get into the base to do what we've come to do. Hopefully, with all of us, we can create enough confusion that we can enter the building unnoticed. We'd been planning to wait until he came out and blow up his craft from a safe distance—because there are so few of us here—but if this is the only chance we'll get, we'll have to take it, risk or no risk."

He said something to the others, and the two women went out.

It was so strange to hear Aghyrian spoken as it should be. Already the linguists had scrambled to change their interpretation of the pronunciation of what had previously been a dead and resurrected language. The way Sarlin spoke sounded nothing like the Aghyrian spoken in Barresh.

Sarlin said, "It may be a good idea for both of our groups to consider all weapons we have at our disposal, so that we can work together."

Yes, that was true. I was beginning to like him quite a bit. He had a practical, down-to-earth quality that I'd missed in all previous Aghyrians I'd dealt with, whether from the ship or in Barresh. Lilona came the closest to a likeable Aghyrian, but even she had that assumed air of authority. I was very happy to see that not all of them possessed this trait.

Thayu talked shop about weapons with him. His eyes widened when Thayu told him about the big guns that Evi and Telaris had. He appeared to be well stocked on devices that could destroy structures.

Thayu found this very interesting. The sudden warmth had made her cheeks glow. She looked much happier now, ready to win some fights.

The other Aghyrian man set about getting dressed to go outside with a sturdy jacket. He clipped on a broad belt with equipment and a helmet with projection visor, while piling the same things next to Sarlin for him to put on.

Not too much later, the two women returned in the company of another group of Aghyrians.

They were all standing inside the door where I was wrestling my coat and boots back on. I felt like a garden gnome amongst all these people much taller than me.

Their gear was lightweight and efficient. Ours was bulky, with thick Mirani cloaks and big packs.

As soon as we stepped outside the shelter, a sound like ripping fabric tore through the air.

"Look!" Thayu said.

I turned around.

The shelter had collapsed into a block of tightly-packed material about the length of my arm. Inflatable shelters indeed. They seemed well-prepared for scouting missions. I wondered how old this equipment was.

The snow had grown heavier. Nicha, Deyu, Reida and Ynggi with the *neshi* and Benton Leck showed up as dark silhouettes covered with a layer of snow.

They looked miserable.

I gestured to Nicha, *Any word from the others?*

He gestured back, *No.*

Damn it. I hoped they were all right.

A couple of Aghyrians came out of the mist.

We were about twenty in all, not counting the *neshi*. It was still a small band of rogues. I asked Sarlin whether the other occupants of the ship were still asleep. I'd seen a lot more people the first time I visited the ship. Where could I expect them to turn up?

"Not so many," he said. "We had a bad infection going through the pods. We lost many."

At least that much of Jayten's story was true. The ship really had been struggling, even back when they came to Barresh. Yet, the captain had never asked for help, and had further doomed many more of the people he had forced to come with him.

"How long did those people spend in the pods?"

"Many years. Some of them were put in stasis when we left."

"Did they know where you were going? Did they agree to come?"

He didn't answer that question, but I saw the answer in his eyes. They had not agreed. What was the chance that those people had voiced displeasure to the captain and had been frozen? That the captain and his cronies had never wanted for them to be revived? That he might even have done something that hastened their death?

I couldn't possibly feel any colder than I already did, but a chill went through me.

"How many of your people are in the base?"

"Besides the captain, there are six."

I stared at him through the drifting snowflakes. So we had—what —a little under thirty people holding *gamra* to ransom with their technology. Only *thirty* people in that entire ship? I found that very hard to believe. There had to be more, up there with Jayten, I was sure of that.

At any rate, they had technology that we couldn't begin to comprehend, and the Aghyrians were not the main group of people we had to contend with. Clearly, there were a good number of other people from other worlds at this base, and they were likely using Aghyrian technology. And we were in between the base and the Tamerian army that was coming up from behind, who were an unknown quantity, dangerous in many different ways we didn't know about yet.

And there were less than thirty of us. It seemed crazy.

Yes, we had *neshi*. I was unsure what we could do with them. Whether they would continue to listen to us or just take off when fights broke out.

We followed the Aghyrians along a narrow path through snow-covered boulders. There was another hot spring in this area, and the *neshi* kicked open the lumps of red fungus as we passed.

We stopped on a hillock.

Ahead the valley spread out through the falling snow, with a view over a brightly-lit square patch of snow that glowed with warm yellow light. At least twenty aircraft stood lined up in the snow.

"What type are those aircraft?" I asked.

"Rixya would know," Thayu said.

"No, he wouldn't," Nicha said. "These are not ours." *Ours* meaning from any of the *gamra* worlds.

Deyu handed me her reader. I had no idea what type of frequency it used, but it showed far more detail than I could discern with my eyes: a flat plain with a couple of squat buildings and the rounded dome that we had also seen last night.

One aircraft had just arrived; the door was open and the lights on. People stood at the bottom of the entry ramp. More people were patrolling the perimeter of the airfield.

A squat building was down near the side of the frozen ocean, with the round dome a little bit to the right. The dome cast a golden glow over the buildings and surrounding snow. It was made of glass or some other transparent material. There was too much light to see what happened inside when I looked at it with my reader, but Deyu's showed an incredible amount of detail. The dome consisted of a number of compartments, each with lots of vegetation in planter boxes. One area looked like a dining room, with little tables and chairs. Another section contained a big table with rows of chairs around the perimeter of the room, like a lecture theatre.

I could see people move inside this area.

"The detail in this scan is amazing," I said to Deyu.

Reida said, "Yeah, I thought so, too. I copied it from the drone and fiddled around with it a bit."

Aghyrian technology.

Well, damn it.

What were we actually doing? These people had possessed today's level of technology fifty thousand years ago. Not just that, they had possessed the technology to leave the galaxy, and settle elsewhere, and come back. And we were telling these people to take a hike, even kill each other, just because their captain happened to be an arsehole.

We have Lilona, a little voice said to me.

Yes, but there was so much more. Because of the disagreement between the Aghyrian ship and *gamra,* the Aghyrians were giving this technology to people who didn't have peaceful intentions. These people made Tamerians who were ineffective and suffered cruel lives, but they were trying to improve on the process and would eventually produce something good—possibly—or dangerous—certainly. These people could build glass domes on freezing worlds and furnish them with verdant forest.

"I don't like the look of those guards," Thayu said, looking over my shoulder.

Yes, I saw them, too, patrolling the airport and the entrance to the building. They were taller than most human body types. I knew the sign: Aghyrians. A lot more than six.

Sarlin crouched on the other side of Nicha. His blew out a breath in a low hiss.

"It looks like there are a lot more people from the ship than just the captain's guards," I said.

"Yeah." He wiped his nose. "They must have been taken off the ship earlier. At times when we didn't see it. Those are our craft, too. Those people are probably not aware of our stand against the captain. All people who are newly awakened have very high loyalty to him. They don't know any better. He is their saviour, because he was there when they were put in stasis."

There was another undercurrent in his statement that I didn't like. Not at all. "What do you mean: their saviour?"

"There was an organism—on the world they called Sekara—an organism that grows on your skin and becomes part of you. It grows into your skin and changes who you are. It makes you aggressive, constantly wanting to challenge those around you. People claim they are happy, but we saw what it did to them. We didn't want to become like that."

And damn, even that tallied with what Jayten had said, only he had painted it in a different light, that the captain had forced people to come. There were always two sides to a story.

A deep chill went over me. "How likely is it that these people will follow you back here?"

"We took their ship. But they can build a new one. Not likely in the short term. In the long term, who knows."

Crap. We needed these Aghyrians so that we could form a stronger defence if that was ever going to happen.

"Getting back to the situation here, what's the plan?" Nicha asked.

"We take the usual approach," I said. "We don't have a huge army with which to fight and occupy this base, so I'll have to go in and use my big mouth. I might take our guest to introduce me."

"They won't let you in," Benton Leck said.

I didn't trust that man as far as I could throw him. "I would love to know what sort of relationship you have with these people. I might ask them."

Benton Leck replied, but his words went right past me as Ynggi drew my attention when he cast a sharp look over his shoulder.

"Anything wrong?"

"You said something about an army?"

Then I saw them, too: grey specks making their way through the snow. If I was not mistaken, it was the Tamerian army running down the mountainside. The first group of them consisted of three people, two tall, one less so, clad in fur cloaks.

Evi, Telaris and Rixya.

"Go! Go now!" Evi called out.

I slapped the *neshi* on the neck. The animal jumped forward, slid down the side of the hillock and broke into a run in the direction of the airport.

I thought, I *hoped,* that the others followed.

We were now on the plain. The knee-deep snowdrift was no problem for the *neshi.* They powered through the white stuff, but the Tamerians were not far behind.

Evi and Telaris had each managed to grab hold of an animal. Rixya had done the same, but he had fallen off and was trying to hang onto the horns on one side while being dragged through the snow.

Neshi were herd animals and, when they felt threatened, they sought safety by organising themselves in a tight group. They ran, flank to flank. There was no stopping them; they ran straight onto the area of packed snow that was the airport.

The guards shouted out. They raised weapons.

I didn't know whether they aimed at us or the army. Deyu didn't give us the option to find out. She fired with great precision from the back of the running animal. Two guards went down.

I wanted to shout at Deyu that these were Aghyrians and that surely the ones put on important guard duty were of the type that could not be killed by a charge gun. I'd seen this before, although it didn't seem that this was common to all Aghyrians.

These ones fell, and did not get up.

I was too scared of falling off to let go and grab my weapon, because I'd be trampled under the feet of the rampaging *neshi.* I couldn't see Thayu and hoped she was behind me. She had to be, because all the other *neshi* were around me, thundering across the airport, weaving between the aircraft.

Directly in front of me, Rixya half-hung between two animals as he was trying to clamber onto the back of one of them.

We were getting close to the building. This part was shaped like a letter L with the entrance in the very corner. The door was shut.

Deyu raised the gun and fired, but the door did not budge.

The *neshi* came to a screeching halt in the corner in front of the building's door. They arranged themselves into a half-circle, horns pointing outwards, flanks heaving with steaming breaths. Nicha dropped off his animal and carried Ynggi to safety in front of the door. Reida also wormed between the animals.

Deyu was firing at random into the Tamerian army to hold them off, standing on top of two *neshi*, a foot on each. "Open that door!" she shouted to Reida.

Evi balanced the big gun on his shoulder. He discharged *foomp*, *foomp*. The flash blinded me. Clouds of steam rose from the ground.

I drew my charge gun and dialled it to a wide setting, discharging at random into the snow. Clouds of steam billowed, but people were already coming through.

Damn, the charge ran out. Did I have any recharges? I searched my pockets just in case—and my hand met the cylinder with the one-charge release weapon that we'd taken off Benton Leck. It wouldn't do much good—because these types of weapons were carried by old women for the scare value, but I pulled it out. I'd never seen one of these things before, but I assumed that the button at the top discharged it, and that the nozzle had to face the enemy.

The Tamerians were running toward us. The *neshi* shuffled and snorted and pushed.

"Stand back!" Telaris fired his big gun. And again.

I pulled myself up onto the back of the nearest animal, held the cylinder up.

Pressed the button.

Benton Leck yelled something to me, but I didn't hear what he said.

I pressed the button again, because nothing appeared to be happening, except . . . a rush of air came out of the nozzle. What the hell?

An odd smell spread through the air. Not just odd, very strong. Sour, like . . .

Nicha, downwind from me held his hand over his nose. "Ugh, what is that?"

One of the Aghyrians was coughing.

And the Tamerians . . . they stopped running. They let their weapons sink. They calmed down. They looked at me.

Well, that was . . .

"You spoiled the work of months!" Benton Leck yelled. His cheeks had gone dark. "Now we'll never get out of here and it's your fault."

"Whatever do you mean?"

"The Tamerians are controlled through a brain implant, but you can override this with smell. No one knew what smells worked in which ways, because most of us have a poor sense of smell, so they hired me to make a dictionary of smells. I worked for months and got one scent that made them listen to a leader. You can only get it from them when they are mortally afraid, so I sent them out on the lake every day. I harvested the smell from them. What you had there was months worth of hard work."

I held up the cylinder in my hand. Looked from its plain metal surface to Benton Leck's face. "Whose side are you on, really? What sort of foul business is this with these men? What makes it all right to send them to their deaths for any aim? You've now told me two different stories that excuse this foul thing."

"I'm telling you the truth."

"Maybe I should ask these Tamerians what they think about you."

His eyes widened. "No, no, it wasn't my fault. They abandoned me on that base where you found me. They used the army to imprison me. I had to collect this substance so that I could bargain with the captain to let me go."

"Captain Kando Luczon?"

Sarlin glared at Benton Leck, who shrank away. "Yes. He's not a very nice man. It was wrong to get involved with him. I didn't know any better. Now all my work is gone and I will die in this hellhole."

"Not if I have anything to do with it."

In fact, if I had anything to do with it, Benton Leck and everyone working here would be dragged before the *gamra* assembly for crimes against humanity. I felt sorry for him, but not too much. A man of his age and experience should really have known better. I guessed he'd been blinded by his own greed, fuelled by rivalry with the Human Tree Project.

Behind me, Reida had managed to open the door, because opening doors was what Reida did best. Right now, I loved the hell out of my association.

The Tamerians showed no signs of aggression. They just waited, watching me.

"So these men consider me their leader now?" I said.

"They will. If you repeat the smell often enough, they'll start to listen more, no matter how much other people try to tell them to do something else electronically."

"Good. We're in this together, right. You want to go home. We're taking the whole army inside."

Reida pushed the door open, just as a group of guards came out.

23

───────

OH CRAP.

All of the guards—there were at least twenty—were much taller than any of us. They wore armour and helmets that hid their faces. It was impossible to tell if these were men or women. All of them wore the same type of belts with equipment that Sarlin and his mates wore. They carried nothing that looked like a weapon but I was sure they were armed in some way.

I was guessing that the last time I'd seen these people, they'd been asleep in the pods in the big ship in orbit. Those pods that were now empty. Jayten had tried to get us to believe that the occupants had died. Heck, even Sarlin had believed it.

The door to the building, that Reida had spent valuable effort opening, had shut again.

Both Thayu and Nicha tensed their hands around their weapons.

"Don't shoot," I said in a low voice.

I had no doubt that these Aghyrians were of the type that were not harmed by charge guns.

They stopped and looked at us. We looked at them.

But then a cracking beam of light shot just over our heads.

People shouted. I ducked between the *neshi*. Thayu did the same.

"Which idiot did that?" I shouted to her.

"One of Sarlin's people."

A firefight was going on over our heads. I spotted Evi and Ynggi between the hairy bodies, too, all of us hiding between the animals.

One beam was met with another. Glancing between two animals, I just saw a beam hit a person in the chest. The person—a woman I thought—balled the light into a sphere and threw it back over our heads.

They all wore the same uniforms so I couldn't tell if this was one of Sarlin's people or not.

I was back in that terrifying moment in the Aghyrian compound in Barresh where I had run into these people before, where I'd dragged myself over the floor and fallen down the stairs to escape this superhuman ability. Where I'd dragged Thayu though the night in the pouring rain into a canoe and had punted all the way to the *gamra* island, where she had collapsed on me with hypothermia and I'd realised how much I cared about her.

The animals were pushing and grumbling, fidgeting to arrange themselves into a defensive circle. They were big and strong and not particularly smart and they were caught in a tight spot.

When they saw an opportunity to escape, they would run. Then they would not care about us. They would stomp over the top of us if we were in the way.

Deyu was looking around. I wouldn't be surprised if she was thinking the same things. Maybe we could use the animals' dash for escape, maybe the *neshi* would ruin our chances. I wasn't sure that any of it was under our control. I'd lost track of the fight between the Aghyrians, I didn't want my team to become involved.

At that moment the door to the building opened again.

Neshi ears flicked up.

Deyu realised what was happening a second before I did.

She yelled, "Get on the animals!"

I grabbed the edge of the *neshi*'s back plate and swung myself up, using one of the shoulder horns.

Nicha did the same.

Thayu jumped onto the back of her animal, dragging poor Ynggi with her.

Reida ran to his animal where Benton Leck still sat, looking miserable.

Deyu herself vaulted onto the biggest animal and slapped its neck.

The *neshi* snorted. It bucked and ran in the only direction it could: into the opening door. And all our animals followed.

A couple more guards came out, but they had no chance to even draw weapons before the herd stampeded in. Clinging onto the back of my animal, I didn't even see what happened to those poor guards.

We entered a low-ceilinged corridor with doors on both sides.

Inside the rooms—when the *neshi* ran past—I spotted benches with transparent basins and medical equipment. Was this where they made Tamerians?

Here and there, people ran out of doorways checking what all the noise was about. Some Aghyrians, but others were Indrahui or Kedrasi or Damarcian. I spotted one African. All watched us with wide eyes as the *neshi* thundered through the hallway.

The corridor ended in a staircase. I was wondering how the *neshi* were going to handle that when the herd came to a screeching halt. The animals bunched together, nostrils flaring and flanks heaving. It would be far too hot for them in here.

All the people out of the labs had run into the corridor and were coming in our direction.

"Quick, get off," Deyu called.

She was already on the stairs. Nicha and Ynggi followed her, and then Evi with the huge gun, and Rixya with his military weapon. Sarlin and his band of Aghyrians had managed to follow us inside as well. The latter ran straight past us, up the stairs and into what seemed to be a large hall.

We followed them and came out into the compartment of the dome that looked like an auditorium. At the top of the stairs stood a large fire bowl from which a healthy fire spread a glow of warmth.

The large table we had seen from outside stood to my left, but it was no longer empty. About twenty people sat around it in a meeting that our arrival had interrupted.

It disturbed me how many people around the table I had seen before.

A representative from PanAf, the African branch of Nations of Earth, a man from Indrahui who sometimes came to the *gamra* complex. A woman from Kedras who I had seen in the Trader Guild offices in Barresh.

Some people at the table I didn't know. I had no idea who the dark

African woman was and had never seen the man who sat next to her either.

Most of them had readers on the table with the same document on the screen, written in Mirani, damn it. There were no Mirani people at the table, although there was one on the first row of the audience seating, amongst a group of Aghyrians and others who appeared to be assistants and secretaries.

This was why the Exchange had detected activity at Tamer: because all these people had been flown in for this meeting. I also realised that Ezhya must have known about this and, in the typical roundabout infuriatingly Coldi manner, had neglected to inform me directly, waiting to see if I worked it out myself.

He couldn't go himself, so he had sent me. I was the most Coldi non-Coldi and I carried the responsibility for billions of people on my shoulders. In this gathering, I was Asto. I even understood Asha's recent pressure to attend the initiation ceremony.

It had taken me this long to realise all these things, and now it was up to me to talk to these people in the name of *gamra*.

As we came up, everyone looked around, and I recognised more people.

Facing me was Jasper Carlson. Next to him sat none other than former chief delegate of *gamra* Joyelin Akhtari. We had wondered where she had gone. I didn't know why I had ever thought that she looked like a fairy queen with her long near-white hair. All I could see before me was a hard-nosed businesswoman, and one with question-able morals at that.

Next to her sat Captain Kando Luczon. Last time I saw him, he'd been an old man, but straight-backed and haughty. Now, he was bent, his face drawn and his skin sallow. He appeared to have lost a lot of his hair, giving the appearance of a skeleton. There was defi-nitely a grain of truth in what Jayten had told us about the captain's health.

As we came in, a few people in the sparse audience shouted for guards. A few came running in, but they stopped when facing Evi's gun. Further shouts did not produce more guards. I suspected they were occupied outside, and two of Sarlin's Aghyrian fighters stood at the top of the stairs.

Sarlin himself sprinted across the room. If ever I'd thought of

Aghyrians as graceful, willowy creatures, he did not conform to that view. Yes, I liked him a lot.

He made for the captain. A few men at the table—I didn't recognise them—jumped up, but Sarlin pushed them aside. The captain pushed himself up from the table, his eyes wide. He shouted something in Aghyrian. He held out his hands as if throwing an imaginary ball.

Several people at the table clamped their hands over their ears. A man who sat at on the other side of Joyelin Akhtari collapsed onto the table. Joyelin Akhtari herself balled her fists on the table.

Whatever the captain was doing to those immediately around him, Sarlin was not affected by it. He grabbed the captain from behind, with his arm looped around the captain's neck. The captain was still shouting at him.

With his free hand, Sarlin pulled a giant knife from his belt. It was a formidable weapon, with a viciously serrated blade with points that looked like they could inflict deep and nasty cuts.

I'd seen the knives on the belts of the other Aghyrians, and understood why they carried them: because they were not harmed by the electronic weapons that everyone used.

There was a moment where I expected Sarlin to drive the knife into the captain's ribcage, but instead, he said, "Tell them."

The captain said nothing. The only way I could tell that he was disturbed was through his flaring nostrils.

Sarlin repeated, "Tell them what you were going to do with this army."

The captain said nothing.

I noticed movement from the corner of my eye.

Two of Sarlin's Aghyrians kept watch at the top of the stairs. They now stepped aside to let through a person in dark clothing.

A Tamerian.

Followed by another Tamerian.

And another one and another one, until the entire army had come in. The men all still looked at me, although their expressions were less intense. I gestured to them, *come closer.* They spread out around the perimeter of the room.

Several people at the table, including Jasper Carlson, looked uncomfortable.

Sarlin said, speaking slowly, "Since you refuse to, I will tell them." He looked at Jasper Carlson. "You represent a rogue element on a world that has recently joined the established authorities. What did the captain promise that you would be able to do with these Tamerians?"

Jasper's cheeks coloured. "He didn't promise so much. We had our own plans." He met my eyes. I had no doubt that he realised that Reida was recording everything.

"But he said the men would be yours?"

"The technology is ours. I don't know about the men . . . at least not these ones." He glanced nervously at the wall of Tamerians that surrounded the table.

"How did that technology work out?" Sarlin asked.

"What do you mean?" Jasper asked.

I said, "You know what I mean. I saw the vile labs that you put together under the guise of medical research. I saw the poor excuses for human beings you created. As far as I know, there are several court processes on Earth running right now to deal with this vile business. What did the man promise you? Why did you even believe someone who had run out on his own people?"

Jasper's eyebrows rose.

"You haven't heard the story? What do you know about the Aghyrian ship and these people?"

Not much, I didn't think.

Sarlin took over. "Whatever he promised you, and you, and you . . ." He looked around the table. Crap. Even Minke Kluysters was there. I guess I should have expected him to turn up at an event like this.

"Whatever the captain promised you, everything he said was a lie. The technology he gave you was not intended to help you. It was intended so that you could do his work. We came back here with a ship that was running on less than a third of the people ideally required to run it. Things were breaking, processes were not maintained. And even then, he kept a large proportion of the crew in stasis, because *we might need them*. We, the rest of the crew, didn't know that *might need them* meant that the captain planned to fight a war, but once we found out, we were clear that we wouldn't support this. Even our small numbers made it a lunatic idea. And we didn't want to fight."

The captain made an angry remark, but Sarlin ignored him.

"We managed to convince the captain that a fight would be stupid—"

Another angry remark. This time, Sarlin hissed something back and pushed the knife closer so that it touched the captain's chest.

"He wanted to take us to yet another remote and uninhabited place, and that was when we split off. I am one of the senior commanders who flew the ship both when it approached your worlds and when we left again. I am not a minor player. I guess I should have taken the step sooner, and most of this could have been avoided, but I never had Lilona's courage. Mostly, I believed that the captain had our best interests at heart. But we found out that he intended to replace us."

I understood. "With the Tamerians."

"You're wrong," Jasper Carlson said. "The start of the Tamerian project was much earlier than that."

Sarlin said, "Yes, because he had given you the blueprint for Tamerians initially so that there could be a race upsetting the dominant majority on Asto before we arrived."

Funny how they used these types of metaphors without having to say *Coldi*. It still left a dirty taste in my mouth.

I said, "That did not work out so well."

"These people here are dumb idiots," the captain said. "Cannot perform the simplest genetic processes. We told you what to do and how to do it, but you didn't listen. And now we've had to spend so much effort making it work."

"It won't work," said a weak voice behind me.

I turned around. Benton Leck stood there. "It won't work, because I no longer have the substance that releases the smell that controls these men." He pulled his tattered book out of his pocket. "And these are my notes. Since no one is paying me, I don't want anyone else to have them."

He tossed the book into the fire bowl.

One of the captain's guards called out, "Stop! Wait!"

He made for the fire bowl, but Telaris with his big gun blocked the way.

Two Tamerians joined him, standing silent, with their hands behind their backs, legs apart.

What?

I stared into the men's empty eyes. "Do you want to say anything in your favour? Do you want to tell us your story? Tell us the truth?"

I had not really expected a reply. None of our experience suggested that they were capable of such.

But one of the Tamerian men stepped forward and said, "Puck."

He balled his fist and thumped it on his chest.

"Puck," the other repeated.

The way they stood there, solemn and sincere, made me choke up inside. What had these people here done to these men? They might not be men in the usual sense of the word, but they were feeling, living beings.

The captain treated them like people he could control at the press of a button and whose opinions he could shape with a single smell. He could make them do anything, even kill themselves in great numbers and not care that the others died.

I didn't know if they knew about Puck, or if Puck meant to them what it meant to me; but I did know when Puck had come to me in the streets of Barresh, he'd dissented, and maybe he'd wanted to tell me something but lacked the language to do so.

After a few moments of intense silence, in which the Tamerians continued to stand with their fists balled over their hearts and the fire in the bowl devoured Benton Leck's notes, Joyelin Akhtari said, "Is this true?"

She was looking at Kando Luczon more than at Sarlin. I didn't know what kind of communication passed between them, but some clearly did. Kando Luczon's face hardened.

Joyelin Akhtari got up from the table. "I think we're done here. We're wasting our time. I wanted a fair deal for those who fall outside the jurisdiction of *gamra*. I don't want any of this." She made a broad sweeping movement with her hand.

There were times I'd distrusted her intensely, because she kept her allegiances close to her chest.

But of course she was allied to the Aghyrians, and many of them *had* been hard done by in the course of history.

Right now, I respected the heck out of this woman.

At that moment, Kando Luczon twisted around. Sarlin was not expecting this and let go of the captain's arm.

I dived for the table, pushing Joyelin Akhtari out of the way. We both fell onto the table.

There was a lot of shouting and screaming around us. Kando Luczon stood in the middle of the room, with the hilt of the knife protruding from his ribs. A dark stain spread over his shirt. His eyes had glazed over.

Slowly, he toppled forward.

Around the perimeter of the hall, all the Tamerians balled their fists and thumped their chests, to solemn statements of, "Puck, Puck, Puck."

Joyelin Akhtari coolly pushed herself up, left the table, and collected her guards and secretary from the audience benches, passing the Tamerian line. Her long elfin-like grey-white hair was the last thing I saw when she went down the stairs.

I balled my fist, put it on my chest and said, "Puck."

He had not died in vain.

24

———

AFTER JOYELIN AKHTARI left, people slowly came to life, stunned, shocked.

One of the captain's Aghyrian guards went to his master's side, but even for me, a number of paces off, it was clear that Captain Kando Luczon would not be answering any questions, giving any more orders and ruining any more lives.

I honestly didn't know whether to be happy or sad.

The "greatest arsehole in the history of humanity" was also one of the most unique people, having lived for longer than any human and having seen both the original Asto before the meteorite hit it and the result fifty thousand years later. There might be others on the ship who had seen that, but the captain was iconic.

"I guess it's up to you to decide what to do now," I said to Sarlin.

"We'll hold council. I suspect we will join Lilona and make sure that our knowledge is shared to the benefit of all humanity."

I nodded. He grabbed both my hands and squeezed them. His touch was cold. I guessed he was probably in shock as well.

Several attending members of the meeting were leaving the room, most of them stunned into silence. They were diplomats, used to civility, polite talk and cups of tea, unused to the spilling of real blood at the meeting table.

Benton Leck had collapsed on a chair where he sat with trembling hands raking through his hair. His lips moved. "My work, my life's work. I will never get a chance like this again. My life is doomed."

He still didn't seem to understand some of the ethical problems with this work.

Well, a *gamra* hearing would take care of it. It would be out of my hands. I would deliver him to his wife, as I had set out to do. I waved at the Tamerians closest to him. "Go and take him somewhere quiet and give him some tea."

To my surprise, they did as I said.

"Are you all right?" Thayu asked next to me.

"I think so." I felt like a lifetime had passed today. "I want to go home. If you can get onto your father some way, tell him to send transport."

I needed to deal with these other people in the room, to make sure they got back home. I didn't even know who was formally in charge of this place. But the African people, the people from Indrahui and Kedras definitely didn't belong here. They needed to be interviewed and referred to *gamra* and then I wanted this facility to be disbanded and investigated.

"Well, you never fail to make an entry," said a dry voice, in Isla, behind me.

I recognised the voice and accent. Minke Kluysters.

He inclined his head to me. "I've heard that no matter how secret the gathering, it's nigh impossible to keep you away. It pleases me that you justify your reputation."

"Well, I'm honoured and I'm not sure I deserve the flattery." I had to admit at being a bit annoyed at his tone. A man had just *died*. "What were you all doing here, anyway?"

He did not answer straight away.

A young man came to bring us each a steaming mug of what seem to be tea. It smelled like tea. I sniffed the steam.

"You can drink it. We have no interest in poisoning you," Minke Kluysters said.

I picked up the cup and sipped. It was indeed tea. Not Barresh tea, but normal earthly tea. Hot and strong. Comforting.

I yearned to be with my association. I was deadly tired, but needed to sort out the mess here first. Who was here for what reasons, how to get home, what to do next.

A couple of Aghyrians arrived to help some of the guests out of the hall. A female guest of a race I was unfamiliar with was very upset.

The sole woman amongst the Aghyrians drew my attention. Her hair was thick and curly, and had the colour and appearance of solid gold. Her eyes were clear dark blue. In my mind, I saw that one photo of myself that used to fascinate me when I was young. It had been taken when I was two or three. I sat in the garden of my father's house in New Zealand, which was then my grandparents' holiday home. It dated from the time when it was fashionable to hypersaturate photos with bright colour. That was what she looked like. That was what all Aghyrians looked like: a taller, more intense, more colourful version of human. I knew what colour my hair would be when it grew back. I was looking at it now.

On the human-tree graphic in the basement under the monument in Miran, my line would be somewhere in between the Aghyrian trunk and the Coldi branch, with some Earth characteristics remaining. My genes would be more Coldi than any other heritage, but my Earth roots—and humanity's Aghyrian roots—would remain.

I didn't know why it was important and why it struck me at this moment, but one of my teachers at Taurus High—an otherwise useless man by the name of Mr Hughes, who seemed to be terrified of teenagers—used to say *In order to know where you're going, you have to know where you've come from.*

And as I watched the woman accompany the poor upset lady to the stairs and watched Deyu—always Deyu who did the dirty jobs—help the Aghyrians wrap their captain's body in cloth, I knew where I had come from.

"What we were doing here?" Minke Kluysters continued the earlier conversation. "For many years, more than I can count, the established authorities—"

"You mean *gamra* or the Coldi?" Because if this was going to be another anti-Coldi rant, then I didn't want to waste my time.

"I mean the people and entities who have been systematically cut out of agreements and deals, because they 'didn't meet conditions'; but when you really look at it, those conditions seem to be engineered with the view of keeping these groups out."

"That's not true." If we were going to go into conspiracy theories, I was wasting my time, too. I had no intention to sit here to listen to arguments about how hard-done-by certain groups were and that it was all the fault of the Coldi. Really, worlds like Indrahui could join, if only they cleaned up their act and abolished their vile life-debt system that was nothing more than slavery.

Minke Kluysters continued, "I am one of the representatives of this loose group of entities which includes most of the worlds and population groups. We are tired of arbitrary rules that prevent entities from joining, especially since a rule to revoke membership when these rules are breached does not seem to exist."

"It does."

"Was it ever used?"

We both knew the answer to that.

"So there are these entities that can never join, populations held back from their potential because they can't travel, and kept in poverty because they can't buy or sell resources."

Here, maybe someone else would have asked him why he cared, since Earth had voted to join *gamra* and the application had been accepted. But Minke was not a man who limited his viewpoint to his own business. It was what made him so dangerous. He was not motivated by pure self-interest. There were other things at play, bigger things, schemes and plans. If I could only figure out what they were.

"I'll show you something."

He pulled a reader out of the pocket of his jacket, turned it on and laid it flat on the bench between us. A three-dimensional holo-projection sprang up, a spidery shape like a loosely coiled ball of hair that was both familiar and unfamiliar to me. It was a depiction of the anpar network, as one could view it at the Exchange. However, its shape was unfamiliar, thinner, with a couple of much longer arms. And the centre of it was not in Damarq.

I looked from the projection to him.

"How much of this has been built?"

"Not all of it. We have this arm and this one." He pointed, letting his fingers distort the strands of light as he moved his hand through the projection. "And these two here. We're linking up these three points, and this branch here will be completed soon."

A rogue Exchange network. *Gamra* had known about this for years. They had stomped on the parts visible to us in Barresh a few times, but of course that was only a small part of the work. With the Aghyrians helping, and the money provided by Minke Kluysters and the ingenuity and work ethic of Indrahui, we should not have expected the network to die.

"When you visited me in my home, I asked you to arrange a discussion with Ezhya Palayi. It seems I was not forceful enough in my demand."

"Ezhya does not let himself be blackmailed, certainly not for issues that have no direct influence on him. His loyalty is to the people of Asto. I could not get him commit to such a meeting." But knowing that this was going on, Ezhya would absolutely be interested. That's why he had sent me here.

"I merely asked you to convey the message."

"Thank you, but I am not a messenger boy. Any messages to him should go through the Exchange." I wished him good luck trying to get past Amarru.

"That woman hates me and will not do her job, which is: to represent off-Earth interests."

"That is not how Coldi society works. It is not how *gamra* works. It may be how Nations of Earth works, but they don't look too kindly upon people who have broken many laws."

He snorted. "Laws? The laws serve the status quo, perpetuated by the bureaucratic organisations who serve only the elites."

"Interesting words coming from one of the richest men on Earth."

"You can joke or try to discredit me, but I'm not part of the establishment, and neither are you. Sure, it is easy enough for us to pretend that we are, because we are enough like them to pass for one of them, because we are white and well off, but all our success is self-made. My father was not rich, you spent most of your life off Earth. Both of us represent the rest of the world, those who are not part of the Nations of Earth elite."

I chuckled. "You represent them by exploiting them?"

"It depends on how far you want to take that line of discussion. Are you responsible for the atrocities committed by the people you represent?" Nations of Earth and *gamra* tried to do the right thing, but that didn't mean that nothing bad ever happened. It would be ridiculous to suggest that those things were my fault, but . . .

"You *owned* these companies that did experiments on people."

"I sold Sandowne before the existence of the cellars came to light."

"They were on your land. Don't tell me you didn't know."

"We were developing controversial cures to crippling illnesses that a single soul in the supposed civilised world had yet to care about. Because they were *African* diseases."

"You were going to make money from it."

"Is that wrong? That's the trouble with people of your ilk. You want everything to come from the good of everyone's hearts. Well, that does not pay the bills. Medical science is expensive and someone has to pay for it. Delving into a disease as unprofitable as the African sleeping sickness is a huge gamble. Do you suggest that people should not be rewarded if the gamble pays off? You lot are otherwise quick enough to lay blame if it does not pay off. There has got to be a balance."

"That's a ridiculous suggestion. People were abducted and taken from their homes. They were disgusting experiments. There is nothing in the world you can say that makes it right to me."

"It was not right, I agree. I owned the company. I did not delve far enough into the operations. I made a mistake."

"You swept it under the carpet."

"Mr Wilson, there is one thing you must understand about Africa, certainly the parts where most of the victims came from: it's nothing like the world you come from. It's a world that has everything in common with the likes of Indrahui where, in order to survive, you have to kill. Your darling *gamra* and Nations of Earth have driven together a group of people who are desperate and who are excluded because of artificial parameters set by rich men in tower offices, which they have no hope of meeting."

"If you are talking about worlds like Indrahui and the Zhori mafia, then it's clear why."

"Let's talk about this mafia, then. They came from a regime that repressed them. They thought they had found safety in the back streets of Athens. They were found, a few years later, by people from that regime, who then attempted to set up a structure that supported the regime that the first Coldi on Earth fled to escape. Why are you surprised that they were not happy, that they went into the only continent populated by people who have been neglected and persecuted in the same way?"

Oh, he played his role so well, almost allowing me to forget that he was one of the richest people on Earth.

"We are Africans, Mr Wilson. We know what the establishment did to our continent. We know that Africa was considered a sacrifice, too far down the trail of desertification to save. We saw the exodus of refugees from the continent, and for many years we saw these people crowd on the southern shores of the Mediterranean Sea, at times mowed down by militias who were of course, always 'illegal', but nevertheless used weaponry that suspiciously looked like it had been supplied by Nations of Earth. We saw the supposedly civilised countries pull up the fences and do nothing to stop this carnage. We saw them trying to stamp out the Sudanese solar glider industry when they did not like it that Africans were trying to help themselves, if only to feed their own families. So don't go on to me about illegal activities and smuggling by some sort of stupid rule that could have been changed back then, and made things so much better."

"So you would have said: give Mr Romi Tanaqan free rein in the Sahara? He would have enslaved whole sections of Africa with the foul life-debt system of Indrahui."

"That is still the trouble with you isn't it? You still don't see that once there is a system you can change it. If you have no system and you have no structure, there is anarchy, and it takes so much more to change anything at all, because nobody cares about the public good."

I had to admit that he was right. And that Nations of Earth had been unable to make much difference in Africa. The likes of PanAf—the African branch of Nations of Earth—had always been hopelessly corrupted.

Minke continued, "So here we have this supposed Zhori mafia, having fled into the cesspool of this continent, having found suppressed, neglected people, and rather a lot of them. Having found these people desperate and hungry, and they did some things that actually changed the lives of these people. Not many things, but it was something. Sudanese solar gliders are rather nifty, you know. They cost next to nothing, they're made from rubbish. And of course the self-righteous authorities try to shut them down. Because they still can't stand that it wasn't an idea that came from them and wasn't administered by them."

"It was because the gliders use material that comes from plants that were illegally imported. Had they put the plants through quarantine, there would have been no problem."

"Oh, by the heavens, do you actually with a straight face hand-on-your-heart believe that?"

No. I didn't. It *was* the only way in which the industry could have avoided becoming the focus of authorities trying to shut them down. But no one at Nations of Earth, not even in the Quarantine departments, would have given a request to import these plants five seconds of consideration. Because there was no big business behind it, because importing was very hard anyway, and because there were no swanky lunches and presentations.

Touché.

"You know this, because you're not part of this establishment. I am not part of this establishment either, much as you despise me and my success. You know I'm right, and you know that it is a big shame on the record of Nations of Earth that they have left Africa in a position like this. The north and central part uninhabitable, dirt poor and at the mercy of anarchy. And now that they're attempting to take control of the continent, much too late, they shouldn't be surprised that people are not terribly happy and not willing to play along with their cheery new rules."

"No, I'm not suggesting that at all."

"Yet you were cheering at the win for the establishment in the referendum."

"Because it is a way to bring structure into what was previously an unstructured mess?"

"Because it is a way to suppress people trying to organise their own structure. After many years, all these people have come together. They are the ones not wanted by the establishment. They are the supposed criminals of all the worlds, who are supposedly preventing the countries, or the worlds, from joining the organisations that they need to join to get ahead. They do not trust any of the establishment. Why should I trust you? Why should they trust an institution and a world that is ruled by a dictator? Why should they trust people who are unwilling to compromise? The establishment has been trying to stamp us out for as many years as we have been in existence. But we are strong, and we are not going to go away. We are solving our own problems, legally or illegally, I no longer care."

Much as I disagreed with some of the other things he said, I agreed with that. We had tried to fight this loose association of entities that wanted an alternate Exchange for many years. They were not going to go away.

And so, in a day of revelations, I came to another conclusion.

I called myself a diplomat, but I hadn't been a diplomat for many years in the sense of the word that diplomats negotiate differences between major disagreeing parties.

Even when Kando Luczon had come to Barresh, I'd always solidly argued from the perspective of the ruling people. I had been, as several people had said about me, Ezhya Palayi's mouthpiece. I'd made no secret about that.

But that position was no longer enough.

If one put a football on a piece of elastic, it would always come back, no matter how hard one kicked it. Humanity was the elastic that held us all together in this way. People could try to flee, but they always came back. Maybe that was the ultimate secret to be learned from the Aghyrian ship's foray out of the galaxy: the call of humanity was strong.

And we *were* talking only about rules. Some rules had good reasons, others less so. And anyway, with certain provisos, if there was going to be a second Exchange, then it would be a hundred times better that it was integrated with the regular Exchange than that travellers across both systems needed to break several laws each time they went across.

A total block, travel ban and boycott rarely worked and hurt only people who didn't deserve to be hurt. We'd tried, and failed.

I said, "Well, just to start off, do you have a manifesto of who you are and what you're standing for and what you want?"

"Bravo!" He clapped his hands. "It has taken you only about ten years to ask that question. It's one that the people here are more than willing to answer. We can go back to the table."

25

IN THE NEXT FEW DAYS, there were moments that I feared I had utterly failed in my mission. One part of me feared that if Ezhya and *gamra* Chief Delegate Marin Federza heard what we discussed, I would be out of a job and they would never speak to me again.

I mentioned this to Thayu and she said, "What do you think Ezhya would rather have? A group or entity that he can negotiate with and learn things from or a group he will need to go to war with?"

Yes, I knew, I knew, but the little voice of doubt was so insistent.

Since Asto had a large army, but had never been keen to wage all-out war, I didn't need to ask Ezhya that question.

Thayu continued, "If Ezhya thought this was an issue he could easily win, he'd have sent a few ships, they'd have blasted a few sites from orbit and he'd have killed the operation. But he's tried that a few times already. So he wanted us to talk to them without actually appearing like he's caved in to talk."

I laughed, and she laughed as well.

We'd been at Tamer for close to ten days, and I'd noticed how her cheeks glowed almost constantly now. And *that* I knew to be a pretty reliable sign for early pregnancy in Coldi women.

"Well then, when we come back, we'll have to inform Ezhya. And also, do you think Lilona will be annoyed by our news?"

"She might, but she might just be happy and congratulate us, or she may say it's early days, and not to get excited yet."

"Yes." Thayu had suffered numerous miscarriages already.

"But if so, we'll try again."

"Yes, we will."

And I leaned over and breathed her scent. Coldi didn't kiss and it rather shamed me that I had once encouraged Thayu into kissing.

Listening, watching, and then acting. That was what my team would have to do.

Strangely enough, it fitted with the changes that I had already made and changes that were coming. Ynggi was excellent at all of those things. Veyada was a lawyer, not a fighter, and we would have Mereeni instead of Sheydu, whose answer to everything had a fuse. Mereeni talked. She tried things; she liked to learn about other people. I almost felt peace with Sheydu's departure, providing I knew that she was all right.

So listening, it was.

Through the long meetings we had, I listened and made a list of all the group's points. Some were big issues and required the entire *gamra* assembly to talk about it. Other requests were smaller.

The Aghyrians asked that the captain could be buried on—they used the term *returned to*—Asto. I had no idea if this was possible, but said I would investigate it. I felt that his death required a monument, no matter how appalling a person he had been. We would learn so much because of him.

Indrahui wanted *gamra* to waive the native persons laws so that it could begin negotiating joining.

Minke Kluysters argued in favour of the poorer cities on Earth, where he had a foothold, and which would be worse off under *gamra* law; for example the Sudanese solar glider industry that was tied up with the war lords of Indrahui. He argued for a relaxing of the quarantine laws to allow suitable crops to be brought to Africa for areas that had not seen much in the way of permanent vegetation for at least fifty years.

When I visited his home, he had asked me to arrange a meeting with Ezhya, and I had laughed at the prospect. Now, I could do little to stop this meeting from happening. I would likely have to be present at it. He said that his house was open.

Minke had an extraordinary sense of seeing big picture developments and I had to make sure that he didn't grab a business monopoly and profit from it. He was that type of person. Not just that, money was not high on the list of things that motivated Coldi. Status was. In a way, status and money were tied up on Asto, but not in the way that money could buy status. Minke Kluysters cared nothing for status. He wanted power and money, preferably without ever being recognised when he went out on the street.

As I had experienced when I had visited him in South Africa, the man was extraordinarily charismatic and down to earth.

He loved heated discussions, yet never yelled at anyone. He could bring the best out of people, and the worst. He had brought a personal supply of whiskey, and we shared a good number of drinks while seated around the fire bowl in the dining room.

He was a formidable opponent, and not one who would give in easily, and one we would have to watch, but one who would talk rather than fight. In true Coldi style, one made friends with one's opponents.

I would have to argue with *gamra* that this group could run some sort of autonomous network, as long as it didn't interfere with the Exchange. We would need to build nodes that integrated the two, and it might be easier for those nodes—I suggested Tamer became the first one—to satisfy *gamra* criteria.

I put my foot down on many issues, such as the Aghyrian ship. Lilona had fled from the dictatorship of the captain. She had told me that she was not the only one who disliked the way he ran the ship. A good number of the captain's people had been in the base. I wanted to make sure that the opinions of all Aghyrians were heard. I requested a full list of the Aghyrian crew and made it clear that there would be no talks until they had disclosed what had happened while they were away and whether there was a chance that some trouble would be following them here from that other galaxy.

There were still a bit under a thousand survivors from the ship, even if most were past middle age. Of children, there were almost none.

While I was talking, the others retrieved and repaired the shuttle. It looked strange on the snowy airfield, and the guards maintained vigilance around it at all times. Only we were allowed to visit. Yana and Taleyu were quite comfortable inside. Rixya joined them a bit later.

I found it harder to negotiate on behalf of the Tamerians.

I learned that the Tamerian program had already wound down, but what was the status of the existing soldiers? Benton Leck wanted a say in this matter. Having worked with the soldiers, he knew how non-human they were, but advocated that they be given physical jobs. In Barresh, they already did a lot of those jobs. I suspected many of them were going to end up in Barresh.

———

When we had tentative agreements on a good number of key issues, it was time to go back.

The shuttle had been repaired and the crew had waited patiently. They were military, and watching and waiting was what they spent most of their lives doing.

Joyelin Akhtari offered the use of their network, but I declined. For one, the military ships waiting would be freaked out and, while there were a lot of groups I had no objection to freaking out, the Asto military was not one of them.

So we spent another week in the tin can eating military rations, listening to Evi and Telaris complain that it was too hot.

I no longer found it too hot and, to my great pleasure, my motion sickness had vanished.

The thought of meeting up with Asha made me nervous. I had sent the documents ahead, and after we had gone through the sling and into the large ship, he came to meet us on the gallery in the hall.

And to my utter surprise he took Thayu's hands and dropped to his knees, his head bent.

I froze, not sure what was going on.

They exchanged a few words which I couldn't hear because of machinery noise in the hall.

He turned to me. "The child will be the heir of the Domiri clan."

Well, that was . . . unsettling, and honouring. But how did he know she was pregnant? And what was more, how did he know this time it would end differently?

I went with him and shared our story. Yes, Ezhya had known that there was some kind of meeting going on. It seemed too coincidental that a number of high profile people were away at the same time.

The thing I'd feared the most—that he or Ezhya would disagree with my solution—did not happen. But I did ask why Ezhya had not contacted me directly.

"You must come to the initiation ceremony," he said.

It was an oddly evasive reply for someone who was normally direct to the point of being rude.

"Yes, I will come," I said. "I would still like to brief Ezhya personally on this."

Heck, I hadn't met face to face with him for quite some time. He used to come to Barresh quite a bit to scope me out and give me infuriatingly opaque instructions. I'd figured his absence was a mark that he trusted me to do the right thing.

"I think we have handled it adequately," Asha said.

That answer, too, surprised me. "Is anything the matter?" Although that was hardly the sort of question that Coldi handled well.

"You are under my responsibility now."

"But we both have loyalty to Ezhya." My heart was racing. Something strange was going on here.

"We do, but how much of that loyalty is rivalry?"

I stared at him. "Is this still about the time that I shot Taysha out of self defence? I thought that matter was dealt with. I'm not Coldi and . . ."

And I understood the issue.

I had not just developed a much cleaner understanding of the *sheya* instinct. I had developed the instinct. Ezhya had failed to visit me, not because he trusted me, but because he *didn't* trust me. Keep your enemies close and your friends apart, was the full version of the proverb that Veyada loved to quote.

Well . . . "I would never . . . that's ridiculous. I don't know why he thinks that."

"The instinct does not *think*."

And in one quick movement, I had wrestled Yana to the wall. That had not been a premeditated action.

"But I have no intention to . . ."

"The instinct doesn't have intentions."

"That's ridiculous."

"It is what it is."

"Does that mean that Ezhya never wants to see me anymore?" I didn't give him the chance to reply. "Why would I want to do . . . It's totally ridiculous."

"I know, but we'll keep you apart because I don't want trouble and he doesn't want trouble. I'll keep you in my clan until your allegiance has settled and then maybe we can avoid the problem."

That was why he wanted me to come quickly for the initiation.

"I will see when I can get time off."

"Yes," he said, and now he sounded more like his usual self. "Go home and recover. You will find that we need to make some changes, your name being one of them."

"Aveya," I said.

"Aveya," he repeated.

———

When we finally came home, we found Veyada and Mereeni in the living room, and Mereeni was so pregnant that she could barely walk.

To my question about whether she had gone through her grumpy phase yet, she joked that she'd done that two weeks ago when "that woman" kept bothering the household about her missing husband.

Her belly shook when she laughed, and she winced afterwards.

I assured her that the husband was back with his wife.

"What, by the way, is happening next door?"

We had to weave between stacks of building supplies on the gallery. The apartment next to mine belonged to a Damarcian delegate who was hardly ever there.

"Renovations, I've been told," Veyada said. He genuinely looked relaxed and happy. At least his mother's departure had not scarred him too much. I should ask how she was, later, when we had a private moment.

Thayu went into the bathroom and checked out a number of interesting things that had arrived during our absence. The main item was a kind of hammock chair that hung from a stand-up frame. Under the chair stood a low-rimmed basin. Next to it lay a pile of folded-up blankets and towels and various substances in bottles.

Thayu stood looking at the arrangements. She didn't move or say anything for a long time.

"Thay'?"

"I never had any of this," she said in a low voice. "They didn't like me so they insulted me by not providing me with things to make me comfortable. When the time came, they locked me in my rooms and came in to give me food once a day. I gave birth on the rug in the bedroom. It made a mess and the rug was soaked. It was an expensive one, too. I just left it like that, and climbed out of the window. Then it turned out that the contract I signed had the option for another child which they wouldn't relinquish, just to punish me."

In the low light of the bathroom, her face looked haunted.

She had never told me any of this. She'd been much younger. I couldn't even begin to understand how horrible that experience must have been.

"Thay', I'm sorry." I closed her in my arms.

"Don't be. You saved my life."

———

Mereeni used the hammock chair two days later when she gave birth to a baby girl. It was, Thayu assured me, a typical Coldi birth, a family affair where everyone came to give support. I'd felt unsure about the implication that we should all attend, but it was not half as disturbing as I thought it would be. Veyada did most of the work, assisted by Eirani, who clearly loved every second of it.

The arrival of Ileyu, who would carry her mother's clan name Ezmi, was a calm affair.

Ayshada was much fascinated by the arrival of this upstart baby in the household.

That evening, when Mereeni lay on the couch, and Veyada sat next to her with the little girl asleep on his chest, he kept running into the room bringing toys and pillows "for the baby".

At one trip on his way to his room, he stopped suddenly inside the door to the hall.

Then he yelled, "'eydu!"

What?

I jumped to my feet and ran to the door.

Sheydu indeed.

She was dressed in her very familiar security black and grey gear. Had she taken another security job with someone else?

There were two people with her, women both, and they stood behind her in that typical pyramid formation. Sheydu was their leader.

"Just checking on the neighbours," she said.

Veyada had come to the door, carrying his daughter.

"That's her, eh?" Sheydu said.

"Ileyu," Veyada said.

She went over to her son, and stroked the baby over her cheek. Ileyu's little hand twitched.

Sheydu smiled, and a tender look came over her face that I had never seen before. It was gone just as quickly when she looked up and faced me. Then I remembered her remark when she came in.

"Neighbours?"

"Asha has bought the apartment next door," she said. "We are moving in."

"We" clearly included the two women with her. One of them was tall and impressive like Deyu. She wore earrings with the emerald stone of the Palayi clan. The other woman was shorter but had an impressively stocky build. She was Vonayi. Elite soldiers.

Sheydu's new association.

I was a bit stunned by this development. "Asha bought the apartment so that you could live next to us?"

"Yes. The building materials are outside and when the pathetic workmen deign to turn up, they'll begin knocking out the wall. For one, Asha doesn't like that proper members of your team have their rooms downstairs."

She referred to Ynggi.

"He also suggested that you need your own guard association."

A position which, clearly, was going to be filled by her and these women.

"But what about Evi and Telaris?"

"They can't come with you to Asto."

Oh.

And that put a whole different perspective on things.

"Does Asha expect me to need it?" Visions of clashes in the Inner

Circle went through my head. Did I really have to go to this ceremony if my visit could upset the hierarchy?

"If he didn't think you needed it, he wouldn't have arranged it."

A typical Sheydu answer.

"Anyway, these are Isharu Vonayi and Naru Palayi, both from the military academy. There will be another layer arriving soon."

Four more guards, a complete three-layered association. "Is that necessary?" But if Asha thought so, it was. "I guess they'll be coming when we go to Asto."

"Yes."

I had looked forward to the upcoming visit, but clearly these people had a different idea of how it would go.

And so it seemed that either there had been a plan for Sheydu all along, or, more likely, Asha had acted once it looked like we might lose her.

She seemed happy, now that she could train her own little army and play with explosives as much as she liked.

———

Life went on.

I went back to visit Lilona and was declared fit for the task we had already performed. Thayu was pregnant, and her moods, her glowing cheeks and her tendency to want to collect cute things was so different from all the previous times that I had a very good feeling that she would be able to carry the child to term.

I was busy.

Of course I had to face the grilling by the *gamra* assembly for failing to quash the opposition yet again. I thought I made a pretty good effort at repeating the sentiment in Minke Kluysters' rant at me. That we'd tried and failed to get rid of the rogue network. That we had neither the means nor the right to do this. That there was a place where Nations of Earth had tried to do the same, a place called Africa.

The assembly voted in favour of talks, which I then had to help organise.

Sarlin brought the big ship into orbit—I heard rumours that Asha had to move one of his vessels to accommodate it—and we started the negotiation about the captain's body which they kept in a pod in the big hall.

Ezhya didn't want it. The Barresh Aghyrians wanted the burial place to be in their compound, but as soon as they started bickering over this, I knew there was only one other appropriate place. He should be buried with the people he'd refused to help and who had fled to Miran. But when I suggested this, several people in the Inner Circle at Athyl acted offended, so it turned out that they did want the monument after all, but were afraid that it would become a symbol for *zeyshi* oppression, since *zeyshi* were legally Aghyrian.

It was a lengthy process but, meanwhile, the captain lay frozen in his pod, and maybe he was laughing over the bickering.

———

It was perhaps two months later that I came home from town to find Thayu standing in front of the mirror-like dark stone in the bathroom.

She was gorgeous, curved and strong, the picture of health. She had stopped wearing tight security uniforms recently. Her lower stomach had begun to swell.

"I've got this," she said, and her eyes glittered.

She pulled out her reader and showed me images of scans of the little worm that would grow into the child I'd never thought I'd have.

I always liked to think that I was emotionally stable, not prone to anger or falling apart, but when I saw that, I burst into tears. And she cried, too, and we spent a long time just crying on each other's shoulders.

———

Thanks for Reading

The story continues with the next volume, *Red Crystal Desert,* in which Cory returns to Asto and the viper's nest of tangled relationships he needs to sort out.

Buy Ambassador 9: Red Crystal Desert direct from the author with delivery by Bookfunnel.

ABOUT THE AUTHOR

Patty Jansen lives in Sydney, Australia, where she spends most of her time writing Science Fiction and Fantasy.

Her career started in earnest when her story *This Peaceful State of War* placed first in the second quarter of the Writers of the Future contest and was published in their 27th anthology. She has also sold fiction to genre magazines such as Analog Science Fiction and Fact, Redstone SF and Aurealis, before making the move to independent publishing.

Patty has written over fifty novels in both Science Fiction and Fantasy, including the *Icefire Trilogy* and the *Ambassador* series.

pattyjansen.com

BOOKS BY PATTY JANSEN

For a complete list of books, scan the image below with your phone.

www.ingramcontent.com/pod-product-compliance
Lightning Source LLC
Chambersburg PA
CBHW060905190726
48286CB00002B/379